THE CRITICS LOVE
KIRK ALEX

Praise for:
Working the Hard Side of the Street –
Selected Stories / Poems / Screams

". . . this is a nicely put together piece of work."

—*BookLore*

"City of Angels? Maybe for that couple of percent of people who get anywhere near that thing called 'fame and fortune.' Everyone else is just trying to get by in a place where, if you don't have the right job and a flashy car, the odds are very much stacked against you.

"This book is excellent. It's full of honest, heartfelt writing that certainly shows a very different view of Hollywood."

—*Paul Lappen, DEAD TREES REVIEW*

"WORKING THE HARD SIDE OF THE STREET— Selected Stories / Poems / Screams is an anthology of powerful, caustic, original tales and poems by Kirk Alex about the ups, downs, and hard knocks of Hollywood's seamy underbelly. The perspective of a "fly- on-the-wall" cab driver provides a piercing realism and insight into the vicious clashes and personal struggles that lie hidden underneath the entertainment capital's glossy, photo-touched exterior. **WORKING THE HARD SIDE OF THE STREET** is recommended as a gut-wrenching read for both its candor and bravado."

—*THE MIDWEST BOOK REVIEW*

BY KIRK ALEX

Zook

Lustmord: Anatomy of a Serial Butcher

Throwback – Book One (of Two) — Love, Lust & Murder Series

Backlash – Book Two (of Two) — Love, Lust & Murder Series

Fifty Shades of Tinsel

nonentity

Working the Hard Side of the Street –
Selected Stories/Poems/Screams

Blood, Sweat & Chump Change — Taxi Tales & Vignettes

Ziggy Popper at Large — Story Collection

Hush-Hush — Holiday #1

Hubba-Hubba — Holiday #2

Hard Noir — Holiday #3

FIFTY SHADES OF TINSEL

Portrait of a Heartthrob

A Novel

KIRK ALEX

TUCUMCARI PRESS

Tucson – 2016

Complete & Unabridged - 2016
This edition contains the extended version of the public park sequence.

Proofreader: Chereese G./April 2014
2nd Edition/Revised September 2014
Copy Editor: G. West
Formatting: Polgarus Studio

ISBN: 978-0-939122-22-6 (pbk)
ISBN: 978-0-939122-23-3 (digital)

TO THE MEMORY OF PEGGY B.

Bait

The women liked him. Gays on both sides, punks *and* lesbians, liked him. Even straight males got off watching Jimmy in action. Jimmy Riff, aka "Tubesteak," aka James Kidd, was hung like Seattle Slew.

"Kidd's got endurance, too," said Benjamin Styles, poverty-row actor/producer. "I've got some terrific footage of Tubesteak fucking Renata's brains out. Unbelievable. You remember Renata, don't you? Renata Blevins? Goes by what these days—Raquel Renoir, or some shit?" He laughed. "Her *nom du porn*, ain't it? One of many."

Edward McFluff only nodded, for he recalled Renata all too well. She had been a columnist on the Industry's biggest gossip rag until she got caught going down on one of the secretaries one day. Not only the boss's favorite piece of ass, but she was lapping cunt in his very own private office. That took balls. Enough to get her shit-canned. Renata "the Dyke" was given her walking papers. Not long after, she ended up in porn. Never mind that she had been in it all along. Strictly managing her porn-star daughter's career, handling her finances. She claimed. Sure. Wasn't long before she started appearing in scenes herself. Yessir: Raquel and Martinique. Mother and daughter act. Second to none when it came to hardcore.

"Dyke liked every second of it," Benjamin said. "Should see the goddamn footage. After hours of steady, hard fucking, Jimmy still had her begging for more. He's beautiful, that Jimmy. Mind you, Renata Blevins don't usually go for dick. Sure, some of these sluts go both ways: like dick *and* pussy. Not a certified muff-diving diva like her. Gotta be something special about Jimmy for a cunt-lapper like Renata to get off. And she paid: better believe she paid good bucks for that meat pole and hard body; those blue eyes. Hell, Kidd is movie star material. Makes a guy like Paul Newman look second rate. Newman is short. So many of these hotshot superstars are short. See Kidd lately? Six-foot-two, last time I checked. Washboard abs. And that ass. Perfection. Sheer perfection. Many a female, as well as male, can't help but salivate at the sight of those athletic buttocks, wanting a taste. You get a taste of that, and it's sheer heaven."

Benjamin Styles knew what he was doing. Inside, he was laughing; outwardly he was as serious as a heart attack. You had to be. Sell the kid. Sell him the way you would a Rolls-Royce, as opposed to a Ford Pinto. Because that's what James Grayson Riff was: a Rolls. Adonis.

His eyes were on McFluff, watching, waiting for any tell-tale signs that he was getting to his carnal needs and cravings for his naive but studly protégé. Must have been. He was sure of it. Only Fluffy was quite good at keeping it cool, concealing it. Had it under control. Old poker-face. That's what it was. Play it any way you want, Eddie, thought Benjamin Styles. I've got your number, amigo. You want him. You know you do.

Edward McFluff lifted the gold-plated phone in the capacity-filled screening room of his posh Beverly Hills mansion and said into the receiver: "Ready when you are, Mr. Pusch."

The lights dimmed.

It was time for the show to start.

The big block letters filled the screen: **A FILM BY R. EDWARD McFLUFF.** A multi-million-dollar production. Producer-director

Edward McFluff's biggest yet. Silence dominated the room as the magic of Edward McFluff enraptured them.

Benjamin Styles quietly maneuvered himself over to the bar. He needed another drink. Reggie was being indifferent, or at least wanting to make it seem that way. He would play it cool and not talk about the kid anymore. Bait the son of a bitch, Benjamin kept telling himself, but don't overdo. He's got the hots for Jimmy. He'll come around.

Edward McFluff, sitting in the front, center recliner, as was his custom, fiddled with the pipe in his hands. He'd filled it with his favorite tobacco, Captain Black, and had not been able to concentrate on the screen at all. His scalp itched. He was perspiring. Mansion had central air, the temp set at a comfortable low-70s, and he was perspiring. He couldn't concentrate on anything but that kid Jimmy.

Angela Bliss, the Ingenue of the Month, forever by his side. Angela was a tall girl. Blonde. Out of Oklahoma or Nebraska, some damn place like that. Got off the Greyhound six months ago to make it in the movies. So far she was only making it on her knees. It didn't faze her any. On the contrary, she was pleased with herself. Look, Ma. I'm with Edward McFluff. She had everything Fluffy liked his women to have, or so he acted: big tits, small waist; ass not too large and hips not too wide; and a face just innocent enough to carry out every one of his perverted fantasies.

Oh, that face. That as yet unmarred, unspoiled, wrinkle-free face. The things he liked to do to it, with it, on it.

"You take care of me—and we'll see what we can do about your career," Fluffy had said to her two weeks ago at that wild bash in the Hollywood Hills. And every second since, Angela made sure she was by his side to cater to his every whim. Recalling some of the things Reggie had had her do still made her blush. But it was all worth it. She would make it to the big time with his help.

She took a book of matches out of her purse and looked at him. Back in her hometown she wouldn't give men like this a second glance. McFluff was pushing sixty. Overweight. Balding. An ugly, kinky six-footer.

She wondered why he was sweating so much.

Benjamin Styles had the barkeep refill his shot glass and downed it in one swift gulp. The booze was free. He would take advantage of it. He thought about the kid and knew it was time to check up on him. Kid had to be kept on a tight rein. Benjamin Styles, with the help of Jimmy Riff's cock, would get back into the stream of things. In return, he had promised to "show him the ropes." He would see to it that Jimmy Riff, or rather, James Kidd, got a start in pictures.

"But you gotta do exactly as I tell ya," Styles had told him. "I mean, you don't ball nobody unless I say so. Got that?'

"Sure, Benjy," the kid had said.

"I mean this town is loaded with has-beens. Every one of them sexually frustrated. Believe me—I know what I'm talking about. No freebies—not as long as I'm your manager. You only fool with the ones who can further your career. Got that?"

The kid had only nodded. He didn't have a worry in the world, and it was enough to piss Benjamin off, for he knew this was the big break he'd been waiting for. And if "The Kidd," Jimmy Riff, wasted precious time with just any unimportant asshole at random, Producer/actor Benjamin Styles would get nowhere fast.

Benjamin Styles, at fifty-seven, dreaded the thought of having to look for someone else to replace the kid. Besides, the chance of finding someone with his prowess in the sack was a slim one indeed. Sure, they existed, here and there, but succumbed to booze or drugs or both, eventually. Ended up O.D.ing, in the slammer, or the bug house. Plenty suicided. Hangings, slashed wrists; blew their brains out—or just plain burned out. The list was long. Kidd was different. Stayed clear of anything that could harm him, pull him down. The other thing that didn't hurt: he was handsome, in a rugged, unconventional way. Not a pretty boy at all, but a man. Had dark hair and a terrific physique. Styles envied that physique, the lean belly. He'd looked that way once himself, years ago, many years ago. Add height to that. And the eyes. The women noticed his eyes. Bluer than Newman's. Kidd had all the equipment. He was a sought-after item, and he was under contract to Benjamin T. Styles: two-bit character actor, two-bit scriptwriter, two-bit producer.

Not many people liked Benjamin Styles. Not many in the relatively small Hollywood circle of movers-and-shakers had wanted to have anything to do with a loser like Benjamin Styles. Only now, things were beginning to change. People he could never reach in the past were trying to reach him. His calls were being returned.

Important people. People who wielded power and demanded respect in the industry. People who made multi-million-dollar deals, industry bigwigs who hired and fired other heavyweights. CEOs of production companies, agents who headed important agencies. People who wanted and desired and needed Jimmy Riff's impressive cock up their ass.

Then there were others who simply liked to watch Jimmy perform and were willing to pay big bucks for it, too. *And guess what, folks? Guess who's got Kidd under his thumb? No one even takes so much as a peek at Tubesteak's ball bat without my permission. No one even gets close to him without my say-so.*

To ensure that everything went according to plan, a close eye would have to be kept on everything Jimmy did. Both night and day. Monday through

Sunday. Even if it meant having to hire private detectives to stay on the kid's tail. Jimmy was costing him money, but Benjamin Styles saw it as a sound investment. Best move he'd made in the thirty-plus years he'd been kicking around in Hollywood.

He stepped out of the screening room, into the hallway. Noticed the security camera monitoring his every move from up high in the corner. He took his little black book out and leafed through it until he came across the private investigator's phone number. Benjamin Styles picked up the receiver. Gold? Was it? Why not? So was the tap in the john, as well as the toilet. When you got money to burn. Phone alone must have cost well over what he'd paid for his beater of a Toyota.

A man's voice answered.

"Nicky Horgan, please," Benjamin Styles said.

"Speaking."

Benjamin Styles felt his blood rising. He was about to blow his top and there was no controlling it.

"Just who do you think you're dealing with, asshole? I told you not to let the kid out of your sight—not for a second!"

"Wait a minute, Mr. Styles—"

"WAIT A MINUTE, NOTHING!" said Benjamin Styles. "I pay you top money not to let him out of your sight! And what the hell are you doing? Sitting in your fucking office when you should be out there protecting my investment!"

"Will you hold on a second," Nicky Horgan pleaded in that Hungarian accent.

"Where did you leave him?"

"If you don't let me talk, Mr. Styles, I will hang up. I promise you I will."

"You do, and I promise you at least a month in a hospital of your choice."

"You are threatening me again?'

"No threat!"

"Will you listen to me? A man's gotta take a shit, shower. I have to get your permission to use the john? That what you're saying?"

"Goddamn straight!"

"That's bullshit, guy!" Nicky Horgan was shouting himself now.

"Listen to me, you slimy little Polack—"

"I am not a Polack! Don't call me a Polack, Mr. Styles!"

"You either do as I say, exactly as I say, or you're through. Got that?"

"You owe me money, Mr. Styles."

"You'll get it!"

"When?"

"Don't worry. You'll get it."

"When, Mr. Styles? When?"

"You like the climate?"

"What's that got to do with anything?'

"Unless you want an escort back to Poland—or to wherever you come from—you do what I tell ya."

"Please, Mr. Styles. I got expenses."

"You'll get every cent," Benjamin Styles said. "That's a promise."

"All right," Horgan said with a sigh. "I'll see what I can do."

"That's more like it." Benjamin Styles paused. "Do you realize how much money I got riding on this? I'll tell you something: Stick it out with me and you'll see the underdog make it to the finish line. I'm talking about big money, Nicky. Big money."

"Whatever you say, Ben."

"That's more like it," Benjamin Styles said. "Where did you leave him, anyway?"

"Mulholland Drive," an exhausted-sounding Horgan said. He wanted to end the conversation. "Got Pete keeping an eye on him."

"Pete?"

"A kid I hired three days ago."

"Got experience?"

"You kidding? Who can afford experience?"

"Never mind that."

"The guy's an actor. Starving. Same as the other two thousand dumbbells in this town."

"Who's Jimmy with?"

"Some fancy broad."

"What she look like?'

"Bleached blond," Horgan said. "Mid-forties. Big tits. Silicone job."

Oh no, Benjamin Styles said to himself.

"I told him to stay away from that Nazi cunt. She's washed up."

"My instructions were to tail Tubesteak," Horgan said. "Nothing else."

"I know," Benjamin Styles said. "That dumb fucking kid."

"Is that all, Mr. Styles? Because I would like to finish wiping here."

"Yeah," Benjamin Styles said. "Do that. Wipe real good. Make it fast. I want you out there right away." And hung up.

⌘

Benjamin Styles lit a cigarillo and began pacing. He was undecided what his next move should be. He couldn't leave the mansion, not this very moment. That would be a dumb move. He knew he would have to figure out a way to get Jimmy away from that sadistic Nazi nympho. Besides, Lisa Koch was through in Hollywood.

She had been a top agent once as Lisa Schwarzwalder. Eight years ago. Then it got out that she was an Ilse "The Bitch of Buchenwald" Koch and Irma "The Beast of Belsen" Grese idolizer; add drugs and too-depraved-even-for-Hollywood ways in the boudoir, and Lisa Koch was slowly squeezed out of the business. She had been forced to sell her agency. The sale had been a lucrative one. However, a good deal of that money was gone now. She had been able to hold on to the house on Mulholland by early sound investments and the periodic sessions of whippings and domination in her custom-made joy chamber equipped with various devices to make her clientele happy with her special brand of sex and sadism.

How could the kid be so stupid? The bitch would surely wear him out, mark him up good. He would have to get her telephone number somehow and put a stop to it.

He picked up the phone again.

Dialed information.

Lisa Koch's number was not listed. Well, he knew that. So why bother?

Benjamin Styles was getting desperate. That dumb fucking peeper. He shouldn't have allowed it to happen. No brains. You only got yourself to blame. You know you can't depend on people.

"Mister Styles?" a female voice said.

Benjamin Styles turned.

Angela Bliss, with lipstick in hand, had stepped into the hallway. Stood in front of a mirror on the wall moistening her lips with a darting pink tongue. I'd like to moisten your lips with something, thought Styles. Sure would.

"What is it, sweetheart?" Benjamin Styles said and felt his cock begin to stir.

"Mr. McFluff would like to see you in his study," Angela said without taking her eyes off the mirror. He guessed the flick was over and Fluffy had other things on his mind. Angela Bliss applied a shade of fuchsia to her lips. Benjamin Styles thought about all the things he'd like to do with this farm girl. The healthy lass with the fuckable ass.

"You know, you got one hell of a set there," Benjamin Styles said, his eyes on her chest.

She seemed to blush.

"Thank you," Angela said.

"I mean it."

"You're so sweet, Mr. Styles."

"I'm a photographer," Benjamin Styles said. "In my spare time. I do portraits. Draw a little, too."

"That must be fun."

"Pretty good at it, if I say so myself," Benjamin Styles said. "Ever do any nude modeling?"

"Well . . ." Her cheeks were as pink as her tongue. She was blushing.

"No," she said, brushing her golden locks out of her face.

"You ever want a portrait of yourself, lemme know."

"Thank you, Mr. Styles. I'd probably have to ask Reggie—"

"Oh no," Benjamin Styles said. "Don't do that. In fact, forget I ever mentioned it. All right?"

Benjamin Styles returned to the bar for a double shot of something strong.

Fluffy

McFluff's study was wall-to-wall books on every subject imaginable. A good portion of it was related to pornography or was porn per se. Picture books, novels, publications like *Playboy* and *Penthouse*, and various others. The gay porn was kept out of sight. McFluff was sitting behind his desk sucking on an olive.

Benjamin Styles cased the wealth he'd always dreamt of having and grinned a wolfish grin. McFluff, The King, knew what Benjamin Styles was thinking, and he was bored by it. Another no-talent jerk crawling about in circles, desperately sniffing around for an opening, a crack in the kingdom to slide inside. Never likely to happen. Styles didn't have it; never would. A certified blowhard who went around intimidating people like a common street thug and never failed to claim that he was "connected" by usually stating something like: *I know people.*

McFluff swallowed the olive and lit an imported cigar. He had decided to give the pipe a break. He left the box open and gestured to Styles.

"Don't mind if I do," Benjamin Styles said, discarding the cheap butt from his mouth and reached in for a Havana. He fired up.

"When can you arrange it?" McFluff asked.

"Depends what kind of arrangement you've got in mind," Benjamin

Styles said. He would finesse this if it killed him. Kidd was his Golden Goose, and this Golden Goose didn't come cheap.

"I thought maybe he could put on a little show for us."

"What kind of show?" Benjamin Styles said.

"What are you asking for?"

"If he's gonna come in here and get a workout . . . ," Benjamin Styles paused, enjoying the aroma of the cigar, "then it's gonna be a little more."

"What do you mean, Styles?" McFluff was getting impatient.

"A part in your next picture."

"Principals have been cast."

"It doesn't have to be a lead role," Benjamin Styles said. "One of the supporting parts will do."

"I'll see what I can do."

"Not good enough."

"I'm not producing this one."

"So what? You're the director."

"Marty Weinstein is the executive producer."

"Makes no difference who the executive producer is."

"Ben . . . ," McFluff paused. "Marty hates your guts."

"You want James Kidd—I want a contract." Benjamin Styles had the door open when he stopped. "No contract, no beefcake." He was bluffing. He prayed to hell it would work.

"Styles, you're too much," McFluff said, smiling and shaking his head. "You think that kid's the only gigolo in town?"

"Have it your way, Reggie. You and I both know Tubesteak's something special. I thought I'd do you a good turn by letting you have him while he still is special. Three, four years from now he'll be nothing but a wasted hustler, a burnout case like so many others in this town. Besides, I don't think I'm being unreasonable. I really don't. Jimmy's worth it. You and I both know it. He'll go far."

"No offense, Styles—but he won't get to square one with you pulling his strings."

"We'll see about that."

"You know what I'm talking about."

"I know exactly what you are talking about."

"You've made a lot of enemies."

"I never slugged anyone who didn't deserve it," Benjamin Styles said, stepping back into the room. "When was I ever wrong?"

"Every move you ever made was wrong. Whatever the reason, you don't go around punching people out. It doesn't work that way."

"The last time I punched anybody out was ten years ago. Ten fucking years ago, mind you. And these assholes are still giving me shit."

"If it were up to me, I'd give you the damn contract; but it's not. I'd be willing to take a chance. I'd give you a break. That's the way I feel about it."

"That's bullshit, Reg. We both know it. All I'm asking for is a co-starring role."

"Like asking for the moon."

"Come on, Reggie," Benjamin Styles said. "We both know you can swing it."

"Let me think about it."

"You do that, Your Lordship." And Benjamin Styles didn't bother closing the door on his way out.

❧

Exactly five minutes later he was in his '69 Toyota climbing Beverly Glen. He was thinking he might even have to slap the kid around a bit to show him who was boss. Goddammit, if he didn't take care of that dick of his it would mean big trouble. Everything down the drain. And Benjamin Styles wasn't about to let that happen.

Whip

Lisa Koch considered small talk a waste of precious time, which she always seemed to be running out of. She had the kid undress the minute he walked through the door.

Ever since she discovered sex, which was at a very young age, she could never get enough. There were many big and varied events that occurred during Lisa Koch's Hollywood career, but before her, this very moment, stood the biggest and the best.

She held Jimmy Kidd's groin in her hands, studying it, unable to take her eyes off of it.

"You've got a beautiful cock, Kidd," Lisa said. "The most beautiful cock I've ever seen."

"Thank you, Ms. Koch," Jimmy said. Stood tall and proud. Felt like a stallion now. King of the Stallions. Jimmy flexed his lats, clenched his abs, chest out. Lisa finally looked up, reaching out with her hand and caressing his massive torso and the thick dark chest hair.

"You're unreal, Kidd," Lisa said. She was so hot she was close to melting. But she didn't want to make any quick moves. She wanted this moment to last forever. "I'm afraid to close my eyes from fear you'll disappear like some mirage."

Jimmy could only smile. "I'm no mirage, Ms. Koch. It's all real."

Her hand slid down from his chest and around to the small of his back. He clenched his buttocks as her soft and moist fingers probed gently, sending something like electric sensations through his body. Lisa Koch knew how to do things. Her other hand stroked his pulsating tool a little harder, but not faster. Lube was key. She had lubed her hands well. Precisely. One should take one's time no matter how difficult, no matter how impossible. This fuck would be a lasting one. A fuck to remember, always. She had plans for this Adonis, for this truly magnificent gift of the gods.

She had both hands on it now and guided it inside her mouth. She was tasting the sweetest thing she'd ever tasted in her entire life, the finest in all-around thickness of shaft as well as the most impressive knob Lisa Koch had ever had in her insatiable mouth; and she'd had hundreds. From matinee idols, rock stars, bit players, studio execs, and heads of state. Jimmy Riff, aka James Kidd, was the Ace of Aces. The best.

His head tilted back, Jimmy was reeling in ecstasy. He'd placed his hands on either side of her head, something like a vise, and squeezed, but not too hard, feeling the fine texture of her hair as he did it. He favored frosted hair, layered. Hers was both. Granted, women her age went for this type of relatively short style to appear younger, and it didn't hurt. He didn't mind. She was great at it. That's all that mattered. He made a conscious effort to keep from applying pressure to her head, for what she was doing felt so damn good.

His hands gripped the top of her head, his jaw tight, teeth clenched, Jimmy knew he would have a tough time holding back. He didn't want to climax too soon; not for a while, anyway. And when I do cum, Jimmy thought, it's going to be something.

Lisa's tongue expertly circled and flicked the knob, making it impossible for him to stand still. She could feel the pressure on her skull now as the kid's fingers continued to squeeze. The kid might cum any minute. She didn't want that to happen, not now. She would have to ease up on him.

Lisa Koch withdrew the hunk of groin out of her salivating mouth and guided her tongue toward the mass of curly hair between the muscular thighs. She knelt directly under him now as her tongue continued to probe under and over to the other side in search of further delights. She loved the smell of him. The kid was wet, sweat pouring from his forehead, from every single pore in his tanned body—but he tasted good, and Lisa Koch wanted to devour every bit of this dream.

Her nose lay nestled between the firm mounds of this fabulous creature, her tongue relentlessly darting deeper and deeper each time. The kid shook, every sinewy muscle that his impressive physique consisted of trembling like one massive human vibrator.

She held on with all her might, clinging to him, her face buried in the kid's ass. She couldn't get enough, and wouldn't know when to stop. She would go on and on with the kid, even if it killed the both of them. It would be worth it, Lisa Koch thought, to go out like that.

Her hands were back on the kid's tool, stroking gently, while her mouth wantonly worshipped the rest of him. Jimmy was surprised, in a way. He never suspected a fine-looking, respectable lady like Lisa could be so good at it. This dame was just a start. Maybe she couldn't do all that much for him career-wise, but she could surely do enough to get him on his way. Besides, it was a first for Jimmy, this type of fuck. A Beverly Hills fuck.

It's *OJT*, Jimmy said to himself. *On the Job Training*. Why he let her pick him up in that bar in Hollywood. It was a start. You took it one rung at a time. He would know how to handle the rest of those fine babes in Beverly Hills and Bel Air, Brentwood and Malibu soon enough. Anyway, he was enjoying himself. He hadn't really expected her to be so aggressive, so sex-starved. But Jimmy Riff, the Kidd, was having the time of his life and nothing else mattered right now.

Jimmy Riff swayed in perfect rhythm to her manipulative fingers.

"I love to fondle you, Kidd," she moaned. "I want to do everything with you. I want to do it all. You're the best, Kidd . . . the best. . . ."

She maneuvered herself under and over to Jimmy's pulsating groin. Her lips were all over it, licking feverishly. She didn't care if he shot his load now; in fact, she wanted him to. She wanted, needed, and desired his creamy juice this very moment.

"Cum, Kidd. Cum in my mouth. I want to taste you. Shoot it, Kidd. Shoot it fast and long and hard. I want to gag on it. I want to swim in it, Kidd. Explode, Kidd. Explode all over me! Shower me with your juice."

Jimmy's erection was a shade of red now, but Lisa Koch was too immersed to notice this. Jimmy was beginning to wince a little from the soreness. The hard tugging and handling only became more severe and painful.

"Hey," Jimmy said. "Ms. Koch?"

There was no way of getting through. The starved female on her knees before him was in another world. She couldn't hear a thing. He might as well be shouting, because it wouldn't have made any difference.

Tug, tug. Grip, grip. The pain was becoming too much.

"Oh, Kidd," she sighed. *"Oh, Kidd."*

He thought of pulling away and hated the idea. He was too close to shooting it all over her; and he wanted to just as badly as she needed it.

Jimmy Riff slowly maneuvered himself over to the sofa, dragging his partner-in-crime right along with him. He sat carefully, holding onto her face to make sure that priceless hunk of meat of his stayed attached to his body, and did not, instead, get left behind in this lady's powerful jaws.

The move hadn't interfered with her assault in the least. She worked even harder, putting everything into it. His most prized possession was a good shade of purple now. Climax or no climax, he would have to do something about it, and fast. He tried pulling away, but it made no difference. He attempted to ward her head away to get her to relent. It didn't work. Jimmy was feeling a mixture of both pain and pleasure. More pain than pleasure.

With an open palm on her forehead, the other hand braced against the sofa for leverage, Jimmy pushed her away and screamed. The teeth around his cock wouldn't let go. The intense, dark eyes looked up at him, begging to let her do what she had to, what she needed to do.

"You have to take it easy," Jimmy pleaded. "Please."

"I will, Kidd," she nodded. "I will." And she proceeded to bring Jimmy Riff to one of the biggest orgasms of his entire gigolo career. The grunt was loud. Every muscle in his body clenching, then subsequently unclenching. Repeatedly. He squeezed the frosted-wet-with-sweat 'do and face in his hands and squeezed hard, pushing her down, goading her to get it, not that he needed to. She licked frantically, did so on her own, wanting every precious drop. She was caught up in it, this feverish frenzy, lapping his thighs, his lean pelvis and abs, his balls.

She reveled in it. And Lisa Koch suspected it was the best blow job she'd ever given anyone.

Jimmy Riff lay against the back of the sofa, spent, exhausted, as she proceeded to lick his genitals clean. She was gentler now, careful and caring. The twinges of pain were gone. And he was thankful.

Uphill Climb

Benjamin Styles hated his car. He hated driving it. He hated the way it looked. He hated it because it was a piece of junk and a constant burden to him. He had spent close to a hundred dollars less than a month ago on a new alternator and the goddamn engine was still making funny noises.

The Toyota puttered up the winding road and Benjamin Styles prayed like hell for it not to break down on him. Where was the justice? Every time he tried to put the pieces together, every time he tried to salvage what was left of his life, someone/something came along and pulled the rug out from under his feet.

Something always happened. Like that time he was up for a part in that crime drama. Pretty big part, too. He had worked for the director before, got along with him. He had worked for the producer, too, on some other picture. They had both told him that the part was practically his. They would contact him in two weeks to confirm it. Two weeks later Benjamin got a letter. *Sorry, Mr. Styles, but we had to hire someone else for the role. The studio insisted on it.*

It was so much bullshit!

Studio, my ass. What the hell they got to do with it! Benjamin Styles had known the main man on the production, the executive producer, and they still wouldn't give him the job.

It's a conspiracy, he kept telling himself.

Benjamin Styles will emerge someday! Benjamin Styles will be the man about town. The star. Hell, he'd been around long enough. Should have been a star twenty years ago.

They don't want me for the gangster flick—so fuck 'em, he thought. So I called Tanner's bluff on that one picture last year. So what? Should have decked the son of a bitch. Just thinking about Robert Tanner immediately caused his anger to rise a notch or two. Benjamin Styles hated the ugly bastard even if he was the top male box office draw in the entire world. And had been for nearly a decade.

Shit, Benjamin Styles should be on that list, and not some dumb Lithuanian by the name of Robert Tanner. They're all assholes anyway, he said to himself. Buncha assholes.

Benjamin Styles' current mode of survival was the welfare department, (the occasional residual check notwithstanding). That weekly unemployment check and the monthly one hundred and fifty dollars he collected from his actor friends who came to his office for casting information. Benjamin Styles was providing them with casting tips via the professional script breakdown service, a service only licensed agents and managers were legally allowed to have. He was charging twenty-five a month per actor. He had four actors and two actresses subscribing to it. That and welfare kept the office going on the seedy studio lot in East Hollywood. It paid for his one-room apartment above Hollywood Boulevard. It put gas in the piece of junk he was driving now. It kept Benjamin Styles alive.

Ten years ago Lisa Schwarzwalder (her real name before she flipped her noodle and legally changed it) could have been a tremendous help to him. Back then she had been one of the top agents in the entertainment industry. But she never had time for Benjamin Styles. She had no room in her agency for new clients. She was always out when Benjamin Styles called.

She was and always would be, Benjamin Styles thought, every inch a bitch. And he would do everything in his power to keep Jimmy away from her and her kind. Besides, she was in no position to afford the exquisite services of James Kidd and his manager.

He would try to feed the engine more and more gas every chance he got; but instead of picking up speed, the goddamn thing would go slower and make more noise. The generator light was flashing now, and Benjamin Styles' shirt was soggy with sweat. He knew he would soon have to stop and take a look under the hood.

He cursed the Koch cunt and he cursed the kid for putting him through this shit. He must have told him forty times: You don't screw nobody unless I say so. You let your manager make the decisions, understand? But what good did it do? That dumb kid was probably getting the whip by now. Just thinking of the whip and what it could do to the kid's body made Benjamin Styles cringe with rage. Goddamn him!

❧

Benjamin Styles pulled over by the side of the road and got out. The engine was smoking. He cursed and popped open the hood. The entire engine was brown, as though a bucket of mud had been thrown over it. What the hell is wrong now? Benjamin Styles didn't know much about cars, never cared to learn, either. But the smell gave him an idea what it might be, because it had happened to him once before when he bought the car from the Jap. The water pump had gone kaput on him. It usually caused the water to squirt out all over the engine.

He unscrewed the radiator cap and knew it was the water pump. The radiator was bone dry.

"Son of a bitch," Benjamin Styles said, slamming the hood shut. He got his sports coat out of the car, palmed the car keys, and walked up Beverly Glen. Benjamin Styles was angrier than a raging bull.

Waiting for Something

Pete Stanfill was weak and spineless; he was also a loser. Those who knew him knew it. Pete Stanfill knew it. Another starving actor trying to make a go of it on food stamps. But food stamps just weren't enough. He had to have pictures taken for his agent, he had to have a resume made; had to pay for the acting lessons. All these things cost money, and he was in the process of earning it, and it made him antsy, antsy and stiff. All over. Restless. They never showed you this part of it in the movies, or on those private detective shows on the tube. Nope.

What was he doing? Sitting in the Volks watching the two-story house on the hill with the fence around it. There was a mean German Shepherd standing sentry at the gate, and that meant he wouldn't be able to get anywhere near the house. No way to get to see what was happening inside, if anything. He wondered what was so special about this guy that Nicky Horgan was paying him ten dollars an hour to watch? And what was the woman's name again?

Mr. Horgan had never even told him. He had given him a B & W shot of the man. Don't lose him, he'd said. About it.

Pete cursed under his breath. Rested his head back. Going to be a long night, looks like, he said to himself, and did not have the slightest idea what was taking place inside the well-guarded compound.

Close Your Eyes

"You like blueberry jelly, Jimmy?" She was in the kitchen reaching inside the refrigerator.

"Sure," Jimmy Riff said. "Sounds good."

He could use something in his stomach right now. In fact, the kid knew he should do something to replenish the spooge.

"Close your eyes," Lisa Koch said. "I've prepared something especially for you."

The kid did as she asked. He was game.

"You got your eyes closed?"

"I got my eyes closed."

"You sure?"

"Yep. I'm sure," Jimmy said. Thinking she must make one hell of a sandwich. His eyes were shut tight. The aroma of peanut butter was in the air. Easy to detect. He'd had his share of it. When you couldn't afford real food, peanut butter saved the day. It was protein. He didn't mind. Didn't add up, though, not when you lived in a house like this, up here on Mulholland, to be serving peanut butter to your guest.

She sidled up to him now, pressing those silicone-swollen hooters close, but not entirely, against his face.

"Open. . ." she said, then guided a nipple toward his mouth. Jimmy was a bit surprised; it wasn't exactly what he had expected. He opened his eyes, staring at the artificially bloated, swollen tits before him covered in peanut butter. Some guys were put off by fake tits, and maybe they had a right to be, and maybe he would have been put off himself any other time. Here and now, it was not an issue. He was smiling. Peanut butter had never looked so delicious. She had to be at least a 34, he thought. Double Ds. Firm, too. Well, not too much so. Fake tits very often were, though. Not always. Usually.

"Not bad for a 46-year-old broad, huh?" Lisa Koch said, while guiding his eager mouth to the right nipple. "Lick, Jimmy, lick," Lisa Koch said, feeling the nipple harden as the kid's tongue continued to flick, circling it, then easing over the nipple itself and taking it full in his mouth and sucking.

Lisa's other hand was between her own thighs now, parting the moist bush and probing inside. Her eyes closed, she was discovering new pleasures, grander sensations; her fingers moving in and out ever-so-smoothly that her own cunt juices made possible as well as the generous amount of lube she had applied in addition. She caressed the clit. God, she loved having both stimulated: clit and pussy lips; but the clit, rubbing gently, giving it considerable attention very often resulted in a sexual experience second to none—but only if the other person did the flicking either with their lips and tongue, or else masturbated her. And of course, insertion, preferably with a live cock, before or after—didn't matter—was the icing on the cake, so to speak. It all worked.

He's the one who should be doing this, she thought. And will be soon enough. Might have to be reminded. They very often did. The clit is number one, lover man. The clit rules. The greatest orgasms are brought to fruition by massaging and being loving and nice to Ms. Clitoris.

She guided her other, perfectly hardened, nipple toward his waiting mouth. "Suck it, my lover man," she sighed. "Get your lunch; get the protein your body craves."

Jimmy had most of the peanut butter licked off her tits and was moving down toward her soft and welcoming belly.

"And down here, Kidd," she panted, "we got blueberry jelly."

Jimmy Riff's wet tongue cleaned out her belly button, tickling her in the process.

"You like blueberry jelly, Kidd?"

"I do," Jimmy said. His mouth moved lower.

"Suck my cunt, Kidd," Lisa Koch said, her fists clenched. "Eat my cunt; eat me out, Jimmy. . . . Suck my pussy. . . ." His mouth dropped lower, his face buried between her tanned upper thighs. His tongue worked and flicked and did so without pause. There was no way for Lisa to control her moans that continued to increase in volume with each nanosecond. And while his tongue tended to the clit and other parts of her cunt, she grabbed the middle finger of his right hand and guided it toward the center of her buttocks and slid it inside her asshole. This was the incredible sensation she had been waiting for. A man who went along with it, a man who was not put off by the butt, who was not above finger-fucking her asshole while at the same time licking and flicking her extremely sensitive clit.

"YES, YES, YES! Oh yes! I knew you'd love blueberry jelly! Suck my jelly, James Kidd! Suck my sweet jelly! Whatever you do, don't stop; don't you dare stop!"

Jimmy Riff, aka James Kidd, wouldn't think of stopping. Not a chance. What kind of man would do that? *Don't mind what she's saying.*

She's feeling the love. In the moment: woman is in the moment. He was getting a lot out of it himself, seeing the power he had over them. Being able to make a woman go nuts with passion this way.

"Finger-fuck my asshole!" the woman demanded. "Eat my cunt! Eat my hot cunt! Then stop long enough to be nice to my butt! Get that tongue of yours inside my butt crack! Do it! DO IT! JUST DO IT!"

Not that he needed to be told. He'd planned on doing exactly that. Knew from experience, women liked to have their asshole played with, licked, sucked, finger-fucked—and plenty enjoyed having a nice hard cock in there as well while they sucked off prick at the other end. Some, more than a few, fantasized about lots of things: one of them being ravaged, fucked thoroughly by several men at once: up the rump, in the cunt, in the mouth—and then sprayed with bountiful streams of *white-hot cum.* Some liked being pissed on, or worse. But you had to draw the line somewhere. There was only so much he was willing to do. At least this one here wasn't asking to be urinated or defecated on. And the rest of it: it was all good, healthy fun. Fucking. Sex. Kinky to boot.

They loved it. One only had to coax it out of them, talk to them, find out what it was that got their motor racing. It took time, lots of time. They were not always forthcoming with this information. This one was. She was old enough, he'd supposed—and that was key. Been around. Knew what she liked and wasn't shy about requesting it.

His tongue serviced the A-hole long enough, and he was back on the cunt and clit, worked it like a vibrator, relentlessly, patiently, covering new ground of the soft, moist vagina flesh. He cupped her buttocks in his strong manly hands, supporting them this way, holding her up in his lap.

The woman had her arms wrapped around Jimmy's sweaty neck, trying to balance herself and to keep from toppling over. Beads of perspiration poured from her forehead, neck, under her arms; from between her tennis-playing, tennis-hardened, muscular, and fit buttocks.

She was due for an encore: you stayed with what works. That same middle finger of his, the pussy finger, returned to the previous erogenous zone: her precious backside, and drove it in deep. *Fuck yes.* He enjoyed doing this as much as he enjoyed driving his thick prick in there—the times the women allowed it. He was eager and willing each and every time—upon request. Some men didn't care to oblige, were even repulsed by it. Not Jimmy Riff. No, sir. Tubesteak was game. It was a great joy and pleasure to service any woman's butthole—so long as she gave her consent.

This one? This one was loving it. *What an understatement.*

She screamed, quivering, holding on tighter than before. There she was, bending her head down, kissing him savagely, hard, on the neck and mouth. Biting, biting. Leaving a trail of hickeys up and down his neck. And that vicious kiss on the mouth, painful enough, to be sure, drew blood. Alas, at that moment, Jimmy Riff had no way of knowing that his upper lip was bleeding; he was too immersed in the moment, lost to it, engulfed by it.

Jimmy withdrew the finger and proceeded to concentrate solely on the cunt until he had it sucked dry—and wondering if it were possible? And the clit? The clit was twice the size it was when they initially started this sex marathon. Twice its normal size. He was sure of it. Nothing unusual there. He'd experienced this phenomena before. You got a woman hot enough, worked on her cunt and clit long enough, patiently enough—and this was the amazing and incredible result: swollen clit; wet love hole dripping with pussy honey.

"Oh, Kidd. . . . Jimmy. . . . Ohhhhhh. . . ."

When Jimmy paused briefly to come up for air, Lisa Koch took the opportunity to return to his face and lips, drawing more blood, blood that she would suck deep into her own mouth with relish.

Jimmy Riff had his feet up on the sofa, lying this way on it himself, while resting his head against the armrest at that end of it, bringing her dark bush directly over his face. At the other end, he had both arms on her shoulders so that she wouldn't topple over and land on the floor.

She was sitting on his face now, her strong thighs firmly clamped against his ears. She wanted to adjust her position in order so that she might get at his rigid member and balls, and he let her: guided her to make it easier for her to have all the access she craved.

His tongue lapped up and down each buttock in turn, found the brown butthole in the center and licked away, probing, searching seeking out what he could not get enough of, while at the other end, her cock-starved mouth worked away on his woody.

And then it happened: tandem explosions! Not unlike two steaming, boiling hot volcanoes erupting, both emitting loud yelps and screams, as they sucked at and wallowed in each other's sweat and fiery lava produced by their way-too-sensitive and overworked sexual organs.

Hitchhike

His arm held straight out, thumb pointing up, Benjamin Styles climbed the steep road. It took its toll. *Goddamn, I'm out of shape. For a former boxer, someone who was fit as a fiddle once, I am definitely in sorry shape.*

At the age of sixteen, handsome, fair-haired Benjamin Styles had been a Golden Gloves boxing champ on the East Coast and drew babes like a magnet. Then had turned pro a few years later; won his share of big purses; was on his way to becoming light-heavy champ. He had made it with just about every starlet back then—East and West Coast—and in between: Vegas cunt, and more than a few European ladies who were drawn to his manly persona. He had been in demand back then, just like Jimmy was now. Difference was, the kid is convinced it will last forever. Dummy. Pure imbecile. Nothing lasts forever. Nothing. Your youth goes, muscle turns to flab, hair falls out, wrinkles and liver spots spoil your once-handsome looks, and there you are wondering what the fuck happened?

But the one thing Benjamin Styles never allowed—as many offers as he'd had in the past from those ballsy enough to approach him—a fruit to put his hands on him. *Nobody buggers Ben Styles.* I'm no fag. Benjamin Styles was a macho motherfucker, a man's man, and everybody around him knew it and he liked it that way. Shit, he fought in front of kings and queens, heads of state from all over the world; cunt fought to hop in his bed; bitches, high class bitches grabbed his cock in nightclubs, restaurants, Vegas events, concerts. Pinching his ass. Literally threw themselves at him. He had been something back then. "In demand," was too lame a description. At least two grand always in his pocket. Walking-around money.

But he had also been arrogant back then. Dumb. As dumb as the kid. He had squandered his dough recklessly, never thinking of tomorrow, never even dreaming that the well would go dry, that a day like today would ever come around.

He had to take a breather, thumb still held high. Look at me. Hitchhiking. No one is going to stop for you on Beverly Glen. Not at night. Not in LA. Not after that slaughter Manson and his sorry lapdogs pulled off back in the '60s. The senseless killings had stayed with the public, not only here, but throughout the globe. Punk Manson and his dipshit followers.

The cars whizzed by. Nobody was interested in picking up a pot-bellied has-been pugilist in his fifties with thinning hair and a soaking wet shirt on his back.

Fucking town is the armpit of America, he thought. And wondered if Charlie M. had been wrong, after all. Pissed off by years of rejection and general mistreatment and disrespect. Same thing he was going through himself presently and had been going through forever. Ask me where the rage and anger and short fuse come from? Go on, ask. He shook his head, recounting the many years he'd wasted in Hollywood, the thousands of dollars pissed away, and nothing to show for it. Wisdom? Hard-earned. Where was it when you needed it most? Good question. Waste of time.

He had even done some collecting for the mob: in Jersey, Boston, New York, Detroit, Vegas—and wherever else he was sent. Bullshitted about his background. Had claimed his mother's maiden name was Spinnell. I got Italian blood on her side. Irish on my father's side. Besides, there hadn't been any need to convince anyone; both groups liked him. For a while. While the going was good. Had made their share off him. Took a dive now and then. Both made heavy jack: Irish thugs and made guys. So did he. Made decent bread collecting, real decent. Because Styles knew how to make them come up with the vig. It never bothered him to break an arm or two. He broke thumbs, fingers, legs. Why not? It was his job. Some of those punks had it coming. Every now and then you broke some mook's jaw or nose and it worked—and lasted. Example. Set one. He did. More than his share. Until that day when the sorriest mook of them all jumped to his death from the roof of his hotel in Atlantic City. Jumped. Wasn't pushed. Jumped without help. On his own. Took a dump in his shorts before doing so. It was the beginning of the end of Benjamin Style's career as a collector. Didn't matter that the dirtbag dove on his own. Nope. Feared Benjy so much he had himself convinced jumping was the easier way out. Never mind that all Benjamin had intended on doing that day was breaking nothing more than a finger on each hand, maybe only the thumbs. Keep the fool from gambling, playing poker and the slots. He was a porny. Made a shitload of money. Gay and straight porn, bestiality. Videos. Movies. Loops. Books and mags. All he had to do was curtail the gambling jonze. Couldn't do it. Swear to God, all I wanted was to put some real fear in his ass. But it hadn't worked out that way. "Can't squeeze a nickel out of a dead mook, can you?" he'd been told by people he was collecting for. Then another deadbeat hurled himself from a freeway overpass and landed on a car below. Crashed right through the windshield. What a mess. All that viscera.

Styles had been in pursuit. A third schmuck stepped in front of a moving train. It was not a pretty sight. More than one witness claimed they saw Benjy playing cat-and-mouse with the vic, enjoying himself. And Benjy Styles' life as a one-man collection agency was *finito*. Over. He was out. Winter Hill wanted nothing to do with him, and neither did the mob.

The times he was flat broke in the past and living in LA, he'd go back east and collect for a while, build up a nice nest egg, and return to the fucking dream factory. Had the acting bug. That's what it was. Wanted to beat it. Show them he was good, that there was more to him than a pair of boxing gloves and brass knucks; more to him than a bully. Always returned to Tinseltown. His pals back East didn't get it, said so. Stay here. What do you wanna go over there where all them fairies live, Benjy? Why? You're a man. Stay put. Move up; you'll move up, but not if you take off whenever you got some dough in your pocket. Listen to us, Benjy, your future is here, not on the fuckin' fake coast. Fuck the movies, Benjy. No offense, but that's for alla them *sissies* out there. Queers. *Capische*. You ain't one of them, pal. You're a paisan; *paisan*, Benjy. Well, half paisan, anyway. What's the diff, eh, boyo?

But he had been a brash young punk back then, a know-it-all, and he liked to show off with beautiful ingenues. He liked to party and have a good time. Life was short. Why not? Live it up. Be happy. Except all the partying was on the biggest fool of them all. Guessed it: one Benjamin Styles. Would never think to let someone else pick up the tab once in a while.

Look at me now. Caught himself. Straightened up, and started walking. Got to cut out that negative bullshit. James Kidd is the way out. Jimmy Kidd would make him a wealthy man again. Put him on top; the same way he, Benjy Styles, had put others on top.

Thoughts of the whip made him drop his depressing past and pick up his pace.

"The fuck are you doin'?"

The German Shepherd continued to pace the grounds on the other side of that wrought iron gate, pausing every now and then to glare at the red Volkswagon and growl. Pete Stanfill took his glasses off and cleaned them with a tissue. He put them back on, looking at the animal and not ever remembering when he'd seen a dog as beautiful and as pissed off as this.

Pete Stanfill's stomach made funny noises, and he remembered he hadn't eaten since that morning. He reached for the worn girlie mag in the glove compartment in an effort to fight off the hunger and deal with the boredom. Pete Stanfill, the weakling, liked to fantasize. And he was good at it. He held a Kleenex in one hand, while the other massaged his growing chubby. He'd look down at the skin magazine, close his eyes, and let his imagination do the rest.

"You've got a great imagination, Petey," those who knew him had always told him. "You should do something with it." Well, he sure was doing something with it now. His imagination would help him forget how broke he was, the empty belly, and the goals he had set for himself and was having an impossible time getting anywhere near.

He unzipped his jeans and gripped his woody.

Pete Stanfill was no super-stud, but he had a good seven inches and he was proud of it. Seven inches of perpetually hard man-meat that never seemed to see any other state. He walked around with a virtual hard-on 24/7. And his only means of relief was by playing with himself.

Girls he had always been crazy about. But he was always too shy and nervous around them, and it ruined things. Tongue-tied. It was frustrating. It was a problem he'd been trying to solve for years. However, a solution was nowhere to be found.

"Drink a beer," a friend would suggest. "Smoke a J, snort some toot." Pete was always afraid to touch any of that stuff. He didn't want to go near dope. He knew damn well what drugs did to a person and wanted no part of it. He might try beer, he thought. He might try beer some day.

He stroked, pausing long enough to run the palm of his hand over the head of his groin. The epicenter of pleasure. It all came down to the knob. This was it. Be good to the knob and you will be rewarded. He was so wrapped up in his fantasy, so into the moment and wanting it to happen, so close to exploding, that he didn't hear the footsteps that walked right up to the window of his car.

"Christ," Benjamin Styles said, shaking is head. Watched as a nervous Pete Stanfill shoved his erection back inside his fly. "The fuck are you doin'?" Benjamin Styles said, grabbing him by the collar. "You're supposed to be watching that house."

"What?" Pete Stanfill said. He didn't know what was going on. Had no idea who this maniac was. "I don't understand."

"You're jacking off on my time, punk, understand? I'm Benjamin Styles, and you're supposed to be looking after my investment."

"I'm sorry, sir," Pete said, shrinking in his seat. "I don't know anything about any investment. Truly, sir."

"The Kidd! That's what 'investment.' Got it?"

"The kid? Mr. Horgan didn't say anything about it."

"Figures," Benjamin Styles said.

"Please. You're hurting me, sir."

"Aw, shut up," Benjamin Styles said and let go. Pete Stanfill stuck his hand inside the black leather satchel on the passenger seat to retrieve something, and before he was able to do so Benjamin Styles thrust his own hand in with lightning speed and gripped Stanfill by the wrist. "Move so much as an inch, punk, and I'll break your fucking arm."

The kid, scared shitless, farted.

"Slowly," warned Benjamin Styles. "We're going to take your fuckin' paw out of there." Pete Stanfill did as told. "Let's see what you were reaching for, asshole." In Pete's hand was nothing more than a black-and-white 8-by-10 glossy of Jimmy. Smiling. Matinee-idol looks. Perfect teeth. Below the image, the block letters spelled out: JAMES KIDD. Benjamin Styles Talent Management; phone numbers to office and answering service.

Styles sighed.

"Mister, all I was told was to watch the house, make sure I tail the guy in the picture. This James Kidd guy. I don't know anything else about it, I swear. When you asked about 'the kid,' wasn't sure what you meant. Nicky Horgan keeps me in the dark about these things. Don't trust nobody. Got this fear I'll call up the *National Enquirer*, one of the gossip rags, and sell what I know about some of these celebrities who live out here."

"You'll know about Kidd," Benjamin Styles said. "This town will know about James Kidd, and so will the rest of the world. Me and him are like Elvis and the Colonel—with real talent. Elvis was overrated, and the Colonel was nothing more than a suitcase pimp. He pimped the poor bastard out for all he was worth in order to pay off gambling debts. Stuck him in all those shitty movies, worked him like a dog. Right into the ground."

He was looking at the restless four-legged killer on the other side of that fence across the street from them as he spoke. The bitch had had the crazy nerve to name him *Blondi*, and every other German shepherd she ever owned, after Hitler's own four-legged beast. Any wonder she was blackballed by the business? "Yessiree, everyone will soon know about James Kidd . . . if I can get to him before that Nazi bitch puts him in traction."

"I'm real sorry."

"How long they been in there?"

"About three hours."

"'About?' What's that mean?"

"Three hours, sir."

"Damn," Benjamin Styles said and walked up to the gate. The dog stood on solid ground, bearing his killer fangs. Benjamin Styles jumped back and wished he had a gun with him, or at least a ball bat, but all he had to fight this vicious animal with were his bare hands. He didn't care for those odds.

He kicked the fence several times, hoping the dog would create enough of a racket to draw the cunt outside. All the dog did was growl and show his choppers, and the fence-kicking was wearing the former Golden Gloves champ out. He turned, looked around for a branch, a big enough rock, something to fight this fucking beast with. He knew he'd have to get inside pretty soon to stop it, if the dummy wasn't getting a taste of the whip by now.

Black-and-Blue

Jimmy Riff's head was spinning. He felt drowsy and weak, and he didn't understand why. Everything was a blur. Maybe it was the glass of milk; maybe she had slipped him a Mickey. But why would she?

He felt pain in every part of his body, particularly around the wrists and ankles. It was not an unfamiliar kind of pain. Just like the time the LAPD busted him for jaywalking. Right down there on Hollywood Boulevard, too. He had been in town maybe two weeks and was used to crossing the street wherever he damn well pleased. Hell, you did it in other cities. Why not here? Was this town supposed to be any different? He'd never even heard of "jaywalking" until he got to L.A.

The cops in their dark blue uniforms had thrown him to the ground, slapped cuffs on him and searched him. That's it, he said to himself. That's what it feels like: handcuffs. She's put cuffs on me. Handcuffed him to a brass bed. Felt like she'd used leather restraints on his ankles as a way of securing his feet to the other end of the bed. On his belly. Spread eagled. But he couldn't see, and he wasn't certain what else she had done to him. Jimmy Riff could only make grunts and similar sounds through the spinning haze and feel the sharp, stinging pain that paid repeat visits across the small of his back.

Lisa Koch stood directly over the presently helpless stud muffin. She wore black, knee-length leather boots with heels, a black garter belt with fishnets, a leather bra, a Nazi officer's cap, and other related Nazi regalia. She held a riding crop and a large red apple in one hand and a vibrator in the other. She slid the pre-lubed vibrator up loverboy's rectum. This seemed to wake him up a bit, and his grunts got louder once he realized what was taking place. He hadn't wanted anything shoved in his ass. *So, it was perfectly fine to do it to me, but not the other way around. That it?*

She posed the question to him, took a good bite out of the apple, and before he could respond or answer she shoved the apple in his mouth. Made a nice gag.

She took her time chewing.

She raised the crop high above her, waited a second, took in a deep breath, and came down with it hard across Jimmy Riff's behind. The hustler's shoulders and back were streaked with blue and red welts and it drove her wild with desire.

"I'll be good, Daddy," Frau Koch said in what was clearly meant to be a sarcastic tone. "I'll be good." Again the crop came down. Leaving a fresh welt. "I'll be good to you, Daddy. . . . Don't hurt me." She was enjoying this scene with this hunk of a man cuffed to the bed helplessly before her. Discipline was the name of the game, and she was the disciplinarian in charge, the one who called the shots, created the rulebook, dominated. Just like her twin heroes: Ilsa Koch and Irma Grese. Two Nazi bitches who enjoyed meting out punishment. Lisa couldn't decide which of the women she admired more. Both equal in cruel and twisted behavior: Ilsa favored prisoners with tattoos; in fact, killed them for them. Cut the tats out and framed them. Irma had a higher murder count. Both females knew how to torture and punish. Both females were feared. The former hung herself in prison at age 60.

Grese was hung at age 22.

Lisa Koch presently was the queen and goddess combined herself, and the massive cock before her but a slave to be penalized and humiliated and dealt with as she saw fit.

Jimmy shook his head, yelling through the apple gag. She reached down, retrieved the apple, said: "What was that? I'm sorry; couldn't make it out."

"No," Jimmy said. "Don't do this. I didn't agree to this."

"Know what you are? Ungrateful. You have no idea how many men, studio execs and legit movie stars: men and women, pay good money for the service. Here you are not being charged and have the nerve to gripe."

"Get the thing out of my ass," Jimmy said. "This is sick."

"I'm wet down there," she said, taking another bite of the apple, and jamming it back in his mouth. Never mind the protests. They weren't valid, after all, were they? She licked Jimmy Riff's behind between breaks in the chewing. Caressed it with the free hand. "The pain is not for naught, my forever loverboy," she said, and kissed him tenderly. "It'll be over soon, Kidd. I won't hurt you. I just like to see you like this . . . at my mercy. . . . Your asshole, your cock, your balls at my disposal to do as I wish. . . ." She held a pocket rocket against her clit. "You cannot believe the sensations, the absolute variety and varying degrees of sensations I am experiencing at the moment. I can't take the pleasure, Kidd. I really can't."

She kissed his eyelashes, his brows; nose, earlobes. What a beautiful man he is, she thought. So beautiful. Such a treasure.

"You've got nice eyes, Romeo. Long, dark eyelashes. . . . So perfect." She was done chewing. Paused to stare without moving a muscle.

"Could use a nose job. Just a minor one. Nothing major, of course. Then again, maybe not . . . of course not. You just wouldn't have the same virile look about you, loverboy, were you to have the bridge re-shaped."

There's too damn many perfect noses in Hollywood, she thought. The kid is just right.

She would handle him with care for a while. Then the whip, the all-infamous whip, the whip that had brought about her downfall in Hollywood. Well, it hadn't been entirely that, the Nazi uniforms and insignia, boots, whatnot, had played a great deal. I'll have to be careful, she said to herself. I don't want "James Kidd" to pass out. Not yet.

A Jack in Hand

"Lemme have the jack," Benjamin Styles said.

"I don't understand," Pete said.

"There isn't a whole hell of a lot you do understand, is there, punk?"

Benjamin Styles was in no mood for conversation, and Pete Stanfill knew it. He still wouldn't like it, whatever it was this nut was about to do to the dog.

"Is it really necessary, Mr. Styles? I mean, to hurt someone's pet like that?"

"Like what?" Benjamin Styles asked, taking the key out of the ignition. "You don't even know what I'm gonna do. Nobody's gonna hurt the fucking mutt, understand?"

"Yes, sir."

"Gimme the jack."

"Yes, sir."

"You gonna 'yessir' me all night long? Get the fucking jack."

"No, sir. I mean yes, sir," Pete Stanfill said, reaching for the tire iron from under his seat. Handed it to Benjamin Styles.

"Keep quiet," Benjamin Styles said, and walked back to the fence. The sentry wasn't about to budge. Not only was he ready to do battle, but couldn't wait to dig his blood-thirsty fangs into Benjamin Styles' throat—if only given the chance. He was frothing and growling. He was ready, and so was one pissed-off down and out unemployable bit-part movie actor, hack screenwriter and motion picture producer named Benjamin Styles, who had never produced a movie in his life. That didn't matter, because his business card said he was: writer/director/actor/producer. You better believe it. That was how Tinseltown worked. You got a bunch of fancy business cards printed up that claimed you were all of those things. It was proof enough. Many did it. Bluffed their way through. Difference was, Styles had a long history in this town, had appeared in many films. But none of that mattered now. He had a Nazi killer dog to deal with.

"I'm gonna ask you nicely to back off," Styles said to the canine, "before I climb over this fucking fence. Got it? Back off, motherfucker."

The dog refused to be stared down. He wanted blood. Was set on it. This was what he had been trained to do. Destroy, tear to bits and pieces anyone who attempted to trespass.

"Have it your way," said Benjamin Styles, and wondered if he'd be able to get up and over before the animal began to tear at his legs as he climbed down to its side? It took real effort, but Styles made it up the wrought iron bars, straddled the top bar. Sat there this way while the dog took leaps, snapping its jaws at him. Styles would lower one of his feet and the dog would lift its head and attempt to jump and take a bite, and Styles would pull the foot back in time.

Son of a bitch. Nazi-worshipping twat and her Nazi pooch. Trained him well. At the least, whoever she paid had trained the psycho animal all too well to reach a fever pitch of rage and fury and need to destruct.

Fine, thought Benjamin Styles, he would do the same. Continue to psych himself up, the way he'd been doing all along. The only way to deal with an aggressive animal like this.

He baited the dog, kept lowering then raising the leg. Would do it longer each time, in that his foot was lower and lower, until mere inches from the frothing dog's jaw.

"Come and get it, you fuck," hissed Styles. "Want a piece of me? Sure you do. Not nearly as much as I want a piece of you, cocksucker." The dog stepped back far enough away, readying for something, a great charge. Smart. Good, real good, thought Styles. This was what he had wanted. Perfect.

"Come at me, punk," said he to the dog, raising his jack high enough. Blondi did exactly that. Ran up. Dug its fangs into Styles' leather boot and Styles swung down with the tire iron, rapping it across its eyes and forehead, knocking it close to senseless.

"Bitch," thought Styles. Dog was on its side, whimpering and making all sorts of weak noises. All huff and blow, like all the other windbags he'd dealt with his entire life.

He turned his head. Could hear, then saw the Stanfill kid standing by the side of his VW throwing up, or at least attempting to. Weak. Kid was weak. This town was no place for weaklings. The dog continued to gasp. Saliva mixed with blood oozing out of its jaw. Another hard whack took care of that. Stanfill was vomiting at last. Good, thought Styles.

He made it up the stoop, crossed the front porch. Front door was half glass. He braced himself against it, leaning his shoulder in. Door was solid and wouldn't budge. No matter. He had the jack. Turned his head away and whacked at the glass, breaking it and making a hole large enough to get his hand inside and turn the knob. He let himself in. He stood in place, waited and listened. Could hear what sounded like a snapping sound that only could be made by a whip. The muffled cry made by a man was the other sound he heard. His investment and future at stake, Benjamin Styles ran up the flight of stairs. He had never been here before. There were doors on the left, as well as on the right. He stood. Waited. There it was: the sound. Crack. The whip was at work. He opened the door and stood there, taking it in: Bitch was in her Nazi outfit: boots, fishnets and all the rest, and she had that infamous whip in her hand. She had his Jimmy cuffed to the brass bed at both ends with a dildo or vibrator up his butt. His back and buttocks were covered in welts. There were bright-red glistening streaks that must have been blood. The sadistic kraut cunt.

Lisa Koch had the whip raised over her head and was about to give her sex slave another lash, when she sensed that there was a third person present. She lowered the whip, turned, facing Styles. Placing her hands on her hips, she wondered how he had managed to get past her fierce Blondi?

"Your mutt's out of commission," said Styles. "I suggest you get him to your vet. Not to save him, because it's way past that point."

"And who the fuck, might I ask, are you? Furthermore, what the fuck are you doing in my house?"

Styles's eyes and concern were with the kid. He cursed under his breath, or said Jesus or both. He had heard enough stories about this cruel ball-buster over the years, as everyone else had, and how merciless the bitch was—but he had never dreamed it was anything this bad. The sheet Jimmy was lying on, Styles realized, was stained with his blood. Yes, he, Benjy Styles, had done his share of beating up people, broke a bone or two, but it had never gotten this messy. And the three who did themselves in? That had had very little to do with him. He'd never physically done the shoving himself.

To be honest, his primary concern had not been with the kid's own health, but what the bitch had done to damage his looks, his body: the goods.

"Blondi," Lisa Koch said. "What have you done with Blondi?"

Styles entered the room. "Take that thing out of his rectum," he said. "Get the bracelets off."

Lisa Koch lifted her Nazi cap, shook her frosted head of hair. She wiped sweat from her brow, then glared at him, demanding an explanation. *"What have you done with Blondi?"*

"Your dog is probably dead by now, bitch."

"What? You killed Blondi? Do you realize what that animal cost me? What it cost to have him trained?"

"I won't say it again: Turn the kid loose."

"Just who the hell do you think you are, buster?"

"You know damn well who I am, lady," said Styles. "I'm his manager. Benjamin Styles. Don't pretend you've never heard of me. You've got just about two seconds to get the cuffs off my boy. Got it? Or *you* get it."

Instead of moving to do as told, she raised the whip and let Styles have it across his torso. The pain was considerable. Bitch knew how to use the whip. Should have been a lion tamer in a circus. Siegfried and Roy could have used her in Vegas.

Then she went for another go. Let the whip fry the air. Styles ducked in time, reaching out with his fist, snagging the whip and tugged on it hard, pulling the Nazi cunt to her knees. He retrieved the whip, held the hilt in his fist, then let her have it about half a dozen times: across her back, shoulders, and face. He walked up, knelt down.

He gripped her by the throat—one-handed, then cocked his right fist, and sent a knuckle sandwich into Lisa Koch's face, that face that had visited so many cosmetic surgeons over the years, that precious and perfect and vicious-looking face that had been given so much tender care over the years—alas, now it was a face with two front teeth missing in its jaw and blood oozing from it.

Lisa Koch lay slumped against the carpeted floor. She was out cold.

Benjamin Styles spotted the key on the dresser and was freeing the kid in no time. He tossed his boxers at him. Jimmy was hardly in any shape to dress himself, but he managed to get into his underwear. Styles found Band-Aids, cotton swabs, and a bottle of peroxide on the dresser. Evidently the cunt had intentions of taking care of his wounds—after she'd marked him up pretty good and gotten her jollies first. He did what he could to tend to the kid's back.

He handed him the cotton swabs and peroxide, said: "You'll have to take care of your own butt, because I'm not going anywhere near your ass."

Jimmy ignored that. Let his buttocks go. Besides, the shorts were already on. Styles helped the kid get into his shirt. Jimmy got into his trousers, socks, shoes, and they walked out of the bedroom, down the flight of stairs and out to the deserted Volks.

Styles helped Jimmy into the front seat. Since that other punk was nowhere to be seen, Benjamin got in on the driver's side, turned the key in the ignition. He made a U-turn and headed in the direction of Beverly Glen. At Beverly Glen he turned south, toward the Hollywood side.

The Contract

Three days of rest and the kid was all right again. And he had but one person to thank: Benjamin Styles. Benjamin had even driven the kid to some clinic and had a doctor he knew take a look at him.

"Don't worry," the doc said, "this boy's as healthy as an ox."

Upon Styles' *insistence*, the doctor briefly explained the dangers of syphilis: that if not stopped in time it could eventually cause damage to the brain, the spinal cord or the heart and blood vessels; and that it can cause insanity, paralysis, or death. "What killed Capone," Benjy Styles interjected.

"But if caught early enough," the doc continued, "and treated with penicillin, permanent body damage can be prevented." Styles had the kid tested for VD. The kid was good. No problem there.

And so James Kidd would be ready to get back into action, action his manager would approve only. Which was fine by Jimmy. He wouldn't go off on his own anymore. It was funny, though, the way that Koch broad had turned on him. He had never expected it, never even dreamed she would do something like that. She could have easily deep-sixed him. If it hadn't been for Benjamin, James Kidd might actually be dead right now.

Jimmy pulled on a beer as a soap opera played on Benjamin Styles' beat-up B&W portable. You couldn't help but notice how small the place was. His benefactor kept it clean, though. Styles was a puzzle. Guy seemed talented, as an actor, at least. Dabbled in painting and photography. Evidence of it was everywhere: Framed photos of all types, as well as framed oils, watercolors, and acrylics, took up every inch of wall space. There were other paintings, not yet framed, on the floor, left leaning against furniture, or else in the hallway against one side of the wall. If he were honest with himself, none of it grabbed him. Photos lacked a certain something, call it pizzazz, or the composition was never quite right. A photographer, any photographer, either had a good eye or he didn't. It had to be in your blood. Something like that could not be taught. You were born with it or you weren't. Jimmy himself didn't have it, knew it, but was not bothered by it. Only when he spotted it, it slammed him right in the gut, hit him right between the eyes. It was the same when it came down to art, paintings. And Styles' efforts in that area? Artwork appeared amateurish to him. Jimmy loved van Gogh, Manet, Monet, could even appreciate Picasso's genius. Styles, on the other hand, had the ability, or lack of, of a grade school kid. Well, Jimmy thought, you're not much of an artist yourself, so maybe it isn't fair to be so judgmental here. Now, the man's history as an actor, and the long list of credits. . . That was impressive. Had to be. Many films with famous stars. Bit parts, to be sure, character roles, but the films themselves had raked in big money and had been popular with moviegoers. Left Jimmy wondering why Benjamin Styles wasn't better known himself. There had to be a reason.

Schwab's

At Schwab's drugstore on Sunset, where Benjamin Styles liked to go in the evening for a cup of joe and to mingle with others in the business, a rumor was in the air. Something to do with Lisa Koch and her two front teeth—which were not there anymore.

Lisa Koch would not say who did the deed. Had initially claimed it was an accident: a trip, a fall; she had walked into something; then it was a home invasion. A prowler had broken in, killed her beloved Blondi, and knocked her out.

The other rumor, and quite possibly closer to the truth: Benjamin Styles's knuckles had had something to do with it. Why the fearless, Nazi-worshipping bitch wouldn't talk wasn't exactly clear. Could be she had payback on her mind and was biding her time. Whatever the truth was (and its eventual outcome), many felt the twisted, hated cunt had it coming. Not only that, it was amusing and fodder for the gossip-mongers.

Benjamin Styles sipped his coffee at the counter, said a hello or two to other has-beens and wannabes. Debated his next move. Edward McFluff was on his mind. The Englishman who got in because he was a conniver. When it came to schmoozing, Fluffy was second to none.

The old saying was: Cream rises to the top. It wasn't true. Not in Hollywood. Bullshitters rose to the top; under-handed trickery got you the big roles and top money. Deviousness and downright criminal behavior (so long as you didn't get nailed for it) was rewarded in this crappy little celluloid community.

Benjamin Styles also knew he would have to relax and try not to think too much about the damn Western. It wouldn't be easy. The part was so damn perfect for him. If only given a chance. There was so much he could do with it. He'd definitely be in demand afterwards. Maybe that's what they're afraid of. They don't want me to make it. Show them up. Wouldn't want me to get too big. They know I'll steal the whole show.

He smiled. Couldn't be helped. Hell, he thought, don't I always?

A black, chauffeur-driven stretch limo pulled up to the curb, drawing his attention. Now who the fuck could this be? Instead of the usual asshole: Hollywood actor or rock star, it was pussy in a mini-nothing skirt and heels. Angela Bliss bounced out, well, her tits did, and she entered and walked right up to where Mr. Styles sat. There was a vacant stool next to his.

"May I join you?'

"Please do," said Benjamin Styles. It was tough to ignore the tanned thighs, the mid-section; halter top and the mounds in it. Those tits were about to give him a boner. And what in hell was that British queer like Fluffy doing with her anyway? Show; it was show. Cover. Sissy was queer. Pole smoker; but there he was, and he and others like him always had a hot cunt like this Angela broad on hand. Those tits looked like they might pop out at any second, and Benjamin Styles would have liked to see it happen.

"Name your poison," he said.

"Coffee. Black," Angela said, brushing her hair back with her hands, while taking in the rest of the place, thriving on the attention she always drew. She loved it; loved being a woman, one men wanted and could not stop ogling. Made her feel good inside; she would even go so far as to say it made her pussy tingle and left it moist.

"Simple enough." Styles waved his hand, which brought the waitress running to his end of the counter. He ordered the coffee for the lass and admired McFluff's latest gofer's incredible figure.

"You're lovely," he said. "Sooo lovely."

"You're sweet, Mr. Styles."

"Call me Benjamin."

"You say the sweetest things, Benjamin."

Benjamin Styles had to laugh. She reminded him of pictures made in the '40s and the many interchangeable dumb blondes who had appeared in them. It has to be an act, he concluded. She's playing the dumb Hollywood bimbo. He was hard down there.

"What's so funny?" she asked.

"You."

"Me?"

The waitress was back with the coffee.

"You got a message for me?" Benjamin Styles asked.

"Mr. McFluff would like to speak with you."

"There's a phone in this place, you know."

"Mr. McFluff would like to see you in his study."

"I've already seen his study."

"It's not something he cares to discuss over the phone."

"Is that so?"

"Look, Mr. Styles, I'm only delivering a message. I don't know what he wants."

"I'd like to put you on canvas, or at the least take some candid photos."

"I thought we discussed this already."

"You know, you ought to be nicer to me. I'm gonna be a big man around here pretty soon, a real wheeler-dealer. With pull. I'll be able to do you a lot of good."

"That remains to be seen."

"Didn't think 'Daddy' could get it up anymore—with broads, that is."

"You're just another chauvinist, aren't you?"

"What makes you say that?"

"It's obvious."

"Oh, I don't know," Benjamin Styles said. "I love women. I love to shag them."

"It's frustrating when you can't find any takers, isn't it?" Angela said. Got up, and took all that booty out the door with her. The limo driver held the door open for her. Watched her climb into the back seat, watched, as did many others from inside the drug store, as Angela hiked up that short skirt of hers, revealing plenty of flank, as she did so. Door was closed. The limo with the ingénue pulled away.

Benjamin Styles sat there. Couldn't help but laugh. All of it had made him laugh. If you couldn't laugh at silly shit like this . . . hell, you had no sense of humor at all. Amazon had shown some brass. That was what had surprised him. Bimbo had some backbone. Not much. Some.

Twenty minutes later his waitress was back and she was holding the phone out to him.

"Hi, Eddie," Benjamin Styles said into the receiver.

"Let's talk," Edward McFluff said.

"Gimme a break, Eddie. You know what my terms are."

"Why don't you come up for a drink?"

"I've got a dinner engagement—"

"Bullshit."

"I'll see what I can do."

"See you in twenty," Edward McFluff said and clicked off.

Styles dialed his home number.

"Hello?" Jimmy Riff answered at the other end.

"HELLO?" Benjamin Styles growled. "You know exactly how you're supposed to answer the goddamn phone!"

"I'm sorry, Benjamin—"

"How do you answer the telephone?"

"Benjamin Styles's residence."

"Right," Benjamin Styles said. "You make sure that's how you answer it from now on."

"I will, Ben."

"All right," Benjamin Styles said. "Listen up: I'm going over to see this big time producer/director. We're gonna talk."

"Sounds good."

"He's got pull," Benjamin Styles said, "and he likes you."

"As long as he's not another psycho."

"He's not a psycho. Eddie McFluff may be others things, but he's not psycho."

"'Cause if he is, I might have to hurt him."

"Why don't you quit trying to sound like a tough guy," said Styles. "He ain't no psycho. And no, you won't have to hurt him."

"All right, Ben. Whatever you say."

"Another thing: Don't leave the apartment tonight."

"Whatever you say, Ben."

"I want you to be there when I call from Fluffy's place. Got that?"

"Got it."

"Better not fuck things up now. Took some hard work and a lot of crow I had to eat to set this up."

"I'll be here," Jimmy said. "Where can I go? My bicycle's still over at that Koch broad's place."

"Don't even mention her name to me," Benjamin Styles said. "Talk to you later."

"Right, Ben."

"Relax and watch TV. You need all the rest you can get. I'm in that *Movie-of-the-Week* tonight. All's I have is two lines, but I steal the scene just the same. I'll be getting a check. Catch the show. Just might learn something about acting."

❧

While going through his pockets to determine what exactly his financial situation was, Jimmy came across the piece of paper with that girl's name, Victoria, the cutie with the strawberry-blond hair who could not stop vomiting at that insane party in the San Fernando Valley upon his arrival in town several weeks back. He debated giving her a call. He had not been physically drawn to her, but it would be someone to talk to, female company. There had been something vulnerable and tender-hearted about the young woman that had stuck with him. Should he dial her number? See how she was doing? What would it hurt? He wasn't looking to get laid; he wasn't after anything, other than his suitcase and the few belongings in it that she had promised to hold for him (while he was being hauled off to the slammer for brawling). Besides, she'd be someone to have a beer with.

Tête-à-Tête

Approximately twenty-five minutes later, Benjamin Styles was pulling into McFluff's Beverly Hills driveway. Edward McFluff stood at the top of his front door steps to greet him.

"I'd like you to see something," McFluff said.

"I've seen the study so many times already, Eddie, I know it better than my own living room," said Benjamin Styles, and climbed the marble steps. Everybody had to have marble steps and pillars and fountains, whatnot. Had to flaunt it. Right in your face. Every single damn one of them. Had so much dough they didn't know what to do with it. Gold crappers and doorknobs. Show-offs. Not only did he resent it but thoroughly hated their guts. "Didn't your current Flavor of the Month give you the message?"

"She tells me everything, Ben," McFluff said, motioning him inside.

❧

In the master bedroom upstairs, in a nest of pink silk and chiffon, with pink lace drapes hanging down from the canopy above the bed, lay the Cinderella from Oklahoma. She didn't have a stitch on. On a large closed-circuit monitor on a wall at the far end of the bed Edward McFluff and Benjamin Styles watched Angela Bliss give her firm nipples close scrutiny. She had her right breast in her right hand, while rubbing the moistened thumb of her left over the areola and nipple.

"She's got to be a 40," Benjamin Styles said.

"Thirty-nine," the director/producer said.

"Thirty-nine just became my favorite number."

McFluff smiled. "Drink?"

"No, thanks," Benjamin Styles said, wanting to remain completely sober during whatever was about to transpire.

Edward McFluff cocked a brow. He had never known this washout to turn down anything free.

"You like her?"

"You have to ask?'

"You can have her," McFluff said, pausing for effect, taking in the other man's reaction. "All night. . . ."

"You got yourself a nice piece of tail there, I gotta admit," Benjamin Styles said. "But, Eddie, this is me you're talking to—Benjamin Styles, remember? Cunt like that is dime a dozen in this town. I can walk into any massage parlor and get laid and parlayed for under a hundred bucks."

"A fine thing like that wouldn't touch you with a ten-foot pole. Nothing personal, of course," the filmmaker added.

"Fuck you too, Reg."

"It's a fair-enough trade," McFluff said, "I think."

"No dice," Benjamin Styles said, lighting one of his own low-grade brown smokes. "You know I'm right for the part, Eddie. I could do a lot with it."

"That was always your problem, Ben. You're always doing more than is required, more than they want you to. Right or wrong?"

"I don't know about that."

"Fuck the director—right, Ben? Fuck the producer! Fuck the lead!

The script, the studio!" Edward McFluff was raising his voice by now. "Fuck everybody—right, Ben?"

"Look—I go in there and I do my best. Is it my fault if the director don't know what he's doing? Is it?"

"Poppycock," McFluff said. "You've been in the game a long time. You know the rules."

"Look—if I'm going in to do something, I'm going in to do my very best; not my second best or third best, but the very best that I am capable—every single time, for every single damn take, no matter how long it takes. How can that be wrong?"

"Sure it's wrong and you know it! You got talent, Ben; you get no argument from me there, but you also have talent for rubbing the people you work with the wrong way. And that's bad."

"That thing with Tanner? I was in the right and you know it!"

"There's no way to get through to you!"

"The son of a bitch acted like an asshole! Treated everybody on the set like dirt. I kept quiet as long as I could, believe me I did. I didn't say a word to him until he started fucking with me. I mean, he started it. He was the instigator, not me. The asshole started it. I didn't back down, simple as that. I didn't take any shit from him. Benjamin Styles takes shit from no one. Not a punk like Tanner: no one!"

"Benjamin Styles can't get work," McFluff said with a sigh. "How about it?"

"What?"

"Is it a deal?"

Benjamin Styles laughed. *Here I am trying to survive, and all this fag has on his mind is Jimmy's cock.*

"I'll even work for scale."

McFluff shook his head hopelessly. "Why do you always make it so tough?"

"I'd be great in that part."

"All right," McFluff finally conceded. "You've got it. Can you bring the kid over tonight?"

"I'll have to see a contract, Eddie."

"Go get the kid. I'll have the contract drawn up by the time you get back."

"Now that calls for a celebration," Benjamin Styles said.

"When you show with the hustler."

"Got yourself a deal there, Mr. McFluff," Benjamin Styles said and left the mansion in a hurry.

❧

First thing Styles did upon unlocking the front door to his modest Hollywood apartment was call out the kid's name. What he got in return was silence.

"Jimmy, where the fuck are you? Jimmy? Hey, Kidd?" He wasn't in the living room, the john, or the bedroom. "Where the hell are you? I got great news, James Kidd." Only, James Kidd was nowhere to be found. Instead, what Styles came across on the kitchen table was a jar of peanut butter, under which was a hand-written note:

> *Ben,*
>
> *It got too quiet around here. Went out for a beer. Back shortly.*
>
> *Jimmy*

Benjamin Styles walked into the living room, the note still in his hand. He read it again, shaking his head. Unbelievable. You tell the motherfucker how to behave, what to do/what not to . . . We had an agreement. Your manager knows what's right. *Do what your manager tells you, goddamn you. Very simple. A simple thing.* Why Elvis was such a success. The Colonel called the shots. The Colonel was the brains behind the dope.

He lowered himself into the recliner, shaking his head as he did so. He crumpled the note, still cursing under his breath, and flung it at the TV set, which had been left on. Waste of electricity. Punk was costing him money by not doing what he was told. Eating his food. He was being used. Fucker was using him, just like all of them out there; just like the rest: Tanner and McFluff, others. Studios made millions, while the real talent like himself behind all the box-office blockbusters got crumbs, if that. Hell, even crumbs would have been nice. He couldn't even get crumbs.

He rose. Downed a shot of whiskey, then another, and left the apartment.

Victoria Chantal

In a singles bar on the Sunset Strip is where they'd decided to get together. Jimmy Riff was working on a beer paid for by the gorgeous strawberry blonde with the captivating smile and figure to go with it. Ah, that figure, that figure he hadn't quite noticed before, not that that was all he hadn't noticed about her. There was plenty of sexual magnetism there, after all, but it went deeper than that. She didn't appear to be your typical LA phony. She wasn't another one of those good-looking but empty-headed females in a cheap, skimpy outfit playing hard to get. That was what he'd liked about her in the first place: she was real. There was something else there, a quality, and it glowed from within. No one who ever knew him as a teen would have ever guessed that Jimmy Riff would or could appreciate a quality like this in a female. It was all right, he thought. You kept certain things about yourself to yourself. It was best that way. Less room for ridicule. But we were all so sure that you were shallow, Jimmy. Shallow. Romeo. Bang 'em and leave 'em, Jimmy. Yeah? If that were true, how is it then that runaround Marcella Blevins had been able to get to him, gotten him to fall for her, then unceremoniously dumped him not only for someone else, but many someone elses?

Think what you want. He'd taken this kind of ribbing from certain people (from both sexes) for quite a few years now. Let it go. It wasn't always easy to do. He had a habit of having these inner dialogues with himself. It was nothing more than a way to reason things out. You had to be your own best friend; had to take a look at whatever troubling situation you were involved in from a number of different angles that hopefully, eventually, resulted in the way one needed to proceed.

One thing he was sure of at this very moment, he liked the fact it gave him a warm feeling inside at having noticed these traits about the woman whose full name she may have mentioned, and probably did, at that party in the Valley that time he could not recall even though they were both drinking brewskies together.

She liked beer, too, would you believe it? He liked that about her as well. No cockamamie out-of-this-world cocktail to impress. And the clothes she had on—nothing exotic or tight-fitting—were quality: a white cashmere pullover that fit her loosely and yet not so loose that it concealed a healthy pair of tits. She wore a gray skirt with that and tan heels. He was drawn to tall women and she was that.

"That was a hard lesson for me that night in the Valley," she said. "Mixing drinks. I had no idea what I was doing. The guy who talked me into going out there, my date, I knew from high school back in Connecticut; we'd known each other for years. I refused to sleep with him, and you saw what he did to get back at me. Those two ladies he was with, with the ridiculous breast implants? Well, it got to me, you could easily say, and before I knew it, I was mixing drinks, and not paying much attention. Ashamed of my behavior that night, to say the least. Sorry you had to see me like that." Then she remembered: "Got your suitcase in my backseat, by the way."

"Thank you for keeping it for me," said Jimmy. "Got some clothes in there; a few personal items; nothing of any real importance, but thank you all the same."

"Thank you for being so kind to me that night."

"You were angelic," Jimmy said, meaning it, truly.

"I was so sick," Victoria said. "Afraid I would puke on you—and maybe I did. I've been trying to live it down ever since. I was totally floored when you called earlier this evening. Didn't exactly expect to hear from you. Had no idea what happened: if you got picked up by the cops or not. Wasn't sure what to do about the suitcase. That guy, Styles? Creeped me out. Shoved his business card at me. Kept saying he was a producer and that he could do things for me, even after I repeatedly pointed out that I was not interested in movies or acting, any of that. I didn't want to have to call him. Paid him more than enough to catch a cab back and pick up his car. I had to practically fight him off. He finally gave up when the cab showed, and left. I was hoping you'd get in touch so I could apologize for my idiotic behavior."

"You were heart-broken," said Jimmy. "We both were. But we lived through it, didn't we? Life goes on."

He was caring. There was no denying it. Her instincts had been right. Instead of making her feel worse by making a big deal about the way she had acted that night, he was kind, just like before. It was this kindness that had drawn her to him. Kindness of strangers. Where had she heard that? If only she were brave and bold enough to embrace him and hold him just now, and have him do the same—this handsome man that she hardly knew anything about. There was no denying the aches and feelings that surged through her being. Maybe in time, she would be able to do something of this nature. Not now. Instead, presently, all she had the courage to say was: "Did those goons hurt you? It made me sick to see it."

"Some," said Jimmy. "I'm fine now."

"I hate violence," she said.

"That makes two of us," said Jimmy. "I do my best to avoid it.

There's times it just comes at you, and there you are—forced to deal with it."

She nodded, wanting to understand.

"Another beer?"

"In a second," Jimmy said, smiling. The girl smiled back.

"What's so funny?" she said.

"You."

He saw her blush, turn her eyes away, and look up again.

"You're probably used to girls buying you beers all the time."

"Not really," Jimmy said. "It doesn't happen as often as you might think. It would be nice if the girl walked up to the guy now and then instead of it being the other way around usually. It's beginning to happen more and more lately, and it's all right."

"You may not be aware of this: it took a lot of nerve on my part to just go up to you that night and offer to fetch you a beer."

That was exactly what made her stand out, what was special about this one. *What you see is what you get.* For that alone, he felt like giving her a big smacking kiss on the lips. Only he thought he'd better not do anything that forward.

How many females (girls and women) had he known over the years who looked as terrific as this woman and were this down-to-earth? How many? How many had been genuine? He'd been to bed with his share: ambitious career women, socialites and hair stylists, coeds and stage actresses, general office workers, and others. Oh yeah; they'd all had their act down pat. They were good at pretending they were human. You'd see one of these so-called "really nice" ladies on the idiot box being interviewed on a talk show, and you were just about convinced they couldn't be anything but the real thing, friendly, sincere, with a heart of gold—then you soon found out after they'd gotten what they were after that they were heartless and bitter, controlling. Deep down hated his gender. Lisa Koch came to mind. One of many. One of the worst, actually. There had been others, lots of others. Shades of Lisa Koch.

Truth was, he could play the game as well as any of them. Sometimes it didn't bother him, other times it did. One thing was certain: he never resorted to slipping a Mickey in anyone's drink, never dropped a date rape drug into anyone's booze. One had to draw the line somewhere. There were things he was not willing to do.

He couldn't help himself now, taking in the girl's green eyes and all that fine, velvety reddish-blonde hair that shone and seemed to change hue in the glimmering lights of the bar. He found himself unable to stop looking at her this way.

"Let me tell you something," Jimmy finally said. "If I hadn't been so preoccupied with hooking up with my lady friend that night, I certainly would have been more receptive and probably would have approached you."

This pleased her immensely.

Jimmy downed a swallow, and added: "You better believe it. You were the best damn looking woman in that house that night. Yes, as sick as you were, puking all over the place and carrying on. Even here, right now, with all of these beautiful ladies, your gorgeous face takes my breath away."

The girl seemed to blush again.

"Better yet," he said, "make that the best-looking lady that I have seen in this town since my arrival."

"Thank you."

"And if that sounds like a line," Jimmy said, "so be it, because it's the truth."

Jimmy pulled on his bottle. Wanted to make sure he got her name right. Having been so out of it at the party that night, her scribble had not been all that easy to make out on the piece of paper she'd shoved in his shirt pocket.

"Victoria Chantal," she said. "Vevrier. Vicki is fine, or Chantal."

"Nice to meet you, Victoria. Name's James, James Riff. Grayson's my middle name. Friends call me Jimmy; Jimmy the Kid was what I was known as growing up by anyone who knew me. Pretty much. Or Gray, Grayson. Sometimes I was called a few other things, too. Tubesteak was one I didn't mind too much. Well, it helps to have a sense of humor to appreciate it."

She laughed a pretty laugh.

"Tubesteak?"

"I'd rather not go into it."

"We don't have to," she said.

"It's not all that interesting," he said. "I had jobs to earn pocket money—after school, on weekends, selling hot dogs at various venues and ball parks. They had these footlong, thick hot dogs. I'd be walking up and down the aisles, shouting: Get 'em here! Get your tubesteak! Cooked and meaty! Tubesteak! Get 'em here, while they last! Get your tubesteak! Two for one! Get your tubesteak, folks! Get 'em while they last! Get 'em while you can! Get two: one for you, one for your best girl! Tubesteaks! Hot, ready to eat! Get your tubesteak!" He paused to catch his breath. "There is another definition that I won't go into."

"X-rated?" she asked.

"R," said Jimmy. "I'll spare you."

Both were smiling. Shook hands.

"Really nice to meet you, Jimmy," said Vicki. "If this is inappropriate, just tell me—"

"Go ahead."

"Can I ask how old you are?"

"Twenty-seven," Jimmy Riff said, still not being able to get enough of the girl's eyes. There was a certain sparkle there: maybe caused by the lights in the bar, or something else. Probably came from within. As he had picked up on it earlier. Some people, certain women, had it. Made you want to get closer, be part of it. It was indescribable. You wanted the person in your life. What it came down to. And it didn't necessarily have to have anything to do with sex, either.

"You don't look twenty-seven."

"How old do I look?"

"Oh . . . I don't know. Younger."

"Yeah?"

"Yeah," she said. "Much younger. What's so funny?"

"That's what everybody says. I still get carded." He pulled on his beer. "Let me guess: you're nineteen."

She nodded. "I'm celebrating my birthday."

"When?"

"Right now. This is it."

"What? By yourself like this? Come on."

"I'm not exactly alone. I'm standing here talking to you, not to mention all the other people in this place."

"Yes, but it's your birthday. Aren't you supposed to be with friends and family—and really celebrating? Isn't that the way it's done?" Not that Jimmy had had much experience at this sort of thing: birthdays and such. Birthdays were non-existent in his family. Nonsense like that was for the rich. Spending money on toys and inviting a bunch of neighborhood brats over to eat you out of house and home was way too costly and a perfect waste of money. Cake? What do you need cake for? You were lucky to get a nickel for a candy bar. *We got better things to do with our money—like subsidize our boozing.*

Well, then, what was going on with this rich girl? (She did smell like money to him.) Why was she spending her birthday like this? And nobody had to spell it out. It was a well-known fact wealth did not guarantee you happiness and other things that we craved as humans.

He was touched by the girl's revelation and felt a need to change the subject for her sake. He raised his bottle. "To a special lady," he said. "My new best friend. Happy birthday."

"Thank you," Vicki said. And they both drank up. She seemed to hesitate just then, wanted to explain something to him, and did not know how to begin. "We're just not close," she said. "My parents and I. . . ."

"Hey," Jimmy said. "I didn't mean for it to sound like the 3rd degree. I understand. There's hardly any love lost between me and my old man, either. So I know about these things, believe me."

She offered to buy the next round. There was no way Jimmy would let her, and paid for the beers himself.

"You just have to be from the East Coast," she said, amused by this handsome lug.

"Yeah?" Jimmy countered. "How could you tell?" It was meant to be funny, because he knew he had an accent so thick you could cut it with a knife. "Brooklyn," he said. "Well, born there. We moved around, up and down, all along the eastern seaboard. Even spent some time in Arkansas, Louisiana, Florida, Maine, Oregon. Old man was a Bible-thumper, to earn a buck. Probably New York State, more than any other place, though. Could never shake the accent completely."

"I know New York," she said. "No reason to shake anything." She liked his accent.

He came close to flubbing it by asking where she was from originally, then remembered her mentioning Connecticut.

"What made you come out to the wild and wooly West Coast? Earthquake country, all that?"

"Art Institute in Pasadena, and, uh, to get away from my parents; mainly to get away from my parents. Not that I'd be missed much. Busy. They are."

He understood. Nodded his head. They drank their beers. The conversation progressed to other subjects. It was clear enough, they had some things in common, experiences they'd gone through while growing up: like getting drunk on cheap wine: Bali Hi, Muscatel, Ripple. While Vicki had usually done her drinking alone, resentful of the private schools she'd had to attend; Jimmy did his while hanging out with the guys in the various towns his father ended up being the substitute preacher at. He also mentioned having spent some time in pool halls and shooting pool and being rather good at it.

"Yeah?" Vicki said, putting her beer down and taking him by the hand and just being tipsy enough by then to do this. "There just happens to be a pool table where I'm staying." She took him outside to a beige Porsche parked in the lot.

∽∞∾

As they headed west on Sunset Jimmy asked her to stop at a liquor store on the way. He went in, grabbed a cheesecake, as that was the only type of cake they'd had there, and a candle. He didn't know the girl all that well, it was true, and neither did she know much about him, but he felt like doing it anyway. It felt right. One kindness deserved another. She had been kind to him by reaching out at that party full of porn Industry types in the Valley, and she had been kind by paying for most of the beers they consumed in the cocktail lounge. She deserved some kind of birthday cake and a candle. The cheesecake came in a box. He had both: cake and candle put inside a brown paper sack, stepped out of the liquor store and got in the new and spiffy Porsche and wouldn't tell her what he had just bought until after they'd continued west on Sunset, passing Beverly Hills, UCLA, Brentwood, and finally they were in Malibu and pulling up to a house on the beach. Nice, real nice.

They were in the exquisitely furnished living room with art on the walls that he actually noticed and liked this time, as opposed to what he had been exposed to back at Styles' place. He even came close to asking who the artist was, but for some reason refrained. The waves were out there; you could hear them, no more than a stone's throw from the rear deck. A jogger ran past. A man and a woman walked hand-in-hand with some type of large dog running around, chasing something.

Jimmy had Vicki close her eyes while he set the cake up on the glass-topped table in the living room. He was in the kitchen for two plates, forks, a knife, spatula, and napkins. He knew it wasn't much of a birthday cake. . . . It was the thought that counted.

"Okay," he told her finally. "You can open your eyes now."

When the girl saw the cake sitting there and the single candle with the glowing, flickering flame in the center it hit her hard. Something like a dry lump of balled-up emotion surged forth and came pouring out in teardrops and flowed down her pretty face. Jimmy reached over with a tissue and wiped her tears away.

"Hey, there now," he whispered softly. "Victoria?"

"I'm sorry," she said.

He rose from his seat. Placed his arm around her and gave her a gentle squeeze. "It's all right," he said.

She was looking up again, smiling. "Thank you," she said. "I'm fine. Thank you."

"Hey, how does that go again? You have to shut your eyes and make a wish, don't you? And then you blow out the candle. Is that right? I'm not exactly sure."

She nodded, and did just that: closed her eyes, made a wish—and blew the flame out. Both had a slice of cheesecake.

"Some combination," Jimmy said. "Beer and cheesecake."

"It's perfect," Vicki said.

Jimmy said: "You've never been with a man, have you?"

Vicki got up, smiling nervously, and found something easy to listen to on the stereo. Music wasn't jazz exactly, but it was close enough, in that it was smooth and soothing.

"Ya never slept with a guy, have you?" Jimmy asked again, but then realized he had no right to ask such a thing and knew it made her feel uncomfortable. "Sorry. I have no business. Dumb question. It's personal." He cleared his throat. "You're nice; I mean genuine. You come across as genuine. Nice is fine, only you're more than that." He was fumbling, and fought what actually felt like butterflies in his gut. Jimmy "The Kidd" Riff, feeling butterflies over someone? There was no denying it was happening. He finally got it. Put two and two together.

"That's what that had been about back at the party in Chatsworth: your date getting back at you for refusing to sleep with him by getting it on with the porn stars."

She nodded.

"Well, I think you're pretty nifty, Ms. Chantal," he said. "I love that name, by the way. Chantal. *Victoria Chantal.* It suites you."

"I think you're pretty nifty yourself, Jimmy," Vicki said.

"That's *your* problem"

Benjamin Styles checked all the bars he knew in Hollywood, gay and otherwise, and didn't start ordering drinks until he reached the Strip. There was no sign of Jimmy and the clock was steadily ticking. How much longer would that prick McFluff wait?

There was only one thing to do: Benjamin Styles was intent on getting drunk. But first he would make one final call. He waded through the crowd in the singles bar and squeezed inside the phone booth.

Angela Bliss answered the phone.

"Benjamin Styles here. Lemme talk to Reggie."

"I'm sorry, Mr. Styles, but Mr. McFluff is unable to get to the phone at the moment."

"What kind of shit is this?"

"I'm sorry, Mr. Styles, Mr. McFluff is otherwise occupied."

I bet he's "occupied," Benjamin Styles said to himself. Probably going down on some wasted stud he got through an outcall service.

"Look, bitch, you better get him to the phone! It's important!"

"It better be," she said. "If you cause me to lose my job—"

"Will you just get him to the fucking phone—now!"

Benjamin Styles studied his wristwatch. A heavily breathing Edward

McFluff growled a "Yes?" at the other end.

"Eddie," Benjamin Styles said, "you won't believe it."

"Try me."

"I can't find the kid."

"That's *your* problem."

"Wait a minute, Eddie—"

"Wait, nothing!" McFluff blared. "I was a fraction of a second from getting my rocks off when the bird insisted I get to the goddamn phone."

"I'm sorry about that."

"Sure you are," McFluff said. "That bloody close. It wouldn't mean that much if I could get it up like I used to. It's been taking longer and longer lately. When it happens—it's a moment. You understand what I'm saying?"

"I know exactly what you mean," Benjamin Styles said.

After a beat, Edward McFluff sighed. "We go back a long way, Ben. You're having a rough go of it right now. You don't need anyone else's shit shoved in your face."

"No apology necessary, Eddie," Benjamin Styles said. "I know you're trying to help." The prick wants Kidd, Benjamin Styles said to himself. He wants him so bad he can hardly stand it.

"Call me when you find him," McFluff said. "You know how to get in touch."

"Don't overwork yourself, Eddie," Benjamin Styles said. "We'll be seeing you soon." He made his way back to the bar. The need for more alcohol wouldn't go away.

❧

Ben Styles had so much booze in his gut he was feeling rowdy. Memories of his boxing days back in Jersey, Boston, NY, flashed through his foggy mind's eye. Styles had the boxer's lumpy brows from having been busted so often he had lost count. Then there was the time two goony punks put his jaw out of commission for a few months by raking a lead pipe across it. He wasn't counting the times his nose had been rearranged. Indeed, he had seen his share of rough days and pain. Didn't matter, because when he had this much booze in him he enjoyed duking it.

His knuckles needed a workout, and tonight they would get one. He would see to it. Win, lose, or draw. Didn't matter. Better to take his frustrations out on some stranger. Wanted to beat hell out of the kid. Had it coming. Sure did. He would maintain instead. *This time.*

❧

Benjamin Styles put away another Jack Daniels-with-beer chaser. He'd lost count of how many he'd had already. He decided on a tall mook. Guy looked like a hardass, maybe a bouncer, who cared?—the nose bent a little, five o'clock shadow in evidence.

Styles stuck his foot out as the guy stepped up to the bar. He tripped but did not fall. He apologized and ordered a drink.

"Hold on there, fag," Styles said. "I believe I have an apology coming."

"Pardon me?"

"Pardon nothing," Benjy Styles said, his nose inches from the guy's startled face. "I said: Apologize, faggot."

"I did," the man said. "I'm sorry."

"You have to excuse me," Styles said. "It's so noisy in here and everything; I just can't hear you."

"That's tough."

"You gonna apologize?"

"I might."

"You got two seconds."

"Who the hell do you think you are?"

"Someone who's about to put you away for a week."

"You ought to really calm down, cowboy."

"Your time is just about up."

"All right," the guy said, shaking his head hopelessly. "I'm sorry. *All right?* Does that take care of it? Because I really am not in the mood to scrap."

"I still can't hear you."

"You got a bad hearing problem, buddy. I suggest you take care of it real soon."

"You man enough, pussy?"

Seething, the man just lunged at him, his huge hands clamped around Style's throat. It took the former pugilist less than a second to break the hold and put the man out of commission. First, a hard knee thudded up his opponent's crotch, and as the individual released his hold, sinking, Benjamin Styles connected with a right/left combo that sent the man reeling back against the bar, knocking down several patrons in the process.

A woman screamed.

Two bouncers rushed in. Beefy muthers. Incredible Hulk types. Stood on either side of Styles. The bartender gave Styles a stare that said: *You had to do it again, didn't you?*

"Fuck it," Benjy Styles said, shrugging. "He had it coming." And walked outside.

"Tell me something I don't know"

Benjamin Styles sat in his Toyota, staring off into space. His head felt like it was made of granite. He didn't get the anger, not really. He'd been angry all his life, it seemed. Why? You're unique. Gotta walk a different path. Stand alone. A man angry is a man unique is a man of strength is a man of power, of determination, of knowledge, of value, of . . . of bullshit.

A life wasted. He reeked of failure. Five times married. Five times divorced. Or should that be four-and-a-half-times divorced? That last one he just walked out on. Kids? Some grown, others in their teens—whose ages he could never keep up with. Grandkids? Couldn't tell you how many he had. Three of the kids and the estranged old lady were living in a house in Jersey he was still making payments on, sending alimony when he was able. Not really because he cared, or did he?

He couldn't say.

If a man didn't care about his offspring, what did he/ does he care about—other than Benjamin Styles? I got three, maybe five years left to do it in.

Would he last that long? He had an ulcer to contend with. Backaches. The once-powerful legs were giving him problems.

He grinned feebly. Shook his head.

For a man who looked like a good, strong bull, there were too many things wrong inside, things others could never see, ailments others should never know about. For if they did, it would surely be the end of "Fearless" Benjamin T. Styles.

He cracked his knuckles. Moved his head from side to side to ease the tension in his neck and upper shoulders.

"Styles?"

Benjamin turned his head. The hard jaw that was part of the scarred face looked like it could eat concrete. Dark features. Not black. Dark. Early forties. Part of the left brow gone. Knife scar or something. Benjamin Styles just looked at him. The man stared back. Dead eyes full of meanness.

"That was a dumb thing you did."

Benjamin Styles inserted the key in the ignition.

"Hear me out."

"My knuckles are sore," the poverty-row actor/producer said, taking in the blood on the skinned knuckles of his right hand, "but not that sore."

"Don't kid me, old-timer," Scarface said. "You wouldn't stand a chance."

Benjamin Styles opened the door and stepped out. Scarface stepped back, smiling, hands raised. "Take it easy now."

"It'll be quick. You won't feel a thing," said Benjamin Styles. "Until after you wake up."

"I'm supposed to be looking after you."

"What?"

"McFluff."

"Huh?"

"That's right," the man with the scarred face said. "I'm Reggie McFluff's boy."

"Funny," Ben Styles said, "didn't peg you for a turd burglar."

"Drop it, all right? The man's paying me good bread to keep an eye on you."

"Oh yeah?'

"Didn't think anybody cared?"

Benjamin Styles got back in his car, turned the key.

"He's willing to take a chance on you. Don't fuck up."

"He's got nothing to worry about," Benjamin Styles said. "I'm keeping my nose clean."

"What about that nose in there?"

"What about it?" said Benjamin Styles. "Just another fag nose that needed rearranging."

"That's a stunt nose you busted up, wise guy."

Benjamin Styles looked at him.

"That's right," the man said. "A stuntman. Morey Grossbard's favorite lollipop." He paused. Said: "You remember Moritz Grossbard? Aka Morey?"

"Shit," Benjamin Styles muttered under his breath.

"Fucked up again," the man said. "Morey Grossbard only runs the studio that happens to be backing this dumb Western Fluffy's directing."

"Shit," Benjamin Styles said again. "I didn't know."

"We learn something new every day, don't we, Mr. Styles?"

Ben Styles was speechless.

"Maybe it can be straightened out. Already talked to McFluff. The stuntman's getting two grand to keep his mouth shut."

"Goddammit," Benjamin Styles said. "I thought Grossbard was still going with that French kid he found in Cannes last year."

"Well, he ain't," the man said. "That's information from the horse's mouth. Anyway, I couldn't give a fuck what these Hollywood assholes do.

Everybody in this town's got shit for brains, as far as I'm concerned."

"Tell me something I don't know."

"Ciao," the scarred one said and left.

Benjamin Styles shifted into gear and slowly, ever-so-carefully, pulled out of the parking lot and drove down the palm tree–lined street.

"I like it"

The pool table Vicki had mentioned earlier was upstairs in the play room, and she took Jimmy around and showed him the rest of the house as well: two bedrooms, two bathrooms. Downstairs again, Vicki opened the sliding glass doors that lead to the patio, a heart-shaped jacuzzi and swimming pool that glowed and shimmered in the moonlight.

"You like it?" Vicki asked.

"You kidding?" Jimmy said. "The kinda stuff you see in movies."

"You do like it," she said, smiling. She pressed a button on the wall and the voice of Billie Holiday filled the room with a much richer, fuller sound than before. "My favorite singer," she said. "I hope you like the music."

Jimmy had never shown much interest in music, never paid real attention, was admittedly ignorant when it came to blues and singers like Billie Holiday, but if this wonderful girl liked R&B, then that was reason enough for him to like it, too.

"I'm glad you like the house."

"It's class," Jimmy Riff said. "I'll have a place of my own some day, maybe a ranch, a chicken ranch; a type of ranch anyway, a small one; something away from the hustle and bustle of the big city. Someday."

Then, with a shrug, he said: "It's a pipe dream."

"It could happen," she said.

"Sure," Jimmy said. "It might rain dollar bills, but I doubt it."

"I don't own the house."

"Whose is it?"

"My dad offered to lease it for me while I went to school."

"Your old man has this kind of bread? What is he? President of GE?"

"He's an investment banker. Wall Street."

"Yeah?" said Jimmy Riff. Came close to saying: That's interesting. Only money never interested him, no more than what he needed to get by. He said: "Money? I'm no good at holding on to it. That is, the rare times I manage to get my hands on some."

"I almost followed in his footsteps."

He looked at her. "Why not? Could do worse."

"I'm not cut out for it. It's what my father wanted me to do. We've had our fights over it."

He walked out to the pool. Vicki followed.

"So what's in Pasadena? What kind of school again?"

"Art Institute."

"You any good?"

She waved her hand, did so with a smile. There was nothing boastful about it. "All you see on these walls is mine."

"Whoa," said Jimmy. Frozen in place. "You're good. I'm not saying it to be nice, either. I said I liked the stuff a minute ago, before I knew who the artist was."

"True," she said. "Thank you."

"You have to live your own life, the way I see it. What's it matter to your old man what you do? Am I right, or am I right? Yes, he's footing the bill, paying for your education, but it's still your choice."

She nodded, readily agreeing.

"It's like me and this thing with the chicken ranch," he said. "People laugh when I tell them. I like chickens, like being around them. I can't even explain it. Spent a few summers on an uncle's chicken ranch up around Portland to earn money, mainly to get away from my father. Parents never gave us a dime; there was no such thing as an allowance. Forget about it. Old man's a semi-retired pastor. Bible-thumper. I believe I mentioned. Big time. Mother was a housewife." Never mind that his running around pushed her over the edge and she took her life. No need to go into anything that morbid at this time. Mentioned he'd worked odd jobs as a kid for pocket money, and one of the more interesting (and educational) was the time he'd spent on the two chicken ranches. "The thing about the chicken ranch I worked at on the East Coast: it was gross. Hens were cooped up, no room to roam, mistreated, abused. What they fed them . . . I can't go into. It's gross. Nothing like the ranch I spent time on in Oregon. I would raise organic chickens the way they do. You get better tasting eggs. People, most people, haven't got a clue what an egg should taste like, what chicken should taste like. But like I said: it's a pipe dream. Was on my way there. Ran out of cash. Didn't want to show up at Uncle Orville's doorstep broke like when I was a kid. This time I wanted to have my own money. I'm not a youngster anymore."

Jimmy took his shoes and socks off, rolled up his pants and sat on the edge of the pool. His feet in the lukewarm water up to his ankles. He sat this way, unmoving, and simply stared at the water as it shimmered and reflected the silvery glow given off by the full moon above. He needed this. To be here, with the woman and the water, both in the pool as well as out there: the vastness of the ocean out there, with all his worries regarding his existence and dealing with lack of money and having a real place of his own to stay, gnawed at his insides. Yes, he was calm, on the surface, and this wonderful girl had had a great deal to do with it. Didn't know her and might not get to truly know her—who got to truly know anyone?—but there was no denying that he enjoyed being with her, around her.

Take it as it comes. See where it goes.

"Back in a second," Vicki said and went inside.

Jimmy stared at the crystal-clear blue water of the pool and wondered if heaven was of the same hue of blue? Maybe not all of heaven, but certainly part of it could be. He wondered if there was such a thing as heaven, after all? He'd always wondered about that end of it. He'd never liked anything that went with all the world's religions: "tradition," garments, brainwashing tactics they all used; the lies to keep the sheep in line, keep them tithing—not for their own good, but for the sake of keeping the various churches/organizations strong. He'd been convinced, from a young age, that it was so much con—saw it first hand, up close; yet, there it was: he could not help wondering if maybe, on the outside chance, that the bit about heaven, at least, was somehow true.

❧

Vicki emerged with two bottles of ice-cold imported beer. Handed him one.

"Thank you," Jimmy said, checking to make sure that the bottle hadn't been opened. It hadn't. You better believe he was being damn careful after what had gone down with that nutty Nazi broad Lisa Koch. There was also no denying he felt a tinge of guilt, because he trusted this girl thoroughly, felt at ease and comfortable in her presence.

"You're welcome," Vicki said, and handed him the bottle opener and sat beside him. He opened the bottle, had a pull. She opened hers, and did same. He had another, and found himself gazing into her green eyes and not able to stop himself from doing it. Mesmerized, transfixed.

Something like it. Whatever it was, he couldn't turn away.

"Tell me what you see," Vicki said.

Tongue-tied momentarily, he said: "Like looking at a gem, something like a sparkling diamond. . . ." He paused, searching for the right words. "I thought the water in this swimming pool glimmered. Compared to your eyes . . . it's dull."

"Thank you." She kissed him lightly on the cheek. Jimmy shook his head.

"What is it?"

"It didn't come out right," he said. "Anyway, you know what I mean."

"I do."

Jimmy Riff looked at the bottle of Heineken in his hand. "You know . . . I can't get it up when I drink too much of this stuff. What I mean is . . . I can get it up, but nothing else, though."

"Give me that," Vicki said, reaching for the bottle.

"That's all right," Jimmy Riff said. "Tonight I'm drinking. Besides, it's already too late. I've had too many."

"You're not going to pass out on me?"

"Nothing like that."

"Can I hug you?"

"So long as you don't expect a roll in the sack," said Jimmy with a straight face. "If there's one thing I don't care for: it's one-night stands."

"I never meant. . . ."

"You can't tell I'm joking?"

He grabbed her hands with his and wrapped her arms about his waist. Said: "How's that?"

"I've been wanting to do this all night," she whispered in his ear. "Just wasn't brave enough. The brewskies gave me the courage to mention it."

"Know something?" Jimmy Riff said. "You make me feel good." And he drew her closer to him. Sometime later Vicki went inside for a couple of pillows and a blanket, and they spent most of the rest of the night this way, lying by the pool with their arms around each other.

The next morning she made them an omelette and drove Jimmy back to Hollywood.

"We've only met"

The Porsche pulled up to the gray apartment building where Benjamin Styles resided.

"About last night," Jimmy Riff said. "I didn't tell the truth: I mean, about the beer. I really didn't have that many."

"Should I be pissed?"

"Please don't be."

"I'm only teasing."

A moment passed. "I want to tell you something," he said. "I've slept with a few women, Vicki . . . had my share. . . ."

"Oh yeah?"

"With the exception of that one up at that party in Chatsworth, Marcella, having been my first . . . With most, with the rest . . . it was sex, nothing more. . . . I didn't want it to be that way with you."

"We've only met—"

"I know."

"I feel the same way."

"Gimme a second," Jimmy said, and ran inside to see if Benjamin Styles was in. He was not. "He's probably at the studio," Jimmy said. "Would you mind taking me down there?"

"Of course not. I've got nothing better to do than be your chauffeur, you know."

"It's not that far, really."

"I'm only kidding."

"I feel great."

"Me, too."

"Yeah?"

"Yes," she said, looking at him with those eyes that hadn't lost any of their sparkle from the night before.

"Will you call me?"

Benjamin Styles Productions. Couple of rundown military barracks–
type structures on either side of the court and parking on Santa Monica
Boulevard across the street from that ancient Hollywood cemetery
where the likes of Peter Lorre, Rudolph Valentino, Bugsy Siegel, Cecil
B. DeMille, and King Kong's favorite girl Fay Wray, among others,
were laid to rest. The guard in the guard shack was as old and decrepit
as the studio itself. Styles' office was locked. Still early. Benjamin Styles
wouldn't be in for another couple of hours, if at all. Who knew?

Jimmy borrowed the passkey from the guard. Let himself in and
dialed Styles' home number. No answer. He walked outside to the
Porsche.

"Is he not in?"

"He should show eventually. I think I should wait for him."

"Jimmy?"

"Yeah."

"Last night was extra nice."

"I guess it was," Jimmy said, flashing that boyish grin of his.

"Will you call me?"

"You bet."

"When?"

"I want to take you somewhere different."

"Oh yeah?"

"I want it to be a surprise."

"When?"

"Soon," Jimmy said, finishing the rest in his head: As soon as I can afford it. He leaned over and kissed her lightly on the lips.

"Thanks," Jimmy said.

"You're wonderful," Vicki said, and drove off.

"Ever fucked a lesbian?"

Benjamin Styles' two-room office was cluttered with magazines: the *Hollywood Reporter, Daily Variety, Los Angeles Times, Newsweek, Wall Street Journal, People, Drama-Logue, Back Stage*, and others, none of which interested Jimmy Riff much.

He sat in Benjamin Styles' swivel chair in the back room. The wall in front of the desk was covered in black & white glossies of actors from film and television, autographed: Duke Wayne, Clint Walker, David Janssen as Private Eye Richard Diamond; Paladin himself: Richard Boone; Lorne Greene and the rest of the cast of *Bonanza*; James Arness as Matt Dillon, Milburn Stone, Amanda Blake, Dennis Weaver and that guy who played Festus Hagen: Ken Curtis; Ward Bond from Wagon Train; Eddie "Cookie" Barnes; Strother Martin, L.Q. Jones, Jack Elam, Audie Murphy, the World War II hero from *To Hell and Back* fame; Elizabeth Montgomery from *Bewitched*; Fred McMurray from *My Three Sons*; even Bogey was up there in his *Maltese Falcon* fedora. Some were of up-and-comers the world would never know about, ham-and-eggers, "friends' of Styles," Jimmy guessed.

Hell, it meant nothing to him. His mind was on the circus that was coming to town, and he wondered if he might be able to borrow enough cash from his benefactor. I bet no one's ever taken her to a circus. Hell, he hadn't been to one himself in years. Something different; something to do. Ringling Brothers & Barnum & Bailey's Big Top was coming to Los Angeles and was not to be missed.

Jimmy Riff propped his feet up on the edge of Styles' desk and folded his arms. What else to do but wait. Take a nap, dream about her. Just as Jimmy Riff was about to doze off someone walked in. She was in her thirties. Had long hair. Light brown or maybe closer to chestnut or blond. Hard face. Not unattractive. High cheekbones and full lips on the pink side. Eyes the color of smoke. A full-breasted woman. Statuesque. She wore biker jeans and black heels. Blue denim shirt with suede elbow patches and colorful embroidery on the sleeves and up above the full hooters.

"Is Benjamin around?" she asked.

"Huh?" was all Jimmy said.

"I'm here for the breakdown."

"I'm sorry," Jimmy said, dumbstruck. "What 'breakdown' is that?"

She walked in the front room, and was back with the breakdown sheet. "This," she said.

"Oh."

She smiled.

"Go right ahead," Jimmy said. "Benjy should be in shortly."

She took a pad and pencil out of her purse, pulled up a folding chair and proceeded to jot down the casting information. Why she didn't do it in the other room he didn't know, and he let her go about it undisturbed. They had a system, probably, Jimmy thought, her and Benjy and the other show business types whom Styles dealt with and knew.

"You an actress?"

She looked up, nodded.

"I have a pretty good idea what it's like," Jimmy said with some sympathy. She smiled.

"Sorry," Jimmy said. "Don't mind me." And he closed his eyes to go back to sleep, only to open them again when a second woman walked in. This one was a brunette.

"The john on this lot is the pits," she said, digging in her purse. "Hi," she said, glancing at Jimmy. Jimmy Riff grinned and closed his eyes. The brunette was equally appealing. Another amazon. Large breasted. Terrific hips, quite a narrow waist. These women took care of themselves, it was plain to see. She had on stylish, beige cords, and a white blouse that was almost, but not quite, see-through. It was sheer enough, he supposed. A darker shade of red nail polish; a modest, if gold, necklace. The faintest trace of eyeliner. He had never been against some makeup, so long as it was not overdone. And in their case it wasn't.

Her footwear matched the other one's, in that the heels she wore were black. This one, too, appeared just a bit on the hard side.

"Mae," the brunette said to the one with chestnut hair, "got a piece of paper?"

"Sure," Mae said, and tore a sheet from her notepad.

"Thanks," the brunette said.

"Tammy," Mae said, "think I ought to try out for this one? It says: A very attractive girl who looks to be no more than 20; Julie is a determined, self-reliant, aspiring young actress. Forced to live in rundown quarters and deal with less than ethical 'producer' types, Julie finds—"

"'Less than ethical producer types?' Not here. Not in Hollywood," the brunette said, snickering.

"Think I could play a twenty-year-old?"

"Eighteen-year-old," Tammy said, "I could see. Twenty? Nope. Not old-looking enough."

The way they bantered back and forth, teasing one another, was contagious, and Jimmy found himself grinning.

"I know," the blonde said, still laughing and looking at Jimmy. "We're terrible."

"Is it really as bad as they say? About the producers?"

"What?" Tammy said. "Man, you have to be kidding me."

"I guess it is," Jimmy said.

"Nobody's that green," Tammy said, nudging her blond friend in the ribs.

"Believe me," the blonde said, "some of these guys are real assholes."

"And the rest are jerks," Tammy said, and both laughed again.

Jimmy Riff wasn't hard down there, but that hardly ever made any difference, for there was no way to conceal the bulge that was his package.

The blonde was the first to notice. And as she kept looking at the hard-to-miss mound in his pants her friend was soon taking in the same thing. Looking and wondering: How long and thick? How enormous? And was the owner any good?

"I'm sorry," Jimmy said. "I'll let you ladies do whatever it is you need do. Didn't mean to interrupt."

"Oh no," the blonde said, "it's just that we've run into so many of these creeps that we can't help but laugh. About all we can do."

Jimmy nodded.

"That's not all I can do, sister," Tammy said. "Remember Harwood? Woody Harwood? The time he cornered me in his smelly little office? Locked the fucking door?"

"Who could ever forget that fat tub of shit," the blond said.

"What happened?" Jimmy asked.

"He got a phone call," Tammy said.

"Huh?" Jimmy said.

The blonde was practically rolling on the floor.

"His telephone rang," Tammy said. "Just in time, too—"

"She picked it up," the blond said. "Said to the little bastard: Here, it's for you, Woody. And rammed it up his slimy balls."

The blond laughed so hard her stomach was beginning to ache. Jimmy was smiling himself. It wasn't the story itself so much, as the way they told it and carried on.

"Shit," Tammy said. "It wasn't a bit funny at the time. Never thought I'd get away from the creep."

"Gotta hand it to you, chick," Mae said, straightening up in her seat, "you did it right that time." And she kissed Tammy full on the lips.

"What's your name, anyway?" Mae asked, studying Jimmy Riff's crotch.

"Want the name I was born with, or the fake stage name Benjamin pinned on me?"

The women traded knowing glances, then looked at Jimmy. "You're not . . . ?"

"James Kidd," Jimmy said. "The one, the only. Please call me Jimmy. Known back on the block as Jimmy Riff."

"This is an honor," the blonde said. Rose to shake his hand. "I'm Ora Mae," she said. "And this is my best friend, Tammy."

"Indeed a pleasure," Tammy said, shaking Jimmy Riff's hand.

"Are you blushing?" the blonde asked.

"You ladies make me feel like I'm some sort of celebrity or something."

"But you are," the blonde said.

"You certainly are," Tammy said, putting her pen and paper down. "Is it true?" she asked, leaning across the desk, revealing a goodly amount of cleavage. "All those stories we've heard about 'The Kidd?'"

"Well, I haven't been here that long—" Jimmy said.

"Long enough," Tammy said.

"Certainly must be," Mae said, laughing. She embraced Tammy and ran her hand back and forth across her lean tummy.

"Ever done it this way, Jimmy?" Tammy asked. "Ménage?"

He recalled the mother and daughter who had tag-teamed him years before back in East St. Louis. Deacon Blevins' wife and daughter, who had seduced him while he was still in his teens. But he wouldn't say. Keep them guessing.

"Ever fucked a lesbian?" the blonde asked.

Jimmy wouldn't say.

"How would you like to fuck the both of us?" the blonde asked.

"First, we'll put on a little show for you—"

"First," Jimmy cut in, "I would have to beg off. And second: I don't think Mr. Styles would appreciate it."

"Forget Benjamin Styles," Tammy said. "Besides, he won't be in for a while."

"How do you know?" Jimmy asked.

"Trust us, Jimmy," Tammy said. She had stood up and was licking his left ear while massaging his shoulders and chest.

"I can't," Jimmy said.

"Yes, you can," the blonde said. "You sexy hunk."

"I shouldn't."

"Of course you should, Jimmy," Tammy said. "You need it like a doper needs dope."

"Like a boozer needs booze," the blond said.

"Like a smoker craves nicotine," Tammy said.

"Like a thrill junkie craves thrills," the blonde said, running the tips of her fingers over the bulge in his pants.

"We've fantasized about you. We have wanted, for quite some time now, to fuck someone like you, someone special; someone built like Spiderman."

She unbuckled his pants, unzipped the fly, and took the horse cock in her hands. At first only ogling, then squeezing the base in her hand. She sighed in wonderment, a sigh that drew the brunette's attention away from nibbling the back of the kid's neck and ears. She, too, couldn't take her eyes off of the kid's rod.

She left his upper head, and moved her tongue down there to the other, the one between his thighs, and ran her tongue ever so gradually, back and forth across the knob, then up and down either side of the pulsating shaft. She was back on the head of his groin, each little lick causing the sensitive and shiny and polished and smooth knob to throb and quiver. For Jimmy Riff, the pleasure was undeniable. How would he be able to turn this down? Was he even capable of it? It hadn't been planned; none of it had been planned. Was he still to be blamed for what was taking place?

He thought of Victoria and how wonderful she was, genuine; someone deserving of a good man—and he so wanted to be that man. Probably wishful thinking on his part. What were the odds of it working out? She came from money; he came from nowhere . . . and was quite possibly headed nowhere. So why not enjoy what was presently available?

It might have been love at first sight with Vicki, although he'd never experienced it before and certainly was no expert when it came to that. Love at first sight didn't mean that suddenly there wouldn't be any problems in the relationship, that they wouldn't have to deal with all the crap that other couples went through. A perfect example was this situation he found himself caught up in and couldn't do much about.

He'd never asked for this ménage, but it was happening. He figured it was wrong for him to be involved in this scene, especially after the loving time he had shared with Vicki. It was more than wrong; it was, quite possibly, betrayal. Guilt ate away at him, and yet there was no denying that he was loving it, engrossed in it, enjoying the moment for all it was worth.

⌘

He looked down at his cock and the soft and moist tongues that took turns covering it with saliva that made him squirm in his seat, and thought: It's all your fault, you randy bastard. I always end up doing what you want.

Gently, he pushed the women away from his erection. They looked up, wondering what was going on?

"What's the matter?" the blonde asked.

"I need some cash from you."

"Bull-fucking-shit."

"You should be paying us, jock," Tammy said, and undid her blouse, revealing a set of perfectly shaped 38s. Then she unzipped her corduroys and massaged the mound through the embroidered pink panties.

Mae undid her own shirt and took it off. The white bra was full and could hardly contain the heavy hooters in it. "When was the last time you saw tits like this? Huh, Mr. Jimmy Riff?"

"Or pussy this fine and juicy?" Tammy asked, taking her panties off. There was a healthy mound of dark hair down there. There was no denying he liked what he saw.

"You don't understand."

"*You* don't understand, jock," Tammy said. "We don't come cheap. You're getting it for nothing. Two beautiful, out-of-this-world luscious pussies free of charge."

"And you expect *us* to pay?" the blonde said. *"Who do you think you're dealing with? A couple of two-bit hookers? We're high class merch, honey. High class and high priced."*

"I'm busted," Jimmy said. "Flat broke."

The lesbians looked at each other.

"Honest."

"How much?" the blonde asked, while licking his right earlobe and worked her way down to the collarbone.

"Yeah," Tammy said, who was back burying her face between his upper thighs. "How much does lover-boy need?"

"Eighty."

"What?" Tammy said, looking up.

"Eighty dollars."

"You're a joke."

"I'm really broke. I could use the cash."

"I can get three good-sized dildos for that kind of money," the blond said, stroking his manhood. "Just as good as this, I might add. Well, not quite. Almost as good."

"I'm sorry, then," Jimmy said, forcing his groin back inside his pants.

"Who are you trying to kid, brother?" Tammy said. "After that incredible flicking job, you're going to tell me that you can turn it off just like that?"

"Benjamin said—"

"What's Benjamin got to do with it?"

"He's my manager."

"Shit," Mae said, shaking her head.

"He has to okay it."

"You're too much," Mae said.

"I'll say," Tammy said, gazing at his crotch. "Give him the damn eighty bucks."

"No," Mae said. "Let's go home and try out that new vibrator." Winked at her friend as she said it.

Ignoring the blonde, Tammy withdrew two twenty-dollar bills from her purse and stuck them inside Jimmy Riff's fly. Then she reached over and dug up two more twenties from Mae's purse and jammed them inside Jimmy's pants pocket. She yanked his footwear off, and was busy pulling his pants down. Mae was already slurping away at the Kidd's massive tool before her friend even had his pants all the way off and had flung them at the corner. Small beads of sweat were beginning to appear at Jimmy's belly button and upper thighs.

"I hadn't intended on charging you," Jimmy said. "I do need the money." And thought: *Now I can take Vicki to the circus.*

"You're worth every bit of it," the blonde sighed. She was kneeling between his thighs, arms wrapped around them, while licking the entire shaft, and then taking about a third of it inside her mouth. She did this for as long as she was able to go on without breathing, but then at some point, had to withdraw, lifted her head up for air, then was back over the large knob, licking, working it with her experienced tongue.

She sucked on the head, removed her hands from his thighs and stroked his shaft with them, while licking and applying saliva to the head. She lifted her face, spit into the palm of her right hand, and ran the saliva over his cock, particularly the bulbous knob. Lotsa lube made the head more sensitive, which in turn resulted in a greater experience. A better suck job, is what it came down to, a more fantastic BJ. And while she busied herself with all of this, her friend, the brunette, was below looking up: her tongue deep inside his hot and hairy butt crack. She couldn't get enough. This was heaven. Most men didn't turn her on, but this son of a bitch was the exception. It always worked that way. Men were average, most of them: clients, johns. You fucked them for money or you let them eat you out; or you peed on them, and did other things with them, to them. Didn't matter. It was a way to make a buck. For her sexual fulfillment she had Mae, and others before her had satisfied her sexual needs.

But this Adonis had that something undefinable. She couldn't put her finger on it, but it was there. Besides, why did everything have to have a label; why did every mystery have to have a denouement. She was having the time of her life, and that was explanation enough.

She left his asshole for the time being, and worked her way toward his nut sack. She sucked on his balls, taking each testicle in turn. The man had large, healthy balls: manly nuts. Built like a real man, and not a boy; not a wimp or weakling. Definitely not a dork. A man, without trying to appear macho or any of that bullshit that she and Mae both hated.

"Mae, don't make him cum," Tammy said. "Not yet."

The blonde nodded reluctantly and allowed his thick prick to slide out of her hungry mouth. Stopping was damn tough, but she managed. She gripped the base of his manhood in both of her hands and squeezed, watching the pulsating veins turn a darker purple than they already were. Lotsa blood in there. Cock was strong and hard. Like fucking wood. Why they called it a *"woody"* in the porn industry. If you couldn't get wood you were out: through. This bastard was all wood: one hundred percent wood. Ready to blast cream. She ached to see him shoot a big load of it, but Tammy had asked her to wait a while. Now Tammy was caressing her thighs, buttocks, which were wet with sweat.

"What do you got, big boy?" Ora Mae asked. "How much? How many inches?"

"I couldn't tell you."

"You don't measure it?"

"Never have."

"Bullshit," said Ora Mae. "Guys like Styles measure every chance they get, not that it helps."

"I don't spend much time dwelling on it."

"You would, if you were small. What about thickness? Diameter?"

"I wouldn't know."

She attempted to get the fingers of her right hand around it, and failed. There was no way. Son of a bitch had one of the thickest dongs she'd ever laid eyes on. It wasn't until she got both hands around it that she was able to get her fingers to connect. Hung? Understatement. Endowed? Not only was he, but his cock did not have any of the usual circumcision scars you saw with most men. The head on it was perfectly shaped, something like a mushroom—and it was a beautiful thing to see and feel: in your hands, mouth, butt crack, or pussy.

He was a great candidate for a caster plaster mold. Men, porn actors, gay or straight, had had dildos made from their dicks—who weren't even as hung as this stud here and whose cocks weren't as nice to look at or as impressive. He ought to do it. She mentioned it.

"I don't think I'd want to."

"Why not? Could be money in it."

"Sounds silly to me," said Jimmy Riff.

Taking her sweet time, Tammy ran the manicured fingers of her left hand over Mae's asshole, sending a rush of ecstasy through her body that was something like an electric current that ripped through her being and set her brain on fire. Was she cumming? Couldn't tell. Whatever it was it was incredibly thrilling. Tammy was not through, not by a long shot. With her other hand she was rubbing the woman's moist pussy. Inserted a couple of fingers inside, gently, slowly, always taking her time, while with her thumb she played with the clit. She circled her thumb over it, non-stop, knowing what it did, knowing for a fact it was paying off and made it nearly impossible for Mae to take all that pleasure without going into spasms. Tammy was relentless.

"Should I let up?" she asked, grinning like a Cheshire cat.

"You do and I'll kill you," said Ora Mae.

"I'm kidding," said Tammy.

"I'm not."

"Just for that, I've got a bonus for you—as part of your punishment."

"Punish me, punish me," pleaded Ora Mae.

"You slut," sighed Tammy, *"you fucking sexy hot slut. . . ."* And she probed the other's asshole with her middle finger. In deep, it went. Ora Mae winced with pleasure. Tammy was merciless in her assault of both: the blonde's clit as well as her butt crack.

"You like having a finger in your asshole?"

Ora Mae was nodding.

"Say so, then, bitch! Let me hear you say how much you like it."

"I love it."

"What about the other? Like having your clit and pussy lovingly massaged? Do you?"

"YES," said Ora Mae.

"I need to hear you say it, you filthy slut. Let me hear you utter the words. Now. Do it. You enjoy having your cunt and asshole finger-fucked at the same time? Is that it?"

Ora Mae was speechless. All she was capable of was moans and yelps, between loud gasps. While all this was being done to her she found it difficult to concentrate on Jimmy's boner.

Tammy stayed with it. It was work, taking its toll on her hands. You did something this strenuous long enough and your hands got sore. But it was worth it just to see her friend squirm in ecstasy this way. You bet. Tammy was loving it.

Ora Mae was cumming, erupting. Great. It was a kick to see her go off, screaming, her entire body quaking: legs, pelvis, chest, head. The way she shook her head was the real kicker, as she had a violent way of doing it: back and forth, her mouth all twisted up in a grimace. It was rewarding to see.

Only Tammy was nowhere near done with her pal. Nope. She withdrew both hands, and got her mouth under the blonde's dripping wet bush. Cunt was hot. This was something she could never resist: had her mouth and tongue all over it: inside and outside the cunt lips, drawing out the muff juice. Then her tongue slid lower, down toward Mae's asshole and licked; around, circling, then inside, probing deep. The smell of her pussy and butt crack drove her insane with insatiable desire. They'd been together more than two years and she still could not get enough of this woman's wondrous orifices.

Her mouth was back on the pleasure box, buried in it. Tammy pressed hard, shoving her tongue way in there, as far as it would go, and wished she had another six inches to probe further. Alas, all she had was all she had to give. It had to be enough. Ora Mae was still yelping and shaking, her thighs wrapped firmly around Tammy's head, while her arms remained tied about Jimmy Riff's neck.

Jimmy was still sucking on the woman's nipples. The hell with this, he thought, reached under her ass and lifted Ora Mae onto the desk. This did not deter Tammy in any way; she kept her mouth against Mae's pussy as if glued to it. Ora Mae reached out with her hands, groping for something, anything, to cling to, as the pleasure was unbearable.

There was Jimmy, she realized, and held on to his shoulders, gripping him with all her might. Jimmy guided his rigid member inside her cunt and did the stroke thing, only his way, the Jimmy Riff original way of pumping a cunt on fire: his were slow and deliberate strokes.

None of that rapid pumping bullshit for him. No. No way. You took your time. It was what made him what he was; what made the women want him and never could get enough of him.

Even when Ora Mae pleaded that he move faster, he refused, took his sweet time . . . until she finally got it and went along for the ride. This was it. Used to it. This son of a bitch knows what he's doing. None of that wham bam, thank you, ma'am—and it's over in ten seconds. This was the way to fuck. And when his strokes increased in speed it was gradual and steady, but not extremely fast, never fast. Speed worked against it. Pump too fast and you ruined it, fucked it up. Spoiled it.

Jimmy took his time, even slightly pausing to see what Tammy was doing down below. The brunette took turns between sucking on his balls and rimming the blonde's rectum. Probe it, suck it, thought Jimmy. There was nothing like it. The experience was one for the books. Why hadn't he set this type of situation up more often in the past? Look at what you missed out on. Two chicks was better than one. Twice the pleasure. Even three might top this.

He withdrew upon Tammy's insistence, and slid it inside the brunette's wide-open mouth. Drive it down, deep. Way in there. Watched her take it. Some pro. They were pros. And loving it. That made it even more of a thrill; that he was able to please these two call girls who sexed it up for bucks.

He was back inside the blonde's hot box. All the way. Strong strokes. Man-meat. Hard prick. Inside her needy cunt. He stayed with it. Now that she was cumming, again, he increased the speed appropriately, and watched her squirm and scream, knocking a stack of phone books off the desk. Tammy had stopped sucking on the blonde's butt and had her finger back in there, adding to it and making it a climax to remember. Mae was wilting and needed them to stop. The climax had been so intense that she needed, absolutely needed them to let go of her privates. She simply could not take anymore. Spent, so spent and exhausted. All she needed was to be held now; held, still, forever like this.

Jimmy did this by instinct. Not because he had to, because he didn't feel obligated in any way, he did so because it was his nature. He held her and gently kissed her neck, up and down both sides of it, her face; planted sweet kisses down her cleavage, burying his face in it, and held her.

Ora Mae no longer made any sounds; relaxed, drifting off into a sea of something calm and relaxing. Heaven. It was sheer heaven. . . . Life at its best. You lived for orgasms like this; you hoped and prayed and ached for orgasms like this . . . and when it happened and you attempted to describe it, words were hardly adequate. No words you could think up could ever describe what she just experienced. And she didn't bother. Her smile, the faint trace of her smile, said it all. . . .

Ora Mae was lying on her back, out of it, in another world. Jimmy pulled out of her cunt and guided his thick cock back inside Tammy's mouth for a while, then he had her stand up, turn away from him, so that her butt was out, while she leaned forward against the edge of the desk. He got down on his knees and kissed her buns, parted them so that her dark butt crack was exposed and buried his face in there. His tongue searched for her asshole, found it, and probed inside, all the while playing, rubbing, teasing her clit with his right hand. His fingers parted her quiff, then entered, exploring, moving in and out for a while. Then his middle finger was back on her clit, for additional teasing. For lube, all he had to do was reinsert inside her vagina, and back out to the clit. It drove her wild. There was moaning; wanting more, wanting something additional.

Jimmy rose. Stuck his middle finger in his own mouth for lube, then stuck it inside Tammy's jaw. Asked her to spit on it. After she did that, and did it well, he inserted this finger inside her butt. It was tight in there, warm; nothing like sticking your finger into a well-built woman's asshole. What a thrill. Nothing beats this, he thought.

"Yes," Tammy sighed. "Do it. Fuck me in the ass. Ream my asshole. My asshole needs attention. Fuck my asshole. I want your monster cock in my asshole."

Some women were like this. They not only needed to have their pussy taken care of and loved, but every now and then they wanted what was taboo, at least here in the US; some were reluctant to admit it, too shy, or something, afraid they would be thought of as cheap and dirty. Some did. Not this one, not here. They were like Lisa Koch in that respect. These ladies were not shy about their sexual cravings and needs. They did not hesitate to let you know what they had to have to get off; what they absolutely needed to blast off and have a great time when it came to sexing it up.

Party? This was definitely a party.

Jimmy pumped her cunt, as before with the other one: they were slow and steady insertions and withdrawals. Sure. He knew what he was doing. Even when they demanded a far more rapid pace he only increased moderately. Nobody tells Jimmy Riff how to fuck. The only reason they demanded faster thrusts was because they hadn't experienced his style of fucking yet—and once they did, they couldn't get enough. That was the way to go about it. Teach 'em how to screw; get the best out of it.

She was requesting that he slide it in her asshole once again. The finger fucking had only whetted her appetite for it. She wanted wood up her butt. Would it hurt? It might. Did she care? Was she aware of it? Where was the lube? You had to have plenty of lube.

"Lube it before I shove this massive meat pole up your behind," Jimmy reminded her. Withdrew and had her spit on it prodigiously. Wanted more saliva. She gave all she had. And if it wasn't enough, whose fault would it be when it caused her to wince in a moment?

He asked for more lube.

"Spit on it, Ora Mae," said Tammy. "I'm all out of saliva at the moment."

The blond sat up, happy to oblige. Small favor to ask after the orgasms of a lifetime she just experienced. Ora Mae worked her mouth, collecting saliva inside it, then spit hard and directly over the head of Jimmy Riff's terrific cock. Jimmy took his hand and spread the moisture evenly over it, then ran it up and down his shaft.

"It'll have to do," he said.

"It's enough," said Tammy.

"You sure, honey?" said her friend Ora Mae. "Because I have more."

"Fuck me, *Kidd*! Don't just stand there," demanded Tammy. "I want it now, while I'm in the mood. Satisfy me, bad-ass."

Jimmy had the head of his groin up against her butt crack. Made a slight nudge at first, gently inserting the knob in. That was the way to go about it. You didn't ram it in there and rupture the woman's anus. Slide it in gradually, by degrees, a little at a time. Inch by inch. To withdraw: same thing. Slowly. No sudden moves allowed. Nothing abrupt or risky.

Then it was back in there. Deeper this time. About halfway in. Not only was the motherfucker hung, but the goddamn thing was thick and half of it in was plenty to get the party off to a good start. He stayed this way, and she matched him stroke for stroke. They had a rhythm going. Stiff man-meat probed her rectum. What a tight asshole. This was too good to be true. Hell, every time he slid it inside a woman's tight rear he felt this way. One never got enough of ass-fucking, especially when they were built like these two.

Prime butt crack, and he was drilling it. He also knew enough to pull out and requested more lube. True, he enjoyed fucking, but not to the extent it hurt anyone.

"Lube," said Jimmy. Drawing it up so that Ora Mae could lean down from the desk and spit on it again. She then repeated the process. This time Tammy had gathered up enough saliva of her own to add to it. Yes; it was looking up. Lube was the key. Whether you fucked them in the round-eye or the vagina. Lube made things a lot easier all around.

"Should do it," said Jimmy, and had Tammy turn around again so that her luscious buns were facing him. He parted her buttocks and slid that thick man-pole inside her asshole. Terrific was how it felt. Tammy was wincing, he could tell, and yet she did not want him to stop.

"I can stop," said Jimmy, "and stick it in your cunt."

"She can take it," Ora Mae assured him. "I've watched her take rubber dildos as large as that. Fucked her with a strap-on myself on more than one occasion—for a john. For big bucks, I might add."

"Don't stop," said Tammy while rubbing her clit. She said to Ora Mae: "Can you help me out?"

"What?"

"What do you mean 'what?'" said Tammy. "You know what I need. Get to it, girlfriend! Now!"

The blond slid off the desk, and was on the floor, kneeling, head up, mouth against Tammy's cunt and clit. She flicked her clit with her tongue. The reward was that Tammy was sighing now, needing it, enraptured by the experience.

Jimmy continued with deliberate strokes, driving his cock in there, gripping the woman's hips and driving it home. It amazed him that she was able to take what he was giving her, but there she was: handling it. He had even suggested he stop and instead enter her pussy, only the woman had been against it. Fine. He was there to please. They had given him the eighty and he would do his part.

❦

He paused. Needed rest. Thought to do the following: withdrew and drew it up against the blond's mouth. Would she take it? After it had been inside her friend's butt? He wondered. Some women wouldn't go that far. Others would. To some it was repulsive; to others, it added a dimension to the overall experience.

"Go for it, baby," said Jimmy Riff. "She's your friend. Her asshole's clean. You know each other."

"This won't be the first time," said the blonde. "She's done her share of sucking cocks that had been in my asshole, too."

"Do it, girlfriend," said Tammy, insisting. "I want to see you suck his cock, knowing it was in my butt. *Do it. Now.*"

The blonde did not need to be told again. Ducked her open mouth over it, relishing the taste. Only it was not easy at first, not because it had been inside her friend's rectum, but the son of a bitch was so goddamn huge. She pulled it out for a moment, sighing: "Fuck."

"What?" said Tammy.

"He's large," said Ora Mae. "This fucking thing is huge. I bet he cums like a fountain."

"Like Niagara Falls," said Tammy, and laughed.

The blonde had it back inside her mouth, and if she couldn't get all of it inside her throat, she managed at least three fourths. Three-fourths was plenty. Jimmy was in Seventh Heaven.

He let her work it a while longer, then slid it back inside Tammy's asshole. His hands moved from her tits and down to the creamy white buttocks. Such a perfectly shaped ass, he thought, and he was pumping the hell out of it.

Jimmy could feel the juice brewing in his loins, about to surge forth, getting ready to erupt. It would be a ton of hot Jimmy Riff cum, a river of certified goo to fill both of their mouths with.

He could feel it now, the lava close to exploding. His spine tensed up, his neck stiffened and his skull got real tight. His entire body froze for a moment. Stiff; he was stiff. Felt it. Moving through his massive groin: surging, nearing the head, and about to blast off into oblivion.

One stroke, two stokes; it was that close. Fuck. Shit. Goddamn. This was incredible. His jaw clenched; his buttocks. He withdrew in time.

"Get it, both of you," he said. *"Get it."*

He guided Tammy down toward his groin, had both of their faces up against it in time as the cum spurted like a fountain, like a geyser. There was plenty; and he watched them lick and suck, watched them eat cum. And it flowed; it flowed like never before. Part of it had to be the fact he'd gone so long without experiencing two women at the same time. Two of them. Even better: these women knew what they were doing. And loving it. The odd part was they preferred to fuck their own kind, lesbians. The other element had to do with it being in this office, and the excitement of being discovered. He had no business doing the nasty here in Styles' production office. . . . But it was too late to have regrets. . . .

"You beautiful bastard, you," Tammy moaned. "Don't go soft on me now."

Her blond friend was saying how tasty he was and that she could not get enough. There was cum on her fingers and she stuck them in her mouth, one finger at a time, and sucked all the cum off, even shoved her other hand inside Tammy's mouth to finish it. Tammy was happy to carry out the suggestion. There was some cum at the base of Jimmy's shaft and balls, and the women went to town to take care of that with their lapping tongues. They worked hard and got the job done.

Tammy was not done, though. Not yet. "Don't go soft on me, like I said," she ordered. "Fuck me in my cunt. I want it in my cunt."

Although at half mast, due to having just shot a huge load of man juice, Jimmy went for it. He was not known as The Kidd for nothing. Yes, he could do it again, this soon. Six times in a row if need be. Or more. Not many men were capable. Well, he was not your average stud.

She sat on the edge of the desk, her legs up, apart. He slid the meat pole inside her cunt. Started stroking. He took his time as before: not only because it was his tried and true method, but to rest up this way. Jimmy was slightly exhausted. Not completely, not entirely, only slightly. It was understandable.

"Fuck me, you bastard," said Tammy. "Fuck me! You cocksucker! FUCK MY JUICY CUNT!" The woman was nuts, but he went for it. It was nothing more than part of the game. Went along. Why not? She deserved to get off.

Ora Mae, the friend, had positioned her face close enough to be able to flick Tammy's clit. This was how they did it: got one another off in the greatest possible way. You flicked the clit or held a vibrator against it, while being fucked: either by your girlfriend with a strap-on, or the way they were doing it now: with a real live meat pole. A gargantuan cock.

Then it happened: Tammy's head hung back, her throat up, extended, in the air, mouth open wide and making sounds: gasps and moans, loud; she was loud. Fuck, Jimmy thought, someone out there or in the office next door is bound to hear. Guess who gets in trouble over it? Benjamin Styles. And Styles takes it out on him.

She was coming, and he was relieved.

"Uh, uh. Oh! Oh! Yes! Yesssssssss! Shit! Oh my God; shit. . . ." She was stiff, still. A smile crossed her face. She wrapped her arms around Jimmy's neck and kissed him on the lips. He reciprocated and lowered her down against the desk, so that she was able to rest this way and calm down.

"We'll have to do this again sometime," Tammy said, and not one of them heard Benjamin Styles walk in.

"Put your drawers on"

"You might try closing the door next time," Benjamin Styles said. He had the same clothes on. He needed a shave and looked sleep deprived.

"What happened to you?" Jimmy asked. "You look terrible."

"Put your drawers on," Benjamin Styles said.

Jimmy did so. Reached for his shirt in quick succession. No sooner had it buttoned, when Benjamin Styles grabbed him by the collar and sent one calloused palm hard across the kid's face.

"You dumb, punk. You dumb fucking punk."

"I wouldn't do that, Ben."

"Didn't I tell you to stay put?"

"I'm warning you."

"Shut up," Benjamin Styles said, and slapped him again.

The women quickly gathered up their clothes and dressed in the other room. The blonde re-entered to stuff a piece of paper in Jimmy Riff's pants.

"You're just jealous, Ben," she said.

Tammy walked up, standing in back of her. Said to Jimmy: "He's been coming on to us for years. He's pissed because we won't fuck him for nothing. Isn't that right, Mr. Styles?"

"No broad is worth a thousand bucks an hour," said Styles.

"We get it—and more," said Tammy.

"I suggest you two slutty, no-talent bitches get the hell out of my office—that is, if you want to keep using the breakdown."

"We can get it somewhere else, Styles," said Ora Mae. "Yours is not the only production company on this lot."

"Entirely up to you," said Benjamin Styles. Itching for a comeback from the loud-mouthed broads. Only both left without saying anything else. He regarded Jimmy Riff.

"Who the hell do you think you're dealing with? Huh, punk?"

"I'm warning you, Styles," Jimmy said. "Get off my back." And broke free of the other man's grip, shoving Benjamin Styles to the far side of the room.

Jimmy had both fists up, ready to duke. He would teach this pot-bellied prick it wouldn't do to badger Jimmy Riff. "You wanna harass me? *Give me a hard time?*"

Benjamin Styles didn't say anything, merely shook his head and grinned.

"Yer gonna get yours, you keep pestering me."

"You know," Benjamin Styles said, shaking out a cigarillo from the pack, "you can get hurt making threats like that."

"I'll let you in on something: nobody owns Jimmy Riff. Nobody fucks with Tubesteak!"

"Settle down," Benjamin Styles said, lighting his cigarillo. "Just do as you're told. Nobody's gonna fuck with you."

"Get off my back."

"What?"

"You heard me!"

"You need me, Kidd."

"Buzz off."

"You need management."

"Fuck you."

"I got too much invested."

"You hard of hearing or something?"

"No," Benjamin Styles said calmly. "But you are."

He seemed to study the ashtray on his desk as he flicked ash into it. Then the former Golden Gloves champ made a hard fist and sent it deep into Jimmy Riff's unsuspecting abdomen. Jimmy Riff doubled over, his face the color of grapefruit pulp. He found himself gasping for air. Nothing was coming in or going out. His mid-section felt as though it had been hammered by a sledge. It was real pain, and there was nothing he could do but let it subside—and in time it would. Only there was no way to stay on his feet. As he began the slow sinking process to the floor, Benjamin Styles delivered a second blow. This time to the kid's jaw, which took him down and left him lying unconscious where he'd dropped.

Break Free of the Bastard?

Benjamin Styles ground out his cigarillo in the metal ashtray. He looked down at the semi-clothed body of Jimmy Riff. There was blood on his mouth and nose. He tore off a paper towel from a roll he had sitting there and wiped Riff's face with it.

He picked up the coffee percolator, which always had water in it, and dumped the cool water on the kid and watched him come to. Then Benjamin Styles walked to one of the sound stages, where yet another lousy television commercial was being filmed by a maggot director who wouldn't give him the time of day, and filched two cups of coffee.

❧

"Here," Styles said, and handed the kid one of the cups. Jimmy had gotten finished dressing and remained slumped in the swivel. The pain wasn't entirely gone. He accepted the coffee without looking up.

"Black," Benjamin Styles said. "Don't remember how you like yours." Indicated the makeshift editing table on the other side of the room. "Cream and sugar's over there, if you want any."

This time Jimmy Riff nodded.

"Be right back," Benjamin Styles said, taking a razor and shaving cream with him.

Jimmy Riff stared at the black liquid in his paper cup. He wiped tears from his eyes and stared at the worn green rug. He would get even with this bastard. He would get back at him. Then wondered if he ever would be able to.

How had he worked things out in the past?

Assholes he didn't care for he simply avoided. Jerks who disrupted his easy-going manner and way of doing things he simply didn't associate with. He'd always been able to handle the situation, no matter what the problem was.

But what did he have here? How insidious the thorn? Could he break free of the bastard? Would he really want to? Styles did have the experience. He might be a certified A-hole, but he knew this town. He's got contacts—or does he? He'd saved his life. Still, no one, until now, had ever had the gall to tell the kid who to make it with and who not to make it with. And it infuriated him.

He drank the lousy coffee and set the empty paper cup next to a stack of mail on the editing bay. Top envelope was from Ma Bell. Jimmy Riff picked it up. Thing was open. He peered inside. In a nutshell: *Unless your bill is paid up by such and such date, your service will be discontinued.*

He peeked inside the other envelope, postmarked New Jersey. Benjamin Styles was behind on his alimony, way behind. A third piece of mail was another bill, accompanied by a letter:

Dear Ben,

Unless we get them the payments for the last 3 months, they've threatened to take the house. I realize there is no love lost between us, but what about your sons? Think of your sons. I implore you, Ben, don't delay. Please send money right away. These people mean business.

Yours,
Ethel

Jimmy Riff left the envelopes where he found them. He crushed the cup and tossed it in the wastebasket. The sorry mook is up the creek without a paddle, Jimmy thought. He sure as hell is. Could be because he's such a nice guy. Don't dwell on it. Waste of time. Instead he did his best to stay focused on Vicki and the circus he would take her to the following night.

❧

Styles was back. He was clean-shaven and had combed what thinning hair remained. That still didn't do much for his appearance.

"Here," he said, and handed Jimmy the shaving gear. "The men's room is across the way. You need a shave."

Headed Where?

Jimmy Riff stepped into the 90-degree LA smog and crossed the narrow, noisy studio street and entered the putrid-smelling restroom. He stepped back out immediately and made a second attempt. Washed his face and shaved. He stared, not long, at the expressionless face with the swollen upper lip in the cracked and grimy mirror.

Where are you headed? Do you know? Have a clue? You going to let your cock run your life? Going to cater to its every whim? Huh, Jimmy? How did you end up in this place, anyway? Marcella. Stopped by to see her, and I thought . . . Hollywood is not your kind of town, Jimmy. . . . This is not your kind of place. . . . You were on your way somewhere else. . . .

He wiped his face with a paper towel and hurried out of there to escape the stench. Once outside, he paused to collect himself, and calmly walked back to the office. Once again, Victoria Chantal, the girl of the night before, was on his mind. Guilt seemed to be knocking at his psyche, just as it had earlier. He didn't know the young woman, had hardly spent much time with her, so what was this feeling of remorse about? What did he owe her, or she him? This was not a relationship; they hadn't even gone out on a legit date, for Pete's sake. What the hell? Yes, there just might be a chance that something could develop . . . but who knew? These things took time. He had a role to play, like it or not, that of the Hollywood hustler. It was but a means to an end. See where it takes you. If things don't work out, move on. Uncle Orville is waiting up in Oregon. Where you were headed originally, anyway.

"They got the hots for you"

"Sure, I can bring him." Benjamin Styles was on his phone. "Anywhere you say. He looks great." Then: "Would I kid you, Eddie? We'll be right over." And he hung up.

The poverty-row jack of many trades, master of none, looked happy for a change. Not that Jimmy Riff gave a shit about that.

"Kidd," Benjamin Styles said, turning to Jimmy, "things are looking up."

Jimmy didn't say anything.

"Where'd ya get that shirt?" Benjamin Styles asked. "Got something better in my car. Come on. Start wearing shirts that match your baby blues. Women go for it. Gives your appearance that something extra." Jimmy noticed finally what the jerk had on: shirt had blue in it. His shirts always had blue in them. Jimmy may have had blue eyes but the color blue never did anything for him. He preferred yellow or red, or even brown—anything but blue. Yes, he had dark hair and blue eyes and women found him appealing, were drawn to him—but he never allowed it to go beyond that. Never would let it go to his head. He had been born with his looks and height and the equipment down there, but so what? *Keep it natural and down to earth, no matter what happens; keep it real, Jimmy.* Always. If he had a mantra, this was it. You were no better than anyone else, simply because you had been given certain qualities at birth. He had also been saddled with certain other qualities at birth: negative ones, invisible scars and a simmering rage, just below the surface—his mother and father's legacy. Bottoms up. Thank you very much. Which he did his best to cope with and stay positive.

And the blue eyes? Mattered very little, if anything. But let Styles go on. The great manager who was taking him places. Yeah. Right. Down the gutter of nowhere.

"You don't know this," said Styles, "because I don't like to toot my own horn: but the name Rock Hudson? I suggested it to his manager. Hudson's real name was Roy something; I forget. Doesn't Matter. Truck driver out of Chicago. As queer as a three-dollar bill. Tab Hunter? Same shit. I made the suggestion. It was my idea to call him that. Someone else gets the credit every time. Troy Donahue's real name was Merle Johnson. I said to his manager at the time: Name the kid Troy Donahue, why don't you, and see him go places. Merle became a star. Orison Whipple Hungerford?" He laughed. "What a fucking handle. I come up with Ty Hardin. Has a nice ring to it. Guy Madison and Rory Calhoun were names I come up with for Robert Mosely and Francis Timothy McCown. Just to name a few. Never got the credit. That's okay, so long as you know you got the best management money can buy. For example, your name: James Kidd is probably the winningest marquee name I ever come up with. JAMES KIDD. Proud of it, if I say so myself. Real proud."

You might be, thought Jimmy, I still prefer Riff. Jimmy Riff. Formerly James Grayson Riff. Even Tubesteak suited him better. Why not? As in-jokes went, it was okay. Showed he could laugh at himself. Never thought he was better than anyone else because of his prowess in the sack. It was Nature's gift. That's all. Just like some are great chess players, or swimmers, or can shoot hoops. His ability happened to be in the bedroom. It was appreciated by certain types. Did he think he was anything special because of it? Hardly. You didn't let a thing like that go to your head—below, or above.

⸎

Benjamin Styles turned out the lights, and they left the office. No sooner had they reached the parking lot, when Styles remembered he hadn't called his answering service. He unlocked his car, reached in for a dark blue shirt on a plastic hanger, and handed it to Jimmy.

"Here," said Styles, "put this on." And re-entered the barracks-like structure his office was in. Jimmy had got into the dry-cleaned and pressed shirt and was waiting in the car. Styles re-emerged, got in himself, and shifted into gear.

"Saul Gold," Benjamin Styles blurted. "Bertram Merrick. Artie Gross. Samantha Unger. Winifred Gale Sacks. Walter W. Roth. Ira Cohen." Lit a cigarillo. "Know what every one of these people got in common?" said Benjamin Styles, looking at the kid. "*You*. That's right. They got the hots for you. Would like to make your acquaintance." He laughed. It was a loud laugh. "All left messages for me to contact them." He dragged on the brown butt. "Right away."

⸎

The Toyota puttered north on Highland, across the heavily congested Hollywood Boulevard. The traffic didn't get on Benjamin Styles' nerves like it usually did. He felt good; no, he felt great. "Guess what else?" Benjamin Styles said. "A friend of yours left a message."

Jimmy Riff looked up.

"The Nazi cunt: Lisa Koch," Benjamin Styles said, "would like you to call her. Wants to apologize."

"Shit," Jimmy muttered.

Benjamin Styles was still laughing, amused by all of it. "Can you believe the nerve of that dyke? *Wants to apologize?*"

Many cars whipped around the Toyota as it neared the on-ramp to the Hollywood Freeway, and more than a few drivers in those cars did not hesitate to give the driver of said Toyota a dirty glare. Styles didn't care. He looked in the rear-view mirror to see what was causing the nasty expressions, although he had a pretty good clue: heavy smoke billowed from the exhaust. Muffler was expelling enough dark fumes, as usual.

"Fuck it," said Styles to himself. What was he supposed to do? It took money to have these imports worked on, money that was in short supply. You had to bear up. Take it. To worry about it wouldn't cause the junker to stop smoking, nor would it keep from losing power, and the car was losing power every day.

The last of the pissed-off motorists zoomed past and honked his horn. Benjamin Styles stuck his middle finger out the window.

"Fuck all of ya!" Benjamin Styles shouted. *"Eat shit!"*

Jimmy Riff smiled, and knew there and then that he was probably one of the very few people who ever even got close enough to Benjamin Styles who might have an idea what B. Styles was about. Was that good or bad?

"I ever tell you what brought that bitch down from her throne?" Benjamin Styles said.

Jimmy Riff shook his head.

"Took some kid, a boy, up to her place one night. . . ." He paused. "Under age. Did what she did to you—but worse. He managed to spit the Granny Smith apple out of his mouth and screamed his head off. A cab driver heard it and called the cops. Saved the kid's life. That's when all that shit about her Nazi worship come out: Nazi uniforms and medals, caps, mementos. She had shit that once belonged to some of her heroes: Ilsa Koch and Irma Grese, and others. Loony cunt goes and names her dog after Hitler's own German shepherd: Blondi. Can you believe it?" Styles spit out the window. Wiped his mouth with the back of his sleeve. "Know where that cabbie is now? Bahamas. Retired. Thirty years old—and retired. The kid's folks had the bucks, see? Saw to it the cabbie was taken care of. . . . She came close to injuring the kid for life, though."

"She do time?"

"Some," said Styles. "Her mouthpiece worked out a plea bargain with the D.A.'s office. Money talks, bullshit walks. You can get away with murder in this town, so long as you have the bucks."

"I never thanked you for saving my life," Jimmy said.

"Don't worry about it," Benjamin Styles said. "Stick with me and I'll make you rich. James Kidd will be a household word. It'll be us living in the Bahamas."

"Mr. Styles is here"

Benjamin Styles took the Barham Blvd. exit and drove toward the city of Burbank. Destination: Inter-Continental Hollywood Studios.

The Toyota pulled up to the studio gate in a cloud of gray smoke. An obese guard stuck his head out with a hankie over his mouth.

"Yes, sir?" the guard said.

Benjamin Styles gave his name and said with great pleasure: "Here to see Edward McFluff."

The guard checked his clipboard, looked up. "Right, sir. Mr. McFluff is expecting you."

That's how it's done, thought Benjamin Styles. You got respect. Long overdue. They called you *Mister* and *Sir*. The way it's going to be from now on. They were on their way. Exactly what he said to the kid sitting next to him in this beat-up clunker: "We're on our way, Jimmy."

The guard ducked back inside his shack, as the Toyota spit and gasped and puttered onto the vast studio lot among new Mercedes Benzes, BMWs, high-end SUVs, Corvettes, and Porsches. There were Ferraris on display as well, Testarossas, Rolls-Royces, and Bentleys. Benjy favored the Rolls-Royces, the older the better. In mint condition. One day he would own one. If that overrated Lithuanian named Robert Tanner could drive around in one, so could he. Why not? His acting chops were superior to Tanner's any day of the week. He knew it, so did Tanner. Why he gave him a hard time on that last picture. The shit. Russian cocksucker. Born somewhere in Philly. Coal miner, they said. But, fuck: he was no real American like Ben Styles. Tanner should have stayed in the coal mines. All he was good for. Fucker had even changed his name from Slowinsky to Tanner. Commie sack of snot.

⌘

Edward McFluff's production company took up the entire single-story building that they pulled up in front of. It might have been a wiser move to park the clunker elsewhere away from Fluffy's building, but what the hell, thought Styles. He knows I'm struggling. No way around it. So the Toyota is a piece of shit, so what? Why hide it? Could have rented a Benzo, like so many phonies in this town, for appearance's sake. Could have, but didn't bother. Whose got the money to waste like that?

Screw it.

They went in.

⌘

Movie posters in chrome frames from the various motion pictures Edward McFluff had been involved in in his vast and varied career covered the wall space. What did it mean? Benjamin Styles wasn't impressed. Maybe the kid was, he thought, but *he* wasn't. Didn't mean zip. No matter how high up you were, you still could slip up and land way down there—HARD. End up taking your life. Like that director the other day: jumped from the San Pedro bridge, because his last three flicks had laid an egg at the box office. And the jumper in question, one Elton Crabstick, had been worth millions, married to a woman half his age, and lived in a five-million-dollar mansion in Bel Air. Left two twelve-year-old twin daughters behind.

Why should he be impressed? Styles had been around too long to know it was all fleeting; like life and love and all the rest of that bullshit. Fleeting.

Still, it would be nice, real nice to be able to make bills and drive a nice car and be able to bang some quality beaver once in a while, like those two cunts he walked in on in his office who were balling this kid standing next to him with his jaw on the floor.

There were two secretaries here sitting behind large desks. World-class beauties—on the surface. Probably sucked dick as call girls during their off hours. That's what Tinseltown was about. Blond bitches chatted on their phones. Too busy to so much as look up.

"Yes?" the blonde on the right finally said.

"Is that any way to greet someone?" said Styles.

"Pardon me?" said the woman.

"I'd like to 'pardon' you," said Styles under his breath.

"Sir?"

"A joke," said Styles. Corrected himself. "Benjamin Styles to see Reggie McFluff."

"This way, please," she said. Rose, and showed him to an office in back. She knocked, then cracked the door. Stuck her head in. "Mr. Styles is here."

"Thank you, Delia darling," said McFluff.

"Yes," said Styles to the woman: "Thank you, Delia darling."

The woman smiled, but it was like the smile of a cobra. Fucking hard bitch, thought Styles. They all were. All of these women who worked here at the studios. Hard bitches. Ball-busters. Chip on their shoulder. Made you wonder where they came from and what made them this way? Not that he gave a damn. Shit on them. Every single one of them. Better yet: shaft them. He thought he wouldn't mind giving her six inches of hard chubby. Wouldn't mind that at all.

He turned away. Bitch wasn't interested. She did give the kid the twice-over. Sure. They all did; the other ball-buster as well. Not only did they look up and down but smiled. They had smiled. Jimmy took it in stride. Must be nice, thought Styles, to be getting that kind of attention from hot broads.

"Would you mind coming back in an hour?" Styles and Jimmy Riff heard McFluff say to the actor who had been sitting on the black leather sofa on their left.

"Not at all," said the actor with the youthful, wrinkle-free face. He rose, and was gone. Another piece of ass Eddie was trying hard to promote, thought Benjy. *The letch.*

"Come in, come in," said R. Edward McFluff, rising himself, hand extended.

Jimmy and Ben entered the opulent office: more posters and weighty and pricey sculptures and do-dads from some vast locales in South America and Africa, and all those other foreign shoots McFluff was known for.

He shook Styles' hand, said: gazing at Jimmy Riff: "So this is James Kidd, *the* 'James Kidd' I've heard so much about."

"Jimmy," Benjamin Styles said, "meet Edward McFluff, one of the top motion picture producer/directors around." They pumped hands.

"Pleasure is all mine," said Edward McFluff. "Please do sit down." That they did. "Anything my secretary can get you? Coffee, tea, imported beer, whiskey, V8, weed? Name it."

"Got any orange juice?" asked Jimmy.

"Orange juice it is," said Edward McFluff. "Name your poison, Ben."

"Nothing," said Styles. "Not when I'm conducting business."

McFluff lowered his behind in the leather swivel behind his desk. Flicked the intercom switch: "Glass of OJ, please, Delia. And a Perrier. Thank you, hon." He was rubbing his hands, and rested his elbows against the blotter, apart. Grinning. Forever grinning, like the certified degenerate Styles knew him to be.

"Thank you," Jimmy Riff said.

"James Kidd," Edward McFluff said the name a couple of times to see if he liked the sound of it. "Has a nice ring to it. Would look great on a movie-house marquee," he said with a straight face. "Ever wanted to be in pictures?"

"Oh shit," Benjamin Styles sighed under his breath.

"Just kidding," McFluff said and laughed. "Pulling your leg."

The secretary whose name was Delia entered with a glass of orange juice and the bottle of Perrier. McFluff nodded in Jimmy's direction. Jimmy rose to accept it. Thanked the woman. "Why, you're quite welcome," said she with a twinkle in her eye, and left, putting definite sway in her hips and behind. She took her time closing the door. McFluff had taken it in, and could only grin and shake his head.

Jimmy had a sip of OJ. He was hungry, and it did feel good to have something in his belly.

"You got a piece of paper for me, Eddie?" Benjamin Styles said with a degree of impatience.

"Ben," McFluff said, his tone changing. He rose. "Want to come with me?" He paused at a door to the adjoining office. Opened it, and waited for Styles to follow. Styles did, wondering what was up. The door was closed behind them.

⌘

Jimmy had another sip of the orange juice. It hit the spot. What he needed. He also needed something else: like a shower, change of underwear and pants, clean socks. He needed to brush his teeth. His mouth felt dry, like cotton. Hell, no wonder. You don't ball two professionals like Ora Mae and Tammy and not take a shower afterwards. Where would he have had the time? Styles had walked in and disrupted the experience. At least he had been able to shave, comb his hair.

Styles and McFluff were in a heated discussion over something. He could only make out snatches through the closed door. He gathered things were not going well for Benjamin Styles, talent manger/producer/procurer/actor/script writer—or something.

There was a screenplay on a corner of the desk nearest him McFluff must have been leafing through before they walked in. Jimmy craned his neck high enough to read the title: *THEY CAME TO DODGE*. He was tempted to pick it up and take a look, but refrained from doing so. Wasn't his property, wasn't his business. McFluff wouldn't like it. The voices in the other part of this office were going up: Styles and the mogul were at it. Close to shouting, but not quite.

"I haven't got much time"

"You have no one to blame but yourself," McFluff said, in this part of the office suite that was equipped with shower and john, refrigerator, coffee pot, a range for cooking, and other appliances. There were no posters on the walls here, and Benjy was glad. Although he was far from happy with what McFluff was telling him.

"Bullshit," Benjamin Styles said.

"Grossbard didn't like it; didn't like it one bit."

"I don't give a rat's ass what he likes."

"The stuntman left and Morey's blaming you."

"How did he find out?"

"Don't ask me," McFluff said, shrugging, "but he did. He doesn't want you on this picture, not even as a walk-on. He hates your guts, Ben."

"No part, no deal," Benjamin Styles said. Opened the door to the other office, and shouted for Jimmy to follow him out the door.

"Wait," McFluff implored. "Maybe something can be worked out."

"I haven't got much time."

"I think I can squeeze you in."

"I'm waiting," Benjamin Styles said, and folded his arms.

"Not much of a part."

"Lines?"

McFluff was hesitant.

"Lines, Eddie?"

"One or two."

"What do you take me for?"

"Ben, you fucked up."

"Eddie, I've been around too long to take this kind of shit. I'm not some dumb aspiring actor looking for a break. I'm good. I've got a solid background to prove it. I've been in pictures with McQueen, Eddie G. Robinson, Chuck Heston, Charley Bronson, Duke Wayne; both Clints: Eastwood and Walker; been in pictures with Presley and Harrison Ford. What the fuck! Been in pictures directed by Don Siegel and Bloody Sam. *What the fuck?* I got a real resume—not fake, *real*—that backs up these *legit* claims. No hype. All solid and verifiable. I did *Big Daddy* on Broadway. Won a Tony! Hear that? Benjamin Styles won a Tony! Not bought, won! Best featured actor award voted by the critics!"

Edward McFluff rolled his eyes. "Ten years ago, Ben."

"What's that got to do with anything? Still have it; I'm still good."

"Good at punching people out."

"What's a Western about?"

"Huh?"

"What's it about if it ain't about fist fights and bar brawls—"

McFluff cracked a smile and shook his head.

"I should be in this picture, and you know it."

"Two, three lines," Edward McFluff said. "Best I can do."

"Should have busted Grossbard's nose instead."

"Ought to be thankful to get anything."

Styles said: "No way to snag one of the principal parts?"

Edward McFluff shook his head.

"What's the character's name?"

Edward McFluff shrugged. "Man #1."

"'Man #1?'" Benjamin Styles said incredulously. "Doesn't even have a fucking name, he's so minor."

"You want it or not?" McFluff said. "I have work to do. Pre-production, Ben."

Benjamin Styles nodded. "I guess so."

That was all McFluff needed to hear. He opened the door and returned to his desk. Benjy followed. Watched Fluffy flip the intercom toggle, and say: "Bring Mr. Styles' contract in, would you please, Delia honey."

Delia did not waste any time getting there. Handed the document to her boss. Could not help herself, smiled at Jimmy Riff on her way out and closed the door. Should he have been impressed? Not really, thought Jimmy. It was meaningless. Pretty much. She was hot; both secretaries were, but he'd had so many women like them. Rolls in the sack. One-night stands. Impersonal and empty. Fun? Sure. Just as the party back at Styles' office with the two call girls. Still, there was a hollowness to it. Left you with a void. Something was missing . . . something he could not put his finger on, exactly. . . .

He looked at Benjamin Styles. Sweating heavily. Pissed, but doing his best to keep calm. It was not easy. They were giving him a hard time. Story of Benjamin Styles' life, it seemed—and Styles had no one to blame but himself. You went around knocking people out the way he'd knocked him out earlier in the day, and this was how it got back at you. You paid. Benjy was paying by struggling to find work, struggling for crumbs. How was he supposed to get him anywhere, when he couldn't even get anywhere himself?

Styles looked over the contract, pen in hand. Lifted his head.

"How many days?"

"One, possibly two."

"How much a day?"

"Five hundred."

"Not much more than scale."

"Getting better offers anywhere else?"

"Make it three days for three grand—" Then, looking at Jimmy Riff, he said: "That includes everything." He re-read the contract. "Plus, I want to lay that farm girl," Benjamin Styles said.

"How many times?" McFluff asked.

"That's cute," Benjamin Styles said. "How long would you want the kid for?"

"A night."

"A whole night," Benjamin Styles said, scratching his chin. "Could kill you."

"Let me worry about that," McFluff said.

"Then I want her for a week."

"Deal," Edward McFluff said. "Pre-production is under way as we speak. Still negotiating the lead. Principal photography scheduled to start in two weeks. You'll get paid like everyone else."

"Bullshit," Benjamin Styles said. "This is no ordinary deal. Fifteen hundred now, fifteen hundred later."

Edward McFluff pulled out the middle drawer in his desk. Reached for a checkbook and slammed it against the desktop.

"No checks."

"You crazy?"

"No, just sensible."

"I don't carry that kind of cash on me," said the film director, "nobody does, that I know of." Benjamin Styles stood without saying anything. Haggling with these bozos was half the fun. Say he allows Fluffy to write a check and the thing bounces, and he's out of luck. Say they drop him unceremoniously, it's happened before—the check bounces so high it gives him a nose bleed, and that's all he ends up with for his troubles. No, sir. You learned the hard way. This was Hollywood, the sleaze capital of the universe. Liars ruled here, con men and scam artists. Snake oil salesmen.

"This is how we protect ourselves against the taxman, Eddie," added Styles. "In this wonderful country of ours. We pay through the nose anyway. Taxed left and right. You, of all people, should understand. Why you left the U.K., isn't it?"

"Give me a second, please," said McFluff, and stepped out of the office. He returned a moment later, sat behind his desk. Delia entered with a white envelope in hand. Handed it to Benjamin Styles. Styles looked inside, then counted the bills. Fifteen hundred, as per their agreement. Only then did he sign the contract.

"Thank you, Mr. McFluff," said Styles. To Jimmy Riff, he said: "Let's go. Air around here is kind of stale." Jimmy rose to leave.

"Pleasure meeting you," said McFluff to Jimmy Riff. To Styles, he said: "I'll be expecting you: 8:00 p.m. Sharp." Winked. "We'll have that drink I promised."

"We'll see you then," said Benjamin Styles, and left with his protégé.

Later, outside in the parking lot, Benjamin Styles gave out a wild hoot, jumped in the air, and gave Jimmy Riff a bear hug.

"I could kiss you right now," said Styles. "You're beautiful."

Jimmy said nothing. What the hell was there to say, anyway? Styles calmed down and they climbed in his car. The Toyota pulled out of the lot, with the familiar gray cloud of exhaust fumes trailing behind. The muffler sounded much louder. Like it might fall off at any minute.

A Room of Mirrors

Up Coldwater Canyon to the McFluff mansion. Benjamin Styles pumped the gas pedal, for what good it did. The Toyota puttered at its own speed.

"Now that you got the bucks," Jimmy Riff said, "think you ought to see about getting a car?"

"Nah," Benjamin Styles said. "Can't afford a decent one. Why spend money on another piece of junk? It wouldn't make sense. Soon as I see some real money I'm gettin' a better car."

Benjamin Styles withdrew a crisp one-hundred-dollar bill from his billfold. "Here," he said. "This is yours."

Jimmy Riff stared blankly at it for a moment, then stuffed it in his pocket.

"You'll get another hundred when I get mine," Benjamin Styles said. "Not bad, huh, Kidd? Coupla hundred bucks for a night's play. Almost called it 'work.' It's not work; it's play." Then he said: "Just do me a favor, Kidd? Don't let the old queen get too worked up, okay? His ticker's liable to quit on him—then where would I be?"

Jimmy Riff said nothing.

❧

The massive wrought-iron gate had been left wide open, and they drove on through. Pulled up to the entrance. Styles took a deep breath, checked his collar and the kid's, and rang the doorbell. The butler, a Mr. Roddy Quilp, a gaunt, old UK geezer who always reminded Styles of an embalmer whenever he saw him, appeared and motioned them inside. He handed Benjamin Styles an envelope with his name typed across the center.

"This is Mr. Quilp," said Styles to Jimmy. "Mr. Roddy Quilp. Mr. Quilp, meet James Kidd—aka Tubesteak."

"The pleasure is all mine, sir," said the butler. "I'm sure."

Jimmy was not certain if he ought to extend his hand, and since the butler, Mr. Quilp, did not appear to encourage something so commonplace and American, Jimmy did not initiate anything.

"You two might as well get acquainted," added Benjamin Styles. "You'll be spending enough time here, working on lines and such, with Reggie. He's quite the acting coach, isn't he, Mr. Quilp?"

"Mr. McFluff is quite the accomplished filmmaker," said Roddy Quilp. "That he is, sir. Many can learn quite a bit by spending time with such a gifted individual."

"And where might this gifted individual be keeping his sagging *'arse'* at the moment, if I might be so rude as to inquire, Mr. Quilp?" Benjamin Styles asked.

"Please read the note, sir," the butler said, in his best British accent.

Benjamin Styles did just that, and didn't like it.

Ben,

The drink I promised you is on a stand to your right. I can't let you have Angela tonight—perhaps some other time. However, I did find someone else to keep you company this evening. You can look up now.

Edward

"Son of a bitch," Benjamin Styles muttered, and looked up. There, next to the butler, stood the beauty. Long, lovely brown hair so clean it shone like tinsel. Early thirties. Another actress. Benjamin Styles grinned, because he recognized her.

"Ariane," he said.

"Hi, Benjamin," she said, and planted a moist kiss on his lips.

"Like I always say: No one kisses like Ariane Dean."

"That's right," Ariane Dean said. "You always did say that."

"Please," Benjamin Styles said, "if there's one thing I can't stand it's a cute broad."

"He hates 'cute,'" she said, facing Jimmy Riff. "Hates anything cute. Well," she linked her arms around Benjamin Styles' waist. "Shall we go?" And she guided an amused Benjamin Styles out the front door to a late model Mercedes Benz. The butler closed the door, and handed Jimmy Riff an envelope. This was something like Oscar night: envelopes were being handed out left and right. What the hell? Showbiz types had their games.

Jimmy Riff studied the note in silence. Afterwards, his forehead furrowed as he paused to digest what he'd just read. Then he followed the butler upstairs to the master bedroom.

The butler opened the double doors. New Age–type, easy listening guitar sounds wafted in from somewhere in the distance. He motioned for the guest to step inside and make himself at home, stepped out himself, and closed the double doors behind him.

"So you're Jimmy Riff," Angela Bliss said. "Pardon me. James Kidd." She was lying in that fancy bed of pink silk: sheets and pillowcases, sheer something or other that hung from the ramada overhead. All she wore was a smile. The room was all mirrors. Everywhere: ceiling, walls; even the long sliding walk-in closet doors in back of her had mirrors. The individual who lived here evidently liked to have viewing access to every angle of himself (and others) while knocking boots. He also seemed to favor the color pink. He liked white a lot; that's what the carpet was and the walls, the ones not covered by mirrors.

"The one and only."

"You must be wondering," she said, observing Jimmy and the way his eyes took in his surroundings: "Which is the fake mirror?"

"Something like that," Jimmy Riff said.

"I think it's that one," Angela Bliss said, and pointed to the wall at the foot of the bed, which was one gigantic floor to ceiling, end-to-end, mirror. "And that one," she said, pointing to the mirror directly in back of her.

She teased her nipples by running the end of the silk sheet back and forth over them, watched them harden. Something else was beginning to get hard, something inside Jimmy Riff's jeans: stirring and growing. She picked up on it, and smiled. "I hear you're quite the stud," Angela Bliss said.

Jimmy Riff shrugged and unbuttoned his shirt.

"So where is he?" he asked.

"Where's who?"

"Mr. McFluff, who else?"

She shook her head. Dreamy-eyed. Whether it was put-on or not, didn't matter, because it worked. "What's it matter? We're here to do as we please."

She sat up, clutching the top of the sheet in her hand against her bosom, while running her tongue across her upper lip. It was deliberate; it was gradual—for effect. It worked, just as the look with the eyes she gave was working. His groin continued to grow in stages, steady and strong. Wood was taking place. Solid wood.

"Come here, sugar," Angela said. "Let lil' ol' me do that for you."

Jimmy Riff moved up to the bed and watched her unzip his fly. She took her sweet time. Jimmy Riff was rock hard by the time she got around to tugging his jeans down to his ankles.

"I love black," Angela said, admiring his briefs. "It's such a turn-on."

If patience was a virtue, she was a master at it. Ran her hand over the briefs that contained the massive member inside and was not in any hurry whatsoever. She concentrated on the large knob long enough to see and feel the wetness that was pre-cum soak through the fabric. She was pleased with herself. Looked up to see that Jimmy was not unhappy about it, either. His eyes were on her and what she was doing, his forehead glistening with perspiration. There was no expression on his face, none that she could easily discern, other than perhaps the one in his eyes that said: *Whatever it is you're doing, keep doing it. . . .*

❧

She kissed the knob through the cloth; they were mini-kisses and plenty of them, a series of quick pecks, performed between the steady rubbing and caressing, up and down with her right hand over the head and rest of the shaft. While she did this, she had her other hand rubbing his backside, up and down, slowly, gradually, then found herself running the tips of her fingers between his buns. She turned him around, and began kissing his behind, kissing the cloth that covered his muscular buttocks.

She turned him around again, so that his groin was in her face, had the tips of her fingers across the top hem of his briefs, one on either side, and began to draw them down, down, down . . . inch by teasing inch, pulling them, tugging on them . . . revealing pubic hair, then more: the large knob of his cock, and the rest of it: balls . . . and more, until the briefs were completely, entirely down to where his ankles were. She got him to step out of them.

Now her eyes were level with his cock. Hard. Like a brick. Like a lead pipe. Meat pole. Thick and veiny. Beautiful. She had to stop, as many had before her, gazed in awe and amazement at the erection before her. It reminded Angela Bliss of the horse ranch she had grown up on; reminded her of the horny bastard stallions who fucked like champs. My God, the size of their cocks. More than once she had fantasized about having one in her mouth. Of course, she had never gone that far; never would, but the thought had crossed her mind. It would have been impossible as well as unacceptable. Society frowned on it. Only now, it was happening; she had a man before her who was hung like a fucking thoroughbred. Had a cock on him only a horse had the right to possess. And it was a cock she was about to taste in her very own mouth. Eddie McFluff and so many of his movie friends had such small dicks that they were like toy dicks, laughable. Puny and pathetic. This was a real man who stood before her, a man with a dick on him the size of three average schlongs.

She would enjoy herself, even though, clearly, this was meant to be nothing more than a show, performance, to be put on for Fluffy, who could not make up his mind about his own sexuality: Was he fag? Straight?—or both? Bi? Liked dick and vagina? Or a voyeur? Peeper. Got his rocks off by watching others fuck? This was Hollywood. She'd never guessed it was going to be like this. And she did her best to play along.

Angela Bliss was ever so grateful. After having had to sleep with Eddie and some of his chubby pals with stubby puds, Jimmy Riff, or James Kidd, as he was going by, was a vast improvement, a dream come true. He was like the Roman gods one read about in books, with his chiseled abs, muscular pecs, and arms. She loved his large hands, the powerful thighs; the tan lines where he had left his briefs on while sunbathing. And most of all, he was modest. She had picked up on it right away. He was not full of himself, like so many men built like him. He did not act like he was God's gift to anyone and this made her want him all the more. In fact, she felt the urge to let him know it. "You don't act like you're God's gift to women," she said. "I like that. . . ."

"Me? God's gift? Never. I'm just me. Jimmy. A preacher's son. I don't think I'm anything special."

"That's what makes you very special," she insisted.

Jimmy Riff smiled. Said: "Thank you. . . ."

He caressed her golden-hued breasts, and pressed his cock up against them. She reached for a bottle of clear lube on the nightstand and held it out to him. Initially applying a stingy dab, Jimmy Riff continued to increase the amount until he had the perfectly shaped tits swimming in it. He teased her nipples by running his thumbs over them, then did the same by rubbing in circular motions his palms over them. There was kneading of said impressive hooters, and squeezing them together, then releasing, then squeezing again. He pinched her nipples with thumb and index finger, then gave a gentle tug.

"Does this hurt?"

Angela Bliss shook her head. She was sighing.

Jimmy Riff climbed on board. He was on the bed with her, straddling her. Maneuvered his cock between the glistening mounds of flesh that were her breasts, and started pumping her cleavage as though it were her cunt. He pressed her tits against his member and continued to pump. It was a thrill to see: the expression on her face, her eyes downcast while she witnessed his enormous meat pole going in and out between the tight-fitting space between her boobs. She was grinning. Looked up. Woman definitely had a wild side to her.

He took her hands and had them replace his own, so that he might explore the rest of her fine, ripe body. While his right hand parted her pussy lips, and with two fingers tenderly ventured inside her cunt that was lubed with her very own hot juices, his other hand, particularly his middle finger, searched for and discovered her other opening on the other side. His left hand was under her backside, his middle finger gently rubbing, then penetrating her butthole.

He withdrew his cock from cleavage and tits, had his mouth, then tongue against her firm belly, gliding, sliding, licking downward, past her belly button; worked its way onto the pubic hair, and lower. His hot breath was on her labia lips, the tongue probed inside her wet cunt, while the middle finger of his left hand continued to slide in and out of her asshole in back. He had his finger in there as far as it was possible, while flicking and playing with her clit. The woman made sounds. Whether her actual name was "Bliss" or not, she was in it: *bliss*, ecstasy, the throes of passion.

She sighed his name repeatedly. This never failed to add to the fun and enjoyment of it. Gave him a certain satisfaction knowing he was making his lover happy enough to have them moan his name and made sex such an intense experience. What it was about. One of the great and magnificent things about being alive. No, sex was not the only reason to appreciate life, but it absolutely was one of them.

"Jimmy. . . ." Sounded like she was about to start sobbing. "My lover man out of nowhere. . . . Jimmy. . . ."

He ate her cunt as though he were licking a ripe and juicy peach, all the while some of the fingers of his right hand inside it pumping back and forth, while the finger that was in her asshole did the same. It was a three-pronged assault, driving her insane with pleasure. It was impossible for her not to cum, and she did: too many times, too often to count: one incredible explosion after another, one blast-off succeeding another. A cluster of sparks and firecrackers and cherry bombs imploded inside her head.

She withdrew, and when he insisted on continuing, she pushed his head back away from her privates; his fingers from both: her pee hole and backside. It was unbearable. Rest was in order. If he wished to embrace her, this was acceptable. He did. Knew from experience this was the thing to do. Held her. Had his face against her neck and upper chest, arms about her neck and waist, and held this woman he knew next to nothing about and yet clung so close to.

This is what happened when you experienced this kind of intimacy; when the fucking was so intense that you became one, united, in the experience. Togetherness was undeniable and totally natural. This was exactly why he was way ahead of so many men. More than a few of those so-called studs out there were primarily interested in one thing: getting theirs. Had no time for foreplay, were not interested in getting the woman's motor going first by playing with her and giving her body the time it needed to get in the moment, with it, by priming them. What so many did was to get theirs, shoot their load, and then suddenly got off the woman and left her there not only unfulfilled and disappointed and pissed off, but wondering what the fuck happened? Just when they were getting into it, getting warmed up, excited, ready for the next phase, the guy was already getting into his boxers, grabbing his shoes and clothes and making his way out the door. To heck with that, Jimmy thought. It was rude, ill-mannered, crude. Ungentlemanly. Idiots behaved this way; men who had no respect for women and did not care how they felt about any of it.

He hated jerks of his gender who behaved in this callous manner. And he would never, ever want to be this way, whether it was appreciated or not by his lovers did not matter. Whether it was taken for granted or not by these women that he was with was beside the point with him. Absolutely. And forever.

They remained this way for a long moment, holding, in place, still. He planted soft kisses on her neck and lips. Kissing her nose, eyes and brow. She reciprocated in kind, then reached over for the bottle of lube. Turned the bottle upside down and poured a good dollop into the palm of her right hand. His groin, forever rigid, was moist from her own pussy juices, but she felt adding lube wouldn't hurt for what she had planned next, and started stroking his groin.

He was lying on his back, she on her side, smiling and looking down at him, while her hand and finger worked his stiffie. This was no amateur when it came to giving a hand job. Not only did she stroke it all the way down to the base, but all the way up to the knob, then stayed there, concentrating on the most sensitive part of the cock. She worked the knob, spinning, circling the palm of her hand over the very top, then did likewise around the rim. She concentrated on the rim, then the entire mushroom-like head of his meat pole.

Jimmy's eyes were closed. He was in another dimension, not here at all. Physically, yes, he was in this bed with this luscious doll from Oklahoma, but his mind and heart were with that girl he met the other night. Could not be helped: Victoria Vevrier occupied his mind's eye. Wondered about her, what it would feel like to be doing these very things with her.

"Penny for your thoughts," said Angela Bliss.

All Jimmy could do was open his eyes and grin. "You're very good," he said.

"Thank you," she said. Then she doubled the pleasure by adding her other hand to the mix. One stroked the shaft, while the other, her right, remained focused on the head.

She said: "When you're ready . . . I want you to shoot it in my mouth."

"You sure?"

"Yes. Let me know when you're ready."

"I can pop any time."

"First, slide it in me. I want it in my cunt."

She stopped the hand job, turned over, so that she was on her knees, and Jimmy drove it inside her hairy beaver and stroked. Her ass, bent over this way, was some terrific sight to witness. Her butthole, as well, looked plenty inviting. But he would do as asked. He slid the tip of his middle finger of his right hand only, then withdrew, held it near his nose to whiff, then inserted it in to his mouth, adding lube, and the finger was back inside her butt crack.

The pumping of her hirsute box continued. Rhythm was there, and it was natural, because the woman was a natural. It was not up to him to do all the work, because a lot of it was accomplished by her, because she knew what was required: matched him stroke for stroke, even though she was on her knees and turned away from him. She knew how to push back with her butt, into him, against his groin, while he stayed with the steady pumping. Then Angela Bliss requested a brief recess, so that they might take a water break. She asked if he were thirsty. Jimmy said he was. When she reached over to the nightstand for a bottle of water, he noticed that the seal was missing. The cap was there, but there was no tamper-resistant seal. He requested a bottle with a safety seal.

Angela shrugged, said: "Fine." Handed him a different bottle. He tore the seal off, drank the water down, while she drank from the bottle she had offered initially. Jimmy placed his water bottle on the nightstand at his side of the bed. They were back in the game, with a slight change of position. Jimmy, suggesting a bit of a break, was lying on his right side, and asked her to do the same, her back up against his waist, while he entered her cunt and resumed stroking her wet pussy.

"I'd just as soon skip that other thing," said Jimmy.

"We can't," she said.

"Why?"

"He's watching."

"So what?"

"I've worked too hard to blow it. What's the big deal anyway? You're getting paid."

"I'd just as soon wrap it up with a blow job and call it a night."

"I said no. He needs to see it. I refuse to disappoint him. I said I would do it—and that's the way it is."

"He's watching?"

"I said he was. You knew it the minute you stepped into the room and saw the mirrors. I pointed it out to you; the man is watching. And we need to shut up about it."

Jimmy lifted his head, looked around, wondered which part of the large bedroom McFluff was hiding in and peering at them from, not that it mattered. This was Hollywood. It went on. Not only did this sort of thing go on here, but hell, in many other parts of the world. When it came to sex, people had some funny ideas. Did it turn him on, being ogled this way? Not really. In fact, it did nothing for him. If anything at all, it made him feel foolish, just a bit. It was silly. The old perv was sitting somewhere, behind one of those large mirrors, in a hidden section of the bedroom, and stroking himself. Let him. What difference did it make?

"Cheers"

In a concealed section of the bedroom, in a walk-in closet, not the one on her right, instead at the far end of the enormous bed, the wall that Angela Bliss had pointed to earlier, there was a two-way mirror. A portly, middle-aged gent sat in a director's chair dressed in a young French student's uniform: shorts, white blouse and black tie, beret on his head, red scarf tied round his neck. White socks, black shoes. The whole bit. A cockapoo with a pink ribbon bow atop its coiffed head gnawed on a dog biscuit treat at the man's feet. Eddie hoped the treat would keep the dog quiet and occupied long enough.

Edward McFluff unzipped his fly and withdrew his limp pecker. He reached for the large bottle of skin cream that he had sitting there on the stand and applied a good portion into his left palm and applied it to the head of his member and began to rub gently, unable to take his eyes away from the live sex show before him. He sipped from a bottle of Perrier periodically and watched as the two healthy young sex fiends performed on the bed as per his instructions. Jimmy was pumping her from behind. Rose to his knees, positioning his stiff prick directly in front of her waiting and open mouth and shot a long and wild stream of cum into it, above and below, but mostly into it. Her face was covered in sperm; the white hot goo dripped down, dripped from her chin, but plenty was inside her mouth and she found herself gagging, literally gagging and slurping it up. She ducked her thirsty mouth over his cock and worked it and worked hard, taking the head and then as much of the shaft as she was able. She withdrew, rubbing the super-sensitive head of his prick, draining him, making it possible for every last drop to drip down inside her hungry jaw.

"Suck it, binty," Edward McFluff found himself whispering to himself, wishing he were in her place instead. "Suck it, Yankee harlot. Nectar of the gods." Bloody bugger had enough cum for two or three, maybe four blokes. How in bloody 'ell do you cum like that? He'd never seen a chap cum as much. What did the bloke eat? How was it possible for any chap to have that much nutsack chowder? It was unbelievable. Too bad he was not a pornie, would not want to go back to that; had got his start in pictures back in London this way: making loops for the peep shows owned by the Krays. No way he could go back to making fuck films.

But this bloody Jimmy Kidd spurted cream like a geyser at Yellowstone National Park. No shit, thought Eddie McFluff.

He reached for the bottle of Perrier, said "Cheers" and was not able to prevent a fart from escaping his expat backside.

Blindfold

The Cinderella from Oklahoma, having polished Jimmy Riff's knob and cock free of cum, handed him a blindfold. She saw to it that the sheet of plastic that covered the bed, that they had been fucking on and pulled half way off, was positioned back on the bed so that it covered it properly.

"More water?" she asked. Was about to hand him a fresh bottle.

Jimmy shook his head. Grabbed the same bottle he'd been drinking from before. Drained it. Water tasted good and was welcome. He felt spent, no denial there. He could have gone again and again, but even Jimmy Riff needed a break after a marathon like that.

Woman had a sip of water from her own bottle, then reached for another blindfold. Reminded Jimmy to affix his. He did.

"How am I supposed to see what I'm doing?"

"You can see well enough through the cloth," she said. He asked what the purpose was.

"Never mind," she said, and slipped hers on. Opened her mouth and waited. Jimmy was waiting too, and someone behind the two-way mirror, an impatient Hollywood honcho sat there with bated breath, wanting the show to proceed. Only it wasn't.

"What is it?" said Angela Bliss.

"It's not my thing," Jimmy said.

"It doesn't have to be. Just do it. He needs it to get off. Do it. Don't make a big deal out of it."

He said nothing.

"Can you go?" she asked. "Need more water?"

"I've had enough water."

"Get on with it," she said. "All over me, big boy. Hose my body with it. He needs to see it. It'll feel good. We can fuck some more, if you like. We'll shower, have a bite to eat, and fuck like bunnies."

Jimmy wished she would stop talking. He aimed his groin, at half-mast presently, and sent a stream on her face. He showered her from the top of her head, over her face, and on down, covering her tits and belly. Her mouth opened wider, as she seemed to want it there, more than anywhere else, and he re-aimed his missile of a cock, while the stream centered strategically into her mouth. She was gagging on it, lapping it, reaching what missed with her fingers and shoving it inside her mouth; down her throat it went. She sucked on her fingers to get all of it, just as she had with the cum-swallowing a moment ago.

"More," she implored. "I want more."

"That's all of it."

"Sure?"

"Got nothing left."

"Press your ass against my face."

He did that. She pushed her mouth into the center of his asshole and licked with her tongue. Deeper and deeper it went. Jimmy, not having any control of it himself, found his cock growing rigid again. He was eighty percent there. Felt on the tired side, but his cock was not paying attention to that. His groin, his penis, wanted more. No, thought Jimmy.

"Put your cock in my mouth," Angela Bliss demanded. Jimmy

turned. She did not wait for him to carry out the request, instead found it with her hands, and stuck it in herself. She alternated, between stroking him and sucking and licking his cock. It was then, at this very moment, that R. Edward McFluff, the pudgy filmmaker with the pot belly, ran out from his hiding place dressed in that French school outfit with his groin poking out of his fly, positioned himself at the edge of the bed, and began to masturbate. His poodle was at his feet, barking like a loon at Jimmy Riff.

"Now, Angela honey," he said. Angela Bliss pushed Jimmy away from her, so that Eddie McFluff could get closer, and he spurted white semen over her body, farting as he did, while at the same time emitting undecipherable sounds from his mouth. He hurried back out when he was done, leaving a steady stream of farts in his wake. "Oh, Fifi, please hush," he said to the dog, and he and the poodle were gone. Jimmy came close to chuckling but refrained. Not entirely, because he was grinning. Sat in one of the puffy and fancy chairs there, and he was grinning.

Angela was lying on her back. Spent enough, herself. She had a smile on her face.

"You're a funny guy," she said, now looking at him.

"Me?"

"Maybe we could repeat this some time. I mean not all of it, some of it. Wouldn't you like that?"

"He might hear us."

"No way," she said. "Right now he's in Mr. Quilp's quarters in the back being flogged with a ping pong paddle for being a bad boy."

Jimmy looked at her without saying anything.

"The two came over from England years ago. It's no secret. The butler was his art director. They were lovers for years; then, out of desperation, sick and tired of Mr. McFluff's philandering ways, Mr.

Quilp shot Reggie in the stomach. Sprayed the two boy toys he caught with him with mace." She pulled open a drawer, reaching for a thick scrapbook. Flipped open some pages to the newspaper clipping. "Here: Bubba Goodrum and Lyle Oland, two West Hollywood street hustlers who had been involved with Reggie in a ménage. Mr. Quilp shot Reg in the abdomen once, then collapsed himself. Had a nervous breakdown and ended up in a nut ward for six months. Eddie took him back, forgave him. Gave him the butler's job. It is strictly platonic between them nowadays. Roddy got religion, was relieved the sex part of it was over. He wanted nothing further to do with Hollywood, period. Being the butler and house disciplinarian suits him just fine. He spanks Mr. McFluff on occasion as a way of paying him back for all the emotional suffering he'd caused him over the years."

Jimmy nodded like he understood. Only he didn't get any of it, nor did he try.

"Reggie, uh, what the butler calls him: Mr. McFluff's first name is Reginald, was really disappointed because he had so wanted to be in my place here with you, only Benjamin Styles, your so-called manager, demanded too high a price: he wanted one of the leads in Reggie's upcoming movie. Reggie couldn't deliver. Morey Grossbard wouldn't allow it; so Reg, Mr. McFluff, had to settle for the next best thing. The way it goes."

"Heart-breaking, isn't it."

"Not really," she said. "So, would you like to get together sometime?"

"What I would like, no, *what I need*, is a shower right now, a long, hot shower," said Jimmy Riff. He gathered up his clothes. She pointed him in the direction of the john, and he walked to it, closing the door behind him.

❧

There had been something unappealing about the whole thing, maybe even disgusting. This wasn't his style, what had just gone down. A plump Hollywood pervert, make that a British transplant dressed like a young French school kid in shorts, a beret on his head, and a red scarf tied round his neck, with his pud in his hand viewing his bedroom antics, then running in there with his crazy poodle named Fifi to jerk off on the woman he, Jimmy, had just been banging, all the while barking like his pooch. It was nuts. Was this what he wanted his life to be about? He hadn't planned on coming to Hollywood to begin with. Not really. Like most, he may have wondered what it would be like to be a celebrity and have money. Because he had needed cash, got off the Greyhound in Hollywood to look up a woman he'd been in love with once, maybe pick up enough of a grubstake to eventually keep moving on to Oregon and his Uncle Orville's chicken ranch. Should have never dropped out of Columbia. Could have hung in there, gotten his degree, and pursued work that paid a legitimate wage. And not this. This nowhere existence was for losers.

He looked in the mirror. Bathroom was large, opulent. Gold taps. Practically as big as Styles' entire apartment.

And he had no business being here. What was he getting for what just went down? And Angela? She had been a good-enough lay, no denying it, but that's all it was: lay. Been there, done that. She meant nothing to him. She did what she did for her reasons, what she was after; he had for his. He didn't want to end up where she was headed: a fuck toy screwing for cash. He saw no future in it. "Fame" was for others. Had enough smarts to see it.

❧

He dressed. Got out of there. The woman was no longer in the bedroom. There was no way to say good-bye. Just as well. Roddy

Quilp, the butler, was nowhere in sight, either. Okay. He walked out the front door. He could hear loud whacks or slaps coming from the butler's quarters, then what sounded like moans, squeals of pleasure, and a man begging for "More!" He wanted more. Needed to be spanked for being a "bad bloke."

Jimmy got into Styles' Toyota and drove off into the night. The BMW that stayed closely on his tail did not have its lights on, and Jimmy Riff, aka James Kidd, had no idea that he was being followed.

Missing Someone

There was a gas station at the northwest corner of Fairfax and Sunset, and Jimmy Riff parked it by the phone booth. The BMW pulled up and stayed out of sight as Jimmy dialed a number. The phone rang a few times until it finally got picked up at the other end. Vicki sounded sleepy. Why wouldn't she be? He apologized for waking her.

"Is that you, Jimmy?"

"Good to hear your voice, Vicki. It really is."

"Glad it's you."

"That place I want to take you? I'll be able to."

"You going to tell me what this place is, or is it still some big secret?"

"I want it to be a surprise, that's all. Special date. Why not?"

"Know something?"

"What's that?"

"I miss that face of yours."

"Really?"

"Yes. Thought about you all day."

"We've only just met the other—"

"I know," Vicki said, cutting him off. "Does it matter how long we've known each other?"

"No," Jimmy said. "Vicki?"

"Yeah?"

"I missed you, too."

Both were momentarily quiet, then Vicki said: "So when are you picking me up tomorrow? Wait, that was a dumb question. You don't have a car. When should *I* pick *you* up?"

"I'll be there by seven," Jimmy said. "Ben, my manager, lets me use his Stutz Bearcat."

"Stutz Bearcat?" Vicki said, and laughed. "You're going to show me up, is that it?"

"It's a terrific machine," Jimmy said. "Your jaw will hit the ground. Wait 'till you see it."

"How should I dress?"

"Casual," Jimmy said. "Wear jeans."

"Jeans? Where are we going?"

"Not telling," Jimmy said. "Besides, you look great in jeans."

"Thank you," Vicki said. "Guess I'll see you tomorrow."

"Victoria?"

"Yes?"

"Are you tired?" Jimmy asked. "I mean, are you going back to sleep?"

"More than likely."

"I just needed someone to talk to. Guess what I'm trying to say is: I wish I could see you tonight."

"Kind of late, isn't it?"

"You're right," Jimmy said. "Just feel like staying up for some reason. Wired. Can't sleep."

He heard her laugh at the other end.

"That's a good-enough reason, isn't it?"

"What's that?"

"For not wanting to sleep."

"Huh?"

"Wanting to stay up."

Jimmy finally caught on. "Actually I feel run down. I'd like nothing better right now than to be able to zone out."

"Take a couple of sleeping pills."

"Nah," Jimmy said. "Can't take no kinda pills."

"Wish I knew what to tell you," Vicki said.

"It's all right," Jimmy said. "I'll go find a pool hall. Shoot pool for a while. See you tomorrow night."

"I'm glad you called, Jimmy."

"Right," Jimmy said, and hung up.

He got back in the Toyota, and drove into the heart of Hollywood. The BMW stayed close on his heels.

"Piss on the Agreement"

One a.m. Benjamin Styles stepped out of his bathroom wearing only a robe. He paused at the open door to his bedroom to stare at the nude woman lying in his bed. Ariane Dean was sound asleep. Long strands of her dark hair covered parts of her face. There was a lock of hair in particular over her mouth that fluttered and was caused by her loud breathing. Woman, in fact, was snoring. Yes, women snored. As bad as some men, even louder. Once the fucking was over and done with, the sucking and diddling and fondling of each other's privates, this was what remained: reality. He had a broad who snored like Curly Howard of *Three Stooges* fame right in his very own sack. He could forget about getting any sleep himself this way—if he let her stay. Or else he'd have to sleep on the couch. And where would the kid sack out? On the floor? Maybe. Wouldn't be the first time. He just better not make a play for this broad. She'd been great, and he didn't want Riff molesting any part of her for the duration of her stay in his apartment.

∽∾∾∽

He closed the bedroom door quietly. Picked up the kitchen phone and dialed.

"Yeah?" Horgan's voice alternated between sounding scratchy and high pitched. This time it was in between, in that it couldn't make up its mind. He didn't sound too pleased to hear from this particular client. "What do you want?"

"Th' hell you doing in bed?"

"Sleeping," Nicky Horgan said. "Trying to."

"I am paying you good money to watch the kid," Benjamin Styles said. "Now what the hell is going on?"

"You ain't paid me a peso in over three weeks," Horgan said, "That's what the hell is going on! I got a family to support! Car payments and insurance! Groceries don't grow on trees, guy!"

"Don't give me that crap," Benjamin Styles said. "We had an agreement."

"Piss on the agreement."

"What did you say?"

"The last time we talked, you said: Don't worry about it, Nicky. You'll get your money."

"That's right. I did say that. I mean to see to it you get every cent."

"You call that an agreement?" Horgan said. "I didn't agree to a goddamn thing!"

"My word is gold, and you know it."

"*Stick with me and you'll see the underdog make it to the finish line,*" Horgan said. "You'll be there with me, in the Winner's Circle."

"You don't have to repeat it word for word," Benjamin Styles said. "I know what I said."

Horgan continued: "I am talking about big money, Nicky. Major bucks."

"Big money is right," Benjamin Styles said.

"Still no agreement," Horgan said. "An agreement constitutes both parties involved agreeing; seeing eye to eye on a thing. I ain't agreed ta nothin'."

"Why don't you go back to night school, ya dumb Hun. Learn to speak American."

"Get yourself another private eye, Mr. Styles," Nicky Horgan said. "Please. I can't afford you."

"You listen to me, you son of a bitch—" Benjamin T. Styles stopped mid-sentence, as one wasted Jimmy Riff staggered into the apartment with a big shit-eating grin on his face and simply sank to the floor.

"I'll deal with you later," Benjamin Styles said into the receiver, and hung up. It pretty much required all the strength in his arms and shoulders to pick the kid up off the carpet and drag him over to the sofa. Son of a bitch was tall, and not light at all. He assisted in getting him to stretch out on his back.

He moved to take the kid's shoes off, only there weren't any shoes there. Kid's socks were on his feet and they were covered in dirt, worn badly. The toes, particularly the big toe, was bleeding. Styles pulled the socks off his feet. Cleaned the cuts with rubbing alcohol, and wrapped the kid's foot in gauze.

When he was done, Benjamin T. Styles slid into his favorite recliner, lit a brown, thin cigarillo, staring off into space. He wondered what to do about the kid.

Fuck It!

Benjamin went outside to see if the Toyota was still in one piece. The car had been left parked haphazardly, with the two wheels on the passenger side on the curb.

He looked at the cars practically glued to his front and rear bumpers and wondered how the kid had managed to squeeze the damn Toyota in without damaging it. Not until he got close enough did Benjamin Styles see the dented rear bumper and both taillights cracked.

He moved to the front. Headlights appeared intact. He cursed and looked inside. The kid had left the keys in the ignition. Styles got in. Turned the key. Motor sounded the same as before. Headlights seemed to work. Tail lights were shot.

He got out, locked the car, and walked back to his apartment. Kid is hopeless, he said to himself. No matter what I say to him, no matter how hard I hit the punk, it doesn't seem to do any good.

How much would it cost to repair the lights? The bumper? Maybe just use the car during the day. Still risked getting stopped by LAPD. That was out. Too ridiculous. No way to get around at night, unless he used the bus. "Rapid Transit." Fuck "Rapid Transit." Buses in LA only ran on major streets. Town was too big to get from place to place on a bus. Took you forever. Hours. If you wanted to get from his building to any of the studios: Universal, Disney, Columbia in Burbank. *Fuck a damn bus!* Cabs cost too much. So that was out. I'm supposed to be a damn producer. I can't take a goddamn bus! What if some of those actors who used the breakdown in his office were to see him? What about others?—production people were to see him waiting at some fucking bus stop like a punk looking to be picked up by a trick? That's what LA and Hollywood punks did, cheap hustlers, waited at bus stops at night and during the day, for some Hollywood honcho to pull up looking for action.

It was way too fucking low, too far a drop. I'd be the laughing stock of Hollywood. They were already saying shit behind his back. Styles kept running ads in the trades regarding his upcoming productions, only none ever took off, nothing ever materialized; no movies were ever produced. He was a joke. They were always talking shit and laughing behind his back. Motherfuckers.

I'll make the kid pay, he thought. I'll have the punk humping every filthy twat and sucking every dirty dick in town. Wait and see if I don't make it stick. You watch me. I'll use the hell out of him. He refuses to fuck faggots? We'll see about that. He'll be fucking *fags and hags*, no matter how old and used up.

I tried to treat him right. Did my best to take care of him. Fuck it!

Payback (Is a Bitch)

Ben T. Styles lit another cigarillo and entered his apartment. A half-dazed Jimmy Riff was sitting up on the sofa and attempting, in all futility, to button his shirt. Ariane Dean was sitting at his side holding a glass of water out to him. There was a look of concern on her face. Maybe it was fear. Styles didn't give a shit. It was annoying; that's what it was. Punk was a chick magnet. Broad didn't know him, but there she was, hovering, like a nursemaid. It was nothing more than an act. They wanted him. Cunts wanted him, the way they used to want Benjamin T. Styles. But no more. Unless there was some sort of arrangement involved. She was only here with him because he'd had that agreement with McFluff. So what was she doing playing nursemaid to the hustler?

Styles said: "It's going to cost you—what you did to the car."

"What car?"

"Don't play games with me."

"Know something, brother?"

"I'm not your 'brother,'" Benjamin Styles said, grabbing the kid by the collar.

"You're a low-life motherfucker," Jimmy Riff said, "like this town."

"You ungrateful sack of shit," Benjamin Styles said, and cocked his arm. Just as his fist was about to hammer into the kid, Benjamin Styles felt a powerful blow against the back of his own neck that spun him and sent him sprawling to the floor.

Styles opened his eyes to see Scarface looming over him with a gun in his hand. The goon looked back, as if awaiting further orders from someone behind him. Lisa Koch stepped out from the bedroom. She gave a nod, and the goon raked the business end of a .357 Magnum across Benjamin Styles' jaw.

The woman, who was missing her two front teeth, knelt down. Said: "Never underestimate Lisa Koch."

"Bitch," Styles sighed, and passed out.

The goon was instructed to escort Jimmy Riff out the door, and this he did.

Lisa Koch grabbed a handful of Ariane Dean's hair at the back of her head, and shoved her face up against hers, so that they were eye-to-eye, nose-to-nose. "You keep your trap shut about what you saw in here tonight," Lisa Koch said. "Understand me, cunt?"

Ariane did not waste time nodding.

Lisa Koch yanked hard on the woman's mane, pulling her back against the sofa, and watched her tumble down and land on the out-cold low-grade fuck 'tard producer/actor/nobody, named Benjamin Twitchell Styles, who had a bug of some sort, more than likely a roach, crawling over his Adam's apple and up his bloody chin. She spit at them both. Vacated the cockroach-infested dump.

A Toothless Star

When Benjamin Styles came to, Ariane Dean was sitting beside him on the floor and dabbing at the cuts on his face with a damp washcloth. Benjamin Styles yanked the washcloth out of her hand and flung it across the room. Then, one piece at a time, he spit his upper dentures out. He was missing three teeth in the upper jaw and the dentures were needed. How was he going to land jobs with this many teeth missing? Glue the dentures together? How? He collected the pieces, cursed in typical Benjamin Styles fashion, and rose to his feet.

"A toothless star," Ariane Dean blurted, without realizing what she was saying. Rose to her feet herself. She thought the observation funny, but only briefly, for the backhand that she received sent her flying in the same general direction that the washcloth had been sent a moment ago.

Benjamin Styles downed a stiff shot of bourbon, and walked outside to his car. All four tires were flat. Slashed. He cursed. Kicked at one of the flats, for the worthless heap of junk that the whole car was, and went down in agony. His foot hurt like hell.

After a while, he remembered the Volks. Had the Pete Stanfill punk picked it up by now? Son of a bitch, he thought. What if I walk the six blocks to discover that it's gone? Punk probably recovered it by now.

He limped back to the apartment and dialed.

"Yeah?" Horgan said in that screechy voice of his.

"You know who it is."

"All too well," said Nicky Horgan. "Give me a break, will you? Why me?"

"Listen," Benjamin Styles said. "You want your money?"

"At four in the morning?"

"Yeah!" Benjamin Styles shouted. "At four in the morning. Yes or no?"

"Of course."

"Come by my place," Benjamin Styles said.

"You come by mine," Horgan said, cutting him off.

"You want your dough or not?"

"All of it?"

"A hundred."

"You can do better than that, guy."

"Two," Benjamin Styles said. "Best I can do."

"Two hundred dollars?" Horgan said. "You rob a massage parlor or something?"

"Just be here."

"The wife won't like it."

"In ten minutes," Benjamin Styles said, and hung up.

❧

Ten minutes later there was a knock on Benjamin Styles' door.

"It's open," Benjamin Styles said.

The door opened, and an exact replica of Nicky Horgan, only much younger, stood in the doorway. Kid was nervous. About 5'11". Bag of bones. Wore black. Looked like a mortician's assistant.

"How old are you son?" Benjamin Styles asked.

"I'll be fifteen next month."

"Where's your father?"

"Mom wouldn't let him leave the house."

"Women," Benjamin Styles said under his breath, and asked the teen to show him where he parked the car.

❧

Benjamin Styles liked driving this '72 Impala station wagon a lot more than he did his own car. It seemed to take a lot less effort to handle the steering wheel, and there was no clutch and gear shift to deal with.

"Nice car," Benjamin Styles said.

"We like it."

"What's your name, son?" Styles asked.

"Nicky."

"Like your daddy, huh?"

The youngster nodded.

"Here you go, Nicky, Jr.," Benjamin Styles said, and handed him two crisp one-hundred-dollar bills. "You give this to your daddy," he said, and pulled up in front of a rundown brownstone at the corner of Argyle and Franklin. Nicky Jr. accepted the money and nodded a thank-you.

"Tell him I should be back with his car in a couple of hours."

Nicky Jr. hesitated.

"Go on," Benjamin Styles said. "He knows about it."

"Yes, sir," Nicky Jr. said and got out. Benjamin Styles was gone before Horgan's son reached the entrance to the building.

"How'd it go with Tubesteak?"

Benjamin T. Styles did 55, 60 all the way up Beverly Glen to Mulholland Drive. The Koch place looked quiet. The glass door had been replaced with all wood.

Styles looked around before opening it. The tire iron was still there where he had dropped it. He picked it up, turned the knob, and walked in.

Dead *silencio*. No one around. Ben Styles found a chair and sat in the dark. Where could the bitch have taken him? He thought about Scarface and knew he would either have to pick up a switchblade or a piece to deal with him. He got his hands on the phone and dialed.

"The McFluff residence," Angela Bliss answered at the other end with so much Hollywood "charm" it gave him a toothache.

"Put him on."

"Who is this?"

"Just get Reggie to the damned phone, will you?"

"Is that you, Mr. Styles?"

"Honey, don't you ever get tired of doing Judy Holliday?"

"Excuse me?"

"Can't you do anyone else? Maybe Garbo, or Gloria Swanson?"

"I don't understand," Angela Bliss said. "I am sorry—"

"Don't be sorry," Benjamin Styles growled. "Just get your Sugar Daddy to the phone."

"He is busy, you know—"

"Goddamned brain-dead cunt!"

"Hold your horses now," she said.

A moment passed, and a heavy-breathing Edward McFluff spoke into the phone.

"Bloody 'ell, Styles! What is it now?"

"How did it go?"

"What?"

"How'd it go with Tubesteak?"

"Fine," an impatient R. Edward McFluff said. "Just fine."

"Good to hear," Benjamin Styles said. "Now if you'll just tell me what the hell you've done with him—"

"Are you bloody mad? It's five o'clock in the morning!"

"Don't tell me what time it is!" Benjamin shouted back. "Your goon paid me a visit earlier this evening with that Koch bitch, knocked me out, and took off with Jimmy. Now I wanna know what the fuck is going on!"

"Kerr is no longer in my employ, Ben," Edward McFluff said. "Haven't the slightest what you're going on about."

"Shit," Benjamin Styles said. "They took Tubesteak, Reg."

"I'm afraid that you're just arse out," McFluff said, and hung up.

"Faggot bastard," Benjamin Styles muttered under his breath, and walked outside. Dawn was clearly breaking and he didn't quite know what to do, where to start looking for the punk.

"Take it easy, will ya?"

Down to Schwab's for eggs and coffee. He was on his usual stool at the counter. The scrambled eggs looked the way Benjamin Styles felt: lousy. He drank the coffee and pushed the eggs to the side.

"What's the idea, guy?" A pissed Nicky Horgan walked up out of nowhere. He unbuttoned the four-year-old black sports coat, revealing a pair of cuffs and a holster with a .38 in it.

"Morning, Nicky."

"Good morning, hell. What's the idea taking off with my wheels?"

"No need to get excited."

"Th' hell you say?" Horgan said, raising his voice. "Wife was late for work this morning. She was in tears, man. Had to take the bus. I couldn't drive her to work—no car!"

"Take it easy, will ya?"

"The hell you say?"

"Everybody's got problems."

"You're my only problem, guy!"

"You want the car keys?"

"Damn right, I want my car keys!"

"Here," Benjamin Styles said, tossing the keys at him.

"I just want you to know one thing: I'm not at all happy at the way you took advantage of my son."

"Nicky," Benjamin Styles said, "I needed the car. Don't you understand? Got a friend that's in trouble; needs my help."

"Do yourself a favor: Help yourself first."

"You like it here?"

"What's that got to do with anything?"

"Fake citizenship papers—"

"All I am saying, man," Nicky Horgan pleaded, "let me be."

"All IDs phony."

"Please?"

"How'd you get your PI license?" Benjamin Styles asked. "Who'd you slip the buck to?"

"I got a family to support."

"You think you're the only one?" Benjamin Styles shouted. "Huh? I *borrowed* the car because someone's life was in danger. Ah, forget it."

"I had no idea. . . ."

"You got your keys. Get out of my sight," Benjamin T. Styles said and sipped from his mug.

"Look," Nicky Horgan said, "that's different. You got the car for as long as you need it. The wife, she can take the bus. I mean, she's not going to tell me what to do, right?"

Benjamin Styles smiled. "Go on," he said. "Get out of here. I don't want your bucket." Added: "I won't turn you in, Pheiffer. Beat it."

Horgan winced at mention of his real name.

"Thanks, Ben," he said and left.

❧

Styles polished off the rest of the coffee and talked one of the actors there into giving him a ride to the nearest car rental agency in exchange for free casting tips.

By the time Benjamin Styles arrived at his studio office at ten after ten, two pissed-off lesbians and a third actor were waiting to get in.

"About time, Ben," Tammy said.

"I apologize for being late," Benjamin Styles said. "Car issues."

"Yeah? What was it the day before?"

"It's too early for this."

"You said ten o'clock," Tammy's blond girlfriend said. "Monday through Friday."

Benjamin Styles unlocked the office door and entered the office without comment. He gave Ora Mae a look that plainly said he was not in the mood for this kind of bullshit.

He took the latest breakdown and handed it to the male actor, one Tevis Wetzel.

"Tevis," Ben T. Styles said, "lock the door, would you, when you're through in here?"

The actor nodded. "Sure thing, Ben."

"Oh," Ben Styles said, indicating the actor who had given him the lift from Schwab's, "Verrill's got my permission to look at today's breakdown." And left.

Buy a Gun

A visit to the McFluff mansion proved a waste of time. In fact, it did nothing but strain their relationship. Reginald Edward McFluff was not interested in his chickenshit problems, nor was Angela Bliss, nor was Roddy Quilp, the butler, nor was Nicky Horgan, nor was Ariane Dean. Who, for that matter, gave a fuck what was happening to Benjamin Styles' life and career? *Not a soul.*

In a coffee shop at Beverly Blvd. and LaBrea, he dialed the PI's numbers: office and home. The office number got him Horgan's answering machine. His Mex wife answered at home. Nicky was not in. Would he like to try later?

Styles picked up two six-packs. Tall Boys. And drove out to the beach. He parked the rental facing the ocean, drank beer, and thought about things. He had a job, but only for three days. And how much of his performance would end up on the cutting-room floor? A good 70, 80 percent. They had a habit of doing that to him. It was frustrating. They kept throwing obstacles in his path, doing everything they were able to keep him from making a comeback. Why? Why did it have to be this tough? What were they afraid of? That he would show them up?

Cream rises to the top. It was a well-known and overused cliché in Hollywood. Only how was that cream supposed to surface when they tripped him up at every turn and made it impossible for him to make any real progress? I can't slow down no matter what, he thought. Now that things are looking up—or were, anyway. Kidd was gone. How would he nail down another job without him? Buy a gun and strong arm his way into a producer's office? Listen, assholes, you're putting me in this picture. It's the least this shitty town can do. The free publicity I supplied you with all them years I was a headliner in the squared circle. I had a following. Drew my share of crowds. Heads of state, royalty. Benjamin "Tough as Nails" Styles was the man they came to see in your crappy, grindhouse B-flicks. I put asses in seats and made a ton of money for everyone, except yours truly. So now, you're going to do something for me: You're giving me a role, something meaty, a part I can sink my choppers into, what's left of them. He cursed under his breath. He'd have to have new dentures made. The cocksucker Lisa Koch was running with had pretty much destroyed his old ones. Was there any chance his dentist might be able to salvage what remained of his dentures?

❧

He was back on the idea of picking up a piece, using muscle to get a role. That was how Sinatra got that major lead in that war picture, wasn't it? Used muscle. *Knew people.* Ended up with an Oscar. If it worked for Ol' Blue Eyes, why couldn't it work for Ben. T. Styles? Not only were his eyes bluer but he knew in his heart of hearts he was the superior actor. Sinatra was weak as a thespian. Man could sing; that he had a talent for, but acting? Don't make me laugh. Never delivered a line Benjy found remotely believable. Not once. Nothing he was ever in. Just another bad actor. And the Oscar? Didn't matter. They gave those away. It was politics. It came down to who you knew, what kind of muscle you had backing you. He, "Tough as Nails," had had support in his corner once, but that was long ago.

So, what was the answer, then? Pick up a rod? .38? .357? .22? .380? Something not too big, but big enough to get the job done and impress them with?

❧

It's the beer. Shook his head and grinned. Don't be ridiculous. You'll end up dead or in the slammer. Gunplay is no way. Tubesteak is the way. Jimmy Riff is the way. Where was he? He polished off the can, cracked the top on another. Even though he had pretty much given up on the idea of shoving the business end of a Saturday night special into some producer's face, he knew that he'd have to have a piece to handle the bushwhacking son of a bitch who shattered his dentures.

He would go see the Anthony Brothers, the lightweight borderline criminal types who owned half the porn shops in the Valley, without asking Nicky Horgan to put in a good word for him. Besides, Nicky was no longer involved with them these days. Never really was, other than the fact he used to supply them with Super-8 loops that they ran in their peep booths throughout San Fernando.

Big Purchase

Two hours later, in an adult bookstore on Lankershim Avenue, Benjamin T. Styles was buying a Smith & Wesson .38 from the clerk in a back room. By the time he reached his office it was 4:30 in the afternoon. None of the actors were there for the breakdown. Just as well. He wanted to be alone.

He locked the front door, and sat in his swivel chair in the back room, sat and stared at pictures on the wall, one pic in particular; it was a glossy B&W taken thirty years ago: in his boxing gear: boxing shorts, gloves on, dukes up. Had his youth, looks, a following: in and out of the fight game. The brass ring within easy reach. All he had to do was grab it. Only it always seemed an inch or two beyond his grasp.

What size waist did he have back then? Twenty-nine? Thirty inches? Packed a powerful punch, in both arms. Shoulders were sinewy with muscle. Had powerful thighs, legs that never tired. They all said his center of gravity was low, what made him such a powerful puncher. He was going places, and did go places—but not far enough. Something/someone kept getting in his way. People were saying things behind his back: *Benjy's his own worst enemy. We reap what we sow.*

Yeah? What was he sowing? When he had dough he spread it around. Generous to a fault. How come no one ever bothered to mention that? Where was *his* now that he was way overdue?

Eyes shifted over to some other publicity shots of the up-and-comer of long ago. Hell. What was the point? It only hurt to be reminded. Why keep the pics up? Why on the wall, right in front of your face so that you can't even avoid noticing? There was purpose: others needed to be reminded of his greatness and ability and endurance. He was still here, plugging away. While others, so many others, fell by the wayside, Ben T. Styles, "Tough as Nails" Styles was clubbing and clawing away. At it. Always at it. I'm no quitter. I don't quit. Quitting's for others, not Benjamin Styles.

He yanked on the middle drawer, picked up the budget for a picture he'd been trying to put together for the past three years. The budget had been revised ten different times. Whenever a potential investor suggested a change, Benjamin Styles was eager to oblige. He had a five-hundred-thousand-dollar budget, a million-dollar budget, million and a half, and so on and so forth. All that work. He wondered if he would ever find money to make even the cheapest version? The phone rang.

"BSP," Benjamin Styles said.

"Benjamin?" the man's voice inquired.

"Speaking."

"Artie here, Ben. Artie Gross."

"How goes it, Artie?" Benjamin Styles said, shifting the ol' charm into gear.

"Can't complain."

"Long time no hear."

"For sure."

"What're you up to, Artie? Working on anything?"

"Producing a sci-fi piece of crap with Ira Cohen."

"Who's backing?"

"Intrepid International."

"Oh yeah?"

"Twelve million. Letting us do as we please. Within reason, of course."

"Location shoot?"

"Shepperton, Tunisia, South Africa."

"Sounds good."

"Not bad."

"How's Kate?"

"Real excited about it. Wants to tag along. Figures we might turn it into an extended vacation. Been married fourteen years, still thinks location shooting is nothing but a picnic."

"Got anything I can do in the picture?"

"Possibly. Can't promise anything."

"When do you start?"

"Two months."

"Terrific. I should be through with this western I'm doing for Eddie McFluff by then."

"When are you going to introduce me to the kid?"

"You know about him?"

"Come on, Ben. Everybody in town's heard of him."

"I guess they have. Tell you what. How about we stop by in a couple of days?"

"Sounds good," Artie Gross said. "See you then, Ben. Nice talking with you again."

"Likewise," Benjamin Styles said. "See you later, Artie."

❧

Amazing, Benjamin Styles said to himself. Artie Gross calling him. Not once, but twice. Artie Gross, the dipstick he hadn't heard from and hadn't been able to reach in over a year. Didn't matter, though. Water under the bridge. Part of the past. Fact was, Artie Gross was another hot property. A highly successful producer at the young age of thirty-seven, after having made only three pictures in eight years. Artie Gross, sought-after commodity in Hollywood, was seeking Benjamin Styles. And all because of James Kidd, aka Tubesteak.

Where could that broad have taken him? Was he still alive even? He held the .38 in his hand. Looked at it. Serial number had been filed down. Piece couldn't be traced to anyone. He stuck it in the holster on his left hip, butt handle out. He pulled his shirttail over it.

He picked up a money order for six hundred dollars and mailed it to his wife. Six hundred, plus the two hundred he gave Horgan, added up to eight hundred dollars. He had spent close to fifty dollars on Ariane and booze. That left him with six hundred and fifty. Rent on the office and his apartment were due in two days. One-fifty apiece. Three hundred dollars. It would cost maybe seventy-five to have the car repaired. A grand total of $1,225; not to mention what it would cost him to have the dentures saved, or new ones made. Then he remembered the .38. That had dented his wallet for another hundred and thirty-five.

He had given Jimmy a hundred. That left him with forty dollars. It would have to do until he got the rest of the cash from McFluff. He would have to find Jimmy. Soon. He was losing money every day.

They Came to Dodge

Not until Styles got in the rented Chevelle did he remember to add the rental fee to the long list of expenses and money owed.

He made the usual rounds: Schwab's, Norwoods, the River Bottom Saloon; Black Forrest, and others. Jimmy was nowhere to be found. He drove up to McFluff's mansion and picked up a copy of *THEY CAME TO DODGE*, in spite of Reggie's insistence that he wouldn't need the entire script. Benjamin Styles persisted until he was given one. His reasoning: he immersed himself completely every time he did a part, and would need to know as much as possible about the character. And this part was no exception.

"We've been over this before," reasoned Benjamin Styles. "You know how I approach a role, any role; no matter how small or seemingly insignificant."

"You've got two bloody lines, for Christ's sake!" Edward McFluff had said. "You don't need a script."

Benjamin Styles had insisted. Edward McFluff hadn't mentioned the kid once, and Angela hadn't even shown her face.

⚬⁓⁓⊙

Benjamin Styles drove home, read the screenplay, and studied his lines. He stayed up all night rehearsing in the mirror, trying out various expressions, delivering the lines a hundred different ways. He was considering growing a beard for the part. This would be one way of getting around paying for new dentures. Whiskers could very well conceal the fact his teeth were missing.

"What do you think of the idea, Reg?" Benjamin Styles asked McFluff over the phone later that morning.

"A beard?" Edward McFluff pondered on the thought. "Maybe, maybe."

"I can just see the guy," Benjamin Styles beamed into the receiver, "Chews tabacky. A great spitter. Spits at everything and anything. Never misses what he aims at. Animals like to be around him, right?"

"I suppose. . . ."

"Well, he could have this parrot on his shoulder, everywhere he goes. They're inseparable," Benjamin Styles said. "See what I mean?"

"Sort of."

"Maybe we could get him a talking bird, give it some outrageous things to blurt out. You have final say, of course. You're the director. You call the shots, Reg. It's a decent role. Been up all night working on it."

"Do me a favor, Ben?"

"What's that?"

"Please stop calling me 'Reg' or 'Reggie?' Please. I only allow me dear mum to call me that."

"No problem, Eddie," said Styles. "Only I've heard others refer to you as Reg and Reggie. Your butler, Quilp, calls you Reg. I've heard that opportunist from Oklahoma call you by your first name."

"I have to run, Ben," the film director said. "See you on the set."

"Right."

～⌘～

Nine thirty. He would have to drive down to the office and unlock it. Don't want to give the dykes a reason to squawk. He reached the office in time and stayed until 10:45. None of the actors showed.

He didn't feel well. Drove back to the apartment, chased two sleeping pills with a glass of water, and slept. Five hours later Benjamin Styles woke up with a throbbing headache. His stomach was empty, but he didn't feel like eating anything. He washed down two aspirin and got dressed. Fifteen minutes later he was in his office studying his lines.

His phone rang. Styles lifted the receiver.

"BSP."

"Ben?"

"Jimmy?"

"It's me."

"Where're you calling from?"

"Can't tell."

"You all right?"

"Sure," Jimmy Riff said. "You'll never believe who I've been with."

"She give you the whip?"

"No," Jimmy Riff said. "She's got nothing to do with it."

"You're not making any sense," Benjamin Styles said.

"I'll tell you about it when I see you."

"When?"

"About an hour."

"I'll be waiting."

Fitch

One hour later, wearing a white suit, nails manicured, hair coiffed, expensive Italian shoes on his feet, Jimmy Riff pulled up in a brand-new Toyota Corolla.

"Where'd you get that?" Styles asked.

"It's a long story," Jimmy Riff said. "It's a gift."

"I bet."

"From one of the biggest wheels in this town."

"Who?"

"Can't say."

"Speaking of wheels," Benjamin Styles said, "Artie Gross called back. Anxious to meet you. I thought we might drop by his place this evening."

"Can't," Jimmy Riff said. "Got something else to do."

"Lately," Benjamin Styles said, "that seems to be your favorite word: Can't do this/Can't do that. Can't. Can't. Can't."

"I really have to make good on this commitment."

"Do you realize who Artie Gross is?"

"Look, I'm trying to help you, but what about Jimmy? What about me? I have my own life to live, you know."

"*You're helping me? Me?* I'm working my ass off trying to get you started in this town—and this is the thanks I get? After all I've done for you? All the contacts? You say you're helping me?"

"You probably saved my bacon. It's quite possible. I'm grateful."

"You're one of the most ungrateful sons of bitches I ever set eyes on."

"You can't say that."

"I just did."

"I give up."

"You'll never make it," Benjamin Styles said. "You haven't got it. No persistence."

"You have it all wrong," Jimmy Riff said. "*You* want to be the star, not me. You're the one."

"Thought you wanted to act."

"Not anymore."

"You don't know what you want, do you?"

"Maybe not." Jimmy Riff pulled out two crumpled one-hundred-dollar bills. "That's for the damage to your car." He turned to leave. Paused at the door. "Forget about Man #1. You're doing Fitch. One of the main roles. Compliments of Jimmy Riff. You can confirm it with the Brit. Now we're even," Jimmy Riff said, and left.

✿

A flabbergasted Benjamin T. Styles lit a cigarillo and scanned through the script nervously. Fitch was third lead. A great part. He dialed Fluffy's number. Had to remind himself not to call him "Reg" or "Reggie" anymore.

"Of course it's true. You got Fitch. Higher-up wanted you. Don't ask why. Just know you got the green light. Found the lead. Negotiating now. We start in three days. See you on the set at 8:00 a.m. Sharp. Sound stage 8."

"Eight a.m. Sharp. Sound stage 8," Styles repeated, to be on the sure side.

"By the way, Ben" said McFluff. "I apologize about earlier, for being cranky about the Reg/Reggie business. Please forget I ever mentioned it up."

How do you feel about being called "Fluffy" then? Styles considered tossing it out there. Instead he hurried outside to his rental and followed the kid to Malibu.

"I love you"

In a flower shop off the Pacific Coast Highway, Jimmy Riff purchased a dozen white roses.

Benjamin "Tough as Nails" Styles parked a safe distance away as Tubesteak pulled up in front of the beach house Victoria Vevrier was renting.

"So that's the 'Stutz Bearcat' you wanted me to see," Vicki said.

"Should have seen the piece of junk I thought I was going to have to drive down here."

"It's nice," Vicki said.

"It's transportation."

She invited him inside, and that's when Jimmy Riff surprised her with the flowers.

"Oh, Jimmy," Vicki said, hugging him, "you shouldn't have."

"It's not something I do every day."

She kissed him on the lips. Then the door closed, and that was all Benjamin Styles could see. He drove back to the apartment to study the script.

⁓

Traffic along Figueroa all the way down to the LA Sports Arena was bumper to bumper, thousands of people on their way to see the circus: Ringling

Brothers & Barnum & Bailey, the Greatest Show On Earth. Jimmy was able to find a parking space, and he and Vicki got in line with all the other patrons. Once inside, the place filled up quickly. Dozens of circus clowns tumbled about, juggled bowling pins and whatnot, while adding to the joyous insanity with a variety of noisemakers, kazoos and whistles. Circus had everything, from Col. Tom Thumb to a flying trapeze act with a star trapeze artist who did, for the very first time anywhere, ever, four, count 'em: *four summersaults*—to thunderous applause and a standing ovation for this impressive feat. There were lions, tigers, elephants, monkeys, horses, dogs; even a parakeet high-wire act. Jimmy got pink cotton candy for them both, and the way Vicki seemed to enjoy herself really made him happy. Without her presence it would have been nothing more than just another night out. Ordinarily, the circus is not that big a deal; maybe for kids it was, but not for grownups. But with her by his side it had been an enjoyable evening.

❦

Later, after he'd driven her back to Malibu and walked her to her door, Vicki said: "I've had the most wonderful time, Jimmy."

"So did I."

"Thank you," she said, and kissed him on the cheek. "Would you like to come in for a while?"

Jimmy hesitated.

"There's beer in the fridge."

"What kind?"

"Imported."

"Deal."

❦

They were in the living room downstairs that faced the ocean and the swimming pool. Jimmy sat on the sofa and picked up the TV remote and turned the set on. A scene from *The Maltese Falcon* filled the screen. He had always liked Bogey and Peter Lorre. Peter Lorre and that funny, awkward way of speaking that he had; and those bulging eyes were a kick, too. The big man, Sydney Greenstreet, had held his own in every scene he was in with Bogey. No easy feat, that one. Vicki appeared with a bottle of German beer. Jimmy thanked her with a smile.

"Jimmy?" she said.

He looked at her as she sat next to him on the sofa. "There's something I've been wanting to tell you all night." She paused. "I think I love you, Jimmy."

Jimmy Riff put his beer down, took her in his arms, and kissed her full on the lips. "You're about the best thing that's happened to me in a long, long time," he said.

"You're so wonderful to me," Vicki said. "Oh, Jimmy." And she held on tighter. "Love me, Jimmy. . . . Please love me. . . ."

Jimmy hesitated. Softly, he kissed her left ear, then gradually progressed to the other, his warm breath arousing her passion which, at this moment, really did not need help. Victoria Chantal was there, needing him. Aching for him to take her. Jimmy kissed her under the chin, her neck; he stopped suddenly and just hugged her this way.

"Make love to me," Vicki pleaded. "Make love to me."

"I don't know if we should, Vicki."

"I want you to; I want you to be the one."

"Maybe we just shouldn't, Vicki."

"*Why?* I don't understand. . . ."

"What if you got pregnant?"

"I won't."

"It's been known to happen."

"I don't care," Vicki said. "I don't care if I do get pregnant."

"I wouldn't want it to happen."

"It won't," Vicki said. "I promise."

Jimmy Riff smiled. "You're not on the Pill, or been taking any kind of birth control—"

"I promise, I won't get knocked up—"

"I want to. . . ." he sighed in her ear. "I'm all out of condoms. . . . I do want to. . . ."

"Then do it, Jimmy. Do it." Vicki had begun breathing heavily by now. She desired him, needed him. She wanted to be taken by this man, not tomorrow or the next day, *but right now, this very minute.*

He would tangle with his own desire and need to make love to her and take a chance on hurting her feelings by simply saying "No"—because if he did make it with her it might also mean the end of their relationship. That's the way it had worked out for him in the past: instances with women where he thought more than just a lay might be possible, more than just sex, some sort of emotional involvement. Alas, after intercourse, Jimmy Riff seldom went back for more. Oh, with some he may have gone back once or twice, but it was rare when it happened. The attraction was no longer strong enough, and therefore not worth pursuing. He would lose interest. Was it the ensuing lack of excitement, or fear of what lay ahead? Fear of giving his heart—if he had it to give? Whatever the answers were, he did not like the idea of doing anything underhanded to this girl. He did not wish to hurt this angelic young woman in any way, not if he could help it.

"You don't know anything about me," Jimmy said.

"I know enough."

"You know very little."

"I know I want you."

And her lips pressed against his. His tongue explored her mouth, and Victoria Chantal pulled on it as if her life depended on it. She inhaled his tongue with every bit of determination that she was capable of; and then it was the other way around: they traded places, as her own tongue found its way inside Jimmy's mouth. She moaned, pressing her breasts into him, clinging to him with a passion and a hunger that had been waiting, hoping, dreaming for years for something like this to take place with the right man, a dream man, just waiting to be released, unleashed like a keg of TNT.

⁂

Jimmy withdrew his tongue and ran it down her neck, biting into it, and dropping lower and lower, down toward the open top of her full blouse. Vicki's head was tilted back, eyes closed, in heaven, as she purred not unlike a kitten having its back stroked, making it obvious she had never before in her life experienced anything like this.

He unbuttoned her blouse and slid his tongue down further to the cleavage and the healthy tits that were super-sensitive to his touch. Her nipples were firm and seemed to be throbbing as he continued to work on them with his warm and moist mouth and tongue, as well as continued to knead and squeeze them in his hands. He continued to suck on her tits, while his hands moved down to the small of her back. He squeezed her firm behind and moved around to the front and undid her jeans. She eagerly assisted with the zipper, pulling the jeans down to her knees, revealing white lace panties, the richly tanned thighs. He squeezed her buttocks, pressing her against his pelvis. Victoria continued to moan, adrift in nirvana: her mind, her entire being for that matter, floating in a sea of ecstasy.

He pressed his hand against the mound, feeling her bush through the thin fabric of her panties. His hand moved up and down, gently, gradually, then cupping the whole of it. His middle finger quested, looked for, slid under, then inside the noticeably moist fabric; searched further for a way past the bushy pubes, found entry, and his finger went in a ways.

His finger probed, entered further, then withdrew. He circled a bit; it was plenty moist and warm inside her vagina. He added a second finger to the process, thus increasing her pleasure. Even so, what he did next doubled it easily. It always came down to the clit. Seek it, pay loving and patient attention to it, and the woman you're with will be forever grateful. The pussy juice he had on his fingers he rubbed over and around the clit. His motions varied: at times up and down, other times he stayed with the circle. Everything he attempted and pursued worked and worked terrifically well. And when he thought additional lube was required, all he had to do was re-enter her pussy and re-supply, for her joy box was loaded with pussy honey, and return to the extremely sensitive clitoris.

And this he did, time and time again. Stay with the clit, no matter what. Stay with it. Take care of it. Adore it.

He knew he was on the right track. No guesswork to it. Her legs, then her stomach shook. Jimmy only smiled, for he knew and rather expected as much. Victoria Chantal was not at all aware of the amused and pleased expression on his face, for she was soaring way up there to notice anything else right now. All she was able, capable of doing, was sighing his name repeatedly: *"Oh, Jimmy. My sweet lover man. Jimmy. . . ."*

The white panties were thoroughly wet, her juices having soaked clear through and dripping. Dripping. He undid his own jeans, and got out of them. He placed his hands on either of her hips, then slowly, always taking his sweet time, began to roll her panties down, past her hips, knees, and cleared the ankles. He ran his hands up, over her thighs, kissed both: right, then the left. He buried his face into her tasty and wet bush, in search of the clit. He parted the pussy hair with his hands, the clit had a tendency to be bashful, and one needed to coax it out for a spell, make it possible for it to receive the attention it craved and needed. He flicked at it, taking his time, taking his sweet time, always and forever. Then he did the circling that he knew he was quite good at. She seemed to be convulsing, her moans increasing, while she thrust her pelvis hard against his mouth and face. They were pressed and stuck together this way: his lips and tongue, and her bush and clit—at one. United. Coupled in a most satisfying way and rewarded mutually. He loved doing this when he liked the woman he was with, and this girl, this young woman, he so enjoyed being with and wanted to please to the utmost of his ability. You went out of your way, at least he did, when he was able to relate to the female's personality; when he respected and liked and was grateful he had someone so personable to be with.

Sex? He was able to sex it up with or without this dimension to it, without this component, but it made it a whole lot easier and satisfying when you felt at one with your lover. It wasn't love; it couldn't be, not this early, this soon, but whatever it was, it was real nice. What prompted him to continue to give of himself in this manner? Her sighs and gasps and calling out his name. The intensity she could not help but experience also gave him the impetus to devote and put into all that he was able to offer, contribute, apply. Yes.

This was certainly the opposite of Lisa Koch, the twisted female who had it in for his gender. The only way she was truly able to get off sexually was by being malicious, venal almost, as well as controlling. She had to hurt, injure, humiliate. The male was nothing more than something like a subservient pet to be kept under her thumb. Maybe some men liked that. He certainly didn't. No way. Vicki was the type of girl he naturally gravitated to. Victoria. Chantal. He liked the name Chantal. The last name was unusual, too. He liked it. Vevrier. A beautiful name for a beautiful woman. Inside and out.

This is what his gut instinct told him about her (in the short space of time that they had known one another). There was no denying it. You paid attention to your gut instinct. The times he hadn't, like with Lisa Koch, he'd paid. And of course Marcella before her, way before. In his teens. He did not disregard his inner voice too often; but the times, the rare times he had, it had cost him—in more ways than one.

Up there, above his head, while his tongue caressed her labia lips and clit, his hands were on her tits, holding them together, squeezing. They were plentiful, and it was a thrill to be able to do this with a nice and full pair of tits like this. Then he lifted his head, moved up to where the breasts were and got his lips around the one, then the other nipple. He looked for her mouth, got his right hand on her face, and guided her lips toward his, and they kissed, while down at the pelvis area, his groin was against her pussy, rubbing against it, grinding. He didn't have his erection inside her, wouldn't want to just yet, and was okay with what was taking place. Drive her wild first; tease and tantalize and caress, until they beg that you to enter, go inside. Let them plead and beseech, and sooner or later, they will. He liked doing things this way. No quick entry for Jimmy Riff. He hadn't been called "Tubesteak" back there in the old neighborhoods solely for selling footlongs. *Tubesteak?* Used to bother him. Not lately. He was fine with it. You had to have a sense of humor in this life and world. Laugh at yourself; because if you didn't, you were in trouble. Take yourself too seriously and the world had a tendency to come crashing on top of you.

His mouth was back down again, needing it, craving her tasty cunt and the juices that flowed and flowed; there seemed to be an endless supply of that immensely pleasurable and priceless fluid called cunt juice. This was what made women so great, in his estimation. This world, this whole damn world would be nothing without women, without the female. Nothing. Life would not be worth living without babes. He'd known it from the time he was a teen, even before. Women were everything. Why men, so many men did not see this, why they could not acknowledge this was beyond his comprehension. And in knowing and accepting this fact about the female of the species, of their worth and importance, of their very existence, is what made it possible for him to go all out to please them, to put forth 110 percent each and every time to make their sexual experience not merely something to remember, but never, ever forget, and always want to come back for more. Perhaps this was what set him apart, once again not so much his size, because other men were similarly endowed. It wasn't that. Because it was also true and a fact, that men who did not have nearly as much as he did down there were in demand and appreciated simply because they took the extra effort, went the extra mile to satisfy their lover. That's what it was. But of course, in addition, if you had size and circumference, this was the added bonus. No denying it. Circumference made a difference. Some women, through no personal preference of their own required that the male have a thick enough cock. It was nature. You couldn't bicker with Mother Nature about such things.

His tongue, hard at work, parted the golden pussy hair and slid deep inside the rosy pink walls of her tasty vagina. Nothing beat this, nothing ever would. For sheer enjoyment; perhaps the actual orgasm, but this licking and tasting cunt and nectar of her joy box, then licking lower and getting inside her butt crack. Always grateful, forever grateful when he was able to do it with someone he could relate to, a female whose company he treasured and thus made him grateful to be alive. What it came down to: moments like this made him appreciate the fact he was above ground. This was, in fact, one of the great things about being among the living and of this world, the opportunity to be able to share an experience like this with someone like Victoria Chantal.

Jimmy Riff witnessed her entire body tremble as he had witnessed so many before, but this one, this one—there was no denying it—he was enjoying more than any of the others. She was not only a mere nineteen years old, but so angelic and giving, so trusting. That was the word, the key; it struck him just then: she was *trusting*. She trusted him, and he reciprocated in every way that he was able. This one female, this person seemed to mean so much more to him. There was no denying it.

He had perfected his method so well over the years, the vibrating of his tongue, and being able to last at it. The other key: endurance. You stayed with it, showed great patience, no matter how long it took. It was her first time, and he would take forever, if need be. He would, of course, last as long as she required him to. His tongue, forever eager to oblige, continued to send her to immense heights. Her reaction, the quaking body and thighs, the moaning and squeezing and whispering of his name, being totally lost in the moment and the act of lovemaking, is what certainly kept fatigue at bay, even though there were times his tongue could have clearly used a break. No way, thought Jimmy. I'm not stopping. He continued to work the tongue, licking inside the pussy, lapping up hot cunt honey, then driving it, drawing it up toward the clit and rubbing, smearing it over it. Drive her insane with every flick and lick of your tongue, Jimmy. Stay with it.

Next thing he knew, her thighs were like a vise around his neck, squeezing. It made it close to difficult to breathe. But no matter, because he would not allow it to deter him. Nope. He stayed with it.

Endurance was everything. She kicked the one leg, the right, out in the air. When the leg came back down suddenly, it landed on the coffee table, knocking their beers onto the rug. Both chuckled briefly at this, not bothering or being able to pay attention to anything but the lovemaking at hand. Pleasure was too great. Close to unbearable. Nearly impossible to take. He could tell by her continued reaction. No matter, because he stayed with it. Her hands gripped his scalp, saying his name, nearly yelling it, pleading with it, as she cried out. Jimmy laughed, let go of the clit, and she released his hair. Then his tongue went in search of the other orifice, her precious and priceless butthole, and went inside. Licking, savoring. A woman's asshole, especially if he truly liked the woman, was the sweet spot. Forever the sweetest spot. He loved doing this to women he was attracted to.

His tongue was back outside again, but continued to circle and lick around, as well as up and down. He returned to the clit, and with the middle finger of his right hand, he probed and entered her tight asshole. She winced at first, was reluctant to welcome it, but then realized that he was being gentle, would do nothing to hurt her, and allowed him to proceed. It was wonderful. She realized soon enough. His finger probed her asshole, sliding inside, then back out again, even as he continued to fight the urge to revisit the clit. Stayed with this for a while, then realized there was no putting it off; Jimmy Riff could not wait any longer. He shed his boxers and inserted his rigid cock into her dripping pussy. He was gentle, as always, and slid it in by degrees. There was the hymen to be aware of. He made it past eventually, and the ensuing thrusting was the result of it. In fact, her pelvis moved much faster than his, and Jimmy Riff, now having been given the go-ahead, was not reluctant to oblige.

Her pussy, so wet by now, had expanded to the point he was able to insert his groin all the way in. It was the thrill of a lifetime. You thought this way every time you made it with a woman who turned you on, one you were genuinely attracted to, but this literally was that thrill of a lifetime. You wanted the moment to last forever; you wanted it to never, ever end. He knew she felt the same, not only due to the reception he'd been getting from the get-go, but she was digging her fingernails deep into his back as he pumped away. Her pussy, although not accommodating enough, it seemed initially, due to the terrific natural lube her vagina and body provided, was just the right size and she did not have too much trouble taking him in, engulfing him like a glove, a warm and moist and welcoming and needy perfect-fitting glove. *Wow.*

Their senses in tune, at one with, united, sweat and body fluids co-mingled. They clung to each other, matching each other thrust for thrust. She may have been a newcomer to love-making, no matter, because she was a quick study, a sharp and willing learner. She had waited years for this moment to happen, and Jim Riff was willing to admit he might have been waiting his entire life as well. Nothing compared to what they were experiencing, nothing on Earth was this pleasurable and intense. One of the great wonders of being alive.

Her thrusts seemed to increase, and he went along with it. If she were able to keep up the pace, he would do his best to accommodate her. Victoria's moans did increase, as she held on for dear life, clung to him with all her might. Her arms were wrapped about his neck, as tightly as she was able. Held him, pressed him against her breasts. She screamed, followed by a long deep sigh. Seemed to freeze up, her entire body froze, locked in, for the moment, for a brief moment, frozen in time; everything stood still for her. She went limp, sighing his name and saying in his ear: "Thank you . . . thank you my sweet, darling lover man. . . . Thank you, my lovely, sweet man. . . ." She seemed on the verge of tears. He looked at her. Was she about to cry? Then saw the smile, the greatest and purest and infectious smile cross her angelic face. She closed her eyes, lying on her back this way, needing to collect herself, needing to rest for a spell . . . just rest and savor what was perhaps the most special and thrilling experience of her entire life.

In fact, she could not move if she had wanted to. Her head was tingling, as were other parts, obviously; it was a combination of having reached multiple orgasms as well as exhaustion, not to mention this close emotional connection there was no denying she felt toward this man.

Jimmy, no longer in her, would allow her to relax, recoup, and recover. She needed it. Would want her to rest after a marathon session like that. He would give her time to enjoy, take in the mellow state a while longer. When he felt she was ready and able, he turned her over gently on her stomach, helped raise her buttocks up, so that she was on elbows and knees, and her enticing ass up in the air. Her waist was slim, the hips flared the right amount. He had his hands on either buttock and parted them a bit, so that the butt crack revealed itself. He loved ogling this, loved being able to gaze and ogle at the wonder of the sight: the butt crack and the hairy bush below, underneath; the wonder of it all. The greatest mystery. There it was: no matter how often, how many women he had been with, it never failed to please and thrill him. It was magical. All of it. A woman with a desirable figure and a raw sexuality that was natural and therefore impossible to ignore. There was no denying it: Victoria had one of the best derrieres he'd ever seen. How was this possible? How could he have been so lucky? Some women had tits that were desirable; some had legs, thick thighs, and beautifully shaped calves; others had a face you could not take your eyes off of; still others had something else: a laugh, a smile, were generally personable;

narrow-waisted and wonderfully wide-hipped.

Vicki? Victoria Chantal had so much that he was drawn to. His eyes were back on her butt crack. Her butthole, and that whole area of her anatomy: the crack and the beaver underneath were undeniably desirous to him. It was just a wonder to witness. A woman shaped like this, a wonderful miracle of a woman. Wow!—is right. And while he admired her figure, there he was hoping she'd had her rest because he could no longer wait for his, to get his end. His balls would start hurting pretty soon if he did not follow through. He needed to get his rocks off. Pronto. There was a huge load of cum brewing inside his nutsack and he would have to blast off pretty soon. Nature had a way of doing things, and one paid heed—or one suffered.

He inserted the head of his cock inside her cunt, while bringing his fingers of the right hand down and under to where the clit was. He would employ the one-two combo: pump with his woody, while at the same time massaging and caressing the clit. His left hand, either the thumb or middle finger, if he were able to pull it off, would be sliding inside her wonderful and miraculous asshole, just as he had done before. It sounded easy, well, maybe not, because to co-ordinate something like this took doing; dexterity, plenty of it.

He was bent forward, doing all three: the clit, paying attention to her butt, while driving his thick and hard meat puppet into her tight pleasure tunnel. Then Jimmy, aka Tubesteak, who couldn't wait to cum himself, inserted his massive member all the way in, and the thrusting was steady this time, all the way. The sight of her bent over this way continued to add to the intensity of the act. He pumped, not being able to do all three any longer. It required too much: both: energy as well as dexterity. He let go of the clit, left her asshole alone for the time being; it was good enough to know it was before him and his eyes were able to keep looking at it, seeing it.

He did lean forward far enough to be able to cup her tits in his hands, but he couldn't keep this up for very long either, for the pleasure he felt at near or about the head of his extremely sensitive groin was just too much and too great. He would be blasting, and soon. Real soon. It would be a load, a double load of hot nutsack cream, a semi full of sperm. He knew it, felt it. Why foreplay was worth it. Not only did it get the woman's motor running, it made it twice and three times as pleasurable for the male.

He gripped her sweaty buttocks in his hands, squeezing them against his woody that continued to pump her sopping wet cunt. From time to time, he would release the buttocks in order to be able to take a gander at her butt crack, forever in awe. There was something about the female butt crack that drove him just plain nuts with desire. He could never explain it or wanted to. The sight of a wonderfully shaped female butt and the tight asshole within those amazing buttocks. And speaking of buttocks, his own muscular buns moved like a jackhammer, getting a workout like no gym could ever provide. The resulting sounds he made deep from within his throat with each pressing fraction of a second totally drowned out everything else, her included. For Vicki was making sounds again, screaming, back in the game, ready for additional explosions. This was the bonus that happened sometimes: the woman, your partner, ready for the encore and willingly going along for the thrills, even though at times the ecstasy of it tended to be almost unbearably intense.

For a newcomer, she was exceptional. He'd noticed it from the start. She was pushing back with her butt, against his pelvis and groin. This is what was required, therefore making it easier on him, so that he was not the sole thrustee. She pushed back against his cock and balls, then forward, away, then back up against him. This was the way to fuck. You worked it like a team, *in tandem*. Move for move, thrust for thrust. United, we reach a greater orgasm; divided, we get somewhere but don't reach the same heights, or something like it.

Then she gave out one final scream and gripped the rug. Jimmy Riff flung his upper body forward, pressing his chest against the small of her back, and wrapped his long arms around her waist. He took a deep breath and held it, while driving his member into her with greater force and held it there, still, stiff, unmoving. His body shook as the hot load of sperm traveled the length of his hard groin, reaching the very sensitive knob-like head of it, and burst forth inside of her. He held on tighter, driving it another inch, or as much as there was left to drive in. Held on; HELD ON, wanting to shoot every last damn drop of his ball-sack cream into her. And it felt like it: his entire load was deep inside her.

～

He was still for a long moment, unable to move. Not a muscle, not an inch. Like a statue. Spent, physically, emotionally, sperm-wise, and every other way. Drained. Exhausted. And feeling good. Nothing tops this, he thought. A long moment passed, and he raised her waist and simply rested his sweaty face against her back. She asked if he was all right. All Jimmy Riff could do was nod.

～

After he'd given himself time to catch his breath, he guided his cock to where her face was, inserted the head into her mouth. Her lips moved awkwardly at first. He was gentle with her, and she caught on. Showed her how and where to flick it with her tongue. Showed her how to circle the rim, then take the head, the knob, into her mouth and suck on it.

Insert it, take it out, then vacuum it back in. It came down to the head, he explained. The head is where all the sensitivity, at least most of it, is located. The knob is where the pleasure comes from: teasing and manipulating the knob. When the guy cums, that's what you want to work on, concentrate on, stay with: the knob, head of the cock. Especially when blowing a guy, and he's coming, concentrate on the cock head, while the cum shoots into your mouth.

She caught on, smart girl, and she lapped up what remained of his cum; the residue. She seemed to be enjoying it as much as he enjoyed watching her do it. Her actions soon gave new life to his groin. Jimmy Riff was hard again. His hips moved as before, facing her mouth. Only he needed to be cautious, as he was too big for her to take him all the way in. She was gagging; the meat pole too thick and massive. At best, she was able to take about half of it in. It was good enough. For a maiden effort. Absolutely. Maiden and gratifying.

She caressed his wet balls, cupping them with such tender care. She ran her tongue from the tip of the head, down to the thick, hairy base and back up again. She wrapped her lips around the bulb, found a pace, and stayed with it. Not until Jimmy held the top of her head in his hands and began to encourage her in this manner, did she step up the action.

For a beginner, this was exceptional, thought Jimmy Riff. And quite uncommon. Usually, very often, it took days, sometimes weeks, maybe months, to teach a newcomer the technique of blowing wood and sucking balls and licking a man's asshole. But not here, not with this intelligent nineteen-year-old.

When she looked up, a bit on the shy side, she saw his chest muscles, his pecs tighten. Veins in his neck were bulging. Sweat poured from his face and armpits. Jimmy Riff was drenched in sweat. He clenched his teeth. Eyes shut tight. His neck and head, his upper body quivered, while he shot a thick stream of cum into her warm and hungry mouth. He opened her mouth enough in his right hand to be able to see the cum shoot inside, and make it down her throat, needing to see it, being excited by it. A heavy load of frothy man jizz. Perhaps not as heavy as the first, but heavy enough, impressive enough. She was grinning, trying to laugh, managed it, being able to make him feel good while doing it. She sucked, taking in all the cum that he had to offer. It was amazing. First the intercourse part of it, now the terrific BJ.

She drained him, and would not stop until she was convinced she had siphoned every last and tasty drop. This she did.

When next she looked up, Jimmy was laughing again, laughing, feeling fine and happy and satisfied. There was a big smile on her face.

Jimmy leaned in and kissed her brow. Vicki reached up with her arms and clung to him, embracing him and pulling him to her. They were lying on their sides, holding each other and looking at each other this way; two happy and contented people, a man and a woman who had found each other. This was how she felt. *Jimmy's the one for me. My wonderful man.* They spent the night this way, entwined in each other's arms.

Fear (of Something)

Jimmy did his thousand pushups and a thousand sit-ups in the morning. There were some people out there this early: joggers, the occasional celebrity walking a dog, others with metal detectors searching for coins and other items of value. Doves glided overhead, diving now and then for food on the water's surface or in the sand.

Breakfast was light for both: scrambled eggs, toast, orange juice, tea. They spent the rest of the morning watching cartoons and eating cantaloupe. Later that day they strolled along the beach holding hands. Vicki braved the water and proved a strong swimmer, so elegant and unafraid. Jimmy remained on dry land. The closest he would get to the ocean was where the water touched the sand.

"Come on, Jimmy. It's so refreshing."

He allowed his feet to get wet. About the extent of it. No amount of encouragement on her part convinced him otherwise.

"What are you afraid of?" she asked. "Sharks?"

"No," Jimmy said.

"There are no sharks around here—that I know of."

Jimmy smiled, then shook his head. "That makes me feel safe."

"What is it, Jimmy" Vicki asked, wading out of the water. He put his arm around her, and they walked back in the direction of the house.

He told her of the time, way back as a kid on Long Island, a neighborhood bully had shoved his head under water and wouldn't let him up for air. Just held him down, pressing on top of his head, pushing him down and kept him there. Jimmy thought for sure he would drown, for when the bully had unexpectedly shoved his head under water Jimmy hadn't been allowed time to inhale enough oxygen.

"I thought my head would explode. When he finally released his hold on me I shot up like a buoy."

"I'm sorry," Vicki said. "What a terrible thing to do to someone."

"I was no more than five at the time," Jimmy said. "Thought I was going to die."

She stopped, facing him. She stood up on her tippy toes and kissed him. "I love you," she said. "I love you, Jimmy: my first and only lover man. I love you. . . ."

She squeezed and hugged him with all that she had.

"You owe me"

Vicki fixed hamburgers for lunch and they ate on the patio. He'd always limited his meat intake, but that was what they had. A good and healthy salad, you hoped, balanced it out. Hell, you had to have protein. Beans were good, he had always liked beans, and fish, but you couldn't eat either day and night.

Jimmy Riff was in a pensive mood. And it had nothing to do with what they were having for lunch.

"Think you'll ever go back to the East Coast?"

"I don't know," Jimmy Riff said. "There isn't much there."

"Don't you miss your family?"

Jimmy Riff shrugged.

"No?"

"Some of them," Jimmy Riff said. "I suppose I'll go back one of these days to visit. The time isn't right just now."

"Where would you like to live?"

"That's a tough one," Jimmy Riff said and swallowed beer. "You make a great burger."

"Thank you," Vicki said.

"I was headed for Oregon," Jimmy Riff said. "Wouldn't mind staying on in Southern California for a while."

"Ever been to Big Sur?"

Jimmy shook his head.

"Carmel?"

"No."

"Santa Barbara?"

"No."

"Neither have I," Vicki said. "We ought to take a drive out there, at least as far as Santa Barbara."

"When?" Jimmy asked.

"Whenever you like."

Jimmy downed the rest of his beer. The phone rang.

"Hello?" Victoria said into the receiver. "Who's calling, please?" Then: "Just a second." She handed the phone to Jimmy. "Your friend Benjamin."

"What?" Jimmy Riff said in a hushed tone. "How did he get this number?"

Vicki found herself shrugging: Your guess is as good as mine.

"Yeah?" Jimmy Riff said into the receiver.

"This is Benjamin—"

"That much was established," Jimmy Riff said.

"How are you, Tubesteak?"

"How did you know I was here?"

"I make it my business to know every move you make, kid."

"Look, I want nothing to do with you anymore. Stay out of my life."

"Artie Gross is still interested. How about it?"

"You got the part of Fitch. What more do you want?"

"I want to thank you for that—"

"My pleasure," Jimmy Riff said. "We're square now. Even-steven."

"I gotta admit," Ben T. Styles said, "Fitch is a great part. But how much of it will end up in the final cut?"

"That's your problem."

"It's your problem, too, Kidd," Benjamin Styles said. "You're my ticket to the top. You might as well get used to it."

"I'm telling you, mister, you're pressing your luck."

"You owe me."

"I owe you nothing."

"We have a contract."

"We *had* a verbal agreement. Which I am presently opting out of."

"A verbal agreement is as good as the other."

"Yeah. As good as the 'paper' it's written on." It was an old Hollywood cliché he'd heard more than once in the short time he'd spent here. The opportunity to use it on a bully such as this Styles character had been too good to pass up.

"You gonna run, Tubesteak? Huh, Kidd? Where you gonna run to? Besides, you gonna give up on the idea of seeing your name in lights? You don't want to see James Kidd up on movie-house marquees?"

"I never cared for the fakery of it," said Jimmy. "The name is Riff. May not sound as good as the one you came up with, but it's mine. It's real. Like me. I like keeping it that way."

"You going to spend the rest of your life running? There's no place to hide, no matter where you end up."

"Look, Styles, I'm telling you for the last time—"

"I just want to go for a couple more parts, enough to get re-established again, that's all. Then you're off the hook. Besides, I think you like that little girl too much to let anything happen to her. If you get my drift."

"So long, Styles," Jimmy Riff said, and slammed the receiver down. He grabbed the beer bottle and flung it toward the sea. "Dammit," Jimmy Riff said, gripping the top of the picket fence. Vicki did not know if she should say anything, or even approach him. She looked at him for a long while, and finally said: "Hon?"

Jimmy Riff stood quietly, his face pressed against the pickets.

"Hon, what's the matter?"

"You try to be nice, you try to help out, and get crapped on every time. Boy, I never learn, do I? I just never learn. What I get for getting mixed up with a character like that." They had him pegged. Did they ever. "You're just a dumb hustler."

"Jimmy? Are you all right?"

Jimmy Riff nodded, and looked at her. The faint trace of a smile appeared on his face. "I'll be okay," he assured her. And put his arm around her. "Would you like to go for that drive now?" Jimmy asked.

"This minute?"

"Why not?"

"You're on," she said. "Your car or mine?"

"Let's take the Porsche," he said. "It's fancier."

⚬⚬⚬

The Cashmere Beige Porsche 911sc pulled out of the garage, pausing long enough for a break in traffic on the busy PCH. Jimmy Riff turned his head to look at the new Toyota sitting there parked in the driveway. "I bought that car for him, too," he said. "Was going to take it to him today."

"Benjamin?"

Jimmy Riff nodded. "The guy saved me from a situation once."

Not only extracted him from the clutches of Lisa Koch but bailed him out of the slammer that time after he'd been arrested at that party in Chatsworth. He'd been jumped by a group of drugged-out porn studs, worked over pretty good. And Benjy's attorney had come through for him the next day, bailed him out. He'd paid him back, he thought. Appeared in that porn flick with Renata Blevins. So why did he feel that he still owed him?

"How long have you known him?"

"Too long," Jimmy said. "That night you and I met at that party in the Valley was the first time I ever laid eyes on the guy. He bailed me out of the slammer after that brawl I got involved in with the porn studs. It seems Mr. Styles is intent on seeing me spend the rest of my life paying him back."

"What will you do?"

"Good question," said Jimmy. "I'll have to think of something eventually."

Victoria nodded her head without saying anything. She shifted gears, and the Porsche roared off in the direction of Santa Barbara.

On Their Tail

Nicky Horgan cursed to himself. The station wagon would soon be overheating and the Porsche up ahead continued to gain speed. They'll be stopping for gas eventually, he comforted himself. They'll have to. **NEXT GAS TEN MILES**, the sign said. Nicky Horgan wondered if he would ever make it.

"Damn that Styles!" he shouted. "Damn that bastard!"

Please God, make them stop for gas. Please. Don't let me get stranded on PCH like this. Please don't. What of the kids? The wife is expecting me for dinner. He knew she would be upset if he showed up late for dinner again, or did not show up at all. It'd happened too many times. In this crazy business he was in, your time and hours were never your own. You spent your life, it seemed, in the car, one way or another. Sitting, waiting, surveillance, or, like he was doing now: tailing someone to God- knows-where. If they kept going they could end up in Bakersfield or Santa Cruz or San Francisco; maybe even further. He didn't know. All he knew was that he had a car that was struggling.

It was no way to do this sort of thing properly. He'd learned, been taught by the best PI's in the business: Choo-Choo Buschitski and Zack Stanton. How he got his experience. Paid his dues, working with pros. If there was one thing they taught him: You didn't pull surveillance alone. There was no way. You had to be able to make restroom stops, and switch off vehicles, have time to change wardrobe. Switching hats wasn't always adequate.

He had a white, porkpie beach-type on presently, and would have to switch that for a trilby. He had a bunch of hats in the back to suit every occasion. But that was not the great fear, far from it. When would the wagon start steaming up a storm and quit on him? And then he'd have to call Triple A, get help. Shit. He just wanted the couple to go back, turn around and return to LA, and make life simple again.

Where was Pete? Pete was having troubles of his own. Used him only when he could afford him. Did his best to keep his hours down. Overhead: you had overhead, and bills. Office rent and apartment rent. Light bills, phone, others. All that he could handle, take care of, if only the couple up ahead, that kid Jimmy—Tubesteak—that Styles seemed obsessed with, and Tubesteak's girlfriend, if only they would turn around and head back.

Where in hell were they going? He'd had her phone tapped. She never said anything about making a trip like this. He hoped for a break.

❧

Ten miles later Nicky Horgan's prayers paid off. He exhaled a sigh of relief as the Porsche pulled up to a gas pump at a mini mart. It was not the smartest thing he'd done in his shaky three-year career as a solo snooper, but he decided to pull up next to the Porsche and gas up himself.

He did not bother looking directly at them, maybe peripherally, but that was all. It was enough. One of them went inside to buy something; Jimmy was at the pump, handling the nozzle. The wide-brimmed hat Nicky had on made him comfortable enough, and he stayed relaxed as far as that went. He popped the hood, undid the radiator cap, face turned away, using caution, lifted it, and the steam shot up like a fire hydrant and remained this way for some time.

❦

The girl was back outside with a paper sack full of stuff. Jimmy was done gassing up. They got in the Porsche and were on the road, heading north. Nicky Horgan refilled the radiator, screwed the gas cap back on. Noticed a roadside food stand selling tacos and burritos. Against his better judgment, he pulled over, bought a burrito and something to drink, and the PI was back on the blacktop again himself not long after.

Love on the Rocks

In a secluded cove, to the left and below the Pacific Coast Highway, hidden from the average motorist, the young couple made love under the clear blue California sky, completely unaware of Nicky Horgan's clicking camera from the cliff above. He was lying on his belly and aiming that camera.

This had been a first for Nicky, witnessing how endowed Tubesteak really was. He had to stop taking pictures for a moment. Maybe the kid was wearing a dildo. Nobody was that big. He re-focused the super-fine lens in search of the strap that should have been around the kid's lower waist. If he was wearing a strap-on penis, where was the strap? He lowered the camera and picked up his binoculars. Looked for it. And found nothing that resembled a strap. He had a condom on, but no strap of any type.

Nah, dummy. Why would a young stud like that be wearing a rubber dick? That's the kid's own salami. Every friggin' inch. Why he's so popular. Talk of the town. Hung like *Seattle Slew*. What Styles said about him. Didn't actually believe it until now. Triple-crown winner. Where do you think the name Tubesteak came from?

"*Maaan*, is he giving it to her," he said to himself. "Is he ever." Nicky wished his wife could see this. Might just show her some of the pics. She won't believe it.

He picked up the camera and used up the rest of the roll, all the while fighting the gas attack. Should've stayed away from that roach coach. He was paying the price now. Never failed. You ate Mex food from a questionable roadside stand and you got trouble, lots of trouble.

⌘

The show over, the kid cracked the top on a can of beer. He and the girl ate beef jerky and sipped from the same can. He also could not help but notice the look of pure love that the young woman had for her man. Reminded him of the way his wife felt about him and never failed to remind him how much he meant to her. The only difference being this kid Jimmy's mind was somewhere else. The girl continued to kiss him on the neck and the side of his face between bites of the beef jerky and sips of beer, and the kid's eyes remained on the ocean out there, or else he was staring off into space. This was the way it happened when you had his looks and body and babes were always throwing themselves at you. Some men were luckier than others, he supposed. It was okay, though. You had to try to be fairly happy with your lot.

Nicky Horgan packed the camera away and chuckled. He knew his wife would have given her eyepatch to be able to get it on with someone hung like that. Nicky lit a filterless Camel and wondered what it would be like to have a dick that size. He also had a far more immediate concern to deal with: the burrito was progressing into a raging hurricane inside his stomach. There was no way to control the farting, either. The goddamn burrito wanted out, or else it was his entire system, his belly and rectum that needed to expel the nasty burrito of dubious origin. He wondered if it was even beef? He'd asked the Mexican woman what it was? She had claimed it was "meat."

"Yes, but what kind?"

"Good meat. *Si, senor.*"

"Beef? Roadkill? What specific kind is it?"

She had shrugged. "Of course it is beef. Fresh beef every day, *senor.* We make the real good and excellent *beef burrito.* Nobody complain."

"That's because they're travelers. By the time the burrito strikes they're halfway to Timbuktu."

There was no way to control the gas. His fear was that if he didn't hold it in, he just might end up shitting his pants. It had happened. Release some gas, a moderate fart, and before you knew it you had boxers full of waste. He found himself cursing under his breath. What was he going to do? How could he even think about sticking around and tailing them?

He would wait until the Porsche was back on the main highway prior to walking to the station wagon and heading back home. He would go against Benjamin's orders and not follow them any further. If Styles didn't like it, he could go fuck himself. Besides, he had the pics, the valuable pics. He should be able to get a healthy sum for them, if not from asshole Ben T. Styles, then from the kid himself. And if the kid didn't care, he would talk to the girl. He could not help but wonder just how well off her family was.

It was then that the turmoil inside his stomach turned into a full-blown emergency. He hurried to the wagon. Prayed that the accident wouldn't happen in his pants. He needed to take a dump real bad. It was painful holding it in. Painful. He felt miserable. Cursed the beaner who had sold him the burrito. He felt it coming on. There was no stopping it. Two feet before reaching the car, he undid his belt buckle, and dropped his pants, and let go. It exploded out of him. It was too much.

His asshole was in pain, burning and in pain. Fuck. Roadside shack. When he was done, he turned around, in search of something to wipe with. Found nothing; could not think of anything. There was no choice: used his boxers to wipe back there. Got into his pants and slowly, gingerly, climbed back in the station wagon.

Adios, My Darling

When morning came Vicki could no longer deny that something was the matter. Jimmy was not being his upbeat and attentive self. There were silences that left her concerned. She had picked up on it the evening before but had said nothing. Victoria Chantal finally asked what was wrong, never expecting that her world was about to fall apart.

"I won't be going back with you," Jimmy Riff said over breakfast in a diner booth next door. Vicki just looked at him. Did she hear right? Maybe he didn't want to go back right away.

"We can stay longer if you like, darling," Vicki said.

Jimmy shook his head. "That's not what I mean, Victoria. I can't go back to Los Angeles. I don't want to."

"We don't have to, darling."

"To get Styles off my back I'll have to go far." He paused. "Either that, or kill him."

"Do you mean that?"

"You don't know the guy," Jimmy said. "He's as nasty as they come."

"I don't think you could kill anybody, darling. I know you couldn't."

"Maybe you're right," Jimmy Riff said. "But he's connected—"

"Mafia?"

Jimmy Riff nodded. "Probably have to go clear to the other side of the world to shake the jerk."

"I have credit cards," Vicki said. "Just say where and when."

"Know why I didn't want us to get it on initially?"

Vicki shook her head.

"Because I knew what would happen."

"What would?"

"It's happening right now," Jimmy Riff said. "I'll make love to a woman once, twice, maybe three times . . ." It was not easy getting it out, saying something like this to someone like her. Too harsh, way too cold-blooded and unfeeling. She deserved better, far better. Destroy the thing you need, before IT destroys *you*. "And it's gone. I lose interest."

Vicki's eyes suddenly welled.

"I'm sorry," Jimmy Riff said. "I didn't want it to be like this."

"Your wanting to get away from that man is just an excuse, then."

Jimmy shook his head.

"If you wanted me to leave, you could have just said so."

"Look," Jimmy said, "I like you. I like you a lot, but it won't last—"

"How do you know?"

"I know, believe me."

"Excuse me," Victoria Chantal said, "I keep forgetting you're 'Tubesteak,' who's been everywhere and knows everything."

"Not true."

"I love you, Jimmy," she said, tears streaming down her pretty face. *"I love you so much. . . ."*

"It hurts me to see you like this. You have to believe that."

"That's just it: I do believe you, Jimmy."

"We wouldn't last."

"Why?" Vicki asked. "Why do you keep saying that?"

"If I couldn't get it up, where would we be?"

She didn't understand.

"I lose interest," Jimmy Riff said. "Fast." He stopped long enough to stare at the ocean outside, how calm the water was, and wished his insides were as calm. "It hurts me to talk to you this way. You don't deserve it, not any of it. I just couldn't go on pretending any longer. That's the way it's always been with me in the past. I get distracted."

"You said that," she reminded him, wiping her nose with a paper napkin.

"My Uncle Orville would send me things when I was a kid; always loved to buy me toys, and my mother would get on the phone and yell at him: Don't you know he'll get tired of it in three days? He'll have that thing destroyed in less than a week. You can't buy anything for that kid. He's never satisfied; always wants something else, always asking for something different."

He was pausing again, searching for words. It was not easy. "I hate to say it," he said, "but she was right. Uncle would buy me a toy, I'd go crazy over it, play with nothing else but that one toy for a couple of days, maybe a week—then lose interest. Take it apart to see what made it tick, and in the process, albeit inadvertently, destroy it. Not only not be able to put it back together again, but would hardly make a conscientious effort." He looked at her. "I've been like that all my life, with everything—"

"Including," she said, cutting him off, "relationships."

She had no idea how close she was. He would never allow himself to forget what he'd gone through early on in his life, the heartbreak, the indifferent way the girl he'd fallen for had dumped him: romanced him, pursued him, and unceremoniously cut him off. He didn't feel like bringing up Marcella's name. It was way too personal. His business and no one else's, really.

Instead, he said: "I didn't want it to happen."

"It's all right," Victoria said, attempting to compose herself. "I understand."

"I do love you," Jimmy Riff said. "Probably never loved anyone as much." And meant it.

"The feeling is mutual," she said. "But what's that got to do with anything?"

A feeble smile crossed his face. "Besides, if you tagged along you'd be putting your life in danger."

"We can't let that happen."

"I'm serious," Jimmy Riff said. "You just don't know how nasty this guy is."

"Tell me: Just how nasty is this guy?"

"It's not funny."

"Of course not," Vicki said.

"He's been hurting people all his life: in the ring, outside it; pushed people off rooftops, broke their legs—"

"Before or after he pushed them off the roof?"

Jimmy Riff ignored the remark and continued. "They say he hit a guy back East."

"He hits, too? That's it," Vicki said, "he's wanted to be a boxer all his life. Wait, he was a boxer, wasn't he? Golden Gloves, or something having to do with gold, or gloves—maybe both."

"I mean, he clipped a man," Jimmy Riff said. "Don't you understand? He did a contract on a dude. A contract the mob paid for. That's why he can't go back East."

"Makes sense," Vicki said. "You 'clip' someone, You Can't Go Home Again."

Jimmy shook his head and sipped his coffee.

"I need you, Jimmy. We can move to Europe. He'll never find you there. We can go anywhere in the world. Money's no object."

"You speak French?"

"Some."

"Spanish?"

"Some."

"Some isn't good enough. How about German?"

"No."

"Or Dutch? Or Italian? Or Danish? Or Czech?"

She had stopped shaking her head.

"Well, neither do I. I can hide here in the States—but alone."

"You're my man, Jimmy. I don't want anyone else."

"Know why he's after me? Wants me to fuck every Tom, Dick, and Harriet just to jump-start his career. And that's what I've been doing all this time—because I didn't care. I did it for the money and I didn't care. But 'Tubesteak' fucked only who 'Tubesteak' wanted to fuck, until asshole Styles came along. See now?" Jimmy asked. "See what you've fallen in love with? A goddamn gigolo."

"I don't care," Vicki said. "I'll always love you, Jimmy." And got up from the table. He watched her walk out of the diner. She walked out there to the edge of the sand, where the soft and gentle waves caressed the beach and sat facing the ocean, her back to him. He knew that she was in pain, and he hated himself for it.

◦◦◦◦

Later that evening, in the motel parking lot, Jimmy Riff walked her to the Porsche. She unlocked the door and looked at him.

"Can I have a good-bye kiss?"

Jimmy nodded, and she kissed him softly on the lips and got in the car. *I won't cry again,* she said to herself, and was partly successful. She did manage to hold back long enough to say: "Will I ever see you again?"

Jimmy Riff looked down at his feet, then up at something overhead. Only there was not much there, other than the usual: sky and more sky. He tugged up on his jeans that did not need it. As Victoria Chantal bravely turned the key in the ignition and drove off into the night she had no idea that James G. Riff, aka Tubesteak, had tears in his eyes.

Lights, Camera, Friction!

Five in the morning, and Benjamin T. Styles was at the studio. On set. Early bird got the worm. Someone once said. He looked good in the Western outfit, even handsome. He wore the gun belt proudly. The cowboy hat was such a perfect fit Benjamin Styles wondered if he might have been born too late.

He would have made one hell of a cowboy. Done his share of kicking ass up and down the real Dodge. Been the baddest bad guy, or the toughest and straightest law-abiding lawman.

❦

Script in hand, his lines highlighted in yellow, the lone cowboy strolled down the Western set, an exact replica of Dodge City back in the eighteen hundreds when Doc Holliday, the Earps, Wild Bill Hickok, Sam Bass, and others were the royalty of the day.

❦

He passed a dress shop, a hat shop, bakery, a storefront with nothing but cowboy attire: lassoes, saddles, spurs, boots, blankets, skillets, coffee pots, and silverware; bridles, holsters, derbies, chaps, jeans—anything and everything that a hard-working cowboy would need to work on a cattle ranch and/or break broncs, mend fences, brand calves. Not only did he favor the way they dressed back then, but the all-around way of life and being seemed simpler. Less gray. Gray was the bitch. Less Graysons and fewer faggots and lesbians. They hardly had any back then, he was willing to bet. There was also no denying that he was romanticizing it just a touch. Well, you couldn't help it. You couldn't see the day-to-day struggle it was to earn a buck working your ass off on a horse ranch or farm, working yourself into the ground on long cattle drives. Shit. The movies never showed you how it really was. If they did, no one would pay to see it. He wouldn't. Although it was nice to look at all of it through rose-tinted glasses. Not that he would ever wear lenses of that hue.

❧

He took a deep breath and readjusted his holster, and a feeling of contentment surged through his body, a long-awaited calm, a state Benjamin Styles seldom experienced, a state that seemed to dissolve all the bitterness and hatred and hostility he felt toward his detractors and enemies, toward the industry and world in general, if but for a fleeting moment. Yes, it was temporary. As much as he welcomed this condition of placidity, he wouldn't allow himself to remain in it indefinitely, for to do so was unwise and could prove dangerous to his well-being and existence. You became relaxed and cheerful, let your facade drop and guard down, and you became vulnerable to all the backstabbing and underhanded tricks this town was so expert at. It was a way of life with these people. There was more honor among the hoods and gangsters and loan sharks and killers back on the East Coast than he ever saw here in Tinseltown. Hell, he had more respect for the average gambling-addicted punk or rapist, or mugger or thief, then he did the average two-faced Hollywood motherfucker.

Besides, keeping your guard up was the first thing they taught you in the Golden Gloves. Keep your dukes up, protect your face and brains. Yes, enough punches absorbed by the kidneys left you pissing blood, but if you took too many shots to the head you were left brain-damaged, punch drunk. End of story. You were fucking done. So you kept your dukes up, unless you wanted to get knocked on your ass. No, he had no use for that. Because *he* preferred knocking the enemy on *their* ass—every time. This was how you not only stayed ahead of the game but remained a player.

⚮

He entered the Long Branch Saloon, and Benjamin Styles was amazed at what he saw. The place was replete with bottles of real booze, authentic labels from the period. It had been McFluff's doing, no doubt. The funny bastard always insisted on authenticity; everything had to be authentic, down to the minutest detail. That was about the only thing he admired about Reggie McFluff. The pole smoker was a perfectionist. An artist to boot. He might be a perverted son of a bitch in the boudoir, but he sure knew how to direct a picture. Give him any genre, any type of film; drop him in any type of country and circumstance—and the degenerate came through for you. His pictures made money. Top stars clamored to work for him. McFluff appreciated skilled improvisers, gave his actors room to breathe and develop and add to their characters. They loved that about him, were willing to take considerable cuts in salary for the opportunity to appear in his films.

Ben envied that about him. The director had the uncanny ability to squeeze and manipulate eyebrow-raising performances out of not only established actors with a track record, but from total newbies, rookies, newcomers who had never been in front of a camera before.

It had to be his lack of machismo, or something. They felt at ease. He was non-threatening. Females did not automatically have their guard up, knowing that McFluff preferred dick to pussy any day of the week, the male round-eye to tits. And yet, he had many women friends. They enjoyed his company, liked socializing with Fluffy, their great pal, brother confessor. Part of it was kissing up; they did this, brown-nosing big time, which (occasionally) resulted in landing major parts in important pictures. Schmoozing. He, Ben T. Styles, had never been very good at it. He was a straight shooter, and it hurt him. He'd been told this time and time again: *You tell it like it is, Ben, and some people are put off by it. Offended. Do it, instead, like every other schmuck in this town: Run them down, bad-mouth them when they're not looking; do it behind their back. Don't stare them in the face when you tell them they suck.*

Plenty in the business called McFluff a miracle worker, a genius. Ben wasn't disagreeing with this assessment of the filmmaker. In truth, he was that, and more. I've always said it. Talent can't be denied. Only then, why was he himself denied? Why was Ben Styles deprived? Look, you're IN for now. A part in a Reggie Edward McFluff production meant instant prestige. Raised people's brows. McFluff had followers. His fans were legion. He was one of those the average person on the street, moviegoers, were aware of the minute a McFluff picture opened. Even if the film eventually did not go on to be a top-grosser, his opening weekends were always impressive enough to keep McFluff landing strong financing from the studios.

Yeah, thought Ben, it could mean Oscar time for him with this Fitch role. One never knew.

He walked over to take a closer look at the labels on the booze bottles and shook his head with a grin: the real deal, down to the minutest detail. How did they do it? He loved it. Stood there admiring the work of the art department, art director, all that the prop people did, as well as the carpenters and others. Movie magic. It was times like this that he loved being part of it, in Hollywood. The greatest dream factory in the world. There was nothing like it, he thought, and was completely unaware of McFluff standing outside the saloon's swinging doors.

Benjamin Styles walked to a table and sat down. The need for a drink was not there this time. He opened the screenplay to the fourth page and began to read aloud. Fitch interested him, a man's man who did not take any shit. A well-respected individual who was easy to respect by not only those who knew him but total strangers. All one had to do was look at Mr. Fitch and you knew right away this was a bad *hombre* not to be trifled with. Those who did paid dearly. It was the way of the West. Law of the Land. Hard life, harder ways. You did what you had to to survive.

He read on. Fitch was in charge of a big-time cattle-rustling outfit. He'd had so much taken from him over the years—by Indians, and others, his family murdered—that he decided to take it back, and then some—from any source, didn't matter. If people balked, they disappeared. And his ranch and outfit expanded fast. Fitch was reaching his goals a lot sooner than expected. He would take over the city and try for mayor. Go legit, turn law-abiding. The Earps did it, why not him? You made your bones any way that you could to get ahead, and then you became respectable and did it the honorable way—on the surface. Look at the Kennedys. Lookit what Joe Kennedy did during

Prohibition. And he was not the only one. Corruption was the American way. You went after the brass ring any way you knew how. If you didn't, you ended up like Benjy Styles, struggling, a Ham-and-Egger. On the lower rung of society. Scrambling for crumbs, leftovers. A food-stamp case. Fuck that. This was why he appreciated Leo Walter Fitch. Scoundrel extraordinaire.

Fitch definitely had his own way of doing things. He would shower the people of Dodge with love and kindness: improve roads, build a new church, school, and a new hospital. He would provide law and order. Bring in doctors, dentists, schoolmarms, plumbers, architects, men of learning, the type of individuals who could promote as well as make growth possible, and . . . Leo Fitch would put Dodge City on the map!

However, only one man stood in his way: a lawman by the name of Clancy Yates. Clearly modeled after Wyatt Earp. Yates was out to stop this wolf in sheep's clothing. He wanted Leo Fitch arrested, tried, hung, and put under the ground, where all good-for-nothing opportunists like him belonged. Why did Earp have so much loathing for him? Because he had been just like him once, and he hated seeing a mirror image of himself repeating his ugliness and all the terrible and underhanded tactics he had committed once himself to advance and satiate his appetite for money and power.

❧

Not bad, for a Western, Benjamin Styles thought. Not entirely original, but if done right it could work, draw audiences. No scrimping on the budget, no cutting back on character development. And if allowed, he could work and improve the script itself. Do some fine-tuning here and there. Nothing major. Just a touch here and there. He loved the damn part, was thrilled at having been given the opportunity to show what he was capable of. Damn right. And on top of everything else, Reggie McFluff was directing.

Benjamin T. Styles sat back in his chair, fingers locked behind his head. He was pleased. Then he wondered who would be playing Clancy Yates? And would the son of bitch give him a hard time and try to steal the scenes he was in? It happened more often than the movie-going public was aware of; it happened too often. Actors were insecure psychotics, especially the ones near the top or at the very top; always in fear of being upstaged, or losing their fan base and therefore having to take less money, even lower billing. Who could it be? McFluff never said, never so much as hinted. Newman? Eastwood? Redford? McQueen? He'd appeared in significant roles with all of them.

Eddie McFluff's portly assistant walked up to the director. Eddie turned, and they left the entrance to the saloon.

"Something wrong, sir?"

Gaffers, makeup people, the script girl and her assistant, grips, two more of the director's assistants, the cinematographer and his cameraman, their underlings, the soundman and his Man Friday, and others, many others, one by one arrived on the set, moving about, coffee and doughnut in hand, sleepy-eyed. It was eight o'clock.

Mr. McFluff did a hand wave in his First Assistant Director's direction, and the First AD barked orders to have the camera set up in front of the saloon, and he wanted it done pronto. No slagging, no ass-dragging. *Time was money.* "I don't give a fuck that it's Monday morning," he shouted into the megaphone. "I want that goddamned crane positioned and ready to go by the time Mr. McFluff is done with his coffee and bagel!"

R. Edward McFluff gestured to his First AD, Sheldon Smedley, to get over to where he sat in his director's chair.

"Now, Mr. Smedley, there's no need for that. Crews who work on my pictures know what's required of them. Let us try lowering our tone and using a more civilized method of communication, shall we?"

The First AD nodded, and from then on resorted to a calmer approach, sans cursing and shouting and berating. It was nothing more than their version of good guy/bad guy. Did it every time. Showed all those involved what a nice man Eddie McFluff was, how much respect he had for his crews. His First AD also loved his role in the process. The fact that he was extremely well paid did not hurt one damn bit. And Edward McFluff hurried to his trailer, with the fifty-year-old Sheldon Smedley, built like a human barrel, close on his heels. Farting as he walked. Non-stop. The rudeness.

"I have to be alone for a minute, Mr. Smelly. Pardon me, Smedley," corrected McFluff, pausing at the door to his trailer. "I'd like to take a dump in private, with your permission, of course, sir?" Went in and slammed the door shut in the AD's face. The assistant director said "Yessir, Mr. McFluff." Returned to where the camera was being set up to supervise the mounting of the crane and rest of the equipment.

Inside the trailer, the director rushed past movie props and relatively cramped quarters to reach the loo in back.

"Christ," Edward McFluff said, as he pulled his pecker out to tap a kidney. "Can't even visit the loo to take a whizz without the curious turd wanting to tag along. He waited a moment, but nothing was happening. He could feel perspiration gathering across his brow.

"Lordy!" he screamed. "For the love of Baroness Thatcher! For Margaret Hilda, the Iron Lady's sake!" The pain in his penis sent him gasping in agony. "Oh Lordy," Reginald Edward McFluff wailed and collapsed against the door. "For dear Maggie Thatcher's sake, I say!" He cried the great lady's name, whom he secretly loved and admired. Same birth place: Grantham; but this was not all they had in common. She stood by her guns, principles. Some in Hollywood, those jealous of him, would say he had none. Fine filmmaker, but runs around like a hound, a dick hound. Some men were pussy hounds. McFluff was a male *culo* hound. Did that discount his work ethic and the absolute attention he paid to detail? Did this cancel out his morals, simply because he enjoyed having a full and varied sex life? Some, rather many, would say yes. Reggie McFluff is a low-life. Wouldn't know a moral if he gagged on one.

Is that so? Why, then, was he able to relate to one Maggie Thatcher? Why did he admire and love her so? He kept it to himself, always would. Hollywood was full of misguided liberals. Imagine him, Edward McFluff, having conservative values. Imagine that! A film director, a gay one, as queer as a nine-dollar bill, able to relate to Maggie Thatcher's conservative approach to doing things!

Only his mind was not on Maggie, Dear Maggie; it was not she who had left him with this malady, but the other female in his life: the ding-a-ling from Oklahoma. Angela Bliss had given him the clap. A clean-looking bird like that had given him the fucking social disease! He couldn't begin to fathom the audacity and carelessness. Goddamn it. Not only did he not wish to believe it, but he absolutely refused to accept it.

How could she? He'd spent his life being conscientious when it came to his romantic interludes, cautious and vigilant. And now he had it. The clap. And Angela Bliss, the bird who engaged in golden showers and swallowed piss for money, had passed it on to him! How could she?

"Damn her!" he shouted. "Damn that hussy!"

Smedley could be heard outside pounding on his trailer door, calling his name.

"Mr. McFluff, sir?"

Eddie McFluff needed to compose himself. It required some doing. He managed to step out of the loo and make it to the door. Unlocked it and cracked it open.

"Something wrong, guv?" Smedley inquired in a hushed tone.

"Goddamn right something is wrong!" Edward McFluff said. "That bitch is wrong!"

His First AD reacted with a look that said: *I don't understand.*

"She's all wrong for the part! Fire her!"

"Fire who, sir? We have many 'bitches' involved on this production. Which bitch are we specifically discussing, guv, sir?"

"The Bliss bitch! Angela!"

"Right now?"

"Shit-can the wench, Sheldon!" McFluff insisted. "Now!"

"Of course, guv," Smedley said meekly, and walked the distance to Angela Bliss' trailer, knocked and entered, to see where she was in costume for the part of a saloon girl. She was being primped by her gay makeup man and hair stylist, a thin Valentino-look-alike of Hispanic extraction by the name of Flaco Pujadas, whom she was testing out various deliveries of her lines with. Flaco did not speak, merely would nod and smile when he heard a version he favored.

"Pardon me, Ms. Bliss," interrupted the First AD, and broke the bad news to her. The welling of tears in her eyes was instant. She shoved Smedley out of the way, and ran out of the trailer to have it out with Eddie McFluff, the ruthless director who had nerve to pull something chickenshit like this after all she had done to provide him with the best she was able in the bedroom, and made it possible for him to experience the wildest times and orgasms he'd ever known in his miserable fag life. Ungrateful ass-hat. Only Angela Bliss had been too late, because Edward McFluff was already in his Mercedes and speeding off the studio lot.

❧

Later, when Smedley discovered the note in his boss's trailer he knew that the director had gone to see his personal physician. Something to do with a nagging headache. His instructions were to carry on until his return.

Smedley looked up, taking in Angela Bliss as she sat on McFluff's sofa, crying her eyes out. She seemed in such agony. Wished there was something he could do to help out. Only Reg called the shots. There was no way to go over his head. Could he talk to Reggie about this? Find out what it was that caused this woman to be terminated like that?

"Mr. McFluff won't be long," Smedley said. "I am sure it can be straightened out, whatever it is. You ought to talk to him when he gets back."

"What good would it do?" Angela said. "He doesn't care. I don't think he likes women. He knows how much this means to me. I have bent over backwards to make him happy, to keep him satisfied in every way possible. You have no idea the lengths I have gone to to please him. I have done things for that man that I never dreamed of doing for anyone; have never done for other men or women that I have known. I am saying some of these things were not pretty to see, either. There are women, hookers, call girls, who refuse to have anything to do with him and his disgusting bedroom antics. The man is a certified pervert, a degenerate. Marquis de Sade had nothing on Reggie McFluff! Nothing. De Sade was an amateur compared to the man you work for! Hear that?"

Smedley nodded his head.

"It's a living; he said. "His pictures make money, fill theater seats."

"That's all that counts," she said. "And you get away with every degeneracy! I loathe this place! I hate, hate Hollywood! I wish I'd never heard of it! It's ugly. The people are ugly. Nothing but parasites," she said. "Parasites!" She wept quietly.

"What about Tubesteak?" asked Smedley. "Do you feel that way about Tubesteak?"

She wiped her eyes with a tissue. Looked up.

"That hustler; what's his name? Jimmy something: James Kidd.

Tubesteak. The two-bit hustler?"

"Two-bit? There's nothing two-bit about Jimmy," she said. "He's genuine. He gives a damn! He's not a user like everyone else in this toilet! He's one of the few people that I have met that I like and have respect for. He didn't fuck me and then roll off! He was affectionate. It means a lot to a woman, to be treated like a human being."

Smedley nodded. "I only meant . . ." his words trailed off. Handed her the box of tissues. She yanked out a handful, blew her nose. Wiped her eyes and face.

The First AD sat on the sofa beside her. He wanted to show her the note.

"Look," he said, indicating the piece of paper in his hand. "He'll be back shortly. He left this, so I know he'll be back. People are waiting; crew is setting up. When he gets back maybe we can talk it over with him. Sure, he's angry about something, but he never stays angry. He's not an angry gent by nature. In fact, he's even-tempered, the guv'nor is."

She was looking at him. "You're right about that: Eddie *is* even-tempered. I like that about him. He's far from my type; does not come close at all, but I appreciate his easygoing manner."

"Of course," said Smedley. "We all like that about him. One of the reasons stars line up to work with him."

Angela was nodding, agreeing, wanting to see things his way.

"Sure," Smedley paused. "I can pretty much tell them what to do for a while." He smiled and shook his head. "Although Mr. McFluff would never allow me to direct a picture all the way through. He never has. I do my share to help out, but take credit where credit is not earned? No."

She did some more rubbing of her eyes and studied the note. Suddenly she felt better. She managed a seductive smile for Smedley and sidled up to him.

"You're the only one who really understands, Sheldon," Angela Bliss said. "You're the only one. . . ." And she had a hand inside his inner thighs, rubbing gently, rubbing, back and forth, getting nearer his groin that stirred inside his trousers.

Not a Stitch On

"Come on, you guys," Sheldon Smedley begged via bullhorn. The rough-looking crew maintained their leisurely pace. "You're getting paid," Smedley implored. "You can do better than that."

The tempo, or lack of it, remained the same. It seemed to take them forever to wheel camera and rig inside and set it up. The DP took his sweet time, as did everyone else. Why hurry? Why bust your balls, when it was just another lousy oater. The picture will get made. What's the rush? So it runs over budget. Whose problem is that? So Fluffy will squawk. Let him. Screw the fag.

"Come on, guys," Mr. Smelly begged. "You can do a lot better than that."

Some of the crew members were snickering behind his back. They knew he had no power unless Reggie was around. Besides, they loved to watch Sheldon sweat, and he did drip sweat like a hog. And smelled like one. Hence: *Mr. Smelly*. Mr. Smelly was squirming. Wouldn't look good if nothing got done while "guv" was away.

"I'll be damned: Sheldon has himself convinced he's directing this piece of shit," a male voice groused. "Guaranteed to be a piece of shit so long as he continues to fuck with people." The crew cracked up, save for one perturbed Benjamin T. Styles and a farm girl from Oklahoma.

"Can't you do something about this, Mr. Styles?" Angela Bliss implored. "It's just impossible to work under these conditions."

Benjamin Styles' jaw clenched and he kept quiet. Angela Bliss grew more nervous by the second. Perspiration was forming across the top and within the cleavage of those impossible-to-miss breasts. I have to figure out a way to speed things up, she said to herself. The idea was to get as much footage of her scene 'in the can' as possible before Reggie got back. She was hoping it would keep McFluff from giving her the boot.

I have to show him what I can do, she thought. Prove that I'm needed. Movie wouldn't be the same without me. He'll see, she thought. Once the dailies come back and open up his eyes. I'll prove to him I'm good, and the only way to do that is to get these professional slackers to work.

"Mr. Styles," Angela Bliss said in her most seductive voice, "you can take that portrait of me. . . . In fact, as many as you like. . . ." Benjamin Styles looked at her. "If you can get these clowns to speed things up."

"When?"

"Now. Get them to move."

"When do we get down to the photography, is what I meant?" he said, all the while grinning like a wolf.

"Whenever you like."

"And you'll pose for me?"

"I said I would."

"I have some of my equipment in my trailer."

"I'll be waiting," said she, and headed in the direction of it.

Benjamin Styles walked over to one defeated Sheldon Smedley seated in the director's canvas chair.

"How long before they get this one ready to roll, Sheldon?"

Sheldon Smedley yanked out a soaking handkerchief and wiped his brow and neck. The portion of his shirt over his gut was wet, as were his pants in and around the crotch region, and in the crack between the oversized buttocks.

He shook his head desperately. "Hour, maybe two. Slowest crew I've ever seen. Three hours gone and we got hardly anything done. It's a shame, Mr. Styles," Sheldon Smedley groaned. "Pure shame."

"Can't lose hope, Sheldon," Benjamin Styles said. "I'll be studying my lines."

"Wish someone would come in and take the whole mess off my hands, or else get them to pick it up before a suit shows," Shel Smedley said, as Ben T. Styles walked to his trailer, where Angela Bliss waited for him.

The Power of Pussy

Less than an hour later Benjamin Styles reappeared on set with a grin on his face and a hesitancy to his step. You'd think he had developed a touch of arthritis in the relatively short space of time he was gone. He reached for Shel Smedley's bullhorn, and said to the First AD: "Don't worry about a thing, Sheldon. Let a *real* producer handle this."

"One should never lose hope," Sheldon Smedley said, beaming, and sat up.

"Listen up, Goddammit!" Styles shouted into the bullhorn. "This thing had better be ready to go in exactly fifteen minutes or every one of you jerk-offs is gonna be waiting in the unemployment line. I make myself clear?"

Fifteen minutes later they were ready. Lights, camera, all in place: script girl, sound man, boom operator, and others. Something had nudged them wide-awake.

"A miracle," Smedley said. "Truly miraculous." Then to himself: "Funny thing is, they do all this for me so long as Reggie's around. They know he can shit-can them, and they don't want that. Nobody wants to get shit-canned."

Ben Styles had his lines down cold, as did Ms. Bliss.

❧

Fitch walks into the Long Branch Saloon and makes a pass at one of the barmaids, played by Angela Bliss. Even though she likes the big lug, she turns him down. Leo Fitch insists and, as always, gets what he wants.

The scene went over nicely. Crew and rest of cast stood applauding. Angela Bliss planted a moist, smacking kiss on Ben Styles' lips.

Benjamin Styles has arrived, Styles said to himself. After all these fucking years, I'm here, where I belong. Finally on my way. I'll win the Oscar; I'll be fucking good in this. I'll take this town by storm. Then an eerie quiet engulfed the scene until Benjamin Styles was the only one enjoying the heretofore moment. He looked up and saw the stocky figure of Robert Tanner, and hatred filled his eyes. The fucking coal miner from Philly; the Russian. Or was he Czech? Not that it made any difference.

"Shit," Benjamin Styles grumbled under his breath.

"Long time no see," the superstar said and grinned. Only it was not exactly a grin. Ben could never figure out the expression. It appeared to be closer to a half-grin, a partial grin, but always spelled the same thing: *Fuck you. You're beneath me, and always will be.*

Maan, did Benjamin Styles detest that self-satisfied look on Tanner's ugly mug. The undefinable expression was a constant reminder that he was a nobody; a lousy bit player. Even if in his own eyes he knew better. Tanner had a way of putting you down, of making you feel cheap and worthless without ever uttering a word. He would just look at you with those dirty-gray coal eyes of his and it was enough. Hey, you can take the coal miner out of the mines, but never the mines out of the coal miner.

He could never figure out how the Russian ever made it so big. He had the facial features of a caveman: greasy dark hair, a Fu Manchu stash he still seemed to have trouble growing at fifty-four.

He realized he'd never seen Tanner with a beard, and it dawned on him that the asshole probably couldn't grow one. Something having to do with his heritage. A mixed bag. Who knew?

Tanner was no more than 5ft. 8, and in the face he looked his age. About the only thing he had going was the rest of him. Robert Tanner had the fit body of a man a lot younger, rippling with sinewy muscle. Not as impressive as Jimmy, to be sure, but pretty damn close. The other thing that made him leery of Tanner was the fact he'd been a bare-knuckle brawler in his youth throughout Philly and the East Coast.

Fuck him, thought Benjamin Styles. I fought in the Golden Gloves. I can take him, if need be. Let him try some shit like he did before and we'll see who goes down. He'll punch the cocksucker in the balls, and then knock him out with a one-two combo to the neck and jaw. Damn right. In the Adam's apple. Balls and Adam's apple. Let him pull some crap.

Thinking of Jimmy reminded him: Why hadn't Nicky reported to him yet? Where was the peeper? Why did he ever get involved with the likes of him, anyway?

"How ya been, Bobby?" Benjamin Styles said. He tried, but was not able, to conjure up a smile, or grin, either. Nothing close. Fuck it. Why pretend to like the asshole?

"Getting seven figures for this one," Bobby Tanner said. "Plus a percentage." And he walked over to Sheldon Smedley. "What's going on, Sheldon? Where's Edward?"

"Mr. McFluff is at the doc's, Mr. Tanner."

"Get him on the phone," Robert Tanner said, and walked back to his pretty blond wife half his age, who held their four-year-old daughter in her arms. A concerned Shel Smedley was soon on the horn, dialing.

"The production's in chaos, a real mess," Robert Tanner said. "Could have stayed in Palm Springs another day."

"Where's Mr. McFluff?" his wife asked.

Robert Tanner shrugged and took his daughter in his arms and kissed her with all the love he had in his heart.

If Benjamin Styles hadn't seen it with his own eyes, he wouldn't have believed it. A prick like Tanner able to show that he gave a damn for someone other than himself. Any way you looked at it, Robert Tanner was considered a heavyweight in the business. Superstar. He created a major fuss everywhere he went. A sensation no matter what part of the planet he ventured off to. He was considered almost a god in Japan. They went for that look Tanner seemed to project: the cold stare, menacing features, strong jawline; every inch nothing but macho. Robert Tanner was one mean motherfucker; at least he wanted you to think that. And the Japanese loved him, as did all of Europe, and other parts of the world where movies played.

Here's what Ben T. Styles thought: Since he fit the bill perfectly, why the hell didn't *his* star shine as brightly? He had the same "don't fuck with me" attitude about him; was good with his fists; not bad-looking. Hell, he looked better than Tanner for sure. Hands down, I'm the better-looking one. The only reason more pussy flocks around Tanner these days is because he's better known. Maybe he didn't have the slim waistline anymore, but so what? That could easily be taken care of. A loose-fitting shirt, and presto: no more pot belly. A few weeks, a month or two at some fitness spa in Arizona, and he'd be as trim as he used to look when he fought in the ring.

So the hell was wrong?

Nothing, Benjamin Styles said to himself. Your time just hasn't come yet. But it will. It's just around the corner. Fitch is but a stepping stone, a start. New beginning. I'll be better than ten Robert Tanners put together. Just you watch.

It was funny, he thought, that whole fairytale about Tanner having grown up in a family of twelve in a coal-mining town of Pennsylvania. There had never been enough money to buy little Bobby shoes, or clothes; not even food. He'd had to wear hand-me-downs that never fit right. And they had stuck him to work in the coal mine when he was nine years old. Ben wondered how much of it was Hollywood hype?—the imagination of some clever PR type? They invented things, covered up your flaws and criminal past. If you were queer they fixed you up with a fake marriage and kept your name out of the papers. And no one was the wiser. Studios had investments to protect. Box office was God. Anything that might potentially hurt a star, or box-office take, stayed out of the papers.

Robert Tanner had been born to a part Czechoslovakian, part Cherokee Indian father, and a Mexican-American mother. Now that was funny, Benjamin Styles thought: a Chech-Mex. Sounded like a breakfast cereal. I'll have a bowl of *Chech-Mex* this morning, ma'am. Thank you. With low-fat milk and a banana. Cup of joe, toast with marmalade on the side, and butter. Chech-Mex. Some background.

The whole Tanner bio smacked of Hollywood hyperbole. Probably thought up by his ever-faithful manager, one Fuzzy Flake. His actual name, not the Fuzzy part, but the Flake part. His manager's actual name was Flake. Normal "Fuzzy" Flake. Now, if anyone ever needed a name change it had to be Fuzzy Flake. But this was Tinseltown, you understand? The Dream Factory. You accepted quite a bit.

However, in spite of what he thought, or wanted to believe regarding Tanner's childhood and background, Benjamin Styles had an iota that it might be true. But even if it were true, Robert Tanner was nothing but a prick. And he hated his guts for having black-balled him for so many years, even if indirectly, from being able to work on pictures Tanner was in. He wouldn't allow the same thing to happen on this picture. He would stay away from Tanner. He would keep to himself, do his part, maybe lay the farm girl now and then, and move on to the next production.

Yep, that was the plan.

He thought of Nicky Horgan again.

He thought of Jimmy Riff. To what extremes would he have to go to persuade him to see things his way?

❧

"I see, Mr. M.," Smedley said into the phone. "Yes sir, I'll tell him." And quietly lowered the receiver. He walked over to the Tanner family Rolls. The super star had his young daughter in stitches with his latest mugging shenanigans.

"Mr. Tanner," Smedley said, pausing, "Mr. McFluff suggested we call it a day. He won't be able to get back this afternoon. He wouldn't say what was the matter. Just having an off day. Not feeling well."

"No sweat, Sheldon," Tanner said. "I get paid whether we shoot a foot of film or not."

"Mr. McFluff also said he'd like to start at eight tomorrow morning."

The Tanners got into their greenback-green Rolls-Royce and drove off the studio lot. One concerned Benjamin T. Styles walked up.

"What was that about?"

"First call 8:00 a.m."

"We wrap?"

Sheldon Smedley nodded. "Afraid so."

"What's going on? Where's Reg?"

"Mr. McFluff is under the weather."

Maybe he's got the clap, Benjamin Styles thought, but didn't find it remotely amusing. What would it do to the production if the old pervert decided to stay away indefinitely?

❧

Benjamin Styles grabbed one of the bottles of booze and took Angela Bliss to the apartment with him. This time, after they balled, he shot portrait-type photos of her. Expended a roll of film, and even sketched her face. The sketches were hardly worthy, and he gave up on the idea.

"Who are you?"

Victoria Chantal sat in the dark in her living room staring at the rushing waves and ocean through the closed sliding glass doors. The house itself was quiet, too quiet. The tracks from last night's and this morning's tears were still there. She hadn't been able to eat anything. She had taken down all of her paintings and shipped them back home. Her suitcase, packed and ready to go, sat beside her on the sofa, about the only things she'd been able to do since her return. She had thought of leaving that morning and decided not to when it dawned on her how hasty a move that would have been.

❧

She refused to accept that Jimmy could do something like this, that he would hurt her this way. He wasn't like the others; he just wasn't. She had felt safe and secure with him. She trusted and believed in him like no one she ever trusted or believed in, before or since. She had felt whole in his presence, a woman.

He'll call. He cares too much not to. What he said about easily becoming tired of things—well, she reasoned, the other girls caused him to get tired of them. None of them probably ever really loved him. They probably just wanted him for his body and what he could do for them in bed. They used him. They never cared about him, how he felt about things, what he wanted out of life. They had essentially wanted sex.

❧

I love him so. . . . I love him more than anything in the whole world. I'll wait for his call. I won't leave. I don't care how long it takes. Then that familiar feeling in her gut made itself known. It surged upwards through her body. She fought, but she fought weakly, and the tears flowed anew. Big, powerful tears that could not be stopped, tears that eased some of the pain, tears that said: I love you, Jimmy darling. I need you to hold me in your arms again.

"Oh, Jimmy," she pleaded, "please come back to me. Jimmy, I need you. I need you, darling. It hurts, Jimmy. . . . It hurts to be without you."

She grew weaker as the tears flowed, yet at the same time the pain seemed a little easier to bear, the burden a bit lighter. Victoria Chantal lay crumpled on the sofa, quietly weeping. The phone rang. She didn't get to pick up until the seventh or eighth ring.

"Honey?" the woman's voice came over the phone.

"Mom?"

"Victoria, honey, where have you been?" her mother asked. "I've been calling for the last two days. Is everything all right?"

Victoria took a second to compose herself.

"Sure, Mom. Everything is fine."

"Where have you been, darling? You had us worried."

"Oh, just out walking on the beach," Victoria said. She felt the feeling in her gut again, stomach cramps, and something additional, but this time she fought and won.

"Mom?"

"What is it, honey?"

"I met him."

"Who, honey?"

"I met him," Victoria said, "the most wonderful man. He's so nice, Mom. You'll really like him," she said, pausing. She was losing the fight. "You and Dad just have to meet him."

"What's his name, honey?"

"His name is James, Mom," Victoria said. "His name is James Grayson Riff." And she burst into tears.

"Honey," her mother said, "are you all right? Victoria? Why did you send your artwork back, hon? Are you not staying in California?"

"I'm all right, Mom."

"Honey, what's wrong? Honey?"

"It's nothing," Vicki said.

"Honey," Mrs. Vevrier said, "you're our only baby. You know how much we worry about you."

"I know he loves me, Mom. I know he does."

"What happened, sweetheart?"

"He's in trouble, Mom."

"What kind of trouble, sweetheart?"

"There are people after him," Vicki said. "Well, it's just one man, actually, but he's threatened to get others after Jimmy unless he does what he wants—"

"I don't understand, honey," her mother said. "Is he in some kind of trouble with the law?"

"No, Mom," Victoria said. "This man is after *Tubesteak*, I mean Jimmy, Mom."

"Why doesn't he contact the local authorities, honey?"

"It's not like that, Mom. Besides, it wouldn't do any good."

"That's what they get paid for, Victoria honey. Have him call the police."

"Mom, you don't understand. It wouldn't do any good. This man knows bad people—"

"You must come home, baby. You don't belong out there. Your father and I never cared for that part of the country. Northern California? Yes. But LA?"

"I don't mean Jimmy, Mom. This other man is in the mafia, possibly, or he knows people who are. He threatened to get them after Jimmy if Jimmy doesn't do what he tells him. He's hurt people before. I'm worried, Mom. They want to harm Jimmy."

"I just don't know what to say, honey. This is terrible."

"He's the nicest guy I've ever known, Mom."

"Come home, honey," her mother said. "Please, baby."

"They might kill him, Mom. I just don't know what to do."

"Let me speak to your young man, honey," her mother said.

"He's not here right now, Mom."

"Honey, come home."

"I will, Mom," Vicki said. "I don't want to leave right now, Mom. He needs my help."

"How can you help him, honey?" Mrs. Vevrier asked. "I don't understand—"

Suddenly the sliding glass door opened and a startled Victoria shot up from where she sat.

"Who are you?" she demanded to know of the intruder. "What do you want?"

"Private investigator," Nicky Horgan said. "I'd like to have a word with you."

"I have to go now, Mother," Victoria spoke into the receiver. "Say hello to Dad for me."

"Did someone just walk in, honey?" her mother asked, still on the line. "Who is it, honey? Honey?"

"I'll call you later, Mom," Victoria said, returning the receiver to its cradle, and did not hear as her mother said: "Your father and I are taking the next flight out. Honey? Honey?"

"I can help…"

Victoria stared at the thin and odd-looking character with the uneven mustache without saying anything.

"I apologize for barging in this way. I didn't mean to make you jump. It just seemed a lot easier than having to pick the front door lock."

"Or you could have rang the doorbell. That's what most people do."

"Some people don't answer their door."

"Maybe they don't feel like talking to strangers."

"Oh, I think you'll want to talk to this 'stranger.'"

"What's this about?"

"Just like to have a little chat with you, Ms. Vevrier."

"How do you know my name?"

"Like I said: I'm a private detective," Nicky Horgan said, drawing a business card; and while he did this, he also saw to it that her eyes caught the official-looking regulation handcuffs, the handgun. It carried weight. He was "official." No matter what Styles claimed about him.

"Nicky Horgan. I'm listed in the Hollywood phone book. May I sit down?"

"What do you want?"

"Chat."

"I'm in a hurry," Victoria said, indicating the packed suitcase. "As you can see. I have a plane to catch."

"Is that so?"

"I have to be at the airport in forty-five minutes."

"Is that so?"

"Are you hard of hearing or something?"

Nicky Horgan consulted his pocket watch. "It is now exactly one o'clock," Horgan said. "A.M."

Victoria Chantal walked in the kitchen and poured herself a glass of water to conceal her discomfort.

"I don't know of any flights leaving this time of night, Ms. Vevrier," Horgan said, "do you?"

"What is it you want?"

"Unless, of course, it's a private plane you'll be boarding."

"This entire conversation doesn't make any sense. Why don't you just make yourself scarce, mister? Leave the same way you broke into this house."

"Your folks got enough dough to buy one, don't they?"

"What?"

"Don't play dumb with me, girl."

"What are you talking about?"

"Did some research," Horgan said. "Richard 'Dick' Vevrier, the big kahuna of Wall Street." He paused, grinning. "One of the top movers and shakers in the world of high finance. Isn't that true, Ms. Vevrier? Isn't it?"

"Would you like me to call the police?"

"I wouldn't do that if I were you."

Victoria walked over to the phone, taking the receiver in hand. "If you're not out in two seconds, I'm calling the police!"

"Jimmy Riff," Horgan said. "Tubesteak. Name make any *sense* to you?"

"What about Jimmy?"

Nicky Horgan indicated with his pinky that she put the phone down, and only then did he continue.

"What about Jimmy?" she repeated impatiently.

"I can help him."

"What?"

"You heard right. I can help. But you need to tell me where he is."

"Did that man Styles send you here? Because if he did, I can tell you both where to go!"

"Calm down, young miss. This has nothing to do with Benjy Styles. I'm strictly on my own. Nicky Horgan don't need nobody like asshole Styles, if you'll excuse the expression. After all, that's what he is, isn't he? *Asshole?*"

"I wouldn't know."

"Didn't Tubesteak ever mention him?"

"All I know is that he's after Jimmy and won't leave him alone."

Nicky Horgan laughed. "That's Benjamin Styles, all right. Once he's got his hooks in you—forget it. He'll use you and keep using you—until he has no use for you. Ya get my meanin', Ms. Vevrier?"

"I've no idea where Jimmy is, if that's what you're after."

"You're lying."

"I don't care if you are a 'private investigator.' You could be the governor of the state; you could be the president—leave."

"So be it," Nicky Horgan said. "I suggest you take a look at these before you make any other wisecracks."

There was some sort of gigantic potted plant that sat on the floor on his left by the curtains. He reached inside his coat pocket and dropped an envelope with a stack of color five-by-eights in the dirt. He dug his hand into the soil, grinding it between his fingers, appreciating the texture.

"Good soil. Rich." He paused at the open glass door. "Nice and rich." And walked out onto the patio, and was gone.

Victoria picked up the photos and was appalled at what she saw: images of her and her man making love. Some of the pictures had been blown up and made to look gross and ugly. It turned her stomach. It was never that way with her and Jimmy. It was always so beautiful and giving when they had sex. She had never felt more alive than when she was in her man's arms and experiencing multiple orgasms. Never had she known anything that came close to making her feel this way. And this creepy man with his pictures had soiled and tainted all of it. This very second she knew she hated Horgan more than anyone she had ever hated in her whole life.

She slid the glass door closed, locked it. Stood there, leaning against it, trying to collect herself. But the fear was such that it gripped her entire being. Her stomach was in knots. She felt acute pain in the back of her neck and her head was aching. Tears and tension, worry, was the cause. A bitter taste rushed up from her stomach. She had attempted to clench her waist by pressing her folded arms against her belly, but it did no good. She would vomit any second. She hurried to the front door, opened it, and saw Horgan sitting in his station wagon, parked in her driveway and waiting. She slammed the front door shut and ran to the bathroom to throw up.

After a while she gathered enough strength to wash her face and rinse her mouth out. She gargled with mouthwash: once, twice, three times—and still did not feel it was enough. She felt dirty inside, so dirty and filthy and used up. The man had taken something that had been a wonderful and memorable experience, something natural and exquisite, to be cherished—and turned it into gutter images she wished would go away. Only she couldn't erase any of it. Men like that creep, and others of his kind who came from the gutter and were the gutter, took the sex act, which was about love and giving and a thrill to be appreciated and enjoyed, and turned it into something repulsive. Like that time a while back at that party in the Valley where she and Jimmy had met. The guy who had taken her there, a friend from back East, never letting on that there would be porn actors present and that they would be filming people in the act. And Jimmy? Had the same curve thrown at him. He'd traveled all the way from the Midwest by bus at the invitation of a girl he'd once been in love with, only to walk in on her smack-dab in the middle of an orgy that was being not only directed by her mother but videotaped by her as well. *This was why Jimmy had walked out on our relationship. Exactly why. It had to be.* She was guessing, but felt she had it figured. Scars. Fear of having his heart ripped apart again.

When you came down to it, it wasn't the sex act that was disgusting, it was they, certain people, who were disgusting, thoroughly disgusting and twisted and made the sex act appear that way. They screwed and used each other and left nothing but unhappiness in their wake and then had the temerity to go around wondering why they were miserable, taking drugs and drinking to drown all that misery, and it never worked. The only thing that worked, she knew it, deep down, from a young age, the only thing, was love. Heart connection. Being genuine with one another, soul mates, taking care, looking out. Was it too mature a take for someone so young? She didn't think so. It came down to logic and common sense.

No, there were no guarantees when it came to love. She'd had her own heart broken a couple of times; nothing as serious as the heartbreak she was trying to get through this time. All she knew was when love worked, the rare times it did, there was nothing better. Nothing was better than having that emotional connection, than being best friends with the one you were at one with. Nothing.

And sex? Sex was the icing on the cake. And it hardly felt like anything close to satisfying when love was missing from the equation. Not for her, anyway. And, she suspected and hoped, for Jimmy as well.

She dried her face, and returned to the living room where she had dropped the pictures. Some had landed facedown on the carpet. Most of the uglier ones had landed face up, and she turned her head away. Walked to a window in front, parted the curtain. The station wagon was gone.

"Leave us alone"

Vicki had never been much of a coffee drinker. However, this night she had consumed cup after cup. She wanted to stay up. Nerves kept her from giving in to her body's need for rest. She would not allow herself to go to sleep. She would never sleep.

She paced the room and drank coffee. He would surely want to talk to her. She was in pain and knew that Jimmy had to feel the same way. He'll call, she said to herself. It's just a matter of time. She had to stay up. There was a deep need to hear the sound of his voice. The night wore on.

The phone remained mute. The coffee eventually lost its effect, and Victoria succumbed to her body's needs. She slept. When the telephone finally rang, it was Benjamin Styles.

"Put the kid on."

"He's not here," a half-awake Victoria Vevrier said.

"Where is he?"

"What?"

"This is Benjamin Styles, goddammit! I wanna know where *Tubesteak* is! I gotta talk to him!"

"Jesus Christ!" Vicki screamed. "Why don't you leave him alone! Just leave him alone!"

"This has nothing to do with you, little girl. Me an' Jimmy gotta talk business."

"Leave him be—please."

"Like I said: got nothing to do with you."

"Please?"

"It's six o'clock right now," Benjamin Styles said, pausing. "I should be ready for another cup of java in thirty minutes. I don't hear from Tubesteak by then, he's in deep shit. You tell him that."

"YOU GO TO HELL!" Vicki screamed at the top of her voice. "Do you hear? You go to hell." Then: "Don't you see what you're doing to him? Don't you see? You've turned his life upside down for no reason at all. You're hurting my man. . . . You're hurting this person that I love so much. . . . Leave us be, please," she begged.

She didn't hear the click at the other end. Styles had hung up. "Leave us alone. Please don't hurt Jimmy. Please, Mr. Styles, don't hurt him. . . ."

Considering Extremes

The City of Dodge. The Lone Cowboy was back. Screenplay in hand, he strolled the deserted streets. There is no denying it, no ignoring it, no phasing it out. The girl's pleading had left its indelible mark. Would he succumb to it?

Hell, no!

She don't know what's going on. It has nothing to do with her. Give up on Tubesteak and all is lost forever. When the time came, he wouldn't get more than a couple of lines in the obit section of the *Hollywood Reporter*:

Benjamin Styles
Bit player. Dead.

They wouldn't give him more than that. Year of birth; year of death. Space is expensive, you understand. You want more space? You have to pay. Run a big ad announcing your death, mister. Go out in Style.

She's got another think coming, he said to himself, if she thinks I'm gonna let it happen. A fucking co-starring role in a Reggie McFluff production! I've been waiting for it all my life! All my otherwise task-after-task shitty life! The name Styles will be bigger than Lawrence Olivier, than Marlon Brando, than Humphrey Bogart, than James Cagney, than Paul Muni, than Clark Gable, than Burt Lancaster, than Kirk Douglas, than Gregory Peck, than James Dean, than Frank Sinatra, than Dustin Hoffman, than John Voight, than Steve McQueen, than Charley Bronson, than Clint Eastwood, than Robert Redford, than Paul Newman, than Duke Wayne, than—*than any of 'em*. THAN ALL OF THEM PUT TOGETHER!

"And the winner is: Benjamin Styles!"

Lights. Glitter. Applause. Fans. Autographs. Limousines. Famous names. Famous faces. Pearl necklaces and diamond rings. Tuxes. Best perfumes money can buy. Expensive cologne. Bow ties. Cummerbunds. Low-cut gowns. Broads. Lots of good-looking broads. Thousands of smiling faces. The Statuette. The headlines would scream out: STYLES WINS OSCAR!

BENJAMIN STYLES BEST ACTOR!

BENJAMIN STYLES FAVORITE!

STYLES: UNDERDOG WINNER!

BENJAMIN STYLES TOP MALE STAR!

If he were to get soft now, none of it would ever become reality. The dream of a lifetime would remain as such, of no value, of no validity; lacking any meaning or purpose. For to go on dreaming without that key element would be stupid and torturous and an exercise in futility.

❧

He looked at his watch. Tubesteak's thirty minutes were up. Benjamin Styles' name wasn't being paged. No one came running up to him announcing there was a call for him. No one said: *Mr. Styles, there is a James Kidd on the phone.* No one said anything of the sort. He would be forced to pursue those extremes after all. Benjamin Styles' temples ached.

⌘

At the far end of the street, the set builders were erecting a sign atop the jailhouse roof. Benjamin Styles eyed the compact brick structure, the single tiny window, the steel bars. This was where Fitch would spend his remaining days. Next to the jailhouse, the carpenters continued to pound away the finishing touches to the gallows. And there, Fitch would utter his final words to the conflicted crowd: "I did it all for you good people." Then someone would pull the rope that in turn would release a hatch, that in turn would send Fitch to his Maker, that in turn would move those in attendance to tears.

A better, more emotion-packed scene had never been written, Benjamin Styles concluded. Better than that: it was critic-proof. A scene, and others like it, likely to move moviegoers the world over.

⌘

Where was Nicky Horgan? Why hadn't the Ben Turpin look-alike called? If Tubesteak wasn't in Malibu, where the hell was he, then? He smiled to himself. The girl had lied to him. Jimmy wouldn't have left her like that. By herself. What had she said? Why don't you people leave us alone?

People? What people?

"Mr. Styles?" Sheldon Smedley said, running up to him.

"Morning, Sheldon."

"Good morning, Mr. Styles," Smedley said. "You're wanted on the phone, sir."

⌘

"'Bout time, Kidd," Benjamin Styles blared into the receiver.

"Good morning, Ben," the man's voice said. "Artie Gross."

"Sorry, Artie," Benjamin Styles said. "I was expecting a call."

"How have you been, Ben?" Artie Gross said.

"Terrific," Benjamin Styles said. "Just terrific. Most interesting part I've had in years."

"Good to hear, Benjamin," Artie Gross said. "How's Fluffy treating you?"

"McFluff? He's great, as usual."

"Been looking at this screenplay, Ben," Artie Gross said, pausing. "There's a part you'd be perfect for. Beautiful character role."

"Sounds interesting, Artie," Benjamin Styles said. "When can I see a script?"

"Right away," Artie Gross said. "I'll have someone bring you a copy." Artie Gross hesitated. "You know something else, Benjamin?"

"What's that?"

"Have a real nice bit part, too, Jimmy, your protégé would be exactly right for."

Benjamin T. Styles covered the mouthpiece and laughed.

"Two or three lines," Artie Gross continued without skipping a beat. "Nice part. Like to read him first. That is if it's okay with you, Benjamin. After all, he's a newcomer. I am sure he'll do all right."

"James Kidd's a natural," Benjamin Styles said, after he'd stopped laughing.

"So I hear," Artie Gross said. "I'd like to read him soon as possible."

"A deal," Ben Styles said. "Nice to hear from you again, Artie. Talk to you later."

～∞～

No sooner did Benjamin Styles hang up the receiver, when the phone rang again. Again, it was for Benjamin T. Styles.

"Speaking."

Winifred Gale Sacks was on at the other end. She wanted to know if he was interested in signing up with her agency. Sacks Talent World-Wide was one of the top agencies in the business.

"I don't have to tell you," Winifred Gale Sacks said, "that I represent the cream of the crop. . . . Speaking of cream," she said, "how's that young stud of yours doing?"

"He's not available at the moment," Benjamin Styles said. "Been rather busy lately."

"When you're hot you're hot."

"Something like that."

"I never told you this—" the woman said, "I always knew you had it in you, Benjamin."

"That so?"

"Believe me. Always felt you had the talent to make it big. If only given the right breaks, I knew you would reach the top. The very top, Benjamin. I would have taken you on years ago, but you know what it's like when you have partners. The shits didn't think you had a big enough name. It's ridiculous. But then again, that's the Hollywood game for you."

"Tell me about it."

"If you're interested, you know where I can be reached."

"Let me sleep on it," Benjamin Styles said.

"Bring Kidd around," she said. "Just dying to meet him."

I bet you are, Benjamin Styles thought. I just bet you are. Everybody in town's just dying to meet the Kidd. And they will, he said to himself. Under my terms.

"Looks like they're ready for me," Benjamin Styles lied. "I gotta run. Call me."

"How does later today sound?"

"In about a week."

"Fine, Benjamin," she said. "In a week, then."

He lit a cigarillo and smiled. He couldn't get over it. Suddenly everybody wants Benjamin Styles. Everybody needs Benjamin Styles. Everybody knows Benjamin Styles had it all along.

It felt great to know you were wanted. He was on a natural high. Floating. It was heady stuff. He was proud of himself. He had finally nailed the rules of the game. The unwritten rules, unidentifiable rules no game book ever contained. Rules that varied from month to month, mouth to mouth. The rules to the Hollywood game. And, he, Benjamin Styles, was finally a participant. One of the players. He wanted to give out a whooping yell. This was what it felt like to be on top of the world.

"Seen Sheldon, Ben?" A rather perturbed Reggie McFluff rushed past with megaphone in hand.

"Like to have a word with you, Reg," Benjamin Styles said.

"Later, Ben," McFluff said, raising the megaphone to his mouth. "Sheldon Smelly," McFluff shouted, "where in the bloody 'ell are you?"

He rushed past a group of extras, past the gathering crew, searching the Western set. "The one finds Sheldon Smelly for me gets a *SAG card, speaking part!*"

No sooner had the director made the announcement, the extras scattered like so many scurrying ants to look for the First AD.

"Can we talk, Reggie?" Benjamin Styles said. "It's important."

"Please. Not now, Ben," McFluff said. "A speaking part," he repeated into the bullhorn. "Find the sweaty bugger." Then R. Edward McFluff's rage doubled when he saw Sheldon Smedley and Angela Bliss, hand in hand, emerge from one of the trailers.

"You conniving, smelly bugger!" McFluff screamed at his rattled AD. "You ungrateful turd!"

Sheldon Smedley froze in his tracks. Sweat poured from his face in buckets. He was too scared to so much as bat an eyelid.

"You should be scared, you duplicitous son of a bitch! You're through! You'll never fart in this town again! Never! You hear me?"

"Yes, sir, Guv'nor."

"Don't you dare 'Guv' me!"

"Yes, sir."

"What were my instructions before I left yesterday? What did I tell you?"

"Well, sir—"

"You're through! You're fired! Shit-canned!"

"Reg," Angela Bliss pleaded, "please, don't—"

"*You*—" McFluff turned, facing the blonde. *"Get off my set! Get off this lot!"*

"You don't understand, Eddie," Angela Bliss said. "It's not Sheldon's fault."

"Off the lot! The both of you! Now! I will personally see to it, 'Sweetie'—" McFluff pointed a finger at her, "that your pretty face never appears on a movie screen. Never! EVER!"

He pointed toward the stunned crew. "I want it ready in five."

He turned to the 2nd Assistant Director and indicated the defeated-looking extras. "Replace them. Every single one." And he stormed off to his trailer, unaware that Benjamin T. Styles had entered with him.

"Contemptuous little bugger," R. Edward McFluff grumbled, and poured himself a drink. "I walk into the screening room and what's the first thing I see on that big beautiful screen? A filthy hussy! Whore! The dailies ruined! Every single take! What's this world coming to? Can't trust anyone anymore! He's never done this to me! Never has he in the past gone against my orders! The cunt put him up to it, no doubt. Well, that's his tough luck. Should have got rid of the bird like I told him to."

"Didn't like the rushes, I take it," Benjamin Styles finally said.

"Damn right!" Edward McFluff said, and poured himself another drink.

"I'd take it easy with that stuff, Reggie. Got a big scene coming up today."

"Don't tell me what to do, Ben."

"Have it your way, Reggie."

"Thank you."

Fluffie downed the drink, and stuck his head out the trailer door. "Somebody get me my First AD. Somebody tell Mr. Smelly I want to see him." And he walked to his desk in back in search of a cigar. Not being able to find one, he wiped the top of his desk clean with a single sweep of his arm, knocking the stacks of scripts and books and pens and copies of various gay publications onto the carpet.

Benjamin Styles leaned in and offered him one of his own third-rate thin types. McFluff made the attempt to light it and got nowhere. A forced laugh surfaced. He held his arm out and watched it shake.

"See what the bloody bitch is doing to me?" R. Edward McFluff said. "Dirty cum-swapping wench."

"She was that bad?" Benjamin Styles said. "I swear I'd have never known."

A beat passed, and the director laughed again. After the nervousness had all but left him, he said: "She'd like to have my bollocks."

The remark made little sense to Benjamin Styles.

There was a knock on the door. McFluff gave the go-ahead to enter. It was Smedley.

"Sit down, Sheldon."

The AD found a place on the sofa.

"How long have you been with me?"

"Eighteen years," Sheldon Smedley said, almost too afraid to look up.

"Tell me," Edward McFluff paused, "how will you keep your raccoon fed now?" A perplexed look appeared on the AD's face.

"How will you pay Madame Alex for those out-call honeys of hers?"

"I'm sorry, Mr. McFluff," Sheldon Smedley said, on the verge of tears. "I should never have done it."

"Forget it, Sheldon," McFluff said, lighting the cigarillo.

"She, she—"

"I know, Sheldon," McFluff said, cutting him off. "Go see if Tanner's ready."

"Yes, sir," Sheldon Smedley said, shooting up from his place on the sofa. He paused in the doorway to say something.

"Get out of here, Sheldon, will you?"

Sheldon Smedley had a big smile on his face as he closed the door behind him. R. Edward McFluff looked at Benjamin Styles.

"It's not that she's bad, it's that she's not clean."

"Too 'used'-looking?"

McFluff grinned and shook his head. "Something like that."

"Fire the makeup guy, what's his name? Flaco? The sissy who looks like Valentino. Fire him instead. Wouldn't that make more sense?"

"Depends where you stand."

"You're not going to fire her, Reg?"

The director said nothing. He picked up his copy of the script and walked outside. Benjy stayed with him.

"You should have seen the crew yesterday when we shot the scenes; went crazy. Stuff was that good. I know I haven't seen the dailies—you can't just scrap it all. The footy is too good to throw away like that."

"Ben," McFluff said, "I have a picture to make. We'll talk about it some other time. Besides, I already have a replacement for her."

"Goddammit, Reggie, how can you do this to me?"

Then he spotted Robert Tanner walking in their direction and

Benjamin Styles remained behind, pretending to be immersed in the script. Only then did he remember the reason he had wanted to have that talk with McFluff. Why hadn't he been told Tanner was working on this picture?

Up and down, he thought. Your emotions are toyed with like a goddamn yo-yo, without any regard whatsoever. He had felt like a million bucks no more than fifteen minutes ago. Now he felt like shit again. Why destroy the dailies? It all seemed senseless. A waste. If I don't get a signed statement from the pervert specifying yesterday's dailies are included in the final print—no more Tubesteak for him.

"Release me, Ben"

It wasn't until after the vicious barroom brawl was shot that Tanner said something about Benjamin's missing front teeth. As ridiculous as it seemed, Benjamin Styles had forgotten all about it.

"What are you trying to do to me, Ben?" Edward McFluff shouted. "I knew there was something else wrong with the damn dailies!"

"Can I talk to you for a second, Eddie?"

"All that footage shot to 'ell!" McFluff went on.

"Can I tell you what happened?"

"Take five," McFluff said to Sheldon Smedley, and stormed off toward his trailer. Benjamin Styles followed in after him.

"What is the matter with you, Ben?" McFluff said, pouring himself a drink. "I don't understand you at all. Not at all."

"Would you let me explain? I can explain."

"You were begging me for a part—begging. You have a co-starring role in a Reginald McFluff production. *Co-starring role.* And you're fucking up something fierce! What in bloody 'ell are you trying to do to me?"

"Will you listen?"

"Why should I?" McFluff said. "Will it make up for the money you cost me? For the time we lost?"

"Sitting in here won't do us any good, either."

"This is I exactly why I didn't want you. You can come up with more ways and reasons to halt a production than any fifty actors put together!"

"You did me a favor. Thanks."

"Don't waste your breath. I had nothing to do with hiring you! I wouldn't hire you if you were the last thespian on earth!"

"Calm down, Reggie," Benjamin Styles said. "It's not good for the old ticker."

"Grossbard's the turd to blame for this," McFluff said, pouring another drink. "You drive me to drink. That's what you do to me. It's way too early to be downing shots like this. Only when you're on the set. I don't need the stress, Ben."

"Grossbard twisted your arm to give me the job?"

"Already behind schedule, thanks to you."

"You walked off the set with a headache yesterday. Paid your doctor a visit. What the word was, according to your boy Sheldon. You're blaming me for that?"

"The big turd said to hire you, so I did. Why the big turd wanted you for a part this crucial is beyond my comprehension." He paused. "He met Tubesteak yet?"

Styles shook his head.

"You sure?"

"I'm sure," Benjamin Styles said, but he wasn't. Something else Jimmy had done without consulting him first.

"That's it, I bet," McFluff said, then grinned. "Let's face it: Jimmy's irresistible."

Benjamin Styles grabbed the director by the lapels of his sports coat and yanked him toward him. "You're gonna hear what I got to say, you kinky bastard. Now, you knew I got bushwhacked by the

Nazi bitch and that crazy schmuck she's been running around with lately, 'cause I told you about it. And you knew about my dentures because I told you about that, too. So don't play '*bloody*' fucking games with me, Reggie. I don't like it." He squeezed and twisted the collar about the filmmaker's neck, practically choking him. McFluff's face was, in fact, turning a shade of crimson. "And I don't like being made a fool of in front of everybody. Do you understand?"

"Release me, Ben." McFluff wasn't asking, he was telling. Benjamin Styles looked at him a moment, then let go. The film director straightened his collar. Discovered a cigar in one of his breast pockets. Lit up. Had a few puffs.

"You don't like the way I do things, Mr. Styles? Leave. Simple as that. Full pay, of course. Just leave. You don't like working with Tanner, you don't like my scrapping the dailies, you don't like my firing that slut—then leave."

"There was no reason to fire her."

Edward McFluff walked to the door and paused. "You been shagging her?"

"What if I had?"

"I forgot: You were supposed to have her for a week. Our agreement."

"Why did you fire her, Reggie?"

McFluff glanced down at Benjamin's crotch and chuckled. "You'll soon find out," he said. "You sure will." He climbed down the stoop, where his AD stood, awaiting further instructions. "You will, too, Shel. You as well."

Benjamin Styles and Sheldon Smedley exchanged looks, wondering what McFluff was talking about. Then the director said: "As of now," looking at Benjamin Styles, "due to sudden revisions in the screenplay, this production is shutting down for a week." He continued on to his

Mercedes. Opened the door on the driver's side. Turned to give Benjamin yet another fixed stare: "I suggest you get your teeth fixed, Mr. Styles." And drove off.

❧

Ariane Dean, attired in the very same dress formerly worn by Angela Bliss, appeared from the same makeup trailer Angela Bliss once enjoyed spending so much time in.

"Ready or not," she said, "here I come."

Only no one was paying attention. Various crews were busy disassembling equipment: lights, sound, camera. The extras, as if in mourning, did a slow walk toward the building that housed wardrobe. Tanner and his family were happily driving off the lot. Sheldon Smedley and his two assistants were preoccupied tending to various details: security guards needed to be instructed to keep an eye not only on the booze and other valuable props in and around the saloon set, but that nothing, absolutely nothing should be moved. "Mr. McFluff is adamant about this."

Benjamin Twitchell Styles walked to his rental. He was not having a good day.

Getting Desperate

Ben T. Styles stopped at the first phone booth and dialed Horgan's home number. Nicky Jr. answered.

"Let me talk to your daddy."

"He's not here."

"Where'd he go?"

"Dad didn't say."

"When will he be back?"

"Said he'd be gone all day."

❧

He dialed another number. No answer. And drove out to the beach. The new Toyota had been left parked in the driveway. The Porsche was gone. He forced his way inside through the patio door. No one home. He opened the suitcase that had been left on the sofa. Woman's undergarments. Blouse, skirt. Makeup. Jeans. Gym sweats. There was a diary. Ben flipped through it. Read a passage here and there. Something about how much "J." meant to her; something about the author of the diary not being able to sleep or eat and thinks about nothing else day and night, but "wonderful" J. She is "thrilled" whenever he embraces her, and his kisses are "heavenly." *Every girl should be so lucky as to have someone as special as J. I have never been so happy. . . . He is kind and considerate. . . . I trust him completely. . . . I would trust him with my life. . . .* Styles flipped through the thing, thinking: *this kid is naive.* There is no such thing as the kind of love she goes on and on about in her diary. He felt like chuckling. Shook his head. Love? Love never worked out for anyone. It was bullshit. Ramblings of a teenage girl obsessed with this idea she has about men. It was romanticized claptrap.

He stopped flipping. Read: *He is afraid . . . to give his heart. . . . I did my best to explain, to convince him that there is nothing to fear. . . . It is so painful. . . . My heart is breaking into a million pieces. I know he loves me . . . if only there were a way to convince him that it's our destiny to be together, to share life and be happy. . . .*

I have not been able to stop crying. . . . I know he is hurting just as much. . . . He has had lovers, many lovers. . . . It bothered me at first. . . . I have been able to accept this part of his life. . . . It happened before we met . . . and if circumstances push him in that direction . . . He is proud and refuses to accept "charity". . . . I have offered to help with money to the extent that I am able and have the means. . . . Should he be forced to sleep with . . . others . . . I will cope as best I can. . . . It will not be easy. It is so very painful. What matters (in the end) is that our hearts are united as one. Eventually, I truly believe this . . . he will be all mine . . . totally. I believe J. is monogamous at heart. Even if it turns out that I am wrong about this part of it . . . I know the others mean nothing to him. I do not want anyone else; I will never want anyone else. He satisfies me in every way. He is my Dream Man; my lover, my soul mate. . . . It is J., or no one.

He was about to close "Dear Diary," when a particular passage struck him, having to do with why there was a "temporary parting" between the great lovers. *Mr. Benjamin Styles has friends in the criminal underworld and has threatened J.'s life if he does not do as he says. This*

*man B. Styles used to hurt people for a living on the East Coast years ago
and knows/associates w/ criminal types who have "done things". . . .*

Ben Styles lifted his head and came close to laughing out loud. *If I
had powerful friends in the "criminal underworld" I sure as shit
wouldn't be in the shape I'm in, would I, little girl? I sure wouldn't
need your boyfriend to get my foot (back) in the door, would I, dumb
young twat? People who have mobsters for pals don't lead a hand-to-
mouth existence.*

He thought about it, and it pissed him off. His "associates," people
he once knew back East, wanted nothing to do with him. He was
persona non grata. End of fantasy.

❧

Styles shut the girl's book. Said "shit" to himself. "Dumb as dirt. . . ."
He'd been in relationships himself. There had been women in his life
who had professed the same kind of devotion . . . only to find himself
served with divorce papers, or worse: catching the bitches in bed with
others. He'd had to kick some butt those times, too. The assholes as
well as the bitches who'd betrayed him.

Love? Why waste time? Never works. Get yourself a steady piece of
ass lined up, arrange it so you can get laid on a regular basis. Now that
made perfect sense. Love? Forget it. If anything, he felt sorry for the
girl. She was being set up for a rude awakening, especially with a hustler
like Tubesteak. How do you think he got his name? Selling wieners?
Idiot broad. They all were. *He's using you.* Bottom line. That's why I
say: Use the motherfucker first. That's how that con is played. Use the
user, before he gets a chance to fuck you over. There was nothing
special about him at all. Just another clown with a big dick. In fact,
lower than most. He fucks for money. Even I won't stoop that low. I'll

fuck a broad because I'm genuinely interested, and money never enters the equation. No amount of money could make me bang a broad I didn't want to bang. And as far as going down on a doll? Forget it. ATM, ass-to-mouth? Forget that, too. As far as spankings and tying them up went? Not my style. That's for perverts like Lisa Koch and Fluffy and that butler of his, Quilp. Roddy Quilp. Fruitcakes. Degenerates. He liked his sex straight up. Nothing sick and twisted that so many Hollywood perverts were into.

He tossed the diary back in the suitcase. Unfastened the ID tag from the handle. There it was: artsy-fartsy business card with Victoria Vevrier's name and Connecticut address visible through the see-through window. He propped his feet up on the coffee table, picked up the phone and dialed Horgan's number again, and got the same response.

He held the ID tag in his right hand, while whacking the end of it against the palm of his left. Repeatedly. Which way do you turn? Jimmy's skipped town. What now? Call the Anthony Brothers? Later. He wondered if beating hell out of Horgan would make him more punctual? Maybe Jimmy and this young Victoria piece of ass just stepped out and would be coming back? He would wait.

He picked up the phone again.

"Sorry, Benjamin," Ariane Dean said. "Got plans. Can't make it."

See? There's "love" for you. He dialed his home phone and got to listen to his own voice: "This is the residence of Benjamin Styles, motion picture writer, producer, actor. . . . I'm not in at the moment, but if you would be so kind to take the time to leave your name and number . . ." blah blah blah.

Fuck. So Angela Bliss had left. He dialed his service: Artie Gross, Ira

Cohen, Sacks, and others, had all left messages for him to call. James Kidd, aka Tubesteak, was in demand more than ever. *Lisa Koch* had left a message, too.

He took the Saturday night special out and wiped it down with loving care and patience. Benjamin Styles wondered what would happen if he and Scarface had another confrontation?

Coast Highway

To spare the Porsche the unnecessary wear and tear and the mileage the odometer would have suffered during the long drive up the Coast Highway, she had opted to rent the Mustang at a car rental agency at LAX instead, where she had left her own car. Should she opt to fly back, the Porsche would be waiting there for her. She was halfway to Santa Barbara by now and had pretty much stuck to the speed limit. There was great tension in the area of the stomach, as well as the back of her neck and shoulders.

The speedometer needle quivered, reminding her she was doing close to twenty miles over the posted speed limit now.

She hadn't dared call the motel where she had last seen him from fear of spoiling a chance to meet face-to-face, be near him, to feel his hand against her cheek, his fingers on her lips. She had this image of squeezing his hand and placing the fingertips into her mouth and kissing them, taking turns, kissing each individual finger, the thumbs, then holding the palms against either side of her face, leaning in and kissing him softly on the lips, then again, harder, with intensity and unbridled need and craving . . . Letting him know how much she desired and lusted after his touch . . . Looking, gazing . . . deep into his eyes and saying: *I love you, my Lover Man; my forever and ever Lover Man. . . . I am yours and yours alone. . . . I need, nor want anyone else. . . . It's only you I adore. . . . Take me. . . . Take me, take me, take me. . . . Ravish me. . . . I want to be ravished by my Adonis. . . . Tubesteak . . . the sexiest man alive; my studly stud muffin. . . . Take me, darling . . . take me now. . . .*

Her body ached for the exquisite smell of her man's body, his golden muscles and tanned washboard abs. . . . She did not have to, but reached down to touch herself . . . to know she was moist. . . . It could not be helped. . . . This is what you do to me, darling. . . . This is the power you have over me. . . . She kept her hand there, unable or unwilling to remove it. She rubbed herself gently. I am lost, absolutely lost . . . and it feels like nothing else. . . . She was floating. . . . Did her best to ignore the fact that her entire region down there, her privates, tingled . . . and the sensation traveled up her spine as far as the base of her skull, overtook the base, then the rest of her brain, engulfing it completely.

She shivered. Her entire body flinched. Shaking and quivering. There was no fighting it. You don't even have to be near, Darling Lover, for me to experience the steady and continuing mini-explosions that take place whenever I think about the way it is when we make love. I am unable to do anything to stop it, nor would I want to.

She decided she better focus on the road, and her hand was back on the steering wheel.

Al Green's "Let's Stay Together" came on the radio. It was perfect. The lyrics of this song expressed exactly how she felt. That's what we should do next time we make love, Jimmy, play Al Green records. . . . She would want to mention it to him when she saw him. Jimmy was not aware of music, by his own admission, and she wondered if he had ever heard of Al Green? If not, she would educate him. All she'd have to do is put Mr. Green on . . . and the rest would take care of itself. She was sure he would love his music as much as she did.

She prayed Jimmy was still at the motel. The needle jumped again. She was doing better than twenty over the speed limit. Watch the lead foot. Highway seemed deserted. Poorly illuminated. She had both hands on the steering wheel, gripping the leather cover. Every now and then a pair of headlights would appear in her rear-view and she wondered if it was the station wagon. Was the private investigator following her?

She gave it more gas, then suddenly released the pedal entirely, allowing the car to catch up. As the VW Bug farted past, she gave a sigh of relief, floored the accelerator anew, and sped off into the night, entirely unaware of the two passengers in the other car.

A Knight With a Few Chinks in His Shining Armor

He crumpled the note he had written and tossed it in the wastebasket. It wouldn't be fair to let her see it. She was hurt enough. Why pursue something that could never be?

He needed her now, this very moment, that he knew. But so what? He would eventually tire of her. How can you be so sure? Look how many times it's happened in the past. Don't be an idiot. None of them were ever like her. No one ever came close. She's an angel. Restlessness set in. Jimmy Riff paced the room.

Why ruin her life? I did enough damage. I led her on. Me, Jimmy Riff, who hates playing games and those who play them with a vengeance, had played the game on her. I won her heart and promptly deserted her. No different from what Marcella Blevins put you through. Remember Marcella? How is it that you're any better? You're not. You're a louse, you bastard. *Hypocrite. You are one worthless effing individual.*

She loves you with every fiber of her being. She loves you completely, entirely, the way you are. She loves you, man. She doesn't care what you've done, where you've been. She asks no questions, seeks no explanations. It is unconditional. She doesn't want to change you.

The only thing she wants in this world is you. YOU. JUST YOU.

If I told her what went down with that Koch woman and Moritz Grossbard, twenty-four hours of non-stop perversion, would she still feel the same way? Would she still think of me as her "Knight in Shining Armor?" No way. How could she? How do you know? Man, even I couldn't take that scene much longer.

What if she doesn't so much as blink an eye? What if it makes no difference to her? What happens if I get tired of her and feel like balling other chicks? You don't know for certain it'll happen. When and if it does—deal with it then.

He finished his beer and crushed the can in his bare hand.

The money Grossbard had given him was all but gone. Like an idiot, he had gone out and bought that Toyota for Styles, hoping to free himself of the man; hoping. He had hoped for too much. Maybe he should have taken Lisa Koch's offer. She wanted to manage him. Exclusively.

"Benjamin Styles is no problem," she had said. "We got the big man in our corner." Meaning Grossbard. How a known and hated Nazi like her was able to pull that off was for sharper heads to figure out. He was certainly no expert when it came to understanding the ins-and-outs of the games these Hollywood people played with one another. "Besides, all that little shit Styles wants is to be a star. A role here and there and he's happy. And Grossbard can provide that. Morey owes me, darling," she had told Jimmy. "He'll take care of Benjy Styles. What do you say?"

Jimmy had turned her down flat. He hadn't even wanted to get back at her for what she had done to him that night. He had felt sorry for her in the end and merely wanted to wipe her from his mind completely. "Will you come again?" Morey had asked. "Who knows?" Jimmy had said with a shrug. Lisa Koch had taken him aside with a bit of advice: "Don't be a complete idiot. This is the best thing that could ever happen to you. Don't be a shit."

"This is a little too much for me," Jimmy had said.

"If he wants you again," she had said, pausing: "there's nothing you can do about it. Hollywood is just a front for organized crime. The so-called talent make the pictures certain behind-the-scenes entities tell them to make. Deals are made, deals only *they* want made."

⁂

He didn't know what to believe. Was it bull? Who knew? What he did know was that now he had two people to worry about. But if Styles was "connected," why couldn't he get somewhere before?

"'Cause he's a canker sore," Grossbard had told him. "You like this asshole? You really like him? All right," Grossbard had said. "He's got a big part. Fitch. One of the principals. Only doing it for you, Kidd. 'Cause I think you're all right. Unique, you might say. Unique I like," Grossbard had told him just before he went down on him. Just one of the many acts that took place that endless night.

"Now that's what I call a 'whopper,'" Grossbard's words echoed in his head.

⁂

He walked to the bus depot and bought a one-way ticket to San Francisco. He had enough money to live on for a week, maybe longer. He'd figure out later how to make it to Portland.

Elke, Betsy & Bill

Past midnight, as the Greyhound cut through the night toward Frisco like some silent and determined and single-minded demonic force. The handful of passengers were sound asleep, save for a couple of teen girls (one black, the other white with blond hair) necking several seats in front of him.

His mind was in a state of limbo; a kind of self-imposed insomnia plagued him. There was too much to think about, too many things to figure out. One never solved anything with sleep (except fatigue). And that was something he would ignore.

Jimmy would glance up now and then at the row of seats to the left of the aisle and the lesbian couple who by now were more than just petting. He could hear and even catch the occasional glimpse of the black girl's head bobbing up and down between the other one's thighs. The blonde had her right leg dangling over the arm rest, while tugging with both hands on the ball cap on her head, pulling it down hard over her ears. The black girl kept going to town and soon had her partner twisting her head every which way, causing her to keep yanking on her ball cap until she finally climaxed and tore the cap to shreds. There was a grunt and major quivering from the blonde, as the black girl continued to finish up, polishing the clit, working it non-stop.

The humor of what he just witnessed should have put a broad smile, or at least a grin, on Jimmy's face. Only it didn't. He was in a world of his own. He hated himself at times like this, when all purpose to his existence seemed to make little sense.

If a man didn't know where he was headed, if a man didn't have a defined goal, or even something close to one, a dream he wanted to make happen, if there was no purpose to his existence . . . What did he have?

He felt worthless, he felt shitty. It's times like this when nothing mattered much: not the exercise, not the sex, fresh air, green apples, or the beauty of plants. He was a plant lover. His entire life. Admired and respected plants. All types. Should have been a botanist. He appreciated bugs, animals, nature. Only the mood he was in presently none of that added up. And pretty girls? Pretty girls were nothing more than a reminder that nothing was ever lasting: not beauty, not anything. Pretty girls got old eventually, like pretty guys: their faces developed wrinkles; liver spots appeared on hands and elsewhere. The Miss Universe of today would end up like everyone else a few short years down the road: going the Botox route, or paying some plastic surgeon big bucks for nicks and tucks that wouldn't, in the end, do much good at all.

Sure, he knew, as endowed as he was, built as he was, he could pretty much have anything he wanted. Within reason, of course. Trouble was, and always had been, he never really knew what it was he was after. The thousands of push-ups and sit-ups, the thousands of miles he ran, even that seemed pointless at times. Futile. What was it for? Now and then he seemed to have an urge to own a chicken ranch, but he wasn't sure. He had spent many a summer working on a chicken ranch on the East Coast. Liked it. Especially the organic one up in Oregon that his Uncle Orville owned. Had

had ideas of his own regarding the raising of chickens. He wanted organic chickens himself. Organic was better: provided you with better-tasting eggs, and chicken meat. Allow the hens to roam freely, feed them properly. Take care of them. His uncle had given a damn about that and he'd learned a few things that had stayed with him. If he had that—would it fill the void? Provide a sense of purpose that he so lacked?

The fucking, he had felt, would make him a happy man. All that pussy, the endless parade of pussy most men could never get and only fantasized about, he got. The one guy so many envied, the head of the *Playboy* empire, Hef? Jimmy pitied. The guy seemed pathetic to him. The women he got, he got due to his wealth and means to put them in his magazine. He, Jimmy, never had to use a tactic like that. They were drawn to him like bees to honey. Without any effort on his part. Well, all but one. Marcella.

Truth be told, being a "chick magnet" bored him. Did nothing but left a gap in his center somewhere. Left him unfulfilled as a man and as a human being. There was more to him. Had to be.

Tell me what I need. Tell me what's missing in my life. He felt like asking someone, anyone. "What's the matter with me?" He dreaded these bouts of depression. For someone who was supposed to be easy going, up-beat, he felt he was spending too much time in the doldrums lately. It's a cycle, he reasoned. It comes around for its turn at bat, just like everything else. You're happy/you're not so happy. Then you hit the pits—blues. Deep down he knew why he felt this way but wasn't prepared to deal with it at the moment. He would have to confront it sooner or later, that much he knew, but not now. I'm the happy-go-lucky kid. The King with the Super Pecker. I'm not supposed to feel this way. Only guys with five inches (or less) are supposed to feel inadequate.

He hated dwelling on the past as much as he hated the current state his mind was in. Someone once said: Never look back. It (the past) might catch up. And Jimmy readily agreed. The past was to be left alone, especially when one's past consisted of so much unhappiness.

He had gone entirely against his father's wishes that he follow in his footsteps and become a preacher. *It's a good life,* he'd say. *You'll never go hungry so long as you know your Bible, son. You'd be doing good work, God's work. Lookit your brother Bill; see how well he's doing. Married, has a family, earns a good living. Never has to worry about going hungry. Provides; that's the key: He provides! Why, you can't even fend for yourself! You and your sisters! One takes her clothes off to earn her keep, the other's in some bug bin somewhere.* Yeah, only he'd left out one thing: He'd molested them both. A preacher did this. Their own father. That was what the fistfight between them had been about, that and his carousing being the reason his mother had committed suicide. Elke was out in Vegas stripping for a living, doing escorts on the side. Betsy was the one who was bipolar, in and out of bug bins on the East Coast. And Bill? Three kids, and number four on the way, meanwhile he was screwing anything in a skirt, just like good old Dad. Getting beaten up by irate husbands and boyfriends, knocking up women, some under age. But he was great at his job, just like Rev. Henry Riff. Had this amazing ability to raise money for any church he was the temp pastor of.

This was how and why they let him slide; elders protected him long enough for him to raise funds that were needed for this and the other: new hospital, daycare center, church steeple, playground. . . . Yes, they did good; but look at the damaged lives left in their wake. And this was what they had wanted for him? No thanks. I can't live like that.

He wondered how his sisters were doing, particularly Betsy. He had always been closest to Betsy, never having told her that he loved her. Why? Somehow brothers, some brothers, took their siblings for granted. He felt terrible for not writing her at the asylum to see how she was doing. She had always worshipped her brother Jimmy. She had never said it in so many words, but he knew, to her the perfect man, the kind of man she wished to be with some day would be like her brother Jimmy: thoughtful, happy-go-lucky, caring and kind, a gentle guy. Never mind that she'd probably never be released. Let her have her fantasy.

Sure, Jimmy thought. *I'm thoughtful. That's me. I care about one person, number one: Jimmy Riff. I'm a self-centered son of a bitch, Betsy. . . .*

He looked up, startled, as the lights on the bus flashed off and on, the bus driver signaling a fellow Greyhound driver headed in the opposite direction. He looked at the lesbian couple. Arm in arm, sound asleep. He turned to his right, staring through the windowpane, at the darkness that went on forever. His eyes welled. That's exactly why you don't look back, he reasoned; that's exactly why, kid.

Some Kid

Kid. . . .

"That's some kid," he whispered, and could not shut off the image of the small Presbyterian church he was seeing again in his mind's eye. A rundown brick structure on a street corner near a black ghetto in some town in the Midwest. Was it near Kansas Shitty? East St. Louis? Small town in Illinois somewhere. Could have been. They'd been to so many towns, chased out of so many places that it was difficult to keep track.

Thanks, Pastor Riff. That girl your son knocked up is seventeen years old. Virgin. Was. Deacon's daughter. She claimed to be nineteen. Had proof. Valid ID, and everything. When they looked at him without saying a word, he said: "You suggesting we should vacate the premises?"

"No, we're saying you should vacate the state."

"Will I be able to obtain a position elsewhere?"

"Unfortunately, yes. You do fine work, and you're good at it; if only your son had kept that thing in his pants, Reverend Riff."

"Temptation is a vicious, vicious demon. My wife and I work so hard to raise our kids the right way: with morals and a strong sense of decency; to be able to discern right from wrong. After all, the boy is considerably younger than her. Can hardly be considered an adult. The young lady is obviously much more experienced in these matters, and older, sir."

"You and your family have a week, Reverend."

"How about a letter of recommendation?"

He was handed an envelope. "Recommendation. With traveling funds."

"Thank you."

"Be gone. Please."

It was not so much as being chased off once again that irked Rev. Riff, but the reason behind it: his son had been laying that sweet tang for one entire month, while he, the Rev., hadn't been able to get near it. Oh, he'd tried, plied the deacon's daughter with gifts and treated her like a queen, but it was his son Jimmy who'd been getting it, not to mention how many others had been dipping their wick all along. And Jimmy knew, if the old man could have, he would have beaten him over it. Of course. The old man was furious, yelling at his wife: "Your son has disgraced us! Caught fornicating with the deacon's daughter! That sweet young Marcella tainted forever now! No decent man will want her! Knocked up! At her age!"

Jimmy's mother, half drunk, as usual, her way of dealing with her husband's philandering, took a quiet satisfaction in their troubles this time. "What's truly bothering you, Henry? That our son Jimmy 'deflowered' that beautiful girl before you'd had a chance to? Oh, for shame."

"That isn't it! Besides, he didn't deflower anyone; she'd been screwing long before we got here! High yellow slut has a rep—and they all know it! This is just an excuse to get rid of us! And her father? The Negro? Married to the white tramp? Deacon Blevins? Beaufort? He's a faggot! Certified! As queer as a three-dollar bill!"

"Of course that's the reason, Henry! Do you think we're blind? That I don't see what goes on? She'd been sitting in the front pew ever since we got here eight months ago, wearing the skimpiest outfits, crossing, and re-crossing her legs! Wearing revealing, low-cut tops, to showcase those large breasts!"

"Her breasts aren't *that* large."

"Large enough!"

"You fail to mention one simple and undeniable fact: she was always sitting next to our son! Somehow she always managed to be around him, near him; didn't matter if it was upstairs, or downstairs in the hall where he liked to tinker with that old piano. She was always there, buying him *Tootsie Rolls* and *Snickers* candy bars! What do you think she was after! *Prick-teaser!* And our son gets the blame! She seduces him, among other men there, many of them, and Jimmy is the one who gets crucified; well, clearly he'd been banging her long enough—but you get my meaning here! She comes on to him, romances him, and we have to vacate!"

"Face it, Henry: You're upset because our son got into her panties and you didn't. Mainly, that's it. The other reason is no different from why we were told to take a walk at all those other churches and towns: Your unscrupulous philandering and carrying on like a common mongrel!"

"*Common mongrel?* I'm accused of being a *common mongrel* now?"

"And let's not forget the dipping into church funds!"

"Why, I did no such thing—"

"Not this time. Not much. Because you got stopped before you could embezzle a serious-enough amount to get yourself arrested and thrown in jail."

His mother had been right, of course, more so than his father. The old man had had his share of knocking up married and otherwise-taken women; and he was pissed because it was, he, Jimmy, who had been doing Marcella. And then Marcella, as was her style, had dropped him like a bad habit and picked up with another member of the congregation, without so much as an explanation. And the embezzling? Had been there all along. This was how the wining and dining of those women had been possible. He'd gotten away with it for years.

"What's going on here?"

Never mind that the uproar over Marcella was bogus; never mind that Marcella's own father, Beaufort Blevins, had been offering Jimmy good money if he would only let him go down on him; never mind that a good third of the male congregants were either half queer or all-out homos and their marriages a sham. But what were you going to do? They had been chasing *him*, and not the other way around. Also, they had been after all sorts of other things, other than his consent to allow them to blow him, but Jimmy had had to put his foot down. The degenerates were clearly perverted. Some were swingers, some into BDSM, which had not interested him in the least; others were into taking it up the backside; pleaded with him to do it, implored him. Here, too, Jimmy refused. He wasn't queer and not about to do anything as nasty as fuck a man in the ass. There were those who wanted to plug *him* in the butt. No way, Jimmy had said. You're not doing that to me. Others still, had baited him with real money if he would only go satisfy "the bitch" they were married to, were tired of, and wouldn't go near. And Jimmy? Declined. Every time. Figured he was with Marcella. They were seeing each other, were they not? Until he and Marcella were busted by the no-nonsense cook in charge of the kitchen, one Willabelle Washington.

Church was upstairs, on the second floor, social hall on the ground floor, commonly referred to as "the basement." Had an old piano, tables, chairs; full service kitchen was in the back, where Henry, Jimmy's father, had gotten him a job as dishwasher. Anything to help the family out. He worked part-time, after school, on holidays and weekends. Wage was slightly above minimum. Willabelle, a stern-looking, tall black lady with some serious junk in her trunk was in charge of the kitchen. Sometimes her eighteen-year-old daughter Cheyenne would help out with preparing meals or serving, or else when Marcella, who was primarily the server, would help in this area: take orders, serve the food. She had just graduated high school, was deciding which college to go to, etc. Willabelle was divorced. She was a controlling, all-business type. She ran that kitchen like a drill sergeant. She and the daughter often fought. They'd argue because Cheyenne, when not serving the food and coffee, would be in the back alley smoking pot. The mother would have a fit over it. "Can't you be more like Marcella?" she'd say. "Or even Jimmy. Lookit that boy: clean cut. Don't do drugs; don't even drink."

"He's the preacher's son, Ma!" the daughter would yell back. "He's supposed to be *all that*: role model."

"Your brother don't fool with dope. Why can't you be more like him?"

"*Worm?*"

"You know that ain't his name," the mother would say. "Stop calling him that."

"Everybody calls him that, ma! *Wormy*! The reason he don't touch weed is because he's dealing!"

"You a lie, girl!"

"Ma, your own son is a pusher!"

"You can't mean Darius?"

"Yes, *Darius*, Ma!"

"He's a bicycle messenger! Delivers documents and such; Western Union telegrams and such! Affidavits and such! Delivers important court documents for that downtown law firm in Chicago! All on the up and up! Legal!"

"Dope; he delivers dope! On his bicycle! See the sneakers he's got on? One hundred-sixty bucks! Where would he get that kind of money delivering summonses? Weed, cocaine, heroin, pills! Where you think I got my pot from?"

And the mother, now infuriated, ran outside, where the two of them had a real knockdown, drag-out: mother and daughter. And Jimmy and Marcella? All over one another. This was a typical mid-morning lull, while the congregation upstairs listened to his father sermonize, doing his best to raise money for a new church the elders had decided to build in a "more appropriate" neighborhood. After weeks of letting Marcella buy him candy bars and suckers while he attempted to play the piano out there in the hall, and watching her spend time with one guy, couple of years older than him, then another in his early twenties, she had been concentrating on Jimmy. Heavy petting was bound to happen, and then some.

They'd go for bicycle rides at the local park, find a thicket or grove of trees away from the bike path and strollers, she'd unzip his pants, reach inside, rub him for a while, feeling his groin stir and grow and would withdraw it, already erect and massive. She'd continue to run her palm over the throbbing head, while in her other hand she would cup his testicles. The girl was experienced. Didn't have to be told anything, not that he would have even known what to say or how to instruct her. He did know certain things he liked to have done: he wanted to see it inside her mouth, sliding in and out, gradually, all of it, if possible. He also liked seeing her tongue the shaft, then go lower, down below, lick and then suck on his balls; take them inside her mouth while looking up at him and smiling. She could do it; knew how. Sucked his nutsack, while with her left hand she would be stroking his massive pole.

The pleasure was incredible, and he also knew it was at these times he needed to withdraw, or else chance erupting too soon. He did not want the thing to happen this early in the lovemaking. Nope. He'd heard enough from other guys, women talking, premature ejaculation was not a good thing. "Not yet," he'd softly say. He'd turn around, his rear end in her face, pushed back against her mouth. He liked having his ass licked and kissed, liked feeling her tongue inside his butt crack. "Lick my asshole, Marcella; my sweet Marcella."

"Mmmmm, Jimmy. . . ."

"Lick it, Marcella. . . ." Then he'd have her plant kisses all over his buttocks. He'd turn around again, and her mouth would be on his cock, lips sucking, the tongue licking. She took him in, all the while making throaty sounds as if cumming. She'd take his hand, guide it down toward her hairy bush. He'd insert the one finger, then two. She'd take his other hand, and guide it toward her rear, between her buttocks, and have him insert a finger inside her asshole.

He'd never known about or even been aware of the clit, the importance of it; you could never, ever underestimate the importance of the clitoris. She had had to literally show him by lying on her back, spreading her pussy lips and pointing to the nib of flesh, about the size of a pencil eraser, at near the very roof of the vagina. "Right there," she'd say. "The most sensitive area for a woman. Rub it gently, but persistently, and when sucking or licking me, you want to concentrate the tip of your tongue on the clit—and stay with it. The best orgasm you can give a woman is to eat her out this way while shoving a finger deep inside her ass, as well as running a couple of fingers inside her pussy, if you can manage." Then she had pointed out he probably wouldn't be able to do all three at the same time. "Slide a finger in my ass instead. Use the fingers of your other hand to part my pussy above the clit, so you can get at it with your tongue, honey. I want you, from time to time, to slide your tongue inside my vagina. Lick the inner walls: up and down and all around, and get back on the clitoris. Then, from time to time, take your finger out of my butt and run your tongue down there, give my clit a break, let it rest for a while, lick my asshole, honey boy. I like having a man's tongue deep inside my butt crack. My butt crack needs love, too, darling, just like my pussy. Bet nobody ever told you as much."

When he didn't say anything, apprehensive and shy, she had gone on: "Well, I'm telling you what I like. I'm not ashamed, either. Wished more girls would do so; because then men folk would know exactly how to please their lady." He would do this, and was a quick learner. Watched her writhe in ecstasy. His middle finger, the pussy finger did its job, staying on the clit, strumming gently, while pussy juices flowed out just below it, creamy and plentiful. She made sounds, a bit too loud, and made Jimmy nervous, while he looked around, wondering if a cop might show or a passerby, and think someone, a woman, was being assaulted—and yet, it added to it: the fucking was far greater because of it.

She came, again and again, convulsing, thrusting her pelvis, saying his name, beseeching that he not stop. "Don't you dare stop now." Then all of a sudden, with both hands on either side of his head, had pulled him down there, wanting, needing to feel his hot breath on her cunt; desperate to feel his tongue on the clit.

Jimmy had obeyed and gladly licked away. Did for her what she had done for him. And his tongue had found its way down toward her butt crack, that sweet spot that he could not get enough of. And when his mouth moved back up gradually enough to get back on the clit, the middle finger of his right hand was inside her asshole, all the way in, while his tongue moved quicker and harder, causing her to have one powerful orgasm after another. This was when she demanded that he enter her. She'd had to say it more than once. Jimmy, being afraid and knowing it would be a way to get her pregnant, was understandably reluctant. "Do it! Now! Do it, Jimmy! Please! My lover man! I need you so! Please, honey! Please, enter me! Put your cock in my hot pussy!"

Truth was, he had wanted to as much as she had needed him to, and did it. Slid it in there. Stroked and stroked. Taking his time, per her instructions: this was where he had learned to do this. *All the way, Jimmy, but take your time, don't rush. There is no hurry. I want to feel you inside me, but save the fast strokes for someone else.* "Fast strokes don't work here, not with me, Jimmy." And then he had exploded; the both of them cumming again, at the same time. "Put him in my mouth now," she had demanded.

"Huh?"

"You heard me, Jimmy. In my mouth. I want to finish you off. I want to taste him. Put him in my mouth. Please."

He did. And it was fabulous. Watched as she made his cock twitch with every lick and alternate caress. He watched her take in the knob, then withdraw, take it back in, pull it out; watched as she worked the cockhead with her tongue, running it around the rim, over, under, and sucked what remained of his cum and her cunt juice, making his groin twitch crazily, it was that sensitive, and a cop had shown up just as they had stood up, Marcella dropping the hem of her skirt in time and Jimmy shoving his groin inside his fly and zipping up his pants.

"What's going on here?"

"I got stung by a bee," Marcella had said, "and my boyfriend was kind enough to suck the stinger out."

The cop had frowned. Stared at them long and hard. "I ever catch you screwing around in this park again, I'll take you in. There's mothers out here with strollers, grandmothers babysitting grandkids. This is a public park, not a lover's lane." To Jimmy, he had said: "What are you gonna do when she gets knocked up, wise guy? Who you gonna go to?" Then he had called Jimmy over, said to him in a whisper: "I've seen her out here with other guys. Watch yourself. I hope you know enough to use a rubber. Never fool with these floozies without protection." The cop had stepped away from him. Stared at them both some more, especially Marcella, as if giving her a knowing look.

Marcella and Jimmy had stood there, not saying anything. The cop had told them to get the hell out of there. They had walked their bikes to the bike path, climbed on, and pedaled back to the city. He would invariably let her take the lead, ride on ahead of him by a few feet, in order to feast his eyes on that bubble butt in the tight skirt. What a sight to behold. Even now, years later, it remained a cherished memory. Something he guessed he'd never be able to shake completely, nor would he want to.

In Stepped Willabelle

It was during another battle between Willabelle and her daughter Cheyenne one Sunday morning right there in the basement kitchen that an opportunity with Marcella had been too sweet to pass up. Willabelle and the daughter were engaged in yet another shouting match over the types of low-class men Cheyenne was seeing. Reverend Henry Riff had been upstairs with the rest of the congregation imploring one and all to give twice and three times as much as before; you see, it was paramount, if plans for the new church were to progress to the next level. Jimmy hadn't needed to be there in person to know what the pitch was. He'd heard it way too often at all the other places and knew it by heart.

"Useless," Cheyenne's mother said to her offspring. "Goin' nowhere! Crack-using good-for-nothing slackers ain't worked a day in they life!"

"Who are you talking about, Ma? Your own son?"

"Darius have him a good job, Cheyenne, and you knows better than to be talking trash about your own brother!"

"I've had just about enough of this crap, Willa!" screamed her kid, and shoved the back door open and stepped outside to light a smoke. "Tune never changes; bullshit never ends."

"'Cause you never learn!" said the mother. "Why I got to keep repeating myself all the time!"

"Are you perfect? Tell me, Willa," Cheyenne shouted from where she stood by the door between hard drags on the butt. "You always done what *your* mother asked? You a lie, Willa! Givin' me a hard time!"

"Why you keep raisin' yo voice?"

"You raisin' yours, ain't you?"

"I'm your mother! You can't talk to your mother like that!"

"I ain't so sure," said Cheyenne and slammed the door shut.

Jimmy and Marcella had been quietly minding their own business. Jimmy was standing over the trough-like sink scrubbing large pots and pans, while Marcella operated the stainless-steel dishwasher. And between all that, she would sneak-pinch his bottom whenever the coast was clear. Although Jimmy clearly enjoyed the attention, it made him just ever so slightly nervous. What if they got found out? Willabelle Washington was no one to be playing grab-ass around. Marcella kept telling him to take it easy. "No need to panic."

Jimmy had sighed. Shook his head. And yet there was no way to disregard the growing erection inside his trousers. Marcella noticed and it made her smile approvingly. She turned her head back, to make sure it was safe enough to do so, and reached down with her right hand in an attempt to rub his crotch. Jimmy had spun away in time, just as the mother dropped another large skillet with the longest handle into the trough, splashing soapy water on his apron and rolled-up shirt sleeves.

Marcella had been able to quickly turn away, looking occupied. She yanked up on the square-shaped upper half of the stainless-steel washer and withdrew a large pot and put it away; she hung various utensils from the metal hanger above the work table that occupied more than considerable space in the center of the kitchen.

By now Willabelle had gone out the back door herself, where the haranguing continued. Marcella had wasted no time grabbing Jimmy by the hand and pulling him inside the walk-in cooler with her. Making sure the heavy door was closed, she knelt, unzipped his fly, and reached in. She had him out in no time. Jimmy had protested initially, but the cool temperature of the cooler had added to the overall sensitivity of his cock head and went with it. Let her do it. She needs it, he thought. Look how hungry she is. No matter how much she got; it was never enough. There was no denying that he was enjoying it himself. You never got tired of being blown, of having your cock sucked, never ever tired of watching a good-looking, light-skinned, mixed-race chick like this lick and suck on your cock.

No denying how pleasurable it felt. My God. He'd look down from time to time, watch her take him inside her mouth, those ruby-red lips wrapped around it, sucking, vacuuming. That's what it reminded him of: a human sucking machine, human vacuum. The need was there, no denying, to shoot cum down in her throat. There was no going back now, no stopping her—or even pretending that he didn't want it. Didn't give a shit, either, that they could be found out any minute now, any second. Didn't matter. He wasn't about to stop her. No way. Maybe he should have. Maybe. Only he couldn't. Now that he was so into it and about to do it. Shoot it; shoot it in her mouth. Fill her throat. It was going to be a tremendous amount. Lots of it. More than ever. The more cum he had to shoot, the longer the climax, the greater and prolonged the resulting pleasure. Yes.

It was on its way. Brewing in his nutsack. About to explode. And she knew it. The girl knew it, could easily tell, because she was grinning, loving it; thrilled by the power she had over him—and loving every moment of it.

Jimmy's breathing increased in tandem of the muted sounds

Marcella made in her full mouth and throat. She looked up from time to time, and he nodded his head each and every single time she did, acknowledging that she was absolutely fabulous at what she was doing. Just terrific. Amazing. What a wonderful cocksucker she was. My Lord! And then it happened: the blast! Up it surged, through the length of his thick groin, up up up nearing the head—and the full load erupting, bursting inside those full lips! Yes! Her mouth was open, as she wanted him to see the cum hose her full on, filling her throat. He watched as she practically gagged on it. There was a truckload of the white-hot ball juice going in there. Then she rewrapped her lips back around the cock head, sucking some more, applying the suction, as before. Vacuuming as much as she was able, draining his nutsack and enjoying the grimaces his face contorted into, she watched and took great pleasure in the gasps and cries and winces Jimmy made while she finished him off. Just as she was polishing, took the back of her right hand, and shoved whatever drops of the cum managed to get past her lips; guided it back inside her hungry mouth. There was some on her chin, and she scraped that amount as well with her index finger and up into her waiting oral cavity. Stood up, just as the cooler door opened, and in stepped Willabelle Washington with a stunned look on her face, her lower jaw dropping and practically hitting the floor. Jimmy's cock, even though clearly spent, was something to behold in its thickness, half-hanging there from his open fly.

"Do it, Young Daddy!"

"You stay put!" Willabelle had ordered Marcella Blevins. *"You ain't goin' nowheres, young lady, until we get this thang cleared up. I need to know what's goin' on here in my kitchen and how long it's been goin' on?"*

Jimmy had pleaded with her: if it got out, his father would be given his walking papers. The divorcee had readily agreed. "Only there ain't no need for that, young man. Willabelle Washington ain't like them other womens 'roud here. I ain't got it in my heart to cause nobody no harm. I ain't no gossip; no sir. Your daddy, he needs his job. I know that, son. And he's doin' a whole lot here for the community, helpin' to raise money for that new church. . . ."

Before he knew what was happening, the woman was fondling him. Soon after, she was down there on her knees, her mouth on his groin, and bringing him back to full mast. And Marcella? She stood there, watching, taking it in. Didn't dare move. Willabelle paused long enough to look up, smiling at him. "How you like that?"

"I can't complain, Ms. Washington."

"Call me Willa, please, young man."

"Willa," Jimmy said. "It feels nice."

"Nice?" she said. "That all? Let's see if mamma can do better than 'nice' for this here white boy." To Marcella, she said: "Get me that step stool, girlfriend, why don't you? Got to have somethin' to sit on. This cooler floor be too cold for my poor knees." The deacon's daughter did as asked, none too happy at the way things had turned out. Willabelle picked up on it, to be sure, only she was not about to let it faze her any.

"Now you stand on over there and watch. Let a woman show you how to please a pretty white boy like this," said Willabelle Washington. "We gone get to the bottom of this 'fore long."

She was back on it, sucking, taking him in. If Marcella was capable, this woman gave it something extra; call it experience, call it a deep craving as a result of having gone so long without. And while she sucked and licked him and worked it with her left hand, her other hand was down there between her thighs, rubbing her pussy.

"Don't you cum now," she warned. "All I'm doin' is gettin' you ready. Makin' you ready, young man."

Jimmy nodded. Looked over at where Marcella was standing. She didn't seem pleased with what she was witnessing, and yet there she was, massaging herself down there and appearing to be getting off.

The black woman stood up, hiked up her dress, lowered her panties. She moved him from where he stood leaning against the wire shelf, took his place, her back to him, and said: "I like it from behind. Not in my ass, young man, but doggy. Since the metal floor be too cold, let's do it this way, standin' up." She stuck her wide ass out, grabbed his groin in her hand and inserted it inside her cunt.

"*Do it, Young Daddy,*" she implored. "*Fuck me, Young Daddy!*"

Jimmy stroked; they were deep thrusts, deliberate and steady. Just as Marcella had taught him, while with his right hand, he reached around the woman's waist, and down there, found her clit and massaged it with his pussy finger. This was it. Willabelle Washington was making a variety of undecipherable sounds through clenched teeth. Once she started cumming it never ended: one orgasm after another,

her entire body quaking, shaking. She had a way of twisting her head back and forth. Finally, she was spent, and Jimmy unloaded himself. Blasted a tremendous amount inside of her.

When the cooler door opened this time, it was the daughter, Cheyenne. Stood there, with a look of shock on her features. She did an about face and exited, and the door swung closed of its own accord. Willabelle dropped the hem of her skirt, and ran out after her, calling her name repeatedly.

Mrs. Blevins

He'd expected the shit to hit the fan right away, for the news to get out and around and his family told to move on, as usual. Only it didn't happen. There was nothing from Willa, other than her giving him the eye, greeting him with a smile whenever she was around. The daughter? The daughter was generally as disagreeable as ever, but she, too, was being nicer to him than was usual. He was fine with that, not that he was interested in anything else from her, skinny and homely creature that she was. Gray teeth from too much pot, or regular cigarettes, or something. The mother had hinted that her daughter had a crush on him. "Forget that hard-to-please Marcella. She be doin' all of them boys all the time, you hear? Ain't nothin' but a ho. I said it, young man. *She a ho.* My daughter Cheyenne do a beautiful white boy like you dirty like that? No sir. Girl is sweet on you, can't you tell?" All Jimmy knew was that he wanted nothing to do with her daughter. The only reason he let the mother manhandle him that time in the cooler was because he'd been taken by surprise and feared his father and the whole family would have to move again, just when he was starting to develop some kind of relationship with this gorgeous Marcella. Falling for her. It was true. At least the mother, Willa, had curves, and was basically a decent person. He had picked up on that right away. Lovelorn. Acted severe and strict, but deep down had a heart of gold. So that hadn't been the problem, other than his father giving him a hard time because he hadn't been able to get into Marcella's panties.

And that was the thing that left Jimmy totally perplexed: Marcella. High-yellow with light-brown hair and natural chestnut streaks had taught him how to make love to a woman, go down, eat pussy; how to make a woman explode in ecstasy—was now completely ignoring him. What was going on? She wouldn't say. She came in, did her job, but was all business. Might or might not say hello and basically ignored him. Was in and out of the kitchen, taking food orders from the people out there in the hall, would return to pick them up as the cook, and her helper, a red-faced fifty-year-old chronic grouch by the name of Jerome Baptiste, took it in. Thin and hunched over. Face red like a lobster. Carrot-haired. Thinning on top. Refused to wear a hat when outside (for protection against the bright sun) from fear he would lose what remained of his precious strands.

Jimmy had to face it: his heart was breaking. He'd never gone through this sort of thing before. He'd been led on, then promptly dropped without a hint of warning. Was it because he'd gotten it on in the cooler with Willabelle Washington? Couldn't be. She'd forced herself on him—and continued to do so from time to time. Marcella had witnessed what had happened inside the walk-in cooler. Saw it with her own eyes. Now and then he made the effort to speak to her, but she never seemed to have the time, not so much as a moment for him. Always on the move, busy, appeared to be, so very. And the rest of the time? On the phone, talking to one of her many male friends, some married, or else had someone. That didn't seem to matter to her. Woman was popular. Jimmy wondered what it was he had done to be dissed and dismissed this way? Only she never would say. Continued to play head games and pull stunts that only managed to underscore how frustrated he felt. He'd call over at her house, hoping to get together and have a talk, work it out; he so desperately wanted to understand what was going on with her; if there even was a relationship anymore. Were they still together? "Is there a chance, Marcella? I'd like to see you."

"You really are love-sick, aren't you, Romeo?" she'd say.

"I can't help how I feel."

"Is that why you continue to do Willa?" she'd say.

"Ms. Washington is a good friend; besides, if I don't cooperate she spills the beans about us and my family would have to move. . . . If we did that, I might never see you again, Marcella. I'm doing it for us. . . . It won't go on forever. She's bound to get tired of me."

He heard her laugh at the other end.

"I'm hurting," he'd say. "You're not being fair, Marcella. I don't make a scene whenever I see you with other guys. . . ."

"They don't own me; nobody owns me, Jimmy. Not you; not anyone. That's the first thing, the most important thing, you have to know and accept about me."

"I do accept it; I do understand. It isn't easy, but I can do my best. . . ."

"This is not a monogamous relationship. We never even discussed the subject . . . so quit acting like we're engaged or something. I date whoever the hell I want to date."

"Of course," he had said, but inside it was quite painful. What could you do? You took it, especially when your emotions were involved and you felt helpless in doing anything about it.

"You are a sweet boy," she had said, after all that. "Why don't you come over to the house."

He did. Only to be greeted by Renata Blevins, the mother. Mrs. B authored a popular lonely-hearts-type column for a local newspaper and worked from home. She was clearly twice his age; she was also a charming 5ft 11 fit natural blonde with curves in all the right places.

Where was Marcella? Gone out. The phone rang, and she said she had to see a friend. Jimmy wondered about that. Where was Deacon Blevins? Playing poker with his buddies.

"Poor boy," Mrs. Blevins had said. Took him by the hand and guided him to the kitchen. "How would you like a slice of cherry pie and a nice tall glass of milk? How does that sound? According to my daughter, you have a sweet tooth . . . and you love pastries. . . ."

Jimmy went along. Sat at the kitchen table while Renata Blevins reached in the fridge for the pie and milk, and he could not help taking in the lady's bountiful rear end. The skirt was just tight enough to accentuate it, and the high heels added a certain unexplainable something that made him crave for a closer look. Of course, he felt guilty at the mere thought. What about Marcella? What would she say if you so much as allowed anything of this nature to take place?

Renata Blevins turned her head, ever so slightly, smiling a mischievous smile. She knew he was observing, and she appreciated the fact he appreciated the view.

She placed the pie and milk on the table before him. Reached for a clean glass, a fork, grabbed a plate. Set the items on the table. Sat in the chair near him.

She cut a slice, served him, all the while saying: "I must apologize for my daughter's behavior. To invite you over and then simply take off without so much as an explanation. . . ."

"It's okay. . . ."

"Well, it's rude. I would think she would be thrilled and ever so grateful to have a handsome, strapping lad like yourself interested in her. . . ."

"I'm probably in love with her, Mrs. Blevins. . . ."

"Please call me Renata. No need for us to be formal; we are friends, after all. You've been seeing Marcella for, what, about six months now?"

"Yes, ma'am. About that. Going on six months."

"Are you sure it's love, Jimmy? Because, you know, they say, it takes on average about two years—for most people. Well, I don't know about most, but I do know that's how long it usually takes me. Two years, give or take."

"I just, I don't know; I'm all mixed up. Not even sure how to talk to her about how I feel. I miss her when I'm not with her; can't sleep at night; don't have much of an appetite. I'm eating this cherry pie at the moment, only because it's hard to resist cherry pie, and because I usually, lately, hardly eat much."

"I'll tell you something, darling boy," said Renata Blevins, "love is the great mystery. We go through life needing it, chasing after it, and when we do get it, we take it for granted, and very often aren't even sure how to hold on to it. Very often, it slips right through our fingers. Love is a puzzle."

Jimmy nodded. Hadn't heard anyone put it quite this way, but what the woman was saying seemed to make a lot of sense. He didn't know. Knew that he was too young probably to get it, just yet.

"Now, look at me and my husband, Beaufort. I didn't love the man when we first started seeing each other, when he started courting me, seventeen, eighteen years ago. And, gradually, I did fall in love with him. Two years it took. But it is also true, that I no longer feel the same way about him. I am not even sure I know what happened . . . nor why I stay in the marriage. He has his life; I have mine. He has his friends; I have mine. We don't relate; we have grown apart. It's the oldest cliché, but so true." She poured herself a coffee, sat back down. She sipped at the coffee, lowered the mug. She leaned in, said in a whisper: "We haven't made love in years. To tell the truth, I believe my husband might even, possibly like, be more comfortable with his own gender. I suspect my husband, Beaufort, is gay. He spends way too much time with other men. And the lack of sex in our marriage, I've already pointed out. . . ." As she said this, she had her right hand over his left, rubbing gently. "You have manly hands. I like that in a man. Such beautiful eyes . . . Square-jawed. A truly handsome, sincere lad such as yourself, and my daughter continues to mistreat you. This is beyond me. I have taught her better than this." She lifted her mug with her free hand, sipped. She lowered the coffee, and placed this hand as well over his. She now had both of them rubbing gently, his palm, fingers. "Such lovely hands; long and sturdy fingers . . . strong. . . ." She inquired if he had ever participated in wrestling or other sports, and wondered if this was how he had built himself up so? Jimmy nodded. Said he enjoyed sports, particularly dodge ball, weights, running.

"That would explain it," she said. Her right hand slid up his arm, reaching his shoulder. She rested it there, massaging gently. "My . . . you do have powerful shoulders. I noticed as much when Marcella brought you over that day. . . ."

"Thank you . . . Renata. . . ."

"You're welcome," she said. "What I would like more than anything right now, is to make your sadness go away. I would love to be able to make your heartache go away, vanish, like a puff of smoke, if possible." She chuckled at the obvious silliness of her own remark; this in, turn, made Jimmy smile as well.

He admitted to already feeling better.

"Is that so? For real?"

"Yes, ma'am," said Jimmy. "The cherry pie is a big help, and of course, ma'am, the company. . . . I do feel better."

"Good," said Renata Blevins. "So then, it is safe to say we are on the right track?"

"Definitely," said Jimmy.

"With your kind permission I would like, if I may be allowed, to proceed and make you feel even better than you presently feel. . . ."

Jimmy was not certain momentarily, then nodded his head. What did he have to lose?

"Please, Renata. Nobody likes feeling lousy. I certainly don't."

"I was so hoping you would say that, dear boy," said Renata Blevins. She leaned in, and kissed him tenderly on the lips. It was merely a light, soft kiss, but it was enough to stoke the embers within. Then she moved over to the left ear, kissing there, planting soft kisses, then moved on down his neck. All done gradually, as she took her time with it. Then moved back up and licked the earlobe, and her tongue probed inside his ear, then back out in back of it, and returned to the neck, in back. She stood, planted kisses all around, until she found his mouth again, and her tongue slid inside. He was not an experienced kisser, but that did not matter. Marcella had probably taught him plenty, but the mother was the true teacher here, and she would show the lad how to be truly loved.

❧

She had him push his chair back, and positioned herself on his lap. She undid the buttons on her blouse, and the black bra, full, Double C cups, were there in his face. She had him unhook the clasp, and the bra was discarded. She guided the one erect nipple in his mouth, let him suck on it, then the other. This would be the beginning of a terrific night of lovemaking, a session of some wild and wanton sucking and fucking. If her own daughter was not able to appreciate this young and randy stud, if her own daughter was so damn ungrateful and callous in the way she mishandled this wonderful young man, she would take up the slack.

❧

She had her head tilted back now, while Jimmy took turns sucking on the nipples, shoving entire mouthfuls of tit flesh in his face. Renata did not have to probe her vagina to know that she was probably moist down there. After all, it had been so long, so very long, of having been deprived. Yes, there had been the occasional tryst, with both sexes, from time to time—and yes, she probably suspected she preferred females to males, with this one exception being this hung kid right here in her very own kitchen sucking on her breasts.

She slid her right hand down there between her thighs, went inside, just to visit briefly, merely to check on what she suspected was taking place: yes, she was moist; yes, she was juicy; yes, it was happening; yes, she wanted to do everything with this James G. Riff, son of the substitute preacher man. She would suck his cock, lick his balls and asshole; and she would have him do the same for her: Lap up her honey dew down there, probe her cunt with his tongue, and drink her cunt juices.

❧

Both were caught up in it; and it was a task to pause long enough for her to get out of the blouse, unzip the skirt, and discard it, so that now she was in garter belt, fishnets and black heels. His own shirt was off, as were his shoes, socks, and trousers. All that this teen stud had on presently were his boxers; and right there, through the opening in the boxers, through the fly, stood out at attention, was this massive erection.

Good God, she loved it. She spit into her right palm, and ran it over the mushroom head of his groin, while cupping his balls with the other. Then it was with this same hand that she permitted her fingers to travel under, slowly, gradually, until they reached his anus. The butt crack.

She inserted a finger inside his asshole. Jimmy jumped a bit at first, not that he didn't care for it, but the sheer surprise of it, and the fact the sensation was unusual and new to him, although rather welcoming, was what did it.

She grinned. "I think you like having my finger inside your butt. Don't you, my darling lad?"

"Yes," Jimmy said. Then reciprocated, and slid the middle finger of his left deep inside this thirty-five-year-old woman's rectum. Happy? Both were. He continued to suck on her tits, while she caressed the head of his prick, making it twitch repeatedly. The sensations that surged through his body were too fabulous, and he had this fear that he might ejaculate prematurely.

"Don't you dare shoot your load before we've had a chance to fuck," she warned.

"I won't," promised Jimmy. "I've never had that problem, Renata."

"Good," said Mrs. Blevins. "Now tell me you love me."

"Huh?" said Jimmy.

"I know that you don't, but I need to hear you say that you love me. Tell me you love me. Please, my lover man. . . ."

"I love you, Renata. I love you dearly. . . ."

"Tell me you want to eat my pussy. . . ."

"I want so very much to eat your pussy, lovely Renata."

She giggled. Kissed him on the lips for the longest time; lifted her head back, looked at him, into his eyes, then kissed him some more. "You are so wonderful; such a loving, sweet man. . . . I am so glad that my daughter let you go. . . . I am."

Jimmy looked at her, grinning. He got it.

Renata continued: "Because if she hadn't stood you up, we wouldn't be doing this right now."

⌒∞⌒

She dismounted his lap, while sliding her face down toward his pelvis. She was on her knees, the palms of her hands made up and down caressing motions over his chest, while she lowered her mouth over the head of his throbbing member. And yes, his member *was throbbing.* It was easy to tell. One flick of her tongue, and his cock jumped. She did it again, and it jumped some more: twitched and throbbed and moved. It made her smile. So did Jimmy.

"My God, I thought Marcella was good. You're fabulous."

"Of course. Who do you think taught her all she knows? I know that you know who it was, but I'm just saying: I taught that girl how to give head; how to tighten her pussy when the male enters her; how to make with the thrusts, so that the man is not the only one being forced to do all the physical labor part of it."

Jimmy's head was tilted back, and all he could do was take in deep breaths. The woman had stopped talking, and her mouth was back on his groin, licking the shaft, all the way down to the balls, and back up again. She had this very efficient and effective method of following with her hand what her tongue did, this way underscoring and doubling and intensifying his pleasure. Then, to top it off, she would do a corkscrew type of twist over the head, that made Jimmy twitch every time; and it was not only his cock that did the twitching, it was his entire body.

"*Wow,*" sighed Jimmy.

She sucked. Glanced up to take in the expression on his face, and continued with the sucking. Then her tongue got lower, past the base of the shaft, and was on his sweaty balls: took one in, then the other. She released the balls, and her mouth drifted below, seeking out his asshole, and the tongue went in, deep and deeper. When she pulled it back out, she nibbled at the surrounding flesh.

"My God, you taste sweet," she said. "So sweet. Love the smell of your sweat. Even your butt crack smells sweet. . . ."

No one had ever said this to him, that he could recall, and it added to the rawness.

Then, just as suddenly, she stopped. Feared he might cum; feared he might shoot his load, and then they'd have to wait a while for him to recover and start anew. She knew a young stud like this would be able to go three or four or five times, without trouble. Maybe even more often. Probably had cum to spare. Living sperm bank. Not a doubt in her mind, but she felt like making him wait all the same. She would fuck him, get off a few times herself, then let him shoot white ball juice down her throat and on her face and tits. This sort of thing always excited her. Liked seeing it in porn movies, and liked doing it herself. Not many women would own up to liking anything of the sort: seeing porn and being sprayed with cum. Hypocrites. She had no time for it. Busy having the time of her life instead.

⌘

She climbed back on his lap, saw that his groin was in her, and she rode him this way: up and down, from side to side, and all around, wanting him to cover every area of the inside of her cunt. Did not wish the slightest crevice to be overlooked. She tightened her vagina walls around his cock and rode him this way. The lube was there, and there was plenty of it. Nothing additional was required.

⌘

Sweat dripped from their brows and necks; a couple of sex machines going at it, oblivious to the rest of the world. This was what it was about: being in the moment. Made life worth living. Made you feel good to be alive. It was one of the greatest things about being in this otherwise fucked-up world. Wasn't it?

"Isn't this great, Jimmy? Isn't this amazing?"

"Yes," said Jimmy. *"YES! I'm loving it!"*

"Fuck my husband," she said, *"Screw you, Beaufort!* And as far as Marcella is concerned: it's her loss."

"I feel so much better, Renata. You were right. I feel like a new person."

"Of course," said Renata. "Sex is like that, when it's exciting and works; when the people involved are compatible. Now, Beaufort and I, we never had it this good. Never, ever—not once."

"Not even once?"

"Of course not! I told you: he's *homo.*"

"How can you be sure, Renata?"

"I am, that's all. Who cares? Didn't he offer you money to let him blow you? He wasn't the only one, by the way, was he?"

"Yes, but how do you know?"

"Never mind how I know. Lets just say that I do. When men go on camping trips that last entire weekends, take sleeping bags with them, but never any of the women they're married to, what is it do you think goes on in those sleeping bags? Huh, sonny boy? Let your imagination fill in the blanks. That's where he happens to be right now, whole weekend. And no, he's not off playing poker, Jimmy. Instead he's playing with some married guy's balls. Look, it's like this: if he wants to be with men, let him. Everyone should be entitled to be who they are. Just tired of the hypocrisy, that's all. I like women, usually; well, stud muffins, too; depends on the guy—if I'm drawn to the guy. Oh, enough about them. Let's just screw our brains out, my lover man. Fuck me!"

They continued on. Decided to change positions. Go for variety, and to give the parts of their bodies they'd been using a break. They moved the pie out of the way, the milk, and Renata climbed up on the table, was lying on her back, and Jimmy was about to re-insert his groin. Only she stopped him.

"Eat my cunt, Jimmy, my darling lad. Suck my pussy and lick my butthole. Suck my cunt juice and drink it in."

Jimmy did not hesitate, buried his mouth between her upper thighs and began lapping the cunt lips, worked on the clit, flicking and sucking and caressing and watching her go into spasms. He stayed with it. It was not easy, as the woman began to convulse and jerk, just as Marcella had, but he was deliberate and determined . . . licked all the areas, her asshole, then back up to the cunt lips, went inside, probing and sucking out the muff nectar, then was back on the ever-sensitive clit.

Worked and worked; stayed with it. Then did the bit with the middle finger of his right hand, inserted it deep inside her butt crack, all the while licking and working away at the clit. And it happened: the woman exploded with a tremendous orgasm and screamed and screamed and sighed and winced, jerking her pelvis. It was all he could do to keep her from rolling off the kitchen table. She kept saying his name and things like: *Oh Shit! Oh Fuck! Goddammit! SHHHIIIITTTT!*

He stood still and let her savor the climax. He would do nothing for the time being . . . and let her come down in gradual degrees. She was lost in it . . . floating. Nothing like a high from a fantastic climax.

Once he realized she was back on planet earth, he moved up to where her face was, kissed her tenderly, all over: brow and cheeks and mouth. She had the biggest smile on her face.

"My lord, I needed that," she said. "Such a sweet, sweet, giving soul. . . ."

"You're a wonderful woman, Renata. I'm so lucky to be here with you . . . so very fortunate to know you. Thank you. . . ."

"No, I'm the one who should be thanking you, dear lad." Then she motioned to bring his still-erect groin to where her mouth was. "Let's take care of you."

"You don't have to."

"*I know I don't have to.* What kind of host would I be if I didn't take care of my *manly stud muffin*? What kind of woman would I be? Only a bitch gets her lover all excited only to leave him with blue balls."

"I'm okay."

"Are you hurting yet?"

"Only slightly."

"Well, you're not getting *blue balls*; not if I can help it. Bring your cock over here. I want it in my mouth. That's an order, young man."

Both smiled. Jimmy slid his cock in her mouth, and the woman gave him a lip lock and worked it back and forth, then loosened up, and took about half of him down into her throat. It was quite a task, but she managed. Withdrew it momentarily to catch her breath. "Goddamn, you're massive. But I'm loving it. I bet you shoot a tremendous load. I can tell; I have a sixth sense about these things. I bet it's a load big enough to fill a coffee mug, or close to it."

He supposed Marcella might have mentioned it to her. Mothers and daughters had a way of exchanging information when it came to their lovers and men in general.

"I have been known to have more than the average guy," said Jimmy. "It's genetics. Just born this way."

"Oh, no need to apologize. I'm saying I'm ready for it and I'm loving it, dear lad; my of-the-moment lover man."

She sucked him back in, then worked the head with the tongue and lips as before, and underscored this method with either hand, in that she took turns. She continued to spit on the head, as well into both hands, and worked his member, which seemed to swell in size before her very eyes. Not that it wasn't large enough to begin with, but there it was: growth, caused, no doubt, by his increasing excitement as well as her increasing enthusiasm.

And she knew one thing right now, this very moment, it was about to take place: the kid was going to spray cum into her oral cavity. She glanced up, saw the expression on his face that said it all. And then it did happen: he blasted a tremendous volume of white-hot sperm into her mouth. He made sounds, just as she made a few herself. She was gagging. Jimmy was in ecstasy, barely able to hold on to the table to prevent from toppling over. His body rigid as he held on to the top of her skull. He jammed it in. She kept up, worked it WORKED IT WORKED IT! The cum sprayed like a goddamn *tsunami of nutsack nectar. Jizzum! Goo! Spunk! Cum.* There was so much it overlapped the lips, covered chin and nose, cheeks. Tits. She worked it feverishly, moving, bobbing, up down, from side to side, all the while rubbing the head against her mouth and the area around it, either cheek and chin, then sucking on the head itself, (while alternately jerking it with fingers firmly, but not too much so, wrapped around the shaft and knob). That was the secret to a great blow job: work (primarily) the fucking head while the sperm is shooting out: *jerk it, while the sperm blasts away! Suck it! Drain the fucker! Drain him! Then jerk it some more!* There she was, grinning a huge grin. *Yes.*

Finally, after she had slowly squeezed out the very, very, very last drop of cock juice, signaling that there was (presently) no more and his cock's jumps and twitches were far more pronounced to the touch than ever before, Jimmy collapsed with a final *"ahhhh!"* against her head; his face, pressed up against her face, right arm under as well about her head, held her in this awkward manner.

He climbed up on the table after a moment, wanting to be more comfortable as well as needing to cling to her. She reciprocated. The lovers craved rest more than anything right now.

Lust in the Shower

They stepped into the shower, and it was not long before they realized they could not keep their hands off of each other. The shower stall was spacious, as was the bathroom itself. There was a jacuzzi, long vanity, and counter. Soft music drifted in from speakers in the ceiling.

She wore a shower cap. Jimmy had no use for one. Worked up plenty of lather as they soaped one another up, washed each other's backs, buttocks, bung holes; then it was on to the front. She saw to it that she got lots of soap on his genitals: cock and balls, then washed his buttocks and butt crack itself. He did the same for her. She turned her back, stuck her behind out so that he might have an easier time of it.

They rinsed each other off, her healthy breasts up against his well-built torso. And there it was: could not be helped. Jimmy was staring at the tits, holding them, then found himself sucking on the nipples all over again. It felt good for her, and she wanted him to go on, as the hot water from above sprayed her full on the face.

He had his right hand down there, between her upper thighs, while the left slid down toward the small of her back, and drifted lower and lower, until it reached the butt cleavage, and parted the buttocks, and the usual middle finger probed, sought out, and found her asshole. It went in. His right continued to gently flick the clit.

They were at it all over again. There was no stopping it. Lust was one of the major forces out there, if not the biggest; perhaps only exceeded by the force of love.

She was moaning again, her head back, eyes closed. She had one of her hands sliding down toward his belly button and beyond; lower it went, until she came upon what she was searching for: his rigid cock. And she began stroking. There was no rushing here, nothing frantic, but it was building into something just as thrilling as what they'd experienced in the kitchen moments earlier.

Jimmy's lips ascended, tongue licking her neck, and moved on up toward her chin, and stopped at the lips. They kissed, the kissing progressing into sucking of one another's tongues. He would tug on hers for a while with his lips and whole mouth, then they would reverse, and she would be the one pulling on his tongue, siphoning it, so to speak, yanking, taking him deep into her mouth.

He spun her around, lowered his face down low enough to meet her butt, then found the crack itself with his tongue. Probed hard, probed deep. In it went. Her asshole. Licking it, eating her butt that he could not get enough of, while his hands, the fingers of both hands worked away on the other side of her: couple of fingers inside her cunt, while the fingers of his right hand massaged, tweaked, and rubbed her clit.

Her moans increased in volume with each passing second. Jimmy stayed with it: determined as always, the way he was taught; remembered not to rush, to only stay with it, seek a good and reasonable pace, and keep it steady. Rotate the rubbing of the clit now and then, but keep it steady, with only one goal in mind: get her off, to see her blast off with more intensity and fervor and power and all-around dynamics than any rocket ship ever sent into space from Cape Canaveral or anywhere else. And he knew he was on the right track whenever he heard her whisper and moan his name, as she had plenty of times already back on the kitchen table, in a beseeching, otherworldly tone. Then he rose.

"Put him in me," she pleaded.

"Where?"

"Pussy. I want to feel that *tubesteak* inside my pussy. Now. Do it."

Jimmy slid it in, all the while staying with the clit. The pumping went on, the caressing of the clit continued. He pumped it, and she thrust her ass back at him each and every time, so that the physical exertion of it was not entirely left up to him alone. This was the way to fuck. It took both parties to do the tango. And bam! She screamed and continued to scream. Cumming! One orgasm after another, as before. This was something truly tremendous. There was heavy breathing and the moans decreased and become softer, lower. . . . She froze, leaning against the shower wall, needing to pause this way and catch her breath. Jimmy did likewise, held her calmly, his face resting against the back of her neck, then gradually covering it with soft kisses. . . .

After she had recovered, she turned around, got a good dollop of lube on her hands and began to stroke him. They were good, long strokes. She took him inside her mouth for a while to give her hands a chance to rest up, then was back to jerking him. Felt a need to see him shoot cum again. It was a real kick, and something she could not get enough of, just seeing the kid's thick meat banana twitching up and down, from side to side, then spraying cum like a fire hose. It was getting there. She could tell just like before. Looked at the expression on Jimmy's face. His own eyes were closed now, right side of his face leaning against the shower wall, with the showerhead above spraying them both.

"Ooooo," was a sound that Jimmy made, clearly indicating the blast was approaching. Not too far off now. It was getting nearer and nearer.

That's when the shower door suddenly flew open, and a stunned and pissed Marcella, dressed in nothing more than a short and revealing bathrobe, stood there with her jaw hanging. To Jimmy she had never looked more alluring: the light-brown hair long and wavy with the natural highlights accentuated only by her golden-hued complexion. If Renata was a looker, and that she certainly was, her daughter was a goddess.

"What the fuck, Mom?"

"Hello, darling?" said Renata with a big smile on her face, not bothering to pause jerking Jimmy for even a moment. "I see you're back already."

"Yes, I'm back!" said Marcella. "In time to see my own mother having sex with one of my boy toys!"

"Watch this, darling," said Renata. "Watch how much cum Jimmy is capable of spraying. He's already unloaded once—in the kitchen. We had a tremendous time; but he's about to explode once more. Probably with as much of the white stuff."

"I know he can cum a 'tremendous' lot, Mom! Do you realize who you're even telling this to? I've been fucking him for months now! As if you didn't know!"

"Either take your robe off, and step in the shower, or else close the shower door. Please, honey, because you're getting water on my carpet."

Marcella pursed her lips, as if to say: *This is unbelievable. What kind of mother does this anyway?*

"Are you for real, Mom? You're fucking one of my beaus."

"Oh, stop pretending to be indignant," said her mother. "You discarded this poor lad like he was a leper or something. You didn't want him. Now, all of a sudden, you're jealous?"

"I'm sorry, Marcella," said Jimmy. "I had the blues . . . after our talk. You weren't around, and your mother was kind enough to offer a slice of cherry pie and milk. It did a world of good."

"Yes, I can see that," said Marcella. At last calming down. She slipped out of the robe and let it drop to the carpet where she stood. "Know what, Tubesteak? This is a good-bye BJ. We can stay friends, if you like . . . but you need to stop coming around my house . . . and fucking my mother . . . just because I am not ready at this time in my life to be in an exclusive relationship with anyone. I enjoy my freedom way too much."

She stepped into the shower, squatting just in time to be sprayed by the heavy load of white-hot sperm that shot out the end of Jimmy Riff's rock-hard member. The women practically fought over who would be the recipient, who would get the most. Jaws open wide, they took it in: swallowing, licking, both tongues converged on Jimmy's cock, taking fast turns sucking on the impressive knob. Jimmy was in heaven; sheer ecstasy, head lifted, wincing; it was the height of pleasure. But he did have the need to look down, actually witness mother and daughter battling over who would finish him off.

They continued to take turns sucking wildly, frantically. First the one would take him in as far as she was able, then the other would reach for his cock and shove it in her own mouth, then Renata would grab it back from Marcella, and jam it inside her own throat, sucking deep and long. The intensity of the pleasure was unbearable for him.

The next thing he saw was absolutely amazing: they licked each other; licked cum off one another's face, even exchanged sperm, mouth to mouth, back and forth. Renata was desperate in her search of cock cream on her daughter's face; and wherever she thought she spotted cum, be it on her neck, chin, tits, forehead, she would dive in with her mouth open and her tongue darting, and lap it up. Marcella would in turn do likewise.

As there was not a trace of cum remaining, they rose at last, the trio hugging each other, kissing and holding on to one another. Smiling. They took a moment to collect themselves, calm down, allow their breathing, their beating hearts, to reduce to normal, and stepped out of the shower. Dried one another off and got into bathrobes.

A Mother's Advice

The kitchen table had been cleared and the trio had decided it was time to have something to eat—actual food this time. Jimmy was having a beef patty, with bottled water. Marcella sipped from a can of diet soda; the mother, sitting to Jimmy's left, had decided on a bowl of healthy cereal with fat-free milk, all the while gently rubbing the back of his hand. Marcella could not help but notice and the pursing of her lips was back.

"You're a great lay, Jimmy," said Marcella. "No one is denying that. . . . There are just too many handsome and randy guys in the world for someone like me to settle with just one boy."

"I already said I accepted that, Marcella," said Jimmy. "I believe I love you. It's just that I've never gone through this before, with anyone. . . ."

"Oh, Marcella, can't you see he's hurting—and just leave it at that? Why rub it in? You dumped him, isn't that enough for you?"

"You have to understand something: my mother has always, ALWAYS interfered in my relationships, and has always felt a need to sleep with my boyfriends. Isn't that so, Mom?'

Renata was smiling.

"She breaks theirs hearts and they come crying to me. I hate to see them suffer so . . . and I . . ."

"Offer 'support,'" said Marcella snidely. "She fucks their brains out and calls it support."

"Doing it with a bit of heart, darling daughter, kindness, wouldn't kill you. We're all human here, aren't we? You don't see your mother going around causing this kind of heartache. It isn't necessary, that's all I'm saying. It's uncalled for."

"Thank you, Mrs. Blevins," said Jimmy. "Sorry, *Renata*," corrected Jimmy. "That's what drew me to you in the first place—your inherent goodness."

Renata Blevins' eyes nearly misted. She leaned in and kissed Jimmy Riff on the cheek.

"This is so very touching," said Marcella. "Only what you don't seem to get, Mom, is if you don't cut someone off, and I mean cut him off, they tend not to get the message, and before you know it, you're stuck with a stalker who won't leave you alone. I've been there, or have you forgotten?"

"We have ways of justifying our rude behavior, don't we darling?" said Renata Blevins.

"You were the one who taught me and explicitly told me: If it isn't working out, end it. Don't get stuck like me for the past eighteen years, in a loveless marriage with a man who prefers to blow guys instead of seeing to his wife's needs."

"Here we go again," said Renata Blevins, "the old tug-and-pull; back and forth. And do we ever get anywhere? You tend to twist my words around, darling Marcella. What I said was: If the man is a jerk, if he is neglectful, if he is a drug-addicted failure as a human being, a perpetual drunk, useless in the sack, is disrespectful to you in public, or disrespectful in general—lose him. Deal him out of your life. What you have done here is merciless, and someone needs to let you know. This is heartless, shameful behavior, to mistreat a wonderful young man like Jimmy here."

Hearing the words spoken with such conviction nearly moved Jimmy to tears. Renata glanced at him. Picked up on it.

"Do you see what you are doing? Do you realize how much harm it does? How would you like it if the roles were reversed—and you were the one being unceremoniously dropped?"

"I *have* been dropped," said Marcella. "More than once, I might add."

"Not by Jimmy here," said Renata.

"Of course not by him, but by others, jerks."

"Well, if you weren't such an easy lay—"

"I like having a good time and I believe in variety. What's wrong with that? Besides, you're putting out mixed messages, *girlfriend*."

"You courted the boy, this good-hearted boy, pursued him for weeks, seduced him, got him used to the great sex: blow jobs and such, all that great lovemaking that I taught you, then suddenly decide to cut him completely out of the loop. This is not right. To go through life leaving pain in your wake. It will catch up with you; that's all I'm saying. There is no need to be this hurtful and malicious."

"I do not need to be attached right now. Why is that such a crime? He is a great fuck, I have already clearly stated as much. Why can't we let it go at that? There are so many women who would be happy to have him, just as I was for a while, and I do wish him luck." She looked at Jimmy now. "I do wish you the best, Jimmy. I mean that."

"So why the jealousy?" The mother motioned with her index finger, back and forth, between herself and Jimmy. "Why make such a big deal out of it?"

"Because you are my mother, that's why. This sort of thing is not supposed to happen! You are supposed to be on *my side*, not his!"

"Your mother is always on your side, darling. It is sheer nonsense to pretend otherwise."

"It would be nice if you would start acting like it."

Renata said to Jimmy: "No matter what I do for my daughter, to show how much she is loved, this is how she comes back at me." She was looking at her daughter again. "This is so unkind of you, Marcella."

"Once again—you're letting a man come between us, Mother," said Marcella. "Just as before. Why you always feel a need to fuck my boyfriends is beyond me; furthermore, I find it totally frustrating and inexcusable. Just, please, stop coming on to my men. *You have to stop blowing my boyfriends, Mom. Go find your own dicks to suck.* Okay? Besides, you prefer pussy. Said as much. She did, Jimmy. Many times. Has she mentioned it to you already? Probably has. She likes to go down on pussy. She loves doing it, as a matter of fact. Loves the role-playing, loves to put on a strap-on and fuck her girlfriends that way; pussy, ass, doesn't matter, or else they fuck her. Digs it. And yet, can't seem to keep her hands off my own studs—that I work so hard to promote and seduce. That's why I get upset. No other reason. And if I hurt you in any way, James, I'm sorry. I thought I mentioned it at the very beginning that I was not looking for anything lasting. I'm way too much in demand, too popular, to be attached to any one dude."

Renata sipped from her bottle of *Perrier*, then reached for Jimmy's hand, lifted it, drawing it close to her face, and kissed it. She had her other hand on it, as before, kissing his fingers, individually, then she took the middle finger, inserted it into her mouth, and began sucking it in as though sucking his groin. It was all so deliberately lascivious and was certain to irk her daughter.

Marcella took a pull from her diet soda. She was shaking her head.

Her mother withdrew his finger long enough to say, "Oh stop pouting, Marcella, like a little child. You're a grown woman, act like it. You're wrong and you know it—to treat this fine young specimen of manhood the way you have been. Can't you see the lad is hurting? He is too much of a man to make a fuss, outwardly, but he is in pain; his heart is breaking. And I, for one, am determined to lighten his suffering and hopefully, eventually, one day soon, he'll bounce back fully healed."

She rose, taking Jimmy Riff by the hand. "We'll be in the bedroom, for phase three of this great healing process. You can stay here and pout, or join us and give the lad a loving good-bye, one he'll remember and cherish the rest of his life. You have a chance to be a giver, as opposed to taking and causing emotional as well as psychological scars, the way you have been for quite some time now. You have an opportunity to make up for it, before *karma* catches up. Mark my words, it will catch up. Entirely up to you, Marcella."

Renata Blevins paused long enough to open the refrigerator door, reach inside for a can of whipped cream, and led Jimmy out of the kitchen. Marcella sat there, contemplating what her mother had said about all of it and decided that maybe, just maybe, she had a point. She would join them in the bedroom as soon as she finished off the last of her soda.

Hollywood-Bound

Henry's wife, on the other hand, had found the incident with the deacon's daughter exceedingly hilarious. Especially when she saw how perturbed it made her husband. Rubbed it in every chance she got. He was upset not only because he had failed at seducing the targeted female but because his own son had been able to. This particular night Henry had wanted to keep arguing about it with his bogus justifications and lame reasons. She'd had enough. Besides, it was getting late and they were out of booze. She wanted to make a run to the neighborhood liquor store before they closed. Jimmy watched her pause at the door and give his father that hard glare: "Face it, Henry, you're losing your touch." And she was out the door.

"Clearly drunk," his father had said. "But there she is running off to buy more."

"Ever wonder why?"

"Why what, Jimmy?"

"Why she drinks."

"Who cares," his father had said. "This is about that underage girl you knocked up, and nothing else."

"She's experienced. She's eighteen."

"She wasn't eighteen at the time, was she, boy?"

"She's older than me—"

"I don't want to hear it, boy. Nothing you say will ever excuse the harm your insensitive behavior caused this family. I'm the one who had to deal with her father, not you, sonny."

"You did? You talked to Deacon Blevins?"

"I'm handling this!" Rev. Riff had screamed. "Keep out of it, unless you want to cause further trouble and bring on additional grief to your mother and me." This was when Jimmy could no longer take it, and had called his father a damn liar.

"What was that? What did you say to me?"

"You're lying! You heard! Liar!"

"I know my own son didn't call me a liar just then!"

"She came on to me! Worked on me for weeks! Plied me with *Tootsie Rolls* and *Twinkies!* You saw her! She must have slept with half the men in the congregation! Wears the tightest skirts! Was always rubbing up against my thigh while I was in that kitchen scrubbing pots and pans!"

"That does not excuse anything! It does not make it right!"

"Look who's talking! How many women, married and/or otherwise attached, have you knocked up on both coasts, not to mention quite a few in between? Exactly the reason we've been kicked out of every town we've ever been in! Your drinking and philandering, old man! And quite a few of them have been under age, by the way! Had to slip out of town under cover of night for that secret abortion!" Surely a fistfight would have broken out between them if older brother Billy hadn't been there to break it up. Alas, two nights later there was no one to step in and the two of them went at it. The mother had never returned from that trip to the liquor store. Jimmy hadn't hesitated to point the finger where it deserved pointing: his father. "You're responsible for this!" he'd said. "You caused it!"

"What's new about any of this?" his father had said. "She's missing.

Happened before. Sleeping off a bender somewhere. Self-destructive; always was. Can't blame me for it, Jimmy! I'm a good provider! Always have been! My kids never went hungry! That's the main thing! Woman's a drunk! Tried so hard to get her to join AA. For years. She refuses. Time and time again, she refuses! She's a lush! And I'm sick and tired of being blamed for it!"

"Accept it! You're the cause!"

"A man has needs," his father had said. "Your mother is inadequate in the bedroom! I don't want to go there; it's not in good taste, especially for a man of my standing in the community."

"You kept shoving it in her face! Going into every detail! Me and Billy could hear it through the wall! In every apartment we rented, every house we lived in! You going into every detail! How you seduced 'that Jezebel'; how you 'penetrated the harlot's bogus resistance'! It's sick! Explains why he's just like you! Sick! The whole thing is sick and twisted! And what makes it worse is the fact you don't even see how hateful it is! How wrong the whole thing is. You would have been better off divorcing her! Instead of carrying on like some heartless degenerate, which is what you are!"

"Divorce? What would you know about divorce? I can't divorce; don't believe in it! I'm a man of the cloth!"

This was where the long-brewing fistfight at last had taken place between them.

"*Man of the cloth?*" Jimmy had mimicked. "Is that what you said? You're lucky you're not in jail for embezzling."

"Embezzling? I did no such thing!"

"Only because they thwarted your scheme before you'd had a chance to put it into action. Someone from one of the other parishes must have tipped them off about your sticky fingers." Elke had been there. Had started to laugh. It had enraged his father enough to where he raised his hand to slap her. It was then Jimmy could not resist the impulse to grab his father by the collar and fling him clear across the living room.

Henry had recovered, leapt at him, and they had started trading punches. The thing that had stopped it was the ringing of the telephone, and Elke picking up the receiver and screaming it was the police. Mrs. Riff had been discovered in a motel room, unconscious, having swallowed a good deal of Liquid-Plumr. "She's in an ambulance as we speak," the caller had said. "Being rushed to Emergency."

It had taken a week of acute pain and suffering before Mrs. Riff slipped into a coma and expired. What had made it worse, the other sister, Betsy, was dealing with a dilemma of her own: she was off somewhere getting the abortion that would eventually push her over the edge and put her in the bug house.

❧

Look back? This was why you didn't look back.

He had moved out West, to Oregon, to spend his remaining high school years there with his mother's brother Orville on his organic chicken ranch. It had taken just as long to get over Marcella, who refused to have anything to do with him. No explanation, no reason. "It was great fun while it lasted, honey."

He had told her that he loved her. "Love, honey boy? What do a couple of young people know about love?"

He'd had no choice but to put it behind him. It hadn't been easy, but you moved on. He also knew he'd stay alert, keep his guard up when it came to this type of heartbreaking female in the future. All of them could not be this way, he had reasoned. There were plenty of good-hearted women out there. One just had to be careful. And he buried his pain. No choice. No point dwelling on anything as unpleasant as what he'd gone through. Besides, he wasn't the only one this sort of thing happened to. Men and women were being dumped every day; there was divorce and whatnot. Love mattered, but love was also a crapshoot, not unlike playing the Lotto. One struck out most of the time, but every now and then you also got lucky. Sometimes couples lasted, marriages worked. It didn't always have to be tears and agony.

For college, he moved back to the East Coast for a couple of years and stayed with his mother's sister, Aunt Irma. Took courses in agriculture, farming, animal husbandry; he toyed with the notion of becoming a veterinarian. There was loss of interest, restlessness, the West tugged at him, particularly the Oregon Coast, and when he received a postcard from Marcella, out of the blue, who was living in California, that cinched it. He had two years in when he dropped out. Contacted his Uncle Orville, who had said: "Come on out, son. We can sure use the help." Bought himself a Greyhound bus ticket and headed West. Felt his money was low by the time he reached LA. Thought he'd stick around long enough to beef up his bankroll. Phoned the old flame from the Hollywood bus depot.

"What are you doing in Hollywood?" Marcella had said. "I'm out here in Chatsworth, thirty miles north of there."

"Can you come get me?"

He heard her laugh at the other end. Sounded a bit on the drunk side and/or high on something.

"You're joking," she had said.

"How do I get out there? I really want to see you, Marcella. Thought about you all these years."

"Cab, Jimmy. Catch a cab."

"I was surprised to get that postcard from you."

"Postcard? Did I send you a postcard? Have the address?"

He said he did. Held the postcard up to the light. Read it off, only she had handed the receiver to the mother before he was finished. Renata sounded truly happy to hear from him. "Frankly, I was kind of surprised to get this postcard from your daughter, Mrs. Blevins."

"We think the world of you, hon," said Marcella's mother. "You know, I divorced that no-good scoundrel husband of mine years ago. Turns out Beaufort is definitely homo. Seduced half the men in that congregation; plenty of them married. I decided I didn't want to take it anymore. Got a job offer with the *Hollywood Herald*; Marcella had always had this dream of being in the movies, and here we are. Why don't you come up, honey. We can't wait to see you."

She gave him directions to pass on to the cab driver, so he wouldn't take the scenic route and overcharge him, and said they would see him when he got there.

Porn Valley Bacchanal

It was a long cab ride out to Chatsworth and took practically all the money that he had. Not to worry. Marcella and her mother were old friends. He could always borrow a few dollars from one or the other and pay them back. He might stick around in LA, see how things worked out for him, before continuing on to Portland and his uncle's place.

It was past 11:00 p.m. by the time the cab pulled up in front of the single-story wood and stucco house with the big front lawn and wide driveway in a residential neighborhood among many other homes like it. The whole affair had an L-shape to it, with the two-car garage on his right making up the shorter part of the L, and the other part of the letter having been taken up by the house itself. Lots of automobiles, SUVs, Jeeps, Humvees, muscle cars, Mercedes Benzes parked in the driveway as well as on the lawn and along the sidewalk. You could easily tell there was a party going on inside; music was loud, people laughing, having a good time.

Jimmy paid the driver and rang the doorbell. A three-hundred-pound black lady eventually answered, inviting him in with a big smile, wrapped her arms around his neck, and began French kissing him between tokes on a doobie. She had on heels for footwear and a large beach towel wrapped around that had her image on it and the words above the image, what Jimmy could make out, that said: *Super Star*. Below the image the words appeared to be *Big Mama Bigelow*. The lady wore a gold necklace and many rings on her fat fingers. Jimmy, not unkindly, turned down the doobie. "I'm a friend of Marcella Blevins. Would you know where I might find her?"

"Marcella? What chu be wantin' with that pig?" said the three-hundred-pounder, reaching for his suitcase, which Jimmy refused to part with.

"She's a friend," said Jimmy. "An old friend."

"You ain't got to lie," said Big Mama Bigelow, glancing at the suitcase. "What chu got in there? You be lookin' for a date, ain't you?"

"A date?" said Jimmy.

"You heard. Got a suitcase full of toys and shit; whips and shit; ballgag' and vibrators. What else would you be doin' if not lookin' to hook up?"

"Well, I have a 'date,' sort of, with her." And disentangled himself free of the large woman and made his way inside.

Living room was packed with people and reeked of pot. There was a mountain of coke on a coffee table that men and women, some squished together on the sofa, and others kneeling on the floor, were snorting with tooters. Something by the *Rolling Stones* blasted out through the speakers.

Weed and cigarette smoke was so thick it gave him belly cramps. He braved his way through the crowd of partygoers. Asked around for Marcella. Half of the people he talked to hadn't even heard of her. One attractive and clearly inebriated coed type in a pair of stylish, tight-fitting jeans and a mane of strawberry-blond hair said: "Martinique?"

"No," Jimmy said. "Marcella, Marcella Blevins."

"No, you mean *Martinique du Maurier*," the woman said. "That's the name she uses; her stage name. How do I know this? My date, whose idea was to come here, introduced me to her earlier, when I was still sober."

"Stage name?" said Jimmy.

"She's well known," she said. "In certain circles. Hey, who are you, anyway?"

"A friend," said Jimmy. "Knew her way back when. . . ."

The girl nodded. Was about to sip from the wine cooler in her hand, then thought to offer it to him. Jimmy shook his head. She had a pull. "I don't know if I should reveal her whereabouts. . ."

"Please," said Jimmy. "The cab I took from Hollywood got all my money. I have been on a Greyhound bus for over two thousand miles . . . and very much wish to see her."

"It's not a good idea. . . ."

"I was in love with her. . . . Probably still am, to some extent. She was my first. . . ."

"Your first? They say you never forget your first love. . . . I wouldn't know. . . ." She stopped herself. "Bet you didn't come two thousand miles to hear that."

"Show me where she is. Please."

She stared at him. Polished off the wine cooler. "Why am I doing this?" She held the bottle up, then turned it upside down. "Don't care for this stuff at all. I'm a beer drinker myself. Would you like a beer?" Jimmy nodded. She said she'd be back in a minute. "Better yet, why don't you follow me?" Grabbing him by the hand, she led him to the kitchen, but not before handing him the empty bottle to do with as he wished. Jimmy banged it down beside the pile of coke on the coffee table and watched the powder spray the air every which way, upsetting the huffers. They continued on to the kitchen. There was a metal washtub in the center of the tile floor half full with ice and beer and wine coolers. The woman extracted a bottle of *Carlsberg* for herself. Jimmy reached in, dug around among the bottles of *Miller, Bud, Schlitz, Pabst Blue Ribbon*, until he spotted a lone *Heineken* and fished it out. Uncapped it. Took a pull. So did the girl. Then said: "Follow me, handsome. *Only brace yourself.* . . ." She giggled. They were back in the living room. Made a right and elbowed their way through the crowd. Made it to a bedroom in back. Door was closed. She placed her hand on the doorknob. Looked at him. "I'm Victoria, by the way. You're . . . ?"

"James. Jimmy's fine. Friends call me Jimmy."

"Jimmy, if things don't turn out the way you expected; if for some reason you feel a tremendous sense of loss . . . for whatever reason. . . . Call me. Victoria Chantal. . . ." And before she could get her full name out, she lost her balance and collapsed against the door, pushing it open, laughing as she did, and dropping to the carpet.

Jimmy looked in. What he saw was enough to cause his jaw to drop.

Bukkake

He should not have been surprised in any way; should not have been shocked at all. Marcella was there all right, on a large round bed, naked, surrounded by half a dozen studs, white and black, and one Chinese-American, who were not clothed themselves. The bed had been covered with a type of blue tarp that she was lying on. Some of the guys had their erections in her: mouth, rectum, vagina; the others were kneeling on either side of her on the large bed stroking themselves in order to maintain those hard-ons.

It sickened him to see it. Marcella, true to form, was up to her old tricks. Hell. What did you expect? Whatever it was, it wasn't this: her, smack-dab in the middle of an orgy: Marcella the center attraction, and her mother Renata running a video camera and apparently directing the show. There was another camera operator, a male, shooting from the opposite side of the room. They had lights on stands placed strategically. The makeup girl, he assumed was the makeup girl, was a woman in her forties, sitting in a director's chair off to the right in the corner reading a Mickey Spillane paperback, smoking a cigarette.

He couldn't move, either. Stood there. The girl on the carpet continued to mumble something or other. "Warned you, didn't I, Jimmy?" she said. "You are one handsome man, by the way. I'm so sorry you had to see this. From the looks of it, you still have feelings for the, uh, lady. . . ." She giggled.

Renata, having heard the girl say his name, did a quick double take, waving five fingers, meaning she needed five minutes and would like to talk to him.

One of the studs turned his head, asking that he close the door. This shook him out of his daze, and he did try. Only Victoria was in the way. He leaned over, attempted to move her, only she refused to be budged. "No," she said. "The guy, my boyfriend, so-called, who brought me to the party . . . is out by the pool doing the same thing; so don't feel bad, my new-found friend. It happens. More than you think. Furthermore, welcome to Hollywood. Better yet: Welcome to Porn Valley, amigo."

Jimmy felt he could have used something stronger than a beer right then. Wished he could have crawled under a rock. He felt ill; a headache, better yet, a migraine, was coming on. Cramps in his belly intensified. Something like a hot ball of pain made itself known inside down there, and began the slow climb up through his lungs and throat. Why he still felt this way, when he hadn't even seen her in all those years, was a mystery. Only it could not be denied. What did it matter that she was screwing a bunch of guys like this? Marcella had the knack, she had the need, and did as she wished. There was no controlling her in any way.

The girl down there had wrapped her arms around his shins and was quietly weeping. *I'm not from around here, you know. I'm not used to this sort of thing. This isn't the way it should be; this is not the way it should be. . . ."*

He stood still, frozen. Feeling for her. Trapped; they both were. And up there, on the bed, the men were switching off, in that the guys who were stroking themselves, were now inside of her: oral cavity, anus, and muff. Hammering home. Marcella was in cock heaven. Her moans and squeals and sighs and whatnot only made his pain more acute.

"Don't cry, mister," Jimmy heard Victoria plead from below. He wasn't crying. Where did she get that he was crying? He may have felt lousy and out of sorts, but there was no way he would yield to tears. "Don't be weak," he heard her say. "Please. Don't be a weakling; not here, not in Porn Valley. They'll crush you. Don't let them see that you're weak; that you have a soft spot. They enjoy crushing people like us. It gives them pleasure to see us this way. . . ."

Marcella looked in his direction, grinning for him, wanting him to see her this way, being gang-banged by these bots. For a brief moment even, she withdrew the large black cock from her mouth, said to him: "*Tubesteak!* Come here. I want to taste you; I want you in my mouth. For old time's sake! Come here, Jimmy. Don't be bashful."

Jimmy had stood where he was, unable to move.

"Could be he can't get wood," one of the studs said, who seemed to be having trouble keeping his erection up.

Marcella laughed.

"I wouldn't talk, pal," said Jimmy.

The stud turned his head, was about to move toward him, when Renata Blevins snapped her fingers. *"No, Lucky! Move out of frame, and you're fired!"* Evidently this was enough to make "Lucky" stay with the task at hand. Marcella grabbed his groin and shoved it inside her mouth, doing her best to make him rigid. It was quite the challenge. She did give it a valiant try, saw it was hopeless, and went for a groin that was already stiff. "Don't like what you see, square muthafuckah?" one of the black studs said. "Get the fuck out, then." It had been clearly directed at Jimmy.

He wanted to; only the tipsy girl, Victoria, was still down there, clinging to him. "Don't go without me," she said. "Please, sir. Mister. Jimmy. Don't."

The studs started shooting cum into Marcella, into her and all over her: the once beautiful light-brown locks with the chestnut streaks that no longer appeared remotely attractive, but matted with sweat and semen. They spurted in her mouth, one after another; all, that is, with the exception of the one they called Lucky, who never made it, and remained in the background, away from the action. Marcella lapped it up, wanting more, wanting it all, and then some. Her mouth wide open, tongue doing things, darting, licking her lips—and beyond. The guy who was inside her asshole withdrew, then guided his prong over to her face and ejaculated: sprayed cum on her mouth, chin, and cleavage area.

The other guy, who'd been pumping her cunt, pulled out, positioned himself over her face and released a tremendous amount of white cum, spraying her face: eyes, nose, hair and mouth, then jammed his groin inside her jaw. Marcella wrapped her lips around it, sucking, draining him as the guy gasped and shook his head.

They took turns, until every single swinging dick was spent. Some lay down on either side of her; a couple of them dropped to the carpet. Lucky, the wise-ass with the limp pecker, in a feeble effort to compensate and/or make up for the lackluster performance, walked over to where Victoria was and attempted to drag her to the bed and have her lick off what remained of the fluids on Marcella and the tarp. Only Jimmy shoved him back, hard, picked up Victoria, and walked her out of the bedroom. He could still hear Marcella laughing mockingly back there, laughing at him for being such a naive wuss. Renata called after him. "Wait, Jimmy. I'd like to have a word with you. Jimmy!"

Aka Raquel Renoir

"I'd like to show you something," Victoria said, grabbing him by the arm and taking him to the backyard where the pool was. There was more partying taking place here. On the left, in the jacuzzi, two former TV stars from a western series were going at it. Jimmy couldn't recall their names, but the guy who played the sheriff was in the water and blowing the other guy who sat on the edge. The guy on the edge had played his deputy; or was it a cop show? He couldn't remember, not that it mattered. Pool was full of naked people, porn stars, as well as stars of the silver screen, fornicating like rabbits. "On the right," Victoria said, pointing to a vacant chaise lounge. "That's where they were. My date and two party girls. Only they are no longer here, obviously," Victoria said. "He never mentioned we'd be going to an orgy in the Valley."

"Jimmy?" It was Renata, Marcella's mother, emerging from the open sliding glass door of the living room. She walked up. "I should explain." She hinted that someone with his looks and ability in the sack could do well for himself in adult films. Jimmy was not interested.

"I still have feelings for your daughter."

"After what you saw back there? You still want her? That *is* love; the real thing."

"I didn't say I'd take her back; I couldn't, but there is no denying the ache is there. I was fine. Seeing her again seemed to reawaken it."

"Poor baby. You'll have to get in line. That kid back there, the one who goes by Lucky Woodcock? He's in your shoes. Fell for my daughter; why he failed to get wood—with all those other studs doing her. Was intimidated, not to mention emotionally crushed. His male ego couldn't take it. I feel awful for anyone who falls for my Marcella and has no idea what he's in for. She does not get attached; there is no emotional attachment for her. It's all about fun and having a good time."

"Oh, I'll get over it. I'm a big boy these days."

"Of course you will. Besides, love is overrated."

"Not what I meant, Renata."

"What is it you're after, dear boy?"

"She sends me a postcard. 'Would love to get together,' it said, 'reminisce about old times'."

"She didn't send the postcard, I did."

This confession stumped him momentarily. Did it bother him? Yes, but not as much as what he'd just witnessed with Marcella and the porn studs. He hand gestured in the direction of the bedroom where the *bukkake* had taken place. "That was not what I expected, Mrs. Blevins."

"Ms. Renoir, please, Jimmy. *Raquel Renoir.* 'Blevins' belongs to my ex-husband. It is not mine. I no longer have any use for it, or him."

"So you're both in show business."

"I write the scripts and direct; she stars. It's worked out for us. Who better to manage my own daughter? I see to it that no one takes advantage of her; that she is not exploited in any way. There's loads of cash to be made here, Jimmy, should you be interested. Fame is within reach. Marcella, *Martinique,* rather, is a top draw, one of the top-paid porn stars in the world these days. Male performers don't make nearly as much, that's true, but someone like you—with that clean and healthy physique, gorgeous face, and sparkling blue eyes . . . you'd be able to fetch top dollar in no time."

"Yes, except she left out a couple of things: herpes, clap, and other STDs," a middle-aged, stocky white guy with a bent nose and lumpy brows said, intruding on their conversation. "The men are paid peanuts compared to what the broads make, *usually*. Talk about exploitation? They're lucky if they last a few years. Before you know it, they're out. Used up, wasted on drugs. Chew 'em up, and spit 'em out. It's the most humiliating way to earn a living. Furthermore, none of them are ever allowed to break into mainstream Hollywood, where the big money is. You want to make it? *See real jack?* You talk to me." He handed Jimmy a business card.

"Who the hell asked you to butt in, Mr Styles? It's really rude of you to do that. On the other hand, rude behavior seems to be your stock in trade. By the way, I don't recall inviting you to this party."

"You should be ashamed of yourself, *Ms. Blevins*. Know what's being done to your daughter as we speak?" The man had said to Jimmy: "They're *whizzing* on her. That's right. Those guys who just hosed her down with nutsack chowder are pissing on her, in her, all over her. Somebody should give the slut an umbrella. She's got her mouth open wide and they're spraying urine in it—for the extended, European version." He laughed. Raquel said nothing. "Golden showers. That's why *Renata* is out here, and not inside shooting it. Let the other camera operator do it. Didn't want to get rained on herself. Say it ain't so, *Ms. Renoir*."

Jimmy looked at her. Was Marcella being urinated on by those dicks-for-hire? Should he have been shocked? When you did porn this was what happened; even more, far worse.

Raquel heaved a sigh. "It's business. Europeans go for the harder versions. We're shooting both versions simultaneously, U.S. and Euro/Asian markets. *Bukkake* is in demand at the moment: *bukkake*, *DPs*, and *anals*. I didn't stay in the bedroom because I wanted to talk to my friend Jimmy here. We have a history. Don't we, *Tubesteak?* We're friends from way back."

Benjamin T. Styles shook his head. "Gotta ask yourself: Want to be part of that low-grade, dead-end scene, or you want to be in legitimate studio productions and thinking in terms of an actual career for yourself? You got my number." He walked off, saying to no one: "With so much easy cunt in this place I should at least be able to get blown."

Love Shed

Marcella's mother had excused herself and left, promising to return, and Jimmy was trying to figure out what to do about his empty billfold situation. Where would he spend the night? Here? Among the hedonists, and risk getting busted and taken to jail for the rampant drugs that were being abused in the place? And what about this girl with him? Victoria? How would she get home? She was in no condition to drive.

"I'm so sorry you had to see that," said Victoria, slurring her words. "Back there. In the bedroom. I feel as awful as you look." She hiccupped. Followed up with a giggle. Then found herself apologizing again, as someone who had had one drink too many was wont to do. "It's either laugh or cry," she said. "I'm not about to start weeping over someone I was never in love with to begin with."

He didn't know what to say to that.

"Bother me?" she said. "Does it bother me? More than I care to admit."

"You still lookin' for a date?" said Big Mama Bigelow, appearing out of nowhere, farting as she spoke. Gas emissions were powerful and loud enough to be heard over the loud music that blasted from inside the house.

"I'm sorry, no."

"Heard you clearly say you wuz lookin' for a date."

"Her date," explained Jimmy, indicating the clearly tipsy Victoria.

"The guy whose idea was to come out here, Bosley —" said Victoria.

"Schitzkowski?" said Big Mama Bigelow. "Bosko? That white boy can't get wood. Shaves his pubic hair to make his dick look big. Lot of them dudes shave their pubic hair to make they dick look big. Dude be hardly big enough. Done a scene with him one time. Had to use a fake dick in close up an' powdered sugar for the money shot 'cause the dude's real dick don't stay up."

"No, the guy I drove up with is Bosley, Bosley Snodgrass," said Victoria. "Goes by Buster Nutsack."

"Nutsack?" said Big Mama Bigelow.

"The name he directs under."

"I know that dude. USC film school asshole. Be actin' like he too good to be doin' hardcore. Be from the East Coast. Family got money; at least he be actin' like it. Can't direct worth shit. Got his nose in the air all the time."

"Sounds like him," confirmed Victoria.

"Seen him doin' toot back here earlier with a couple of them skinny white bitches with fake tits be like blowed-up balloons. They be sayin' them tits growed all by they self since the last time I seen 'em; was two or three weeks ago. Don't nobody's boobs grow like that on account they gain' some weight. Tell me about it. Who know better than Big Mama Bigelow?"

"As you can see she's in no condition to drive herself home," explained Jimmy. "We'd like to find him so she can talk to him about getting out of here before the place is rousted."

"Rousted?" said Big Mama. "You sho talks funny. Where you from, anyway?"

Jimmy shrugged.

"Don't know where you from?"

"We traveled a lot."

"This is the Valley, honey," Big Mama assured him. "Ain't nobody gettin' '*rousted*.'" She reached down and grabbed him by the crotch. Said: "Follow me." Jimmy had no choice but to do as this clearly high and unpredictable big lady demanded, taking him past the right edge of the pool and the tool shed located way in the back in the right-hand corner of the yard. Victoria staggered along, shaking her head at the insanity going on all over the place. She couldn't wait to get out. First, she would let Bosley know she was leaving. That would be the right thing to do, wouldn't it?

They reached the shed. Big Mama finally let go of his crotch and opened the door. Many tools hung from hooks on the right wall: trowels, pruning shears, claw hammers, locking pliers, crescent wrenches, saws, drills, and drill bits. There were shovels, rakes, a lawn edger, bulb dibble, seeders, a hedge trimmer, a hose trolley on the carpeted floor, couple of hoses, watering cans, a tree pruner, a power mower. The left side of the shed contained an editing bay with three video monitors. On that same side of the shed was a hideaway bed that had been pulled out and there were three naked and sweaty, writhing bodies entangled on it in passionate activity. The two women were on the slim side, although their surgically enhanced breasts were enormous. There was a man there, about Jimmy's age, in the middle, sandwiched between the females. He noticed them watching and didn't seem to give a damn one way or the other. Jimmy saw the look of anguish on Victoria's face and felt the need to get her out of there. Only she was not budging.

"Tol' you the muthafuckah be no good," said Big Mama Bigelow, and left. Jimmy decided to do the same.

Big Mama Bigelow
Leaves an Impression

He stood, pretty much in shock, at what he witnessed next: Big Mama dropped her towel and walked back in the direction they had just come from, in that it was the deep end of the pool. Paused at the steps to the diving board, her rapidly deteriorating condition making it a challenge to negotiate the steps. She made the effort at last, climbed up the half dozen steps, taking it one step at a time, and made it finally to the top. No one paid attention to her from down there in the water. Two Filipino-American types were directly below, gay men evidently, preoccupied with each other. Big Mama Bigelow, the naked three-hundred-pound porn superstar, walked out to about the end of the board, turned with great caution, and squatted. As before, she was farting, releasing a tremendous volley of methane. And then something else followed that was not gas. This was where the shock for Jimmy Riff came in. He found it difficult to believe what he was about to behold. And he still refused to accept it as it progressed directly into that. The people down below in the water, immersed in whatever activity they were participating in, had no idea what was about to befall them. It was no different for the two gay male Filipino-Americans doing the dog paddle and admiring one another directly below the diving board. It was not until one of her large logs landed on the gay couple that all hell broke out. People were shouting, a woman screamed, another fainted at the sliding glass door. Up there, though, Big Mama Bigelow remained calm, collected, determined, as she continued to squeeze out additional logs. Then started pissing; a great waterfall of urine poured out. The Filipino-American males wasted no time swimming out of harm's way and climbing out of the presently contaminated pool.

Someone, a white dude in bathing shorts, who had been sitting at the patio table, yelled at her to stop. She paid no mind. He reached for a small item in his folded trousers and climbed the steps to the diving board and sprayed her with what appeared to be mace. Big Mama lost her balance, and dropped down into the water.

It turned out she was not a very good swimmer. Only no one was willing to jump in to help her on account of the floating waste. The two gay Filipino-American men were digging around inside their swim suits and were swiftly extracting what appeared to be waterproof plastic pouches from which they further extracted a small handgun each, badges, cuffs; yanking out as well fake dildos that they tossed aside.

The guy with the mace was promptly cuffed and read his Miranda rights. Jimmy snapped out of his daze long enough to fetch a lifesaver in the shape of an erect penis and tossed it in the water for Big Mama to latch onto and paddle herself to the edge of the pool where she stayed, breathing heavily, doing her best to catch her breath, whereby she remained, dazed and confused, disorientated, as though on a bad LSD trip.

Jimmy Riff realized that it was clearly time to vacate the premises. He turned his head, saw that the ruckus had drawn Victoria outside, and he waved to her to follow as he crossed the yard and re-entered the house through the patio entrance. He elbowed his way through the packed living room. Exited out the front door. Victoria did same. Caught up. Pleaded with Jimmy to drive her home.

"What about Bosley?"

"Don't make me take a cab. I'll pay you—in cash money."

"Your date? Remember?"

Her date appeared. Hurried after her. He was shirtless. The three were in front of the house, standing in the driveway.

"Vicki! Who's this guy? Where you going?"

"I'm leaving. You didn't tell me it would be anything like this."

"Said it was a party with showbiz types—"

"They're porn people, Bosley!"

"If porn isn't showbiz, what is? It's all show business, honey! Entertainment! Done to make a buck!"

"Drugs and orgies! I never would have come if I had known!"

"Who is this guy you're leaving with?"

"*A friend!*"

"I bet! Well, you got here with me and you're leaving with me. I'm taking you home; I'll drive. Gimme your car keys."

"I'm not going anywhere with you."

"You just met the guy. You're choosing him over me? Someone you've known since childhood? I don't get it! It's insane; it's nuts!"

"I'm disgusted, thoroughly disgusted with you at the moment!"

"Are you fucking him? Did she fuck you? Hey, buddy, I'm talking to you?"

"We just met. I don't know the lady. She begged me to drive her home. There is nothing more to it."

"Bullshit!" He grabbed Jimmy by the arm. "She never give *me* any!"

"Not that. You don't put your hands on me," said Jimmy. The guy got the message and let go. "I want nothing to do with any of this. Renata and her daughter are friends from way back. Only reason I'm here. This woman, your date, or friend, whatever she is, started talking to me. She's too drunk to drive. She begged me to help out. There is nothing more to it. My 'girlfriend,' in fact, the one I once was involved with is back there in one of the bedrooms—being done by a bunch of guys. So I don't feel particularly good right now, pal. Understand? I don't need your problems. You want to take your 'sweetheart' home? Be my guest."

Jimmy started to walk off.

Bosley Snodgrass suggested the three of them snort some toot.

"There's plenty."

"I don't do dope," said Jimmy. Didn't bother mentioning that the undercover dicks had just arrested someone in the backyard, nor did he want to know how the jerk could've missed it. He wanted to get going. Had no idea where he was headed, so long as it was away from here.

"What? You square? You shittin' me? Don't do free toot? You don't know what you're missing," said Snodgrass. Called Vicki.

"I have no use for your drugs, Bos!" said Victoria.

"*It's free toot!* Hell's the matter with you? Nose candy! Blow! Free! *Let's party!*"

"Forget it!"

Victoria Chantal followed Jimmy, calling after him. He had kept to his right, had begun crossing the lawn. "You're not going to make me call a cab? Here in the Valley? It can take forever. And even longer to take me to Malibu. It will take way, way too long to drive me out there. I don't feel good. Jimmy? Please. You're not going to leave me stranded like this? I realize we just met. I know no one else. . . ."

She followed after him, stumbling as she reached the lawn, tripped on a sprinkler, and went down. Jimmy turned, walked back, helped her up. She had cut herself, skinned a knee. Elbow was bleeding. He wiped the blood with his shirttail. Wanted to get peroxide and Band-Aids for her. Only she refused to go back inside.

"You're hurt."

"Only my pride," said Vicki. Bosley Snodgrass waved his hand, then flipped them both off and returned to the party, saying he was looking to snort some dust.

She shook her head. Walked off. Continued crossing the lawn in the same general direction Jimmy had been heading in a moment earlier. She was mumbling to herself. "I'll take myself home; that's what I'll do."

Jimmy called after her. She stopped.

"You're in no condition," he insisted. She waited for him to catch up where she stood in the middle of the lawn.

"Hey, wise guy," said a male voice emerging from that side of the house. It was too dark and he was too far away to make out what he looked like— until he got closer. "What was that wisecrack you made back there on the set?"

Jimmy looked at him. It was the guy who'd had trouble getting wood. Drunk.

"You made the 'crack,' pal, not me."

"Maybe next time you'll think twice before you open that big mouth of yours."

"Can't take it?" said Jimmy. "Don't dish it." It was then the guy Marcella's mother had called "Lucky Woodcock" leapt at him, swinging with some type of black club or one of those long flashlights. Jimmy blocked it with his suitcase, and swung with his right. Lucky went down, dazed. "He was easy," said the Chinese guy. "Too easy. Would you like to try that on me?" Jimmy saw him step out from behind the tall hedge. More trouble from the porn gallery.

"Who the hell are you?" said Jimmy.

"Lucky's friend," said the Chinese guy. "Name's Iggy Gu."

"You're kidding?" said Jimmy.

"You seem to think this is funny."

"No," pleaded Victoria with the Chinese guy who went by Iggy Gu. "Don't hit him. Jimmy, let's please go, now. Please." Saw that Jimmy was about to get beaten up. She staggered back inside to get help.

"For some reason everything is funny to you, isn't it?" said Iggy Gu.

"No, just your stage names. I can appreciate the humor."

"That don't mean shit to me," said the Chinese-American.

Jimmy lowered his suitcase to the ground, waited for the guy to make his move. Only he didn't, one of the soul brothers in back of him did. Guy was bare-chested. Gym-rat type with steroid bloated arms and pecs. Thick neck. Had tats on his massive torso. One that resembled Dr. Martin Luther King, the other appeared to be Malcolm X, or was it? Jimmy couldn't be sure. Although he was sure of one thing, he had great respect for both: King and Malcolm. Probably the latter more so than the other. He had read the autobiography on the Greyhound on the way out. But what did any of that matter now? He was in the process of being ganged up on. Jumped. For no legitimate reason he could think of.

"He's mine, Toby," said Iggy Gu to the soul brother.

"I got this square muthafuckah," said the soul brother. "Actin' all superior and shit. We in there workin', makin' a living, and this square muthafuckah be actin' all high and mighty. Wanna know what my name be, punk? You be askin' everybody's name."

"I didn't ask for any of this," said Jimmy. "I'm against violence. The lady requested I drive her home."

"That right?" said the black guy. "Lyin muthafuckah. Know who you be talkin' to, chump? You talkin' to *Toby Dick*. Laugh at that. All attitude an' can't back up nothin'. Who the fuck you think you is? Makin' fun of my white brotha Lucky Woodcock cause the dude can't get wood during a scene! What you don't seem to know, muthafuckah, that was his old lady in there, that fuckin' ice queen Martinique du Maurier, or whatever her fuckin' name is! That's right: *his old lady.* Dude be in love with her. Probably had no business bein' in the scene; why he couldn't make his chubby!"

"Oh, I know all about her," said Jimmy. "She pulled the same stunt on me, years ago, when her name was Marcella Blevins."

"You know the bitch?" said Toby Dick. "You a damn liar. You insult my homies and thank you can just walk away! No, muthafuckah, you gots ta pay! Got you an ass-whuppin' comin' to you, punk!"

"I may be a few things, Mr. Toby Dick, but a *'punk'* is not one of them."

"You exactly that, dude—one sorry-ass punk!"

Toby Dick moved in, threw a punch that Jimmy easily ducked. The stud followed with a kick that was short of its intended target, Jimmy's lower belly, by half a foot, although close enough for Jimmy to grab the man's ankle, yank on it, pulling him to the ground. He leaned in, punched him in the face once, twice, then delivered a hard elbow to the side of his thick neck. That was all she wrote. Iggy Gu went for it: kicked Jimmy somewhere in the head, and Jimmy went down himself, dazed plenty. Rose to about his knees, when the Chinese karate porn stud delivered a kick to Jimmy's midsection that flipped him over, knocking the wind out of him.

Benjamin T. Styles leapt out the front door, with Vicki following. Styles wasted no time and whacked Iggy Gu with a sap across his brow and down went Mr. Gu. Out like a light.

When Styles looked up, he saw two police cruisers quietly rolling down the street toward them. A number of neighbors had begun to emerge from their respective homes, taking in the ruckus. Styles did what he could to stir Jimmy awake, grab him, pull him up, but it was no use. He was way too heavy and not entirely coherent.

"Don't worry, kid," said Styles. "I'll put up bail. I'll get you out."

"Take her home," said Jimmy. "Don't let her drive. Please, Mr. Styles."

"It's under control, kid," said Styles, grabbing Vicki by the arm. Victoria freed herself long enough to grab Jimmy's suitcase and she and Styles hurried off down the street, away from the squads. Victoria kept turning her head, looking back to where Jimmy was. "We can't just leave him. Sir!"

"He'll be fine," said Styles. "It's the assholes back in the house who might end up doing some serious time on account of all the drugs and shit. 'Boyfriend' will be fine. I'll get my lawyer on it."

Back to the Present

Styles had bailed him out the next day. He was beholden. He owed him. Knew it. And he'd paid him back by accepting Renata's offer to do a film with her (so long as Marcella was not in any of the scenes with him). Figured he and Styles were even. Only it was a bitch trying to free himself of the albatross the man had turned into. Controlled his every move. Like he owned him. I've got news for him—and the rest of them. Nobody owns Jimmy Riff. He'd find a way to disentangle. No one was going to tell him who to make it with, how to live, especially not someone like that.

Deep down he knew he could have taken care of Styles that day in his office; he could have knocked him out for sure. He'd done it to others, the times he'd had to defend himself when assaulted by punks whose mothers were being romanced by his philandering daddy. He hadn't liked hitting anyone. That was the last thing he'd ever wanted, to be like old man Riff, chasing attached women, and when faced by irate husbands and/or their sons, acting indignant and blaming the woman, acting like he had every right. "If these 'love-starved ladies' weren't getting it at home, what was the matter with making them happy?"—had been his father's reasoning. "What about Mom? Look what it's doing to your own wife? You don't see the suffering your callous actions are causing?" Henry had finally done it, though. Woman switched from booze to *Liquid-Plumr*. Swallowed enough to end it. This was why you ran from it; why you didn't look back. It wasn't pretty—and no, you never could run from yourself, no matter how hard you tried.

No denying he was also running from some other things, too. Victoria Chantal. No doubt what he'd gone through with Marcella Blevins had had something to do with it. My psyche won't let me forget. The female version of his father. Love 'em and leave 'em. He didn't want to get burned again. That's what it was. So he ran. Saw that something genuinely good was actually taking place in his life; but that didn't matter, because Marcella had left a scar that cut deep. . . . What was the cliche? Something about the first cut being the deepest. Never mind that Vicki was not Marcella. Vicki; Victoria Chantal . . . was so close to the way he himself actually was . . . aching for that one person to be with, stay with. . . . Unlike his father and brother Bill; closer to the way his mother was. Never mind the numerous trysts and romantic encounters that meant nothing. There was a chance for something real with Victoria Chantal, something lasting and true, a heart connection; to have a good-hearted female on his side, be best friends with. All the way. Through everything. Good times/bad times. Ups/downs. Only his psyche, whatever that consisted of, call it self-preservation, wouldn't let it take place, would not allow it. . . .

Leave it. Let it rest. Dwelling on it accomplished only one thing: left him feeling psychologically exhausted and perplexed.

He hadn't hit Styles because the time hadn't been right. He was back on that. Styles. Overbearing creep. Worse than any overbearing female. You could always walk away from a woman who behaved this way. But with a guy like Styles, the only way to get him off your back was to duke it out. Knock him on his ass. Badgering son of a bitch. He hadn't slugged him that time in his office because he had owed Styles for helping him out and saving him from Lisa Koch, no matter that the man had had an ulterior motive. There was always an ulterior motive when it came to Benjamin T. Styles and his "kindnesses." Still, there was no denying he had gone in and extricated him from her clutches; quite possibly saved his life. Knew it. Never denied it.

But now things were changing, Jimmy thought. *Everything is different. If the louse refuses to let up, comes looking for me and continues to disrupt my life, I'll have to deal with him whether I like it or not, mob or no mob.* Some people, like Reverend Riff, all they understood was violence, a punch in the mouth, the backhand across the face; the only way left to communicate with a barbarian like that.

❧

He jerked his head from the quasi-dream state just as the bus pulled into an all-night gas station adjacent to a greasy spoon. *No,* he thought, *Styles not what's bothering you right now. You know what it is, Jimmy. You know exactly what's eating you.* . . . He wondered what Vicki was doing now, and to what extent the ex-pug would go to get his way.

Blackmail

Her eyes barely open, hands on the steering wheel, she snuck in snatches of shut-eye here and there. Needing more of it. Zooming headlights coming at her from the opposite direction were a nagging reminder to abandon the idea of allowing sleep to take over. Even so, she had next-to-no confidence that she would make it to Santa Barbara without yielding to her body's need for rest and crashing the rental, and it didn't seem to bother her any. It would solve all her problems, eliminate the pain. Everything was falling apart, it seemed. Her parents would be coming soon, and if that guy ever showed them the candid stills that would be the end of her. *I might as well be dead.* She would never be able to look either parent in the eye after that. And even if she could, she wasn't sure she would want to.

And how would Mom react? What would Dad say? It would just destroy him to think his "little girl" would do such a thing. Her nerves giving way, her legs began to shake. Her stomach was so tense and tight that she was unaware of the Mustang weaving: to the right, onto the gravel shoulder, and back over to the left, crossing the yellow line. Her eyes watered and she turned the radio up. *You really did it this time,* she said to herself. *You sure did.* And she punched the accelerator.

Pete Stanfill's Blues

Pete Stanfill adjusted the horn-rimmed glasses and withdrew a Kleenex from the box and held it near his erection. Irritated was how he felt when he saw what the car was doing up ahead. It was going to be that much tougher to keep stroking if he had to pay attention to the road.

The Mustang slowed down unexpectedly and he was forced to let go of his groin in order to downshift. He looked over his shoulder and was thankful Nicky was still snoring away in the back seat.

The car ahead picked up a steadier pace, but the weaving continued. He shifted again and resumed stroking. The porn star he'd once seen in a skin flick, the girl he'd fucked so many times (in his mind's eye), he thought of again. The scene from the film continued to unfold inside his head. The way she had plopped down on the bed, squeezing her tits and rubbing the nipples, then fondling her crotch. The guy in the scene had stood at the foot of the bed, massaging his enormous hard-on. The blond porn star had looked up at him, smiling enticingly, while gyrating her pelvis. The camera had moved in closer on her crotch as her hands covered her golden bush. She was wet and her pussy glistened.

"Fuck me, big boy," she had said to the actor in the scene with her. "Fuck me. . . ." Never mind that the dork in the scene hardly had six inches.

And she had begun to finger-fuck herself, her tongue darting in and out of her mouth. The guy had mounted her, only Pete Stanfill saw himself doing the deed instead, inserting his pulsating groin in her, and sliding it back out again. His forearm moved faster. His breathing got louder.

"Oh yeah," Pete moaned. "Oh, bay-bee. . . ."

He recalled the actor's meat going in and out. He could distinctly see the hairy balls slapping away at her sweaty ass, his buttocks pumping.

❧

He reached for the skin mag in the glove compartment and opened it to the centerfold, unaware of the VW's weaving. A glance here and there at the pictures in the magazine just didn't make it. He needed to have a better, longer look at the centerfold and pics. The longer his eyes lingered on the buxom, dark-haired model with the amazing tits and hairy beaver, the worse his weaving got. It was becoming too difficult to control and beyond Pete Stanfill's driving capabilities. His cock was cement hard and he would cum any second, and nothing else mattered: not being found out by Horgan, who lay sleeping in the back seat, not swerving over to the side and getting stuck in some ditch, not swerving far enough in the opposite direction into oncoming traffic and causing a smash-up, even if it meant getting killed.

Besides, he had jerked off on the highway many times in the past and nothing ever happened. He might have come close to side-swiping or hitting another car, but so what? He had always managed to careen out of harm's way in plenty of time.

He had to climax; he had to shoot juice into that tissue; he had to feel that sensation, that wonderful, grand sensation that never lasted long enough.

A jeep sped past, a pickup truck. Both honking their horns and having to veer over to the shoulder to avoid a collision. Oblivious to it all and so close to ejaculating, Pete Stanfill's wrist moved faster and faster, drawing him nearer and nearer to the moment. A semi threw him, made him jump in his seat with its blasting foghorn, and Pete lost control of the steering wheel. He applied the brakes out of nervousness and witnessed the VW Bug slide into the gravel shoulder on his right and down into a steep-enough ditch, slamming into a tree.

Nicky Horgan came awake with the impact that sent him hurtling into the front seat, his head cracking the windshield.

"The hell you do, guy?" Horgan said, after he'd regained his equilibrium.

"Darn it," Pete groused. It was not so much the damage to the car that made him angry. He had come so close to shooting his load.

Nicky Horgan staggered out to inspect the damage. The front of the car looked like a V. The right headlight demolished.

"Nice going, guy," Nicky Horgan said, and opened Pete Stanfill's door. Pete Stanfill looked up at him.

"Out."

"Wait a minute," Pete Stanfill said in protest. "You don't know what happened."

"I know you almost got us both killed, guy. *Out of the front seat.* Get in the back."

Pete Stanfill had little choice. Did as told. He was relieved Horgan hadn't caught him jerking his meat.

"Just hope it starts up again," Horgan said. Got behind the wheel and turned the ignition. Engine wheezed and sputtered. Horgan cursed. He tried again. Motor caught, and he steered the car back up on the blacktop.

"You get fifteen now," Horgan said without looking back.

"You said thirty dollars, Mr. Horgan. And we only go as far as Santa Barbara."

"I lose her, you only get fifteen," Nicky Horgan said. "I don't want to discuss it."

An angry Pete Stanfill closed his eyes and tried to sleep. Blue balls plagued him.

Home-Free

There was a lot on Nicky Horgan's mind. Blackmail was something he had never attempted before. Plenty of opportunities had been there all along—here in the United States, not so much in his native Hungary, which he got homesick for every time he thought of. Even when he didn't think of his native country, there was a homesickness he could not shake entirely.

He had lived in the U.S. since the mid '60s. Lots of years. And he still missed the people of his homeland: the customs, the picnics and the great food that was present at those fun outings. Ah, the food. How he loved it, yearned for it. Began to picture the various dishes in his mind's eye he'd missed out on over the years, Hungarian cooking his Mexican-born wife had never been very good at. Don't think about the food, don't think about Europe. It will only make you sad. Besides, there are enough Hungarian restaurants right here in Southern California. Expensive, but there. Not the same as being in Europe. . . . It was better than nothing.

To go for a visit. Now there was an idea. It took money. Everything took money. There was an old saying: No money, no honey. True, true. It would be nice to visit, see the people, places he grew up in.

Wouldn't be so nice to re-visit and be reminded of the poverty. All due to Communism. The Communists had a way of destroying everything and taking everyone's joy away. That was all totalitarianism was ever good for. Spreading misery; anguish and unhappiness. "For the good of all," they said. Asshole Marxists. His country was just fine until they rolled in with their tanks and APCs, took over.

He detested them: Communists and Communism. The loathing was so strong he could not even put it into words. It was because of them you could not even breathe freely, from fear a family member or neighbor would turn you in for supposedly having been critical or said something negative about the government. You could never buy anything like a car or even your oldest boy a bicycle. Not even a bicycle! It was no life.

Why did he have to think of Mikhail? He must be seventeen now, he was fairly certain, but did not know when the boy's birthday was; never did, other than the month. And every September he would send his son a present. His wife had married an engineer a month after they divorced, and it had been a traumatic experience for Nicholas Pheiffer.

Serafina was a plain-looking Mexican girl he married some fifteen years ago in San Diego just prior to his visa expiring. Believing her to be a citizen of the U.S., he had proposed matrimony—only to discover to his shock and dismay she had snuck into the United States without papers. She was illegal. He remembered that night so well, the night his new bride with the black patch over the left eye broke the news to him—their honeymoon night—that she was a native of Chihuahua, and not a U.S. Citizen.

"Chihuahua?" Nick had shouted. *"Chihuahua? What do I need with a one-eyed whore from Chihuahua?! I have no use for a one-eyed wetback*

from Chihuahua! I didn't travel all the way from Europe to marry a beaner from Chihuahua!"

He had begun to slap her, to take it out on her. He ranted, vented his rage: "You think I crawled on hands and knees through a Commie minefield, crawled under barbed wire and scaled over a brick wall for this? They shot at me with machine guns, I tell you! *Machine guns!* The Bolshevik pigs shot at me just because I didn't like their system of governing our people! *I lived through all that to marry a Mexican lettuce picker without papers?"*

He recalled the night, remembering it vividly in his mind's eye, the night he got away from the Reds. The border guards had opened up on him with sub-machine-guns. He had managed to get away with only a flesh wound. When he was forced to stop running and tie a swatch of cloth around his leg in order to keep from bleeding to death, he could hear the drunken guards laughing themselves silly. They were having a grand old time: guzzling vodka, joking. To them it had been nothing more than a bit of target practice.

He recalled lifting his pant leg in the motel to show Serafina the scar where he had been hit. "You think I survived all that to end up with you? Why do you think I married you?"

However, both had soon been in tears as she told of the hardships she, too, had endured. The fourteen kids in the family, starvation, life in a shack with a dirt floor. No plumbing or running water. Picking lettuce, grapes, and strawberries for next to no money. She had been raped, not once but twice, and cut in her eye by the filthy *coyotes* who had driven her and a truckload of her countrymen across the border into the United States. She had risked life and limb to help her family out, her poor parents and siblings, two of whom had decided to cross into Arizona and had been found dead in the desert. Her two brothers abandoned without water and died of dehydration.

It had been more than enough to soften Nicky Horgan's heart. They had spent the night together in each other's arms. It was the following morning that he had changed his name to Horgan, borrowing it from the motel desk clerk, obtained fake IDs, and relocated to Los Angeles, and the two of them began life anew.

The hell he'd gone through, all the misery, all the shit he'd had to endure, caused him to hate Styles with a vengeance. The threats, ribbing; slandering him simply because he had ordered an Eastern European dish that night with Styles, a client, that lousy, friggin' night he and Styles got stone drunk on Southern Comfort six years ago in that restaurant on Fairfax—that night he spilled his guts to Styles believing he had found a friend, an American to be trusted. Instead, Styles had turned on him, got his hooks in him and used him, and continued to use him as he pleased.

❧

Well, things would change. Things would be different from now on. Nicky Horgan had plans—and he had Benjamin Twitchell Styles to thank. Through this Vevrier girl, he would obtain the needed cash to start his business. A business so unique, so unusual, that he felt downright proud of himself for having thought of it. Sure, he'd had his failures in the past. Sure, the door-to-door selling of marital aids hadn't gotten him far, monetarily speaking. Peddling Bibles hadn't worked out, either. Too many people had the Bible already. Very few people would hardly allow him to deliver the entire sales pitch. It had something to do with his voice.

"Scratchy. Squeaky-sounding," his drama coach had told him years ago when Nicky had had grander illusions. "You'll never make it," the instructor had told him.

Nicky Horgan patted himself on the shoulder now for having had enough sense to see it as the truth, and not allow himself to waste his life pursuing something he wasn't qualified to do, unlike so many others in Hollywood; unlike so many idealists who were wasting their lives away. And Benjamin Styles was a prime example, and so was the kid in the back.

Nicky knew that Pete Stanfill didn't stand a chance of making it in the picture business. But why tell him? They never listened anyway. Besides, it kept Nicky Horgan's drama workshop from going under; it kept his wife and four kids fed and clothed. Nope, he said to himself, you haven't done badly at all. You own the actors' studio, a detective agency; you're married to a woman who still loves you, and you have four fine kids. For a Hungarian who is not legally supposed to be here, you haven't done badly at all.

Still, the acting classes he gave three nights a week (private detecting permitting; he had others fill in the times he was unable to be there) wasn't enough and merely kept him going. The students never seemed to stay around long enough: something about the way he taught, not enough experience or something. He had also allowed Styles to fill in from time to time, which had been a mistake. The number of students never remained the same; the average was tough to nail down. One week there might be anywhere from fifteen to twenty in the class, the next week under a dozen. It was frustrating as hell.

He wanted to buy land in Arizona, build a house out there. He wanted to get his family out of the seedy brownstone at the corner of Franklin and Argyle, the armpit of Hollywood. The mansions where once the reigning Kings and Queens of the Silver Screen resided. The prison-like fortresses had names like De Mille Terrace, Griffith Gardens, Lombard Court. . . . These days it was almost like being in the ghetto. Welfare recipients lived in these tiny hovels. Apartments that had once been spacious, plush, desirable, had been divvied up into cramped singles and one-bedroom flats, and the people in them existed like so many crowded rats in a sewer.

He glanced back at Pete, who was snoring away, and regretted not having made a better deal with him. Why did he have to offer him thirty dollars? Why not ten, and free acting classes for a month? Stanfill had stayed at his acting school the longest, God knows why, but he was certain he could have talked him into taking less than thirty dollars. And now, if it meant having to go further than Santa Barbara, he would have to convince him to go along. If not, he would figure out a way to leave him behind. No matter what happened, he could not let the girl get away.

The word *blackmail* sounded a bit harsh, and he didn't like to use it. Nor did he see what was about to take place as such. It's not really blackmail, he concluded. I borrow four, five thousand from her to get the business off the ground, then pay her back, or give her the choice of becoming a silent partner. Can't be any fairer than that, he reasoned. Is life fair?

Then he sighed to himself. "Bullshit." B.S., Bullshit Styles, is sure to interfere once he finds out—only he won't. He's got no way of finding out where the girl is staying. Besides, dummy, he said to himself, he hasn't got any pictures. You do! Christ, he doesn't even know about the pictures! You're home-free. Relax. Enjoy the ride.

He felt his pocket for the envelope. He wanted to look at the photos one more time. His hand dug into his right pocket, the left, inside the sport coat. No envelope. All pockets were empty.

Then a finger tapped him on the right shoulder. Nicky Horgan jumped in his seat.

"Looking for this?" Pete Stanfill said, holding up the envelope.

Nicky Horgan yanked the envelope from his hand and stuffed it inside his coat. His lower lip was twitching. Nerves.

"Know something, Mr. Horgan?" Pete Stanfill said casually. "Smells like blackmail to me."

"Dammit," Nicky Horgan cursed under his breath. He had broken out in a cold sweat.

A Message to Victoria Chantal

Dawn was breaking as the Mustang pulled into the motel parking lot. Victoria cut the engine and waited in the car. She stared at the door with the number 6 on it. It had been their room, their Eden.

She took a hanky out of her purse and dabbed at the perspiration across her brow. Flipped the overhead mirror and checked her face. She looked terrible. Exhaustion will do it every time. Worry, sleep deprivation; not to mention all the sobbing she'd been unable to control.

She checked her makeup. Applied a touch of lipstick, eyeliner. Ran her brush through her hair. It was no great improvement, but it was something and would have to do.

She got out of the car, took a deep breath, and walked up to the door. She held her hand directly in front of her face, about to knock. She waited, and felt the resurgence of sweat across her brow and scalp. Victoria bit her lower lip and rapped at the door with her knuckles. Not a sound came from within the room.

"Jimmy?" she said, and waited. "Jimmy, darling?"

She knocked again. Walked to the motel office in desperation. The door was locked, the color TV blaring away inside. A guy in his twenties with dishwater-blond hair and a goatee was stretched out on the counter, sound asleep.

She rapped on the glass part of the door until she woke him. His eyes closed, he raised and shook his head. Victoria continued to knock on the glass until he finally sat up, did open his eyes, and magically came to life. He hopped off the counter, unlocked the door and courteously ushered her inside.

"I really am sorry," the night clerk said, "but we don't have any vacancies. You're more than welcome to spend the night here, if you like," he said, indicating the sofa in the lobby.

"I was here last night," she said. "Room 6. Do you remember?"

The clerk produced a joint and lit up. He offered her a toke. When Victoria shook her head, he helped himself to a long one.

"Let's see," the clerk said, releasing the smoke. "Last night. . . . Right. *Right*," he said, recalling. "Didn't you stay with that dark-haired guy, looks a lot like that movie actor from years ago? Seen him on the *Late Show*: Tyrone Power?—or maybe not. You guys kept your neighbors up all night. Knockin' boots."

"Nobody complained to us about it," she said.

"They complained to me—the next morning. Reason they never said anything to you two, they were enjoying the audio too much."

This nosy clerk was saying more than she wanted to hear. She may have been embarrassed, but she was also tired of his attitude and chatter.

"I locked myself out," she said. "Can you let me in?"

The clerk held out the joint again.

"Is that all you know? Toking on that poison?"

He shrugged his shoulders.

"Try knocking," he said.

"I did."

"Try again."

"Can you please let me in? I don't have all day."

"I don't know," the motel clerk said, and sucked on the joint.

"Would you like me to file a formal complaint with management? I can. And will. How would that make you look?"

"Stay cool," the clerk said irritably, and got the pass key off the rack. "Just stay cool. Romeo should be in his room. Still got the key. All you hadda do was knock loud enough. Probably drunk and passed out. You two can put the brew away, but got the nerve to complain because a man likes to toke on weed now and then. What gives? What happened to live and let live?" He scratched the back of his neck, said: "Whatever."

He walked over to #6, shaking his head. Gave it a loud knock. When he didn't get a response, he unlocked it.

"Thank you so much," Victoria snapped and hurried past him, shutting the door in his face. The joint flew from his mouth as the startled clerk jumped to avoid getting hit by the banged up red VW that suddenly braked to a stop inches from where he stood.

"Goddammit!" he cursed, as Nicky Horgan stepped out of the car, flashing the fake badge. "Why the hell don't you watch where you're going?"

"Hastings. Homosexual," Nicky announced, walking up to the clerk. "I mean *Homicide*," he quickly corrected.

"Big titty," the clerk remarked. "You should still watch where you're driving."

"Knock it off," Horgan said. "The young lady who pulled up in the Mustang—where'd she go?"

"Let's see that badge again," the clerk said. "You're about the *squirrelliest-sounding* plainclothes cop I've ever seen—and I've seen my share."

Horgan unbuttoned his coat to the extent that his .38 was revealed. All it took usually. One image was worth a thousand words.

"Better sober up. Fast. Or we go downtown."

"The ball-buster's in there. Room #6."

The PI walked to the door. Pete Stanfill climbed out of the VW to stretch his legs, and Horgan spun in his direction.

"I told you to stay in the damn car!"

"Yessir," Pete Stanfill saluted, and reluctantly climbed back in. Nicky Horgan was about to knock on the door. Noticed the clerk still hanging around. "Make yourself scarce, or I haul you in for possession of narcotics."

The clerk took a walk. Nicky turned the knob and stepped into the room.

Dearest Victoria

Victoria Chantal was lying on her back on the bed. Still. Eyes shut. A tear wound its way from either eye down the sides of her face and onto the bedspread. She held a crumpled piece of paper in her hand and opened her eyes long enough to see who had walked in. Her fears easily doubled, yet she was unable to move any part of her anatomy. She felt as though she were paralyzed: her body, every inch of it, immobile. She could not move a finger or bat an eyelid. She felt a need to do both: run *and* remain put. Still. She did wish she could make everything disappear, including herself. Most of all, she wanted to scream—but even this seemed impossible.

In her mind's eye all she saw was a vortex of darkness that she was adrift in, a bottomless pit. Her body continued to tumble and spin through the air as if on some out-of-control amusement park ride.

She didn't give a damn about the pictures anymore, didn't give a damn about being blackmailed. Didn't give a damn if her parents found out, or even if this man Horgan beat the shit out of her. In fact, she wished he would. She wished someone would pounce on her, hit her hard, bash her face in. She wished someone would do something to her, make her vanish. Eradicate her and her miserable life from the face of the earth.

"We meet again, Ms. Vevrier," Nicky Horgan said with a smile on his face. "What you got there?" And he extracted the wad of paper from her hand. "You look happy this morning, Ms. Vevrier," he said and read the note. Many words were crossed out and other words written over them. This was the gist of it.

Dearest Victoria,

I know one thing: You will always be in my heart, no matter how far apart, no matter what happens. What I feel for you is eternal and will never fade. The truth of it is, Darling Girl, you were it for me early on. If not from the very first in that house in the Valley, as I was still out of sorts from that other situation and doing my best to deal with it, but certainly once we got together in that lounge on Sunset Strip. You were the one for me, the good-hearted, sweet lady I have been longing for my entire life. I knew it then, just as there is no denying I know it presently. I could no more do anything about it back then anymore than I can now.

Yours,
Jimmy

After he'd finished reading it, Nicky Horgan remained standing there, staring at the piece of paper. For some damn reason he couldn't move. He wanted to look up, to look at the girl, and he couldn't do either.

He glanced at the wastebasket by the end table loaded with empty beer cans and beer bottles, and among them many wads of crumpled paper. He picked one up: it was a different version of the message he'd just read. He did not have to go over the other crumpled balls of paper to figure out what was in them. This kid, Jimmy Riff, was conflicted, to say the least. He needed and loved the girl, this easily came across, but had some innate fear that it would falter and fall apart eventually . . . and he could not exactly put into words how shaken it had all left him, shaken and afraid and in great emotional pain. His "solution" had been to run.

"He, uh," Horgan stammered, "he must care for you." He had yet to look up as he made it inside the bathroom and splashed his face with cold water. When he finally looked up his eyes were welling. *What have I been doing all this time?* he said to himself. *What have I done? I have been on this young woman's back the same way that rotten son-of-a-bitch Styles has been on mine. And for what? Cash? To start a business? So how different from Benjamin Styles am I?* Just because Styles wanted to be a Hollywood movie star that was no reason to make people miserable. That was no reason to inflict pain, to use people!

Nicky was shaking his head. "Dammit," he sighed. "Dammit all. . . ." He was holding onto the sink for support, his head bowed. Tears streamed freely, uncontrollable. The feeling in his gut wouldn't go away. He felt shitty. He felt sorry for the pain he had put the girl through, too ashamed to look in the mirror again.

Money, he thought, money makes you do stupid, awful things. Money. Money to feed your family, money to give your kids a break, a better life than you'd had. The bottom line was that was no reason to behave the way he'd been behaving. *Blinded by the dollar.* This was not the reason he had emigrated to this great and wonderful country. For all of its problems and flaws, America was still the best country in the world. He still loved his new country; he loved the flag so much and for what it stood for.

He gripped the vanity until his knuckles turned white. His wiry body shook, and he was gritting his teeth, clenching his jaw. He hated himself right now, hated what he had allowed himself to become.

"How much do you want?" he heard the girl ask. Victoria had walked up. From her hand, in clear plastic holders, the credit cards dangled practically down to the floor. In her other hand she was holding a checkbook. When Nicky Horgan did not look up, she said: "How much, Mister Private Eye?"

"I'm sorry," Nicky Horgan said, his tone so low it sounded like a whisper. "I am so sorry."

"What did you say? Can you please speak up?"

"I just had no idea what was involved here," Horgan said, without looking up. "I had no idea. . . . I am not a blackmailer. You must really love the guy," he said. The tears flowed. He wiped his eyes against his sleeve, then yanked a few tissues from a box there on the counter and blew his nose. He dropped the wad into the wastebasket. All the while not allowing her to see his face.

"The pain I must have put you through. . . ."

"It's quite all right," Victoria said, being flip about it. "You were just doing your job. I've got money. Loads of it. Filthy rich, as they say. Well, not me, my family. My dad. Ever wonder what it would feel like to be in such a position? Huh, Mister Horgan? I always had the best: dolls and doll houses, gowns, schools and nannies, tutors; "proper friends"; the vacations on the French Riviera and Monte Carlo, trips to Spain for the annual Running of the Bullshit; world cruises; finest money can buy."

Her forehead furrowed, and she was squinting now. She would not allow herself the fleeting release tears often yielded. Not now; she wouldn't cry anymore. And she fought not to break down, the way she'd done before—and she was losing the battle.

Nicky Horgan finally looked up. He handed her a wad of tissues and Victoria wiped her own tears.

"Life is just a bowl of cherries," she said. "Isn't it?"

Frisco-Bound

"You've got to admit," Victoria said, "it's out there. Just a tad."

Nicky Horgan smiled. It didn't bother him that she found the idea amusing, even hilarious. But he knew this idea would work. He would make it work.

He had made her promise to keep it a secret and not reveal the concept to anyone before he'd had a chance to get the business started. He had gotten her to snap out of the funk she was in and it made him feel better.

"You sure it will work?"

"Not a doubt in my mind," Nicky Horgan said. "How many people get a chance to build their own coffin? I want to give more people that opportunity. Caskets normally cost anywhere from—" and he gave her the lowest at the low end, to the highest at the other, that ran in the thousands. "But if you take my booklet," he held the notepad up, "and add the cost of the materials, you can build one for under $80, way under. That's quite a savings."

They were sitting on the edge of the tub. He held what appeared to be a home-made instructional booklet in his hands. The sheets were stapled together, the text typewritten. The cover was a glossy photo of a nice looking but inexpensive wooden coffin that had been cut out from a publication and pasted on. Nicky stressed that the booklet was nothing more than a demo, a prototype of the actual manual he would eventually have typeset and printed by a professional.

He had it open to the first page.

"It's so simple to build a coffin that I made the instructions sound complicated," he said. "For example, in the booklet I say pick up part 7 and attach it to part 8, using items 17 and 18. All that means is to nail two pieces of wood together with a hammer." He flipped to the last page. "I include a warning: If you plan to be more overweight than you are now when you die, you should increase the depth by two inches for each twenty-five pounds of weight gained."

Victoria nodded her head, even though she did not quite know how to take this off-the-wall plan of Horgan's. At least it kept her mind off of other things, and that had to be worth something.

"But what do you do with the coffin until that time comes?" said Horgan. "It can be used as a liquor cabinet, coffee table, a cabinet to keep your stereo in, or store your guns in." He read the last line: "Or if you're short of beds and your mother-in-law's coming to visit. . . ."

The whole damn screwy notion of it had put a smile on Victoria's face and kept it there. "It sounds crazy enough to work," she said.

"I sell the booklets for about $4.50, explaining how to design and build your own coffin. They can buy the parts/materials themselves, or—should they choose—order the parts through me. I'd like to have the cover done by a professional designer, same with the interior text, then have it printed up to look real nice, sharp. It will have a bar code on the back, ISBN, everything. Spine will look sharp, back cover: all of it. Takes dough. You see," Horgan paused, "that's why I needed the money. The pictures were never my idea. He thought, Styles, he could keep Jimmy in line through you. I had no choice but to do as he said. I am not legally supposed to be in this country, and he knows this. He knows everything: about my wife, the phony IDs." He produced the fake PI photostat, the phony cop badge. "It's illegal. I know. I can go to jail for it. I only use them when necessary. I worked for licensed and bonded real private detectives and know the score; actually, still work for them when they call. I could easily pass that silly exam the government requires. Problem is they would have to take a look into my background and I would be deported. This would be very painful, a mess. My wife is a native of Mexico; and my kids; what would happen to my kids?—who were all born here in the United States." He scratched his head. "Do you see how awful, what a mess; the way he had me cornered. I have five mouths to feed, not including myself, not including the one on the way. . . ." He stared at the tile. "What's a guy supposed to do? My so-called acting school is nothing more than a storefront in a seedy part of East Hollywood. My 'detective agency' is also located there, in one of the small offices." He looked up. "I am sorry I caused you all this grief."

He stood up, took the envelope with the photos, and dropped it into the sink and set it on fire. He then scooped up the scorched remains with a couple of tissues and dropped it all in the toilet and flushed it away. "That takes care of that set."

He paused at the john door. "The negatives are at the house. You have my word: I will destroy them as soon as I get home."

"What will Mr. Styles do to you?"

Nicky Horgan shrugged. "He doesn't know about the pictures." He paused. Opened the front door. "I'm through doing his dirty work for him." He shook his head. "The man is sick. A basket case. The obsession to become a star is eating away at him, destroying him. He'll end up in the nut house for sure . . . if someone doesn't kill him before he cracks. The man has a knack for making enemies. He's stepped on too many toes, destroyed too many egos."

"I always heard they protected their own," she said, remembering that Jimmy had told her that Benjamin Styles was "connected."

"They?" Nicky Horgan said. "Who's *they?*"

"His friends," Victoria said.

"A psycho like that hasn't got any friends, not real friends."

"His gangster friends," she said. "Isn't he connected?"

Nicky Horgan laughed. "That's a myth," he said. "That's what I heard first, too. All a fabrication. Lies. No one wants anything to do with him. Not the mafia, not the Irish hoods on the East Coast, not the studios, not even his own family. He did some work for the mob awhile back, some thugs in Boston, Winter Hill, but he was such a—if you'll excuse the expression—he was such a fuck-up, loose cannon, that they told him to get lost. I mean," Nicky Horgan said, pausing, "look at it this way: If he were connected, don't you think he would have made it already?" He looked at her.

"Right?"

Victoria nodded.

"He was bluffing all along," she finally said. "Threatening Jimmy, getting him to do what he wanted. Using him."

"Sure he was using him. Benjamin Styles uses people like you and me use toilet paper. Uses them up and flushes them away. He's a cruel man," Nicky Horgan said. "That much I know."

"I have to tell Jimmy," she said. "He should know that this man is acting alone. The authorities: cops, FBI, would surely be able to do something about it."

"Worth a try," Nicky Horgan said, and stepped outside. "I'm truly sorry for having caused you all the trouble. So long now."

"Wait," Victoria said, walking toward him. "Don't go yet." She held her checkbook in her hand, searching her purse for a pen. "How much would you need to get your do-it-yourself coffin-building business started?"

"I beg your pardon?"

"How much?" Having found a pen, she began to fill out a check. "I don't have access to unlimited funds, but I'm sure I can help enough to get you started, at least."

"Please, don't," Nicky Horgan said. "It isn't necessary."

"I feel like it."

"I couldn't take your money."

"Wait a minute," she said. "You got it all wrong. I am not going to let you have it just like that. You'll have to earn it. *How much?*"

He quoted her the amount.

"I have a proposition for you." She paused. Handed him the check for close to the amount he needed. "If you help me find Jimmy."

He studied the check for what seemed a long time.

"Well?"

"You got a deal," Nicky Horgan said.

They shook hands.

On the Hunt for Tubesteak

Pete Stanfill sat low in the front seat pulling on his pecker, unaware of the clerk, who was watching and grinning from behind the counter. No sooner was he ready to cream into the Kleenex when Nicky Horgan and the girl stepped out of the motel room and walked past the VW on their way to the motel office.

Pete Stanfill cursed and stopped what he'd been doing. He sat up in his seat and put the porn magazine away.

Inside, Horgan grilled the clerk like a true professional and got the answers he needed.

"Sure. Ty Power, or one of them other Hollywood matinee idol types from way back. Had that about him. Similar. Good-looking guy. Asked how far it was to San Francisco and how much and how long it would take? What time the bus came through and how to get to the depot. Didn't seem too sure where his head was at. Said women were trouble. Nothing but trouble. Me? I said I liked that kind of trouble. A real nice dude. Sounded like he was from New York; maybe Jersey or Boston. East Coast, anyway. Know what I mean? Said women were always throwing themselves at him, caused him grief. Me? I wished I had some of his *grief.* Know what I'm sayin'?"

"Absolutely," Nicky Horgan said.

"Yeah," the clerk said. "You got it. Absolutely."

❧

Pete Standfill was given a check for a hundred dollars and was relieved he didn't have to go with them, wherever it was they were headed.

Nicky Horgan called up his wife to let her know that it looked like there would be a slight glitch in plans; he also mentioned having gotten the start-up funds for the new sideline.

"When will you be back, Nicky?" said his wife. "That's what I want to know. I am over here by myself with the kids and my husband is gone all the time."

"Can't say exactly when, honey, but as soon as I can wrap things up here. You should be used to it by now."

"Nicky, I will never get used to it," said his wife. "I miss you."

"I love you and the kids, honey," said he into the receiver, but his wife had already hung up at the other end. Then he and Victoria decided to give the beach house a ring. Victoria dialed the number.

"Bet you anything he's there," Nicky Horgan said.

"Mr. Styles?"

He nodded. "Waiting."

Victoria handed him the receiver. A gruff voice came over the phone.

"Hello? Hello?"

When Nicky Horgan kept mum, the voice said: "Son of a bitch."

The line went dead.

Stabbed in Malibu

"Son of a bitch," Benjamin T. Styles repeated, the receiver still in his hand. Who could it have been? His gaze shifted toward the glass doors. Dawn was breaking fast.

He sat up in the sofa. Yawned. Rubbed his eyes. He found milk and a box of corn flakes in the kitchen. The small of his back plagued him: a sharp, stinging pain that kept him from sitting still. He stood up, bent forward, fingers extended, only being able to touch his knees.

He did this several times, pulling himself forward as far as possible. It did very little for his back. He ate breakfast standing up. A new pain, much sharper, raked across the inner walls of his stomach, and for a second he thought all the cereal would come back up. Bitter-tasting bile shot up through his throat, finding its way into his mouth. Benjamin Styles stood over the sink, waited. He spat, and continued to spit as the awful-tasting belly juices kept coming up.

He hurried to the bathroom to deal with the inevitable: the vomit came charging out of his mouth before he could reach the toilet. It spattered his pants, shoes, and some got on his shirt. He felt like cursing. Instead, he sighed: "Dear God. . . ."

Leaning over the side of the tub, the vomit poured from him in sudden spurts. There appeared to be traces of blood mixed in. He couldn't be certain and didn't want to think about it.

"Dear God," Benjamin Styles repeated when it finally stopped. He felt a little better. Still weak and wobbly, sweat dripped from his weather-beaten face. He washed the beard over the sink without once looking in the mirror.

"There stands a defeated man," he heard something like an echo announce, a female echo. "Benjamin T. Styles, the macho man who turned to pudding."

The voice sounded familiar. Definitely a woman's voice. It had to be her, he said to himself. It's the bitch. It has to be. He turned. Could see her standing in the kitchen. Had a smirk on her face.

"Despicable pudding, at that," Lisa Koch said.

Benjamin Styles remained quiet and realized he'd left his gun on the sofa. Scarface was standing in the hallway, not far from the open door to the john.

"Kerr," Lisa Koch said from the living room, where she had relocated her nasty self. "Bring him out here. Like to have a chat with him."

"Come on out, Styles," said the henchman, stepping into the john. "You heard the princess."

Benjamin Styles feigned a severe cough, throwing Kerr off-guard, and lunged at him and grabbed him by the collar of his sports coat.

"You sure are a mule-head, Styles," Kerr said, the barrel of his .357 buried deep in Benjamin's stomach.

"Let go of the skins," Kerr said with a fiendish grin, "or get a belly-full."

"Need a glass of milk," Benjamin Styles said, finding his way back into the kitchen. "Ulcers, you know."

"How sad," Lisa Koch said.

"Life," Benjamin Styles said. He filled a glass with milk, all the while his eyes searching the kitchen counter for a knife, a blade sizable enough to stop Kerr—permanently, if necessary.

"Would you hurry it up, lady," Kerr said. "I don't think I can stand to look at this pitiful creep much longer."

"Where's Tubesteak?" Lisa Koch asked.

Benjamin Styles shrugged, raised the glass of milk to his lips and sipped. Made a face. Never cared much for milk. Not even when he had it with cereal, the rare times he had cereal for breakfast.

"Come on, Styles," Lisa Koch said. "There's money in it for you if you produce the kid."

Benjamin Styles had another sip. Didn't taste any better.

"Grossbard," Lisa Koch said. "Are you at all familiar with the name?"

"Slightly."

"Riiiiight," Lisa Koch said with a wide grin. "He misses Jimmy so much."

"Don't we all?"

"Enough of this shit," Kerr said, stepping up to Benjamin Styles, ready to strike him down with the Magnum.

"Kerr!" Lisa Koch screamed. "You had better stop right now. Right now, goddamn you! Put the goddamned gun down!"

"You're fucked!" Kerr snapped back, lowering the piece. "You know that, broad?"

"I'll drink to that," Benjamin Styles said.

"Shut up, asshole!" Kerr said. To her, he said: "You are one fucked-up broad."

"I'm flattered," Lisa Koch said, using a quiet tone this time. "Better understand this: You're paid to be my bodyguard, to do as I say. I hope that's simple enough for you to understand, because if it's too difficult—"

"Shut the hell up," Kerr said, cutting her off. "Take care of business." He faced Benjamin Styles. "I don't like you, man. I don't like you at all."

"The feeling is mutual."

"The feeling is mutual," Kerr mimicked. "You make me sick. Mr. Macho, who beats up fags and gigolos. Mr. Macho, Tough Guy, who thinks he can kick ass, instead has ulcers up the ass."

Benjamin Styles squinted, the washed-out blue eyes staring at Kerr, seeing right through him. And this infuriated Kerr all the more.

"The hell you staring at, asshole? I should have knocked all your teeth out."

Benjamin Styles' clenched his jaw. He raised the milk to his mouth. He had stopped staring at Lisa's bodyguard.

"Grossbard's got the hots for him," Lisa Koch said. "Simple as that."

"Nothing's as simple as that anymore," Benjamin Styles said.

"Listen to the 'poet laureate,'" Kerr said.

"Kerr, would you shut your mouth, please?" Lisa Koch said.

"Hurry it up, then," Kerr said. "I'm getting bored."

"Have to admit," Benjamin Styles said, "I am, too."

"Look," Lisa Koch said, "this is just a friendly visit. Grossbard wants to see him. He'll take care of you. Another good part for sure."

"Tell him I'll see what I can do," Benjamin Styles said, forcing himself to finish the milk. He turned, facing the sink. Made it look like he was washing out the glass. "Fitch is a great part," Benjamin Styles said. "I thank him."

"You hear that?" Kerr said, the sarcastic tone in his voice steadily feeding Benjamin Styles' seething anger. He wanted nothing more right now than to get his hands on Kerr. He felt like ripping him apart.

"The *nobody* thanks him," Kerr continued. "Make sure the studio chief gets that."

"Christ," Lisa Koch said. "Why don't you shut up?"

"The jerk's a two-faced creep like the rest of you dildos."

"You don't like this town?" Lisa Koch said. "Get the hell out."

"You talk loud, mama," Kerr said.

"And you're a pain in the butt." She turned to Styles, who appeared to be rinsing the glass out. In fact, what they didn't know was that he was waiting for the hot water to get hotter, much hotter; only then would he fill the glass to the brim.

"Look, Styles," Lisa Koch said, "I'll let him know how much you appreciate it." She paused. "But if either of us had any sense, we'd be working together."

Benjamin Styles cleared his throat. He looked as though he were in pain. Kerr found it amusing.

"With the contacts I have, and I still have a few, you know I do, we could get a lot for Tubesteak's services. He could get us pretty far. Not only get us back on our feet again, but to the top—*and we stay on top this time.*"

"It's funny," Benjamin Styles said. "You're all singing the same tune now."

"Get smart, Styles."

"Oh, I am," Benjamin Styles said. "Fitch is but a start. And just think, I did it without your help."

"See how much further you get."

"Koch," Benjamin Styles said, "you turn my stomach. Low-grade opportunist. Where the fuck were you when I needed you? When I had my youth, looks, when I had the potential to *really be somebody?* To be a leading man? Why didn't you ever return my calls? You had the power back then. With your help I could have been on top years ago."

"You're a trouble-maker, Styles," Lisa Koch said. "Always have been. Face it."

"How's that? With all the sick shit you're into? I'm the 'trouble-maker'?" Ben T. Styles laughed. "We won't even go into the Nazi obsession. Hey, with all my shortcomings, and I guess I have a couple, you won't ever see me going around praising a bunch of psychopathic cutthroats like that."

"You can still make it. Right role, right project. It's not too late. You can do it. I can name six thespians right now, your age, who are making big bucks, breaking box office records—and not one has ten percent the talent you have. Think about it, Ben," she said, and walked to the door.

He might have thought about it, if the cramps and acute pain in his belly did not have him bent over the sink, nearly causing him to drop the glass with the hot water.

"Let's go, big mouth," Lisa Koch said to her bodyguard. "Let the pitiful bastard be."

"I sure will," Kerr said. He grabbed Benjamin Styles by the collar with the free hand, the other still had the piece in it, and yanked him up against the range. "The saying goes something like this: "Sticks and stones will break my bones, names will never hurt me. For some reason I never went along with that. You called me a 'turd burglar' once, *faggot*. I cripple punks over less."

"How do you feel about being called a 'shit stabber,' then?" Benjamin Styles said, and threw the hot water in the thug's face. Kerr grunted in agony, jumped back, shaking his head, as if it was supposed to ease the stinging, burning pain in his eyes. Styles stood in place, taking in the antics. Kerr continued to hop around like a crazed gorilla stuck in a cage way too small for his size.

Benjamin Styles liked what he was seeing and did nothing for the next couple of seconds or so, and just took it in. That instant Kerr's gun came up and he squeezed off a sloppily aimed shot. Styles slapped the gun out of the man's hand and followed through with a hard fist to his stomach. He was equally as proud of that one as he was of the hot water trick. Kerr groaned, thudded against the refrigerator, and hit the floor.

Benjamin T. Styles was grinning, pleased with himself. "Like I said," he muttered, "a fucking sissy." He moved to pick up the gun that was about ten feet away from them both, and Kerr, with all the effort that he had left in him, kicked his one leg out, tripping Styles and bringing him down to the floor with him. Styles threw another punch, to the mouth this time, trying to shake the hold Kerr had on his left leg. Kerr wouldn't let go and just held on. Styles smacked him again and again, struggled to break free and grab the weapon. But Kerr would not concede. The cramps in Styles' belly wouldn't go away, and he wished this goddamn Kerr would stay down; he was getting tired of throwing punches. Kerr's face was just about covered in blood, water and blood, and he was still holding on. Styles made one final effort to break free and it didn't work. He turned for one brief second to try and get his left hand on the .357 Mag on the floor.

Styles stopped throwing punches, his hands were sore and the last thing he needed was to break them, and decided if he had to drag the punk in order to reach the gun, well, that's what he would do. He dragged the heavy bastard for about two feet, got his hand on the Magnum, and turned back in time to see Kerr drive a switchblade through his forearm.

"Jesus!" Styles groaned. Managed to whirl back toward him and rake him across the mouth with the barrel the same way Kerr had done to him that day. The blow had finally done the job. Kerr lay spread out across the kitchen tile. He was out cold. A bloody mess.

"Shit," Benjamin Styles sighed, gritting his teeth. The goddamn switchblade was in his forearm and hurt like a son of a bitch—and he was going to have to yank it out. Slow and easy, he thought. Easy, easy. He stuffed the piece in his coat pocket, got his hand around the hilt of the switchblade, and withdrew it from his arm. He cursed to himself.

When he looked up, Lisa Koch was standing over him with a bottle of hydrogen peroxide in her hand. Styles tore his sleeve off and poured the peroxide over his wound. The pain was excruciating. As expected, Lisa Koch stood there with a smug look on her face. Styles glanced up at her, and she knew enough to step back, away from him.

"His kind you kill," she said, indicating the unconscious Kerr.

Styles withdrew the .357 from his pocket and held it out to her. Only she didn't want any part of it.

"Take it," Benjamin Styles said. "You want him dead? Kill him, then."

"No thank you," Lisa Koch said. "A murder rap is something I don't need."

"Who does, bitch?"

"Until we meet again," she said, and walked outside. Styles found a towel to wrap around his forearm and walked out himself in time to see her get into her Beemer.

"Lisa," Benjamin Styles said to her, "I ever see you again . . . I'll kill you."

Black-Balled

It was two days later, after having gotten his new dentures, that Benjamin Styles got a call from Sheldon Smedley.

"I'm to inform you that there's been a delay, Mr. Styles."

"What's going on, Smedley?"

"I'm not exactly clear on the details, Mr. Styles. All I can do is relay the message I've been given."

"All right, Smedley," Benjamin Styles said, and had thought nothing of it until a couple of days later when he received a similar call.

"Further delays, Mr. Styles," Sheldon Smedley said.

"What the fuck, Smedley?"

"Mr. McFluff is re-casting some of the minor roles."

"I see," Benjamin Styles said. He was genuinely concerned. Wondered what Reggie was up to. Didn't like it one bit. "By the way," Benjamin Styles said, "seen that Angela broad recently?"

"Ms. Bliss? No, no I haven't, Mr. Styles."

"The ol' pecker been dripping any lately?"

"Beg pardon?" Sheldon Smedley said.

"Allow me to break it to you as gently as I can, Sheldon ol' boy: what you have is what I found out I had, oh, not that long ago—"

"Beg pardon, Mr. Styles?"

"The clap, my boy. You have the clap. Thanks to our ever-giving and kind Ms. Angela Bliss. The Ingénue of the Year has given us the clap."

"Oh no," Sheldon Smedley said.

"Oh, yes," Benjamin Styles mimicked. "That's why Reggie was so pissed that day. That's why he fired her. Finally makes sense. See you at the free clinic," Benjamin Styles said, and dialed Reggie McFluff's home number.

The butler answered. "Mr. McFluff is out, sir."

Click. The phone went dead.

Desperation time.

Days gone by. No sign of Tubesteak, no sign of his girl, no sign of Nicky Horgan. Benjamin Styles had a sneaking suspicion the Polack was up to something. He only wished he knew what. Every time he called his house, the foreigner's beaner wife had the same pat answer for him: "Nicky not home now. I am sorry, *senor.*"

"Where the hell is he?" Benjamin would ask, only to get the familiar reply: "I no say, *senor.* I am sorry." And she would hang up.

The one time the Polack's son answered and had begun to explain that his daddy had left a message, the woman had yanked the phone away from him and given him a slightly different version of the same pat answer: "Nicky say he will be out of town on business."

Click.

It infuriated the hell out of him. That's nerve, thought Benjamin Styles. She had never met him, and had hung up on him close to a dozen times already.

❧

He took a drive by the Polack's school, a stucco rat hole in East Hollywood. A hand-made cardboard sign had been left in the large storefront window:

407

CLOSED FOR REMODELING
N. Horgan.

Closed for remodeling, my ass, Ben Styles thought. It had been too long since he had last heard from the squirrelly loser. Just too damn long.

⸙

First thing he did was put air in the bald tires on his Toyota, then he got on the phone to the car rental place and ranted and raved until they finally came and picked up the Chevy. This way he saved himself a bus ride back to his place. Then he got in the Toyota and drove to the corner of Argyle and Franklin.

The stench in the shoddy apartment building didn't improve his present take on things one bit. He climbed the stairs to the fourth floor and had to pause against the railing to give his legs a rest.

He knocked on the Horgan family's door.

"Who is it?" he heard Nicky Junior say.

"Manager," Benjamin Styles said.

He heard the latch being unfastened, and the door opened.

"Like to talk to your mother for a second," Benjamin Styles said, and wedged his foot inside to keep the kid from closing the door on him. "It's all right. Get your mother."

Junior went inside and soon returned with mom.

"What ju want?" Mrs. Horgan said, pulling a tight mint-green blouse over a swollen belly. Hair was a mess. The black eye patch didn't help any, either.

"I'm an associate of your husband's, Mrs. Horgan," Benjamin Styles said. "May I have a word with you?"

"What ju want?" she repeated. *"I don't have time."*

"May I come in?"

She studied him silently.

"Please?"

She opened the door all the way to allow him entry.

"Thank you," Benjamin Styles said.

"I am busy," she said. "Nicky call but he dun tol' me where he eez. That so much I know. I cannot help you, Mr. Stills."

"Styles," Benjamin corrected. "With a Y. Styles."

"I tol' ju many time' before," she said, returning to her pile of dirty dishes in the kitchen sink. "Nicky say nothing. He work with ju sometime is all I know."

A boy of nine, a girl of five, and a girl of two were creating such a ruckus that Benjamin Styles had a tough time hearing her. He stepped into the kitchen.

"He must have said something," Benjamin Styles insisted. "You don't know how important this is."

"Importante?"

"Yes," Benjamin Styles nodded. *"Importante. Mucho importante."*

"Si," she said, and rinsed off a large skillet. "Si."

He waited for her to say something else, instead she continued with the dishes, only pausing now and then to swat a roach with the dishrag. Situation was hopeless, as far as Benjamin Styles was concerned. Frustrated was how he felt. Debated using force. Grossbard would cut him completely loose from the picture if he didn't produce Tubesteak.

"Don't you understand, goddammit," he said, raising his voice just a notch, "my life depends on it."

She froze. Looked at him with that single eye. "Ju don't say nothing in my house! Ju understand? Ju show respec'!"

It took him a moment. Styles said: "I apologize."

"Ju go," she said, and returned to the dishes.

"Won't you help me? Your husband is working for me. Nicky works for me. He's on retainer. Understand? We have an agreement." And he caught himself trying to talk like her. And he hated himself for it, just like he hated spics and their language and everything else about them. It was an invasion of America, no different from all those cockroaches in and around her kitchen sink and counter. His country was being overrun by ignorant wetbacks like this unclean bitch who was clearly carrying another illegal beaner inside her large belly. What the fuck? Didn't she and Horgan have enough brats running around already?

"He was supposed to contact me days ago," he explained. "It's been a good while. What is happening to him? Is he in trouble?"

"Trouble?" she said, pausing. "What ju mean?"

"Maybe Nicky is hurt," Benjamin Styles suggested, using his talent as a film actor for dramatic effect.

She searched his eyes out and saw the genuine concern there. She picked up a kitchen towel and wiped her hands. The youngest waddled up to her, clinging to the woman's legs. Mrs. Horgan lifted the little girl in her arms and gave her a smacking kiss on the lips.

Her one good eye was back on Benjamin Styles, who looked as though the world were on his shoulders: the salt and pepper beard, the worrisome peepers, the shoulders hunched. She felt sorry for him.

"Nicky call long distance," she finally said, and sat at the kitchen table.

"Long distance?" said Benjamin Styles, his ears perking up.

"Si," she said, and nodded.

"Where from?"

"He never say. But—" she kissed the girl again, and released her. "Ju play with Belinda," she said, then looked up at Benjamin Styles. "He say he come back soon."

The woman rose to her feet, grabbed a teaspoon from the wire dish holder, reached inside the refrigerator for a jar of baby food, and called out to the two year old. To Styles, she said: "Ju talk to my husband when he come back." She walked into the living room part of the setup, calling: "Juanita! Ju come eat!" The kid must have run off into the bedroom, where she could be heard laughing hysterically and causing mischief, and the mother ran in after her.

"Thank you," Benjamin Styles finally said, and couldn't wait to get away from the noise and smell of unwashed diapers and pesticide.

Bad Hombre

It was hot. Heavy smog hung over the city, but the air was nowhere near as bad as the sickening odor he'd just left behind.

Benjamin Styles paused in front of the ugly gray structure and looked up just in time to see the woman duck back inside the window.

He got in his car and made it look like he was leaving. He drove east on Franklin and made the first right and parked in the alley. Then he ran the length of it back to the apartment building. He found the garage entrance and made his way inside through the basement.

❧

Styles had his ear glued to the door and could faintly hear what the woman was saying:

"Ju tell him to call his wife," was all Mrs. Horgan said, then put the phone down. "Junior," she said, calling out to her son. "Ju no say nothing to dat man. Nicky say he's a bad hombre. He make much trouble for us."

"Okay, mom," Nicky Junior said.

"I mean it, Junior. Say nothing. We let Nicky talk to him. That's all," she said. "Go with your sisters." When she heard the loud knocking on her door, she said: *Jesus Cristo.*

"You better open up, Mrs. Horgan," Benjamin Styles said, "or I'll have the Immigration up here before you can say Chihuahua."

He waited a while, not long. Heard the chain being unlatched, the door unlocked. Styles stepped inside.

"Open sesame."

Woman's forehead was furrowed. Once again, she invoked her Savior's name. Knew she wasn't supposed to, but could not help it. She rubbed her hands together, then called out to the youngest one. The little girl happily wobbled across the worn carpeting to her mother's waiting arms. Mrs. Nicholas Horgan scooped the child up and carried her to the living room. Styles followed. Serafina Horgan sat on the sofa. Looked up at Benjamin Styles. "You will call Immigration?"

Benjamin Styles nodded and picked up the phone.

The worried woman said something under her breath in Spanish.

"I don't want to," Benjamin Styles said. "But I will . . . unless you cooperate. I don't want to hurt Nicky. We are compadres, don't you know? Drinking buddies. *Cervesa.*"

"Cervesa?"

"Si," he said, and realized he was doing it again. For someone who hated the language, he knew too many words. "I want one thing," he said. "I need to know where he is. I hired him to keep an eye on someone. I want my money's worth. I want the number you just dialed."

"*Numero?*"

"Si," he said. "*Numero.*"

She sat there quietly, staring at the playpen in the corner full of unwashed diapers, at the grimy figurine of the Virgin Mary atop the portable black and white television with the bent rabbit ears. Jesse, her nine year old, appeared immersed in the stack of vinyl records next to the ancient turntable and was anxiously going through them. The eclectic collection consisted mainly of Hungarian and Mexican singers and musicians. Some were American: Sinatra, Jerry Vale, Engelbert Humperdinck, Ruby Keeler, Louis Prima. Very few were contemporary. To her mother's annoyance and discomfort, he put on Prima's *Please No Squeeza Da Banana.*

"Honey, not that one. . . ." she said to the kid. Only the boy hadn't heard, or maybe he had, and left the record on anyway.

"I'll call Immigration," Benjamin Styles said. "I swear I will. You and your children will have to go back to Mexico. I'm desperate. . . ." He paused. "Believe me."

The five year old scribbled away in her coloring book with a red crayon. Her nose needed wiping and Styles wished someone had enough sense to do something about it. Ignorant foreigners and their army of rug rats. Didn't have a clue as to how kids should be brought up. The scene made him nauseous. All of it: clutter, odor, cramped quarters. He didn't have the means to live in comfort himself, but both his office and apartment were clean, organized. Clothes he wore? Clean. Boots? Shined. You took care of where you lived and how you presented yourself.

He proceeded to dial.

"*Senor,*" she pleaded. Motioned with a hand to wait a second. *"Por favor."*

She walked to the kitchen. Reappeared with a piece of paper. Her face was buried in the hand towel. She handed him the piece of paper and sat on the far side of the *Kool-Aid*-stained sofa. Not until Benjamin Styles dialed the number she had given him did she lower the hand towel from her face. Her good eye had begun to well, and she blew her nose into the towel and stuffed it into a plastic laundry bag at her end of the sofa.

"Nothing will happen to him," Benjamin Styles promised. Then, into the phone, said: "Nicky Horgan, please."

"Do you have a room number, sir?" the man at the other end said.

"No. No, I don't."

"One moment, please."

"Sure," Benjamin T. Styles said. He took his little black book out and jotted the number down, and handed the piece of paper back to Mrs. Horgan.

"*Gracias*," he said.

"Sir?" the voice at the other end said.

"Yes?"

"I am afraid Mr. Horgan is not in his room at the moment. Would you like to try later?"

"Yes, I will," Ben Styles said. "Thank you."

He walked to the door. "Don't worry," he said to the woman, and left.

Aspiring Assholes

As absurd as it sounded, it was true. He was being black-balled again. The bastards were fucking with his head. I'm strong, he said to himself. I've seen a lot of shit, been through a lot. But goddamn. . . .

He sipped at his coffee from his usual spot at the counter and stared blankly at the aspiring actors in the coffee shop. It was seven in the evening. Schwab's was packed. Aspiring actors, he said again, and it dawned on him how much he had begun to hate the term. *Aspiring assholes* was more like it. If they weren't assholes now, they were surely to become assholes down the road. That's what this town did to people: turned them into rectums. Cruel, ruthless, and way too ambitious for their own good.

No matter how well-intentioned and good-hearted they might be upon initial arrival; it made no difference, they all got hard sooner or later. And if one didn't get hard enough . . . one never survived. Granted, he may not have been entirely naive and pure in the beginning, coming out from the East Coast with his background and "Tough as Nails" moniker . . . but the steady slide down the slippery slope of sleaze didn't exactly sit right with him, either. You ignored it; did your best to shove it aside, swept it far enough under the rug so that it didn't gnaw at your conscience. You had to—for your mental health and well-being. Truth was, he never would have made it to his mid-fifties had he allowed himself to remain innocent and pretty.

Pretty boys, like pretty girls, always got fucked. He recalled the time a producer offered him a part in a major motion picture if only he, Benjamin, would allow the producer to go down on him. Benjy had been in his early twenties. Newbie. Wet behind the ears. He had declined politely at first. The producer wouldn't take no for an answer and had started tugging at Benjamin's crotch. Styles remembered punching the sick bastard in the nose and knocking him on his ass. Word was soon out. The pugilist was trouble. He's a nut. Forget his popularity with fight fans. Don't hire him for anything. It was the start of his Hollywood rep.

Throughout the years he managed to land bit parts here and there on productions manned by "straights." The fags didn't want anything to do with "Tough as Nails" Styles, not that all of them had wanted to ball him. They detested the "uncouth and out-of-control animal" for the pain he had inflicted on one of their own.

It was stupid, this dwelling on the past; a waste of time, he concluded, and motioned the waitress over for a refill. Ariane Dean walked in with a handsome stud her own age and pretended not to see him.

"Ariane Dean," Benjamin Styles shouted loud enough for everyone to hear. He didn't give a shit. Wasn't about to let the phony twat walk past him as though she didn't know he existed. Ariane Dean faked a smile and walked over. She kissed him on the cheek and said to her male companion: "The most talented character actor I've ever seen."

It was meant as a compliment. Benjamin Styles hadn't cared for it. He was leading-man material, and always would be.

"And this stud muffin here," she said, holding up the dark-haired man's hand, whose own fingers were interlocked with hers: "has the makings to be one hell of a leading man."

Styles had heard it all before. Had seen many like the young stud with her come and go. Buncha sprinters. Candy asses.

"How's Fluffy treating you?" Benjamin Styles asked.

"He's a gentleman, as always," Ariane Dean said, searching about the coffee shop with her roving eyes, anxious to get away from this over-the-hill loser. "This is one smooth production," she said. "Robert Tanner is just wonderful." She turned to her escort. "Isn't he wonderful, Radley?"

The Flavor-of-the-Month nodded.

"I just bet he is," Benjamin Styles said.

"Weren't you working on that picture, Mr. Styles?" she asked.

"Still am," said Styles, and sipped from his mug.

"What part?"

"Fitch," Benjamin Styles said.

"What?" her escort said.

Benjamin Styles lowered the mug, and looked up. "Fitch."

The actor chuckled, as did Ariane Dean.

"Must have it confused with some other Western," the actor said. "I was signed on to do Fitch two days ago."

The mug in Benjamin T. Styles' hand suddenly became so many shards of crushed porcelain, the hot steaming coffee spreading across the counter and dripping onto the crotch of his pants and tile floor below.

"Careful," the actor said. "Could burn yourself that way."

"So long, Benjamin," Ariane Dean said, and the two left to join a group of show-biz types in another section of the coffee shop.

Ben T. Styles sat there, unmoving. Stunned. In a daze. He couldn't budge for the longest time. Finally, he reached for a napkin and dried his hand. He rose and walked outside.

"Nice seeing you again"

"Well, well," a different, nonetheless familiar, female voice said from behind. Benjamin Styles walked to his car without turning. "Just the man I want to talk to," Angela Bliss said.

"You gave me the clap," Benjamin Styles said, showing no expression.

"I know," Angela Bliss said.

Styles took in the face. She looked terrible. He would have said something, commented, only he didn't give a damn. She wasn't doing Judy Holliday anymore, and he was grateful. She had lost quite a bit of weight. Hair was unkempt and appeared unwashed. The excessive dark eye makeup and lipstick made her look like a cheap hooker. Woman had rings under her eyes and was on edge, nervous. Rumor was she was working for an outcall service these days. No surprise there, thought Styles. Nor did he give a damn. All he knew he had to step back to avoid her breath.

"You got nerve," he said at last.

"I know," she said, flashing a dumb grin.

"I ought to slap the shit out of you," Benjamin Styles said.

"On the contrary, you'll want to kiss me after I tell you what I did."

"I hardly think so."

"Can we talk?"

"Another dose I don't need." He unlocked his car and got in.

She walked to his side of the car and stuck her head in before he'd had a chance to close the door. The idiotic grin remained. Bitch was losing it. Booze and pills, he figured. Most of them succumbed to it. This broad was no exception. Made the cash. Easy come, easy go. Dumb-ass whore was throwing her life away.

Benjamin Styles leaned his head back, away from her. He didn't need to feel any worse than he already felt, and that's what her foul breath did to him.

"I hear you're not on the picture anymore."

"What's it got to do with you?"

"I gave Grossbard a healthy dose."

Benjamin Styles inserted the key in the ignition.

"He don't fuck broads."

"This one he did," Angela Bliss said proudly.

Benjamin Styles looked at her. Suddenly he felt better.

"You're kidding?"

"Nope," she said. "Not this chick." She was laughing now.

"That *is* funny," he said.

"Angela Bliss refuses to get mad—she gets even." Then said: "I got plans to get back at the rest of them schmucks. Can we talk?"

"That's what we're doing."

"I was hoping you'd buy me breakfast."

"Some other time."

"Look," she said, "I know you got fired and I know Grossbard's got enough pull to bar you from every studio in town. They've done it to me. The only thing I could get is work on amateurish independent projects with shoestring budgets—or porn. That's crap. I didn't come here for that. We're in the same boat. . . ." she said. Stared down at something. "Shouldn't you be getting new tires pretty soon?" She dropped the tires. Said: "The sick things Reggie had me do. I was his slave the whole time I was with him. I let him exploit me. . . . My fault. . . . What did I gain by it? What a cold bastard."

Benjamin Styles thought she would cry.

"I didn't mind," she said. "So long as he delivered on his promises . . . which never happened. He used me to get to the young studs he had the hots for. . . . Asshole. Bunch of fucking parasites. You're used and discarded. . . ."

She looked at him. "You're about the only straight shooter I've met since I came out here."

She stared at the ground again. "I feel awful about what happened. There never was any bullshit about you."

"The one thing I could never tolerate."

"Me neither," she said, and stared at the passing cars on Sunset. Gazed at the smog-enshrouded hills above. "I may have given Jimmy a dose, too. I don't think I did, but if I did . . . tell him I'm sorry." Then she thought: *I couldn't have given Tubesteak the clap. I got it two days later from that dyke agent.* She couldn't even remember the woman's name.

"No," she said. "I'm sure I didn't pass it on to Jimmy."

"Look," he said, "whether you did or didn't—let's not discuss it. Period."

"Don't worry," she said. "I wouldn't do anything to harm the only two real people in this shitty place."

She finally looked up. "Listen," she said. "Would you have a cigarette?"

Benjamin Styles gave up a cigarillo and lit it for her.

"Thank you," she said. "Nice seeing you again." And walked away from the car.

"What would you gain by it?" Benjamin Styles asked. "I couldn't be of any help to you."

"I'll feel better," she shouted back. "I'll feel a lot better. I am going to give Hollywood the clap!"

She walked to the corner and stuck her thumb out.

Benjamin Styles pulled away from the curb, and the Toyota merged with the heavy evening traffic on Sunset Boulevard.

Dry Hump

In a bar in the San Fernando Valley Benjamin Styles was getting plastered. Someone would be getting hurt soon, he concluded, that someone being Reggie McFluff.

He had signed a contract, sure. But it wouldn't make things right. They could settle out of court. But that's not what he wanted.

He had studied Leo Fitch and had come up with ideas for the character: nuances, expressions; invented his background—and had gone on believing every little detail as though he were a real human being. To Benjamin Styles, Leo Fitch was indeed real.

He, in fact, had become Leo Fitch. He knew the lines forwards and backwards. Better than that, he could recite the entire script word for word. He knew everyone else's lines, everyone else's background down to the smallest bit part. He had studied the history of Dodge, done research, read books. He knew everything there was to know about the town. Never mind that Fitch was, for the most part, fictional, invention, but he accepted the premise because, after all, it was only a movie. Even John Ford said, when asked if pressed to choose between fact or legend . . . that he would go with the legend.

Styles understood this. Because if you told the real truth about more than a few of these legendary men of the West like Doc Holliday, Earp, and others . . . audiences would be appalled by some of the lowlife behavior. None of these cocksuckers were as pure as certain books would have you believe. Most of the exploits were exaggerated, and the chicken-shit behavior swept under the rug. History books? Rife with fabrication and outright lies—unless they supplied footnotes and facts that could be backed up. Which, very often, was rare.

His beard itched. Posed problems. He had never cared for beards. A 'stache he didn't mind. But this beard business was nothing more but another annoyance he'd had to tolerate for this role he had been contracted to portray. And now his dream had been flushed away, not unlike so many others he'd hoped and wanted to see come to light.

Ben Styles felt rage. He felt he had been violated and disrespected. He wanted to kill. Kick some ass, at the least. Break a nose, dislocate a jaw.

All Benjamin Styles wanted, just once, was a break. A lousy break. Dammit, was that too much to ask?

He ordered another mug of beer. When turned down by the bartender, Styles picked up his empty pitcher and flung it at the man. Barkeep ducked in time and the pitcher shattered the large mirror in back of him. Styles was promptly dealt with by a couple of burly bouncers and tossed out on his ass on the sidewalk outside, but not before they'd plucked his driver's license from his wallet that would be returned to him upon reimbursement for damages.

Later that night in a gay bar in Hollywood, as he leaned over to sink the 8-ball with the cue in his hands, an over-eager queen walked up from behind and wrapped his arms about Benjamin Styles' waist, pressed his crotch against Ben T. Styles' backside and began mock-pumping.

The dry hump lasted long enough for Benjamin Styles to thrust his behind out, knocking the bewildered homosexual off-balance, then Benjamin Styles pivoted and whipped the thick end of the stick across the side of the fag's face, breaking the cue in half, one end of which went flying and hit another sissy in the chest.

Styles wasn't done, not by a long shot. As he reached down to grab the one who had made the lewd advances by the collar, a sharp, stinging pain in his right knee made its presence known and pretty much stifled any additional moves he had planned to make.

The welt across the fag's face was a purplish, ugly thing. His eyes were wide, stunned and hurt, indicating without so much as a word that he did not want a second helping. He was scared to death.

Benjamin Styles released his grip, and walked out of the place. Why he had set foot inside a queer joint he was at a total loss to explain. Maybe he had just felt like going in and fucking up some queer, beat up a pole smoker, kick a shit-packer's ass. Whatever the reason, he didn't care—because to him it didn't mean a fucking thing.

He walked to his car.

Willing to Kill

By the time he reached the Horgan family's apartment, Benjamin Styles was drunker than he'd ever been before. Place was as cramped and disheveled as ever. His nasal passages were congested, and he thanked God he wouldn't have to smell the pile of diapers over in the corner where the washer and dryer were. Being in the vicinity was bad enough.

The youngest of the kids had been left in the playpen in the living room, banging a baby doll against the wall in back of her. The kid's diaper was loaded and needed to be changed. Styles didn't like seeing it.

"What ju want again?" Serafina Horgan asked.

"Don't bother me," Benjamin Styles muttered, and picked up the phone to dial.

"*Como?*"

He stopped, and looked at her. "Don't speak that Mex shit to me. You hear?" He wasn't in the mood to tolerate it. And he would make damn sure he didn't utter a word of spic from now on. The woman nodded and walked back in the kitchen.

"You want to do something worthwhile?" Benjamin Styles said, looking at the child in the playpen. "Your kid's carrying a load, for crying out loud. Should at least have enough sense to take care of it." And he finished dialing.

The woman was back with a clean diaper and tended to the child.

"That you, Polack?" Benjamin Styles said into the receiver.

"Don't you ever learn?" an irritated Nicky Horgan said. "I am not a 'Polack'; nor am I 'Bulgarian,' nor am I a 'Hun,' or a 'wop.' You're the 'wop.'"

"Part."

"Good for you," said Horgan. "I was born in *Budapest*. That's in Hungary. Not Poland, or anywhere else. *Hungary*."

"What's the difference? You're still a Commie foreigner."

"I am not a Communist, Mr Styles. You are out of line, sir."

"You listen to me and you listen good," Benjamin Styles said. "I'm willing to deport your whole fucking family myself unless you do exactly as I say."

"I hear you, Ben."

"What are you doing in San Francisco?"

"Playing tourist. Taking in the Golden Gate Bridge."

"I'm desperate, motherfucker!" Benjamin Styles shouted. "You better know it. Fuck sending them back. I'll wipe them out! You hear that, *Polack*? You hear it? I lost 'Fitch' because Tubesteak isn't here. The son of a bitch is costing me! My career just got derailed because of that punk!"

"What 'career' is that?" Nicky Horgan wanted to know.

"Come here!" Benjamin Styles said to Nicky Junior, and yanked him by the arm. "Got your Daddy on the phone. Talk to him."

"Ben?" Nicky, Sr. said. "What are you doing, Ben?"

"Dad?" Nicky Junior said into the receiver. *"He's hurting me. . . . My arm. . . . Dad."*

"Hear that, *foreigner*?" Benjamin Styles shouted. "I'll break his fucking arm!"

"All right," Horgan screamed. "What do you want? What is it?"

"I want James Kidd back. I want to do Fitch."

"Ben, I don't know where he is. We've looked all over for him."

Benjamin Styles was now twisting Nicky Junior's arm and had the teen in tears. Styles stuck the receiver into the kid's mouth. Serafina Horgan made an attempt to pull her son away; instead, she got a backhand across her face that sent her reeling back in the direction she had come from.

"Talk to your old man," Benjamin Styles said to Nicky Junior.

"He hit mom, Dad. He's gonna break my arm."

"Ben," Nicky Senior said. "I'm pleading with you. Please don't."

"I don't want to hear that crap," Benjamin Styles said.

"All right," Nicky Senior said. "I'll cooperate, man. Please don't harm my family. That's all I ask."

Benjamin Styles released Nicky Junior and the kid ran over to console his mother.

"Talk," Benjamin Styles said.

"I came out here, to San Francisco, to find him; not because of you, but because of the girl—"

"What girl?"

"Jimmy's girl."

"Get to the point."

"I don't think he knows how much she loves him. I wanted to find him for her. Victoria is hurting bad. She needs to see him."

"Still not telling me what I want to hear."

"Well, we looked everywhere. The Tenderloin, all the strip joints. Wasn't long before we got a lead. He did a two-day quickie for some porno people. They were very pleased with him and wanted him to do another one, until they found out he had a social disease. The other performers hadn't liked that at all."

"Get to the point, goddammit," Benjamin Styles said. "Where is he?"

"Then I talked to a transient. He saw Jimmy get in this fancy Bentley in the alley behind the burlesque theatre. Couldn't make out the two ladies who sat in the back seat; it was too dark. Didn't get a good look at the guy who jumped out of the car to help him out, either."

"Who are they? Where do they live?"

"That's the problem. No one knows who they are or where they live. As far as what they look like: it was late at night, impossible to see. Pretty much."

"What about a license plate number?"

Nicky Horgan hesitated. "That," he said, "we got."

"You dumb fuck! Why didn't you say so in the first place? Why give me all that other worthless information? You got the plate number; that's all that counts."

"How do we know he's with them?"

"Find out! You got the plate number and you got contacts. You're in the peeping business! I'm not the gumshoe! Get the address, names, then the phone numbers! I have to spell it out?"

"Won't be easy," said Horgan. "I'm out of my element here." Only Horgan was lying, stalling. He knew the women were sisters and their father, having been murdered years before, had been one of the biggest providers of porn in the nation. His company was headquartered in Chatsworth, but the Rodales, never having been able to relate to the LA and Valley scene, had always maintained their primary residence in Northern California. Solange Rodale, the widow, having inherited the business, had others run it for her. Stepdaughters Emerald and Saphyre did their share to help out.

"Do it."

"I will," Nicky Horgan said. "I'll bring him back. But you need to hear what I have to say to you, Mr. Styles. My family better be all right, guy. I might not be a professional boxer, and I might not have your punching power. . . . You better believe me when I tell you I have enough strength to pull a trigger."

Benjamin Styles took it in, then quietly said: "You got three days to bring him back."

"Just you remember what I said."

"Three days."

"Let me talk to my wife."

"Three days," Benjamin Styles said, and ended the conversation.

Marin

If this was it, what everyone was supposedly after, top of the heap, The Life, he didn't want it. Didn't need it. He would have preferred something more modest. It wasn't Marin, an upscale area north of San Francisco, that disinterested him, so much as the too-rich-for-his-blood 30,000-square-foot-French-style mansion. Mansion, hell; it's more like a palace, he thought, as he stood at the second story window, taking in the manicured topiary and grounds, tennis and handball court, putting green, miniature golf course; there was even a go-cart race track, not to mention a wine cellar downstairs, home theatre, library, and gym, that sat on 7.5 acres of land.

He should have been impressed, he supposed. He was, about as impressed when he pretty much saw the same back in Bel Air and Beverly Hills. Didn't faze him, and he was okay with that. Could do without the opulence and the overhead and headaches that came with it.

Jimmy stuck his head out the window and sent a glob of saliva high into the air and watched it descend to the ground below, missing the Vietnamese gardener by mere inches. The weathered face of the gardener stopped briefly to consider what had just whizzed past his ear, and resumed trimming the rose bush.

Jimmy Riff stuck his head out over the sill in order to make some sign of apology, but the old man never looked up. Jimmy had had no idea that anyone was even down there.

There was a light tap on his door, and a Vietnamese woman, as old and weathered as the landscaper outside, walked in carrying a food tray. Jimmy's eyes stayed on her as she lowered it on top of the fancy, antique dresser, bowed humbly, and left.

Could have said thank you, said Jimmy to himself. The easy life has turned you into a jaded prick. That's what it is. Better watch it.

Jimmy Riff yawned, stretched his arms, and ate the turkey sandwich at the window. While polishing off the bottle of imported Dutch beer, his second, the shiny Bentley pulled up to the entrance. A boy of no more than nineteen, wearing the standard chauffeur's uniform, hopped out. He, too, was Vietnamese. He had one leg. Reached inside for his crutch and hopped around the back of the auto and opened the rear door on the passenger side.

Now, there's a brave little son of bitch, Jimmy thought, studying the driver. He had seen the kid ride a bicycle with that one leg as well as anyone with two. Four days ago, when the rich widow's two daughters picked him up in the Bentley and brought him here, he had witnessed the kid do an assortment of things around the property— and never, ever in less than a great and happy mood. There was always a smile on his face. Kid had energy and good vibes to spare.

There was a lesson to be learned. In the future, if he ever got down on himself for whatever reason, not that it was the norm with him, he'd have to remind himself to remember this young Vietnamese guy who had but a single leg to stand on, whereas the rest of us, most of us, had two, and didn't go around with a grim look on his face.

Impressed? Yes. People like this impressed him. Not tennis courts or wine cellars, luxury autos, or his own prowess in the sack. Attitude. It was attitude.

The widow emerged from the front door at last. The statuesque lady wore black: heels, fishnets, skirt, blouse, black gloves, and veil. The veil pretty much obscured her features.

Quite the intelligent woman, the few times he heard her speak in what sounded like a French accent. Oftentimes Jimmy felt less than worldly in her presence. She used words he was not familiar with, named places she had been to that he had never heard of. She never talked down to him; had too much class to do anything of the sort. If he ever felt socially inadequate at times, it was through no fault of hers. She spoke to him as though he were her equal in every way.

He watched her thank the kid with a nod and climb in the back seat. The Bentley pulled away. Jimmy watched it travel the quarter mile of winding gravel road toward the wrought-iron gate and could not help but wonder where the lady was headed.

Curious was how he felt about this well-kept, auburn-haired fortyish woman. There was something enigmatic, something unexplained about the Widow Rodale. She had said nothing the night the twins brought him over and introduced him to their stepmother, merely had greeted him with a wan smile. Of the twins, as before, Emerald had been the only one who had spoken to him, although relatively quiet herself.

The daughters were twenty-five. Both were. They would be the same age, wouldn't they—since they were twins. Pretty. Both had their deceased father's eyes and high cheekbones. Both looked like they came off the cover of *Cosmopolitan* or *McCall's,* or some such popular publication—only much better, because the twins had curves; they were built. The usual, way-too-thin models used by *Cosmo* and all the other overrated fashion mags had never moved him much; just as the air-brushed, overly made-up models who posed in Hugh Hefner's *Playboy* rarely had him raising a brow, or raising anything else, for that matter.

But in the face department? Yes; the widow's adopted girls were appealing.

And the widow herself and her idea of sex? Well, he had never encountered anything like it before, and found it rather amusing, more than anything. She preferred to do it in the evening, once, twice at the most. She liked to take Jimmy by the hand, lead him to the john, and this was some john: larger than most apartments he'd stayed in, with jacuzzi, large tub and shower, vanity and bidet. The wall on the side where the sinks were was one large mirror. Carpeting was plush, thick; felt like you were floating on a cloud as you walked on it.

And the taps and handles? Made McFluff's place look like a pauper's hovel.

But this well-preserved woman would guide him to the john; she'd have him stand over the toilet, gently unzip his fly and release his member from within. She would caress him softly, taking her time, until his groin rose to full mast, then she would point his rock-hard member at the toilet bowl and wait for him to whiz. She got some sort of inner satisfaction, a charge, from watching urine arc over and down into the water in the bowl. Holding a man's hard cock while piss poured out of it was Widow Rodale's idea of sex. So far.

⁊∽∽⁊

Jimmy Riff went along with the routine, what harm did it do, after all?—and was not able to stop smiling through it every time. And the widow? The widow would look up at him, from time to time through that veil, with a pleased expression of her own.

She had a habit of breaking out in a sweat before each session. She'd offer him beer or coffee, water or tea, or whatever libation he preferred, so long as he peed to her satisfaction—and the longer the stream of piss, the more contented and fulfilled and elated this made the woman. Often times she would remind herself (with hand gestures) not to rush the pumping of liquids into him; she would remind herself to take her time, walk slower to the bathroom, gradually unzip his fly, and take her sweet time in handling and prying out this wondrous organ that she appeared to be enamored with.

Once, even, while softly and slowly stroking him, while flicking the head of his groin with either thumb, she took a hand of his and placed it on her chest so that he would feel her heart beating away like a snare drum.

This is okay with me, Jimmy thought. He came around. If it makes this wonderful lady happy, who am I to judge? Who am I to snicker and look down my nose, not that he ever would. People had their little quirks and fantasies. Could be that she had loved the late Mr. Rodale so much and she was unable to have actual sex with anyone else; and this was how far it ever got. Who knew? It was fine with him.

⤜∽⤛

After each session she would take her sweet time, once again, to unbutton his shirt and relieve him of it. Hang it carefully on a wood hanger; undo his wristwatch and place it carefully on the counter. Untie his leather shoes, and pull them off and leave them outside the bathroom door (whereby one of the help would shine them and bring them back and leave them there); she would have him sit on a stool, and take each sock and roll it off; she then would run her hands up and down the one leg, then the other. She did this slowly, taking forever, then gradually, inch by inch, would pull his trousers down, all the way, until they cleared his ankles, and had them completely off and would carefully hang them on a hanger. Then came the boxers. Down they went. There was no denying the inner joy and unmistakable satisfaction she derived from each phase of the process.

She would have him step into the jacuzzi with bubbles floating and billowing. Taking a sponge in hand, she would run it across his back, up and down, across one shoulder then the other. She would have him stand up in the jacuzzi, and run that large sponge across his chest, under the armpits and down, down one leg, and up again, and get the other.

Of course, Jimmy would not be able to help himself, and he'd be as hard as a ball bat. She never said a word, never removed the veil, merely kept that small smile on her pretty face. The Widow Rodale was something else. Jimmy had never been treated this way; and who would have thought that anything of this nature would turn him on and leave him panting for sex, for the real thing?

Of course no such thing ever happened during these sessions. But she stayed with it. And that sponge got nearer and nearer to his genitals. She rubbed his balls, under them, then ran the sponge up along the shaft; circled the head that left it throbbing. *Damn*, thought Jimmy. How is this possible? Woman is driving me nuts with sensations I'd never known possible.

Instead of taking him in her mouth, or masturbating him, she'd let go of his meat pole and have him turn around while she ran that sponge over his buttocks. And never, ever did she rush. My God, said he to himself, this woman knows a thing or two about foreplay. This was it. He'd thought he was some sort of master at it. Look what she's doing.

I can't stand it. It was a good thing that he never had premature ejaculation issues, because his balls were aching to get off. He felt like fucking. If not her, someone.

She ran that sponge and cleaned the one muscular bun and cleaned it thoroughly. Ran it around in a slow circle, then progressed to the other. When done, she would open both, and ran the sponge up between Tubesteak's buttocks. She slid it up and down, tenderly, across his butt crack. Moved lower, and got the testicles anew.

Then it was on to the legs: upper thighs, lower legs. She washed his neck, face. Shampooed his hair. She gripped the hand shower, and rinsed the shampoo and soap off. That was not enough washing for the Widow Rodale, it seemed, because she had him step into the shower and rinsed him off some more.

When she was convinced he was clean enough, she had him step out and dried him off. Ah, she was so conscientious about all of it: drying his hair and face, neck and shoulders and chest. Belly, legs, completely; then she focused on his privates: nutsack, groin, buns, and bunghole.

He was handed clean clothes to wear: sharp, top of the line by the world's finest fashion designers: Gucci footwear; silk shirts and dress pants flown up from shops in Beverly Hills. To get into later. For now, she preferred he got into the white and fluffy bathrobe. She left him to dress himself.

Mind this? No; he didn't mind it at all. It was nice—for what it was.

Now, as turned on as he clearly admitted being, Jimmy also wondered if he would have the patience to go through the routine on a regular basis, every week; month after month? He doubted he wanted to be owned in this manner; because that's what it felt like: ownership; a kept man, who wouldn't be allowed to get his rocks off. In a way, he had to admit, it was a tad cruel. Had to be. His gonads ached after each session. You simply could not do something like this to a man, any man, drive him to these heights . . . without allowing for some sort of release.

After he'd gotten into the robe, she'd have him follow her to the step-daughters' bedroom. Emerald and Saphyre had begun to sleep in the same bedroom, not the same bed necessarily, ever since their father's death. The trauma had taken a heavy toll. Saphyre, he would come to learn, hadn't spoken a word since the tragedy, and Emerald had remained numb inside. He'd watched the widow kiss them on the forehead, hug each one in turn, say good-night on her way out.

He had stayed on because initially he had wanted to, because she'd had her own physician give him a check-up that proved, once and for all, that he was clean, no STDs, taken care of his swollen lip and sore shoulder as a result of having been ganged up on by those misguided punks connected to the production. On top of all that: he had been well compensated for his burlesque routine.

Probably the greater reason, more so than the others, why he remained, had to be curiosity. His. Regarding the widow. A day did not go by that she didn't pay either her deceased husband's grave a visit or stop by a particular eucalyptus tree at the local park, placed a fresh wreath or flowers, said a prayer. He wished to understand. His compassionate nature steered him in this direction. Was there a way to lessen the widow's plight and burden? Sex? It was not that. Yes, he found her appealing. There was magnetism, to be sure, but carnal relations with her—beyond what she got a charge out of from the times she bathed him and enjoyed piloting his groin while he urinated—he was not after. In his heart of hearts, he was not cultivating this. When he asked Emerald one morning over breakfast, after the widow had left in the chauffeur-driven Bentley, what it was about, how her father, the widow's husband had died, and why the tree? What was the significance of the tree?—she had been cagey. He did not press the issue, merely requested the use of her wheels, a Corvette, and she consented.

❧

The next time the widow departed, post-breakfast, Jimmy followed. The first place he tailed the Bentley to was the public park. The one-legged driver remained behind in the car. Jimmy had stayed put in the Corvette and kept his eyes on the widow as she walked to that tree, carrying a bouquet of roses with her. She set the blooms down close to what looked like a memorial, with other flowers there, some wilted from previous visits, evidently, a wreath. There was also a chrome cross. His eyes stayed on her. Watched as she knelt, seemingly in prayer. Stayed this way for a long moment. He saw her withdraw a handkerchief and wipe her eyes, rise, and return to the car.

❧

He followed the Bentley on to the cemetery. Stayed behind in the Vette long enough for the widow to go walking in search of a grave. He stepped out, and followed on foot without being spotted by her. He waited hidden behind a tombstone while the woman went through the same familiar procedure: leaving flowers, kneeling, praying, or saying something. He watched as she wiped tears away, then blew her nose.

There was something else he could not help noticing, even though it brought on a good degree of guilt, the woman's figure. She did have a voluptuous behind, and the narrow waist only added to it, thus making it very difficult not to take in. And the legs? Never bare, in a type of hose, very often fishnets. Strong thighs, athletic; it was obvious. Supple calves that

439

curved down into beautifully shaped ankles. This was a fit woman, and feminine in every way. The guilt he felt could not be denied, no more than the carnal urge that proved just as stubborn at last. I'm only human, he thought. Kept telling himself. *It won't go past that.*

What could you do? Be a gentleman. Push them both aside: lust *and* guilt. Look at your surroundings. You're in a cemetery. The woman is dressed in black, has been dressing in black for years, and was here to pay her respects to someone she had loved a great deal. He would do the only thing there was *to do*: behave.

It was not until she left the grave, did he walk up to take a closer look at the name on the marble stone:

Clement Tristram Rodale

Year of birth, year of his passing. Underneath, the legend read:

Loving husband and father.

We miss you so.

Jimmy hurried back to the Vette in time to see the luxury auto pull away, and drive down the gravel path toward the cemetery exit. He hopped in, and followed.

⤜∞⤏

The sign by the side of the road said: San Quentin. He followed the Bentley up into the parking lot. Watched as the woman got out with what looked like a care package. She may also have been carrying a Bible with her. She entered the prison. Jimmy considered going in himself but doubted he would have gotten very far. He also considered walking over to the chauffeur and asking what it was all about; who was it the widow was seeing here, out of curiosity. But thought better of it. Didn't think he would have gotten anywhere there, either, or that it was even his business. He'd only done what he had so far out of curiosity. But you know what they say about curiosity and what it did to the cat.

He stayed in the Vette, waited. An hour later, the widow was back outside, walking to the Bentley. This time they took him to a homeless shelter; actually, it was a battered women's facility. He watched as the one-legged dynamo popped open the trunk and the widow reached in for a bundle of clothing and took it inside. The woman was a giver. Had a heart. All the crap you heard about the rich being jaded and unfeeling was wrong. Some may have been, just as plenty of poor were A-holes, too. Just because you had money didn't mean that you were a rotten human.

She was out soon enough, and walked to the Bentley. Jimmy followed them back to the house. The adventure was over.

Only the thing ate away at him, the visit to San Quentin nagged at him. What was it about? Who was she visiting? And how often? What was going on? And what was up with the tree? Why that particular tree? Was that where her husband bought it? Gasped his last breath?—Right at the foot of that eucalyptus? He had questions, and hoped to dig up an answer or two. He would not be able to leave this place until he found out what was going on.

Basilio Garcia

He asked Emerald to tell him what it was about. The visit to the grave he understood well enough; but what about the tree? Why that tree? And who did her mother visit at the prison? "Can you tell me?" he said. "I'd like to know."

Emerald popped in a video, a years-old copy of a local TV station news broadcast that told how her father was slain by the man her mother had been visiting regularly (for years) at San Quentin.

"She was able to forgive him after what he did?" said Jimmy when the video was over.

"That's my stepmother," said Emerald. "That's the kind of woman she is."

Jimmy was at a loss. Sat there. Speechless. Stunned. Finally: "That's amazing."

"The man, Basilio Garcia, thought he was doing the right thing, trying to save her from a sex maniac; believing he was saving her life."

"Instead, he shoots the only man she has ever loved," said Jimmy.

"The love of her life. . . ." said Emerald.

"Wow," said Jimmy, from truly being out of words at the moment. "Incredible. Tragic, but incredible."

"He was a good man," said Emerald. "Our dad. Self-made. He never let the money go to his head. Rarely spent time in LA. Hated it out there. He had people running his various businesses." She paused, looking at him. "Would you consider doing a favor for us?" she asked.

"What is it, Emerald?"

"She needs to be pulled out of her shell. You've seen her; doesn't go out except to visit his grave, visits the tree, the prison. Now and then she stops by the shelter for battered women . . . drops off items, good clothes, shoes. She actually goes to thrift stores, will buy up a bunch of stuff and take it over there. Come Christmas time, everything she buys is brand-new."

Jimmy studied her face.

"New," she said. "On Thanksgiving, Christmas, New Year's, Mother's Day, she's over there with food; has presents for the kids."

"What is it that you need, Emerald?"

"Thank you for allowing her to bathe you, and especially for being kind enough to let her hold your cock while you pee," she said. "She has never done this sort of thing before with any man, other than my father. It is tremendously rewarding to her in many ways. . . ."

He waited. She had to eventually come out with it. And did.

"Would you consider making love to her?"

Jimmy sighed. He was being asked at last. And yet his gut instinct said not to. It had been fun; but he also knew his heart belonged to someone else. He needed, and wanted to be with his girl. There was no denying it. Sex without that heart connection was enjoyable enough; it was good enough—but why settle for "good enough" when it could be and was great with the person he wanted to be with. That's what it was: He missed her. He'd tried so hard to bury these deep feelings that he had . . . and there was no use. The thing nagged at him. There was a chunk missing in his makeup; there was a hollowness, a void that only that other person's presence could fill.

"There are any number of guys who would gladly do this for you," said Jimmy.

"We would pay," said Emerald.

"Guys who would do it for nothing," said Jimmy.

She walked over to the entertainment console, shoved another VHS cassette into the video player. He did not know what to expect, until he recognized one of the names, one of the very first names that appeared on the screen: Raquel Renoir, starring in *Confessions of a Muff-Diving MILF.* The name that followed was, of course, Martinique du Maurier, the daughter. His own stage name, which Styles had had a hand in creating at the time, had been Shane Felsen, appeared next. Third billing. What did it matter? His goal had never been to be a porn star, or even act in porn. The tape looked old, grainy, and had suffered tremendous wear and tear from having been viewed so often. This was the first time Jimmy had ever seen the video he did that time to pay back Styles the attorney's fees and for having bailed him out of jail after he'd been arrested at Marcella's mom's place in the San Fernando Valley. Renata Blevins, or should he refer to her as *Raquel Renoir,* had pleaded with him to make other videos with her and her daughter, appear in their various popular productions, and Jimmy had turned them down. Decent money had been offered, and he had said no. Now he was viewing the footage, a scene with Martinique's mother only, as per his request, as he had not wanted to be anywhere near the daughter, sexually at least. By his own admission, the scene was quite hot, quite possibly as steamy as his very first encounter with her in her kitchen back when she was married to the deacon and living in that house in East St. Louis. He was viewing it for the very first time and wondered how his hosts had ended up with it.

"My stepmom has a *jonze* for you, as you may have guessed," said Emerald. "Our film distribution companies handle Ms. Renoir's productions. Her titles do well. She is a very popular MILF and has a strong following. As you may or may not know, the acronym MILF stands for Mother I'd Like to Fuck. How exactly my stepmom, Solange, came across this particular title, I'm not certain. Perhaps she noticed you in one of the stills from the video while okaying pictures for the catalogue before it went to the printer. She was transfixed and phoned San Fernando Valley and requested a copy of the video be Fed-Exed. . . . Of course, once we pointed out that you were one of the male strippers we had recently hired here in San Francisco, she was thrilled, desperately wanted to meet you. She was sexually frustrated; could not bear to have sex with anyone other than her husband, so she would look at these adult videos, usually this particular one that you're in, whenever the sex drive was too overwhelming to ignore, and masturbate; get off, then cry herself to sleep . . . because she missed her husband, my dad, so much. . . ."

Jimmy had to admit, the story moved him. Recalled the hell he went through and the tears he had shed when Marcella dumped him years before. It was not difficult to relate to any of it. We had needs. Whether you were male or female. The sex drive could not be ignored. About the only time one did not have to deal with it was when a person was too ill, or in the ground. It was one of the most powerful forces out there. Came a close second only to love. Love was still about the strongest. He did not know what to say.

"She hasn't been attracted to anyone since my dad's passing, not even in a fleeting way . . . until you came along. . . . Your uncanny resemblance to my dad." She indicated a framed photo of her biological mom and her father on the end table. Jimmy failed to see the resemblance, other than dark hair, blue eyes, ruddy complexion. Both were smiling in the photo, as were the two teenage girls standing in front that they had their arms around. A happy family. Said Emerald:

"You stirred something in her, feelings; reawakened something deep down that had been dormant for so long. . . . So many years now. . . ."

Jimmy shook his head. She had no idea what she was asking.

Emerald said: "Her psychologist has suggested that the lovemaking take place at the tree where her mate was killed."

"Wait a minute. . . ."

"Is it morbid? Possibly."

"Possibly?"

"It could very well be," said Emerald. "But who am I to second-guess a psychiatrist."

"I thought you said he was a psychologist?"

"Yes. One or the other; what's the difference? This is what he suggested. I was there during that particular session: love, better yet, a reenactment of the ravishing, at the foot of the tree—would quite possibly help to get her to snap out of her doldrums."

"You mean pretend rape?"

"Yes."

The thought of rape was unpleasant to him, pretend or otherwise.

She said: "*Defilement* would be a better description. Rape is too ugly a way to describe what they did. She enjoyed being ravished by him. It was nothing more than play acting."

"How often?" asked Jimmy.

"That, he didn't say. He was not specific on that score, Jimmy."

"And we have to do the whole reenactment thing out there?"

"If you would please consider it," pleaded Emerald. "It would mean so much to us."

"Us?"

"Me, her, the family."

"And it's sure to bring her out of her shell?"

"According to the psychologist she's been seeing now for years."

"Carry her off and ravish her out there?" said Jimmy. "That's it? Nothing else? Nothing more? I won't be asked anything else? Because this is it for me. I have obligations; I need to return to being true to myself. I don't even know who the hell I am anymore. I broke a girl's heart, a wonderful, caring girl's heart. And that isn't me. That's not who I want to be—ever. Let some of those other studs behave that way. Just because I happen to have a certain ability in the sack doesn't mean I have a right to be rotten to people who love me."

"I think I'm in love with you," said Emerald. "Truth is, all three of us probably are."

"Emerald, look; listen to me: you *like* me. *Like.* There's a difference. Because you hardly know me. And as far as your mother goes: This is *lust*, nothing more. She's attracted to me, but it's not anywhere near love, real love—it's *lust, desire.* Not that there is anything the matter with desire, you understand. Only please do not confuse it with love. Love is what my girl Victoria feels toward me, and how I feel about her. It took me a while to stop being in denial about it. I don't know why this is the way it works with so many guys, but that's the way it is. It takes time . . . to fall truly in love . . . but when it happens that's it, the real thing."

Emerald was tired of hearing about this other woman and wanted him to stop it. She had her stepmother on her mind. Her stepmom's well-being and happiness was of primary importance.

"Will you do it, then? Is that a yes?"

Jimmy was not saying.

"What about the cops?" Jimmy said. "This is a public park. We get caught bopping around in our birthday suits we get busted and hauled off to jail."

"Not if done at a certain hour."

"What about transients and peepers, and all the other perverts who roam these parks out here, not to mention the Zodiac."

She laughed.

"Who?"

"That guy: the Zodiac."

"That was years ago."

"Haven't you ever heard of copycat killers?"

"You're funny."

"Not by intent."

"Will you please do this for Mom?"

He was being pushed into compromising his true self. What it was, what it came down to. There was no bullshitting about it. There was no question that it was a worthy cause; and yet . . . By helping the widow he would be hurting himself, in that there was always a price to be paid by participating in something you did not entirely feel right about.

The women, all three of them: stepmother and her adopted daughters were decent women, good-hearted souls. No question there. If he didn't have feelings for the one he'd left behind, if he did not feel the way he felt about Victoria Chantal . . . it would not have been a problem at all, not an issue whatsoever. . . His conscience ate away at him.

How would he explain it to Vicki down the road, should they ever reconnect? What would he say? He would want to be honest with her. How would it go? Wasn't it enough that he had already broken her heart? She was a one-man woman; they were rare enough. . . . Yes, I slept with the widow because she was existing in a sort of shell ever since her husband had been murdered. Well, you could hardly call it an existence. And I did what I did to help. . . . Out of kindness. . . . It was nothing more than that. Attractive? Solange? Of course. Very. Even for an older woman. I've been there before, with Marcella's mother,

Renata. I find these women quite appealing. The difference in our ages was never an issue for me. If a woman was attractive, fit, took care of her appearance—and on top of all else was fairly intelligent . . . There was no denying he found these traits most appealing, more so than a female half the age who was in essence shallow and basically heartless. I did what I could to get her to rejoin the human race and have some kind of fulfilling life.

Yes, Vicki. I'm damned. I slept with the mother. Again, it was nothing more than a favor. The woman was a widow, as mentioned, and a caring person. They, the daughters, Emerald, anyway, because the other twin daughter, Saphyre, has stayed mute since the death of her father, pleaded with me. . . . She hadn't been with a man since her husband's murder. . . .

He had to stop himself from going on in this manner.

To Emerald, he said: "What's going on with the flowers? All the flowers your mother collects and then visits all these different places?"

"I'm not at liberty to say."

"I'll let you know," Jimmy said, and left.

Blooms for the Forgotten

He would find out exactly what was going on with all the flower collecting. In the morning the widow was chauffeured down the long drive and off the estate. He watched her go from flower shop to flower shop and place bundles of flowers into the trunk of the Bentley. He tailed them in Emerald's Corvette as they drove to various supermarkets and mom-and-pop neighborhood grocery stores collecting additional flowers: bouquets of roses, tulips, daisies, chrysanthemums, gardenias, and others.

He wondered what was going on? The trunk was full to capacity, then more flowers were placed in the backseat, while she sat in the front with the chauffeur.

There was no more room for a single bloom, and that's when they proceeded on to what looked like a rest home, and another, and another, with several bouquets, and would remerge empty-handed.

He still did not have a clue. Did the widow know this many people who stayed in these rest homes? He watched the Bentley pause at a bus stop where a homeless lady sat with her shopping cart full to the top with her belongings, a beagle on a leash by her feet. He watched as the widow pulled up with a bouquet, and handed them to the woman. He watched in amazement what took place next: the homeless lady's face took on a big smile, nearly in tears. The widow hugged her, and returned to the Bentley. Jimmy watched this scene transpire many times over. He tailed the Bentley to recovery homes, cancer support groups, visit shut-ins, shelters. And when all the flowers were gone, he watched the widow visit other flower shops and stores to collect more.

It was dawning on him what was going on. But he felt compelled to go inside just once and see for himself what exactly was taking place. He waited until the Bentley appeared to be empty of flowers late in the afternoon, and followed on foot as the widow entered one of the rest homes. He paused in the lobby, out of sight, and watched and eavesdropped on the widow as she spoke with a desk clerk, asking if there were anyone here who hadn't had a visitor in quite some time; anyone who did not have family or friends to come see them. The clerk, an elegant black lady, had a smile on her face; evidently, she knew the widow and pointed out several residents she might wish to visit on the first floor, down the hallway.

One lady was lying in her bed watching something on the TV perched high on a shelf. The widow entered, saying with a smile on her face: "These are for you." Handed the flowers to her.

"The flowers are beautiful," said the elderly rest home resident.

"*Oui*, except you are much more so," said the Widow Rodale. She leaned in and hugged the woman, and kissed her on the cheek. A tear appeared and slid down the woman's face. The widow wiped it away with a white hanky.

"Thank you."

"You are quite welcome," said the widow. Jimmy stood back, his own emotions getting the better of him. Kindness always got to him; anywhere, anytime. Acts of kindness moved him very often to tears. Some tough guy; some stud. I never claimed to be macho, Jimmy thought. And as far as being a "stud" . . . That was never my definition. I have sex because it's a rush, but that does not mean I am heartless.

More tears flowed from his eyes, and he turned away to get out of there before the widow discovered that he had been spying on her.

There were other places he followed her to. The cancer support group was the toughest. A hospital. Once again, the widow appeared at the front desk with her bundles of flowers, greeted the receptionist, a personable young woman, who directed her down a hallway to the elevator. He watched the widow board the elevator. Stood there as the elevator stopped at the second floor. He climbed the steps, three at a time, made it. There was another desk and a clerk. He stopped, asked where the lady with all the flowers had gone to. Was directed. He made a left, then a right turn, and down the hallway he went.

In a waiting area with a TV up on the wall near the ceiling, were a group of women, cancer patients obviously. Some in wigs, others wore ball caps to conceal the hair loss. He watched Mrs. Rodale pass out bouquets, giving each of the women a good hug. Some recipients wept openly. It was the kindness, the caring way the widow had about her. Some had met her, it was obvious, before; others were new to her and were introduced by these ladies who knew her.

The widow's own eyes welled. Once again, Jimmy was moved. A lump, a strong and hard lump moved up his throat and got stuck there. Tears were hard coming. It happened. Kindness. This was kindness.

There were giving souls in this world, this at times crazy and unpredictable world we lived in. So much kindness and caring people. Not all of it was about ambition and greed and wanting to own and hoard material possessions. Not all humans were like Ben T. Styles, and others of his ilk, chasing after something as pointless as fame, as ultimately worthless as an Oscar statuette; having top billing in a crappy Hollywood movie.

Just then he spun around, forcing himself to get out of there before he started bawling like a baby.

When he returned to the mansion, he entered the living room where Emerald was reading a novel. He let her know that he had followed her mother all day, watched her pass out flowers to residents at rest homes; give flowers to homeless, at shelters, the cancer center.

"Your stepmother is a giver; she's kind."

"Always has been this way," said Emerald. "Why my father fell in love with her. Yes, she is beautiful, and they had a fabulous love life, but really, truly he fell for her due to her kind heart and selfless nature. Money never meant much to her. Yes, she is aware of its importance in the world, and realizes one needs it to have some kind of stress-free existence; but they were never obsessed with money and wealth and owning things. She would be just as happy as if she lived in a hovel. In fact, when my father met her, working in a Montmartre cafe, working as a waitress, that was exactly how she lived, in a tiny apartment, taking care of her elderly mother who had Alzheimer's. She had no idea that my dad had money when they began to date and fell in love. My dad had gone off to Paris as a way to deal with the untimely death of his first wife, my mom."

He asked if her biological mother had been French as well.

"No. She was American. Fallon, my mother, was hired as a stripper here in San Francisco by my dad at the same burlesque theatre you were hired at for the male revue. She did so as a way to survive. My dad fell in love with her. She left the stage when they married. It was a good marriage; both were monogamous. As is my stepmom. My dad never strayed. I know; it's funny to be in the kind of business he was in and at the same time be monogamous."

"I suppose it is," Jimmy said. "Not unheard of. I have a tendency to lean in that direction myself. Always felt I was like that. I was in denial about it. It takes a while for a person to realize what he is about, truly about, who he is."

"Yes it does," she said. "It's like that for so many of us. We think we want to be this way and that way. We try this and the other, because we see others behaving a certain way, until our true core beliefs surface and we settle in, finally."

"Well, distractions are plentiful out there. I don't knock people who are swingers, who can handle being that way: nudists and people in porn; the ones who need multiple partners. I've tried living that way . . . and it's no good for me."

She nodded her head.

"What about you? Your sister?" he asked.

"I can't speak for Saphyre," she said. "I suspect I'm like my parents. I'm young, and not so sure. But I believe being with that one true person is probably the way."

Jimmy said: "With regards to this thing with your stepmom: Go work out the details and get back to me."

Emerald wanted to hug him and say thank you. He allowed it. Even though he was about to go through with it to the best of his ability, there was no denying he felt his conscience gnawing at him, that he was also betraying someone who meant a lot to him. There was no easy answer here; no easy out. The daughters had spared him from a beating in the alley that time, had they not? Didn't the woman they called mom deserve some happiness herself after all the happiness she was giving others? Even so. . . .

Monsieur Jimmy

The whole thing had been worked out, planned, down to the minutest detail. He had been given a sheet of paper with typed instructions. He would wear some sort of dark masquerade mask over his eyes, wield a dagger. He'd have the widow's wrists bound, and lead her to the tree, where she would be secured. He'd tear her black mourning clothes off, including that dreadful veil, and proceed to ravish her. He'd force her to fellate him. He'd do all sorts of other things to her: perform oral sex, etc., drive her to orgasm after orgasm to make up for all the years she had gone without, while she twisted her head, making sounds through the gag, fighting him, supposedly.

He shoved her against the tree. Bare breasts and face against the bark. He'd ordered her to embrace the tree, ignored her feeble protests and lame attempts to resist, and slapped a pair of handcuffs on her wrists on the other side that would keep her put no matter what she did or said to get her out of the situation she was in.

It did not take long for the widow to start responding to his moves. She was clearly receptive; and Jimmy had to admit, he was getting into it himself.

She loved having her buttocks caressed and asshole tongued, while a finger or two gently rubbed her clit and her pussy juices flowed and the moisture poured out of her in generous torrents. She had gone so many years without; all those years of being deprived—by choice, of course, but without, nonetheless. And she was making up for it now; this was her body's way of saying it was all good; it was about time. Yes! Long overdue! The moisture dripped and oozed out; oozed out and dripped. So much of it. Covering Jimmy's hand. He paused, to shove the fingers in his mouth and lapped up the cunt juice. He sucked his fingers, then returned this hand to her pussy and worked away on the clit, while his other hand stayed with her wonderful browneye. He had one gentle finger inside, probing, then added a second finger, as he knew he'd have to prepare the asshole so that it was flexible enough to take the length of his throbbing and quivering cock eventually. Not now, though, not now.

Take your time, Jimmy, he reminded himself. Yes, he was nervous about being found out, nervous that some San Fran homeless guy or wino would happen along and disrupt the works. He was tempted to yank the eye mask off, but left it alone. Make her happy. It was one of the prerequisites.

The widow swayed her hips, rotated her buttocks. At times she would even make partial thrusts, her pelvis moving in, then out, as though humping the tree itself.

Jimmy lapped up some more of the juice that flowed from her hairy cunt. And it seemed, that no matter how much he drank in, savored, and licked, there was more of it, an endless supply of pussy juice on the way. Lube. Natural lube. Best there was. He thought to rub some of it inside her rectum. This ought to help down the road. He continued the process, guided the cunt cream under and up, up into her tight asshole. She was loving it. Her intermittent moans and gasps continued to underscore this undeniable fact.

He stopped for a minute to give both of them a chance to rest up, and to kiss her face. He removed the gag only enough to be able to kiss her on the mouth, and she lapped him up hungrily, sucking in his tongue in the most wild and wanton way. Woman was desperate. Her hunger had no bounds. Even though he should not have been surprised to the extent that he was, he had to admit that he might have been taken aback just a bit. But why? The poor lady had gone without this natural of functions for six long years now. Not six weeks, not six months—*but six years*. Without.

He understood.

Then it was his turn. His lips sought out her tongue and pulled it inside his mouth, vacuumed it in, while he sucked it. This was replaced by biting of the lips; they took turns: biting each other on the lips. The lip nipping was dropped for hickeys, which they rotated indulging in. He had the first go: up and down her neck, witnessing her wince many times in pleasure, and she, in turn, reciprocated: biting one earlobe numerous times lightly, then hard once, making him succumb to the sensations it sent throughout his body, then she worked on the other.

Raw sex. Animal-like. Nothing else came close to describing what was taking place. Surprised even him that it should turn out to be this explosive. Yes, he had found the woman attractive from the get-go: wide hips, narrow waist; the tanned thighs and calves athletic and strong, and her kindness had moved him. He had felt so much compassion for her, the situation, the nasty blow fate had dealt her, but he had never expected anything like this, nor for it to be this thrilling. Another lesson in a long line of lessons: *Never judge a book by its cover*. No preconceived notions if you can help it. Don't assume. Never assume anything.

Trust your gut instincts. Go by that. Only his gut instincts had been dozing upon having been originally introduced to this woman by

Emerald and what she would be like during sex, not that he had given it much thought, actually. Not in the beginning.

Guilt? It was there. He had to admit. This would be it for him, as he had stated to the daughter. Only while he was at it, he would follow through and do his very best to make it a memorable experience for the widow.

Enough foreplay. It was time. She needed him to enter.

"I beg of you, Monsieur Jimmy," the widow pleaded. "*Entrez!* Enter! *S'il vous plaît! Maintenant!* Right now! I desire you *inside my pussy!*"

The request was louder than he thought was appropriate for the location. What if a loon heard them, a "Good Samaritan," as before, and came at them? It made him nervous as hell and he wasted no time complying. Once again, he considered yanking his party mask off. Let it go. Instead, whispered: "Of course, Solange. Can you please lower your voice? We're in a public place."

"Sorry, Jimmy," said she. "I will try. I wish to cooperate, but it is not easy to stay calm. . . ."

His initial move was to ease the knob in, and he took his time. He suspected it would be snug inside, and it was. *Very. Snug. A tight fit.* But the lube, all that natural lube, so much of it, made it possible for him to continue on in: one third, halfway, and then the rest. Just about the entire length of him was in her, and he heard her gasp: her cunt, and her entire body recoiling, to some degree, then there was a long moan that escaped her mouth as she nodded her head in quick succession.

"Yesss," he heard a nearly silent cry leave her lips. "Please . . . Jimmy, *mon amour. . . . Merci, Merci!* Please. . . . Go, go; you must. YES."

And he proceeded. As far as his groin would go, his nuts slapping the bottom of her cunt. They were good strokes, done with every confidence (now that he knew she had no trouble welcoming quite a bit of him).

This one, too, requested a quicker pace, only Jimmy was deaf to it. Nope. He took his time. Not too slow, but steady and deliberate. She'll accept it this way. He knew it. They all did. And loved the payoff. Always.

Not only did his style of shagging result in a more dynamic climax for the female, but served a dual purpose as well, one just as valuable, if not more so: it kept him from shooting his load prematurely. And you never, ever wanted to do that. Not if you wanted to see your lover's eyes go from one of admiration to one of resentment and downright loathing. And who could blame any woman for resenting it? How could you take the time to turn the woman on, and then leave her in the lurch? Unfulfilled and frustrated to the point she wouldn't want to have anything to do with you ever again.

❦

Jimmy continued driving it in there, and pulling back out again, the head of his cock sending sensations to his brain that felt better than anything he'd ever experienced. This was sex, fucking, at its best—and felt better than anything else that was available out there. Tell it to the druggies and boozers. You can't. What was the matter with them, anyway?

Forget all that, thought Jimmy.

He had his hands on either hip, looking down, taking in the widow's healthy buttocks, the butt crack, and the hairy bush below that, watching his groin disappear inside, and slide back out again; pumping, driving it home. Her tone was rising again; she was saying things in French. As much as he loved hearing it, it truly made him nervous and apprehensive.

"Solange, please," he whispered in her ear. "Someone will hear. We're in a public park."

"I do not care," said Solange Rodale. "I am loving this so much. Half a dozen years of getting myself off with vibrators and dildos, rubbing my clitoris . . . what a waste of time. Years and years of feeling repressed about so much: bitter and angry; I was, Jimmy. Please understand. Angry at fate; angry at the world."

"I do get it," he said.

"Fuck me, darling man," she begged. *"YOU MUST FUCK ME."*

He responded, not verbally, but physically, by jamming it in there, practically lifting her off the ground every time by an inch or two. Again and again. Out, and back in there—and the woman would be off the ground and moaning and saying things in her native tongue.

"The cock: this particular cock is very good to me; I must confess, Monsieur Jimmy," she sighed in a tone that continued to escalate by degrees. "I do not care who will hear," she said. "I have been patient and I have been lady-like. But no longer, *mon dieu.* No longer!"

He decided the only thing to do was to ignore the noise she was making and concentrate on the task at hand. What else was there to do? There was no way he could stop her from being noisy. She had managed to slip the gag off, not that it had done much good to begin with; and when he attempted to cover her mouth by placing his hand over it, she simply shook her head. Even bit down on one of his fingers at one point.

Well, that was no good. He needed his fingers, especially the middle one—that he had down there on her clit, and rubbed; stayed with it, concentrating on working the clit, while his hard-as-a-lead-pipe groin worked her cunt.

He saw it happening; he saw it taking place. Felt it. Her breathing quickened, her moans and all the other sounds she uttered went up in volume. Her body was quaking: thighs, buttocks, feet, mid-section and upper body and head—all quaking violently. She was screaming now, way too loud, screaming as the ensuing eruption could no longer be kept in check. This was something like witnessing a volcano blasting lava with a series of both: *explosions* as well as *implosions.* One after another. There was no point in trying to keep track how often her body went from quiver to quiver, twitch to twitch, because the series of orgasms protracted: the ripples and all the various manifestations taking place with very few lapses and/or next-to-zero pauses in between, all linked together by an invisible, yet all-consuming, mighty force. No way he was going to stop, either. She shook. Did her best to throw him off, it seemed. The orgasms were too intense and violent. He held on. Jimmy had his arms folded about her waist and stroked with determination and single-mindedness.

She was crying now; he was sure of it. Crying. Uttering things in French.

"Oui! Oui! Of course! *Je t'aime!"*

He slowed down by degrees, but not entirely. Her explosions went on. Even after he paused, and it was wise to do so, her eruptions did not cease. She was heaving at this time; her belly going in and out, while she gasped, her tears pouring.

She requested that he free up her hands , as she needed to embrace him, as well as be embraced by him. He pressed his thumb on a lever on one of the cuffs and it flipped open. She spun, the free handcuff dangling from the wrist that had the "locked" cuff on it. Solange Rodale was clinging to him; her face buried in his chest. Yes, she was crying. He held her this way.

When she looked up, she had a smile on her face.

"Do not worry, Jimmy," she said. "I am happy. The time for sadness has passed. Enough sadness already. We must be joyful. What life should be about. Yes, there is sadness sometimes—but life must also be about other things."

She lifted her face, her luscious lips needing to kiss him. And this they did. And while doing so, she had taken his groin in her hand and was stroking him. The pole was rigid; he needed to get off himself, and the woman knew this.

She knelt down, her back against the tree, and took him in her mouth. All of it? Not quite. It wasn't possible, but that didn't matter. She handled enough of him: the head, and then some. She licked; what an expert licker. Worked the bulbous head with her tongue and lips, then would alternate with either hand. Adequate amount of lube remained; and to compensate, add on, she spit on the knob and continued the business of blowing him.

Then she spun him around. Jimmy was the one now against the tree, his chest anyway, while she rimmed his bunghole and continued to stroke his groin with her hand.

Her tongue drifted lower: inch by inch, then under; and she was back on his groin with her hungry mouth and tireless tongue. She would glance up from time to time while she did this, to take in the expression on his face: his eyes shut, and the rest of the expression on his sweaty countenance gave a good indication that she was definitely on the right track. Her method was impossible to resist. This certainly gave her a solid feeling of satisfaction inside and the determination to stay with it until he got off.

Jimmy blasted. A load. It was tremendous. He was leaning against the tree for support, grunting in ecstasy, while watching her work it as he sprayed cum into her open mouth.

It was unbelievable to witness. This beautiful woman sucking his cock and gulping cum with so much genuine fervor. The more he laid on her, the wider her grin and the more she craved.

He should not have been surprised. This is what happened when you went without. The sex drive had to be dealt with; lust and desire had to be fed. Just like when your belly was empty and you were hungry for grub: food was the only answer. She had gone hungry for sex for so long; hungry for a good boff and taste of cock and cum that it finally resulted in all this. And he, Jimmy Riff, had been the grateful recipient.

Even though he was spent, and there was no more ball juice to be had, there she was lapping up his balls and surrounding area. My god. She couldn't stop. And he loved watching her lick him all over with that able tongue. She worked his upper thighs, belly area; under the nutsack and butt crack and buttocks.

❧

Finally, it was done. Both were exhausted and a break was in order. He pushed the eye mask back so that it sat half-cocked atop his forehead. They had a blanket there that they sat on and drank purified water. Only it was not long before she wanted more.

"Are you up to it?" the widow inquired.

Why she bothered to ask even he could not understand, because all she had to do was take a gander down there between his legs. He was hard. The meat pole was standing at attention.

Lust Is a Must

They'd wiped each other down with a towel; wiped the sweat and other bodily fluids off, and the widow was requesting that he pull the mask back down over his eyes and she be secured to the tree once again. He was not certain that he wished to repeat either of the requests. What if they got found out? So far they'd been lucky.

"What if someone should happen by?"

"Someone will not happen by," she insisted. "This is a free country, and we are making love."

What about before, he thought. How could you have forgotten? But he did not say anything, from fear of bringing up a bad memory for her and ruining her fantasy, and quite possibly having the effort fail at helping her recover one hundred percent. So he would do it. And did. The ridiculous eye mask was over his eyes. She was secured to the tree, in that the loose cuff was clamped back on the left wrist as before. The widow did not waste time shifting into her act, the protestations genuine enough to be convincing. Her fabulous ass was back out there, sticking out: voluptuous and inviting.

"This way again?" Jimmy said.

"Of course," she said. "I never get tired of a good thing. Have you not noticed?"

"I noticed," said Jimmy. All too happy to oblige, after all. "What would you like? What is it that you desire?"

But he knew. The widow was after sodomy now.

"You need ask?"

"Oh," Jimmy said. "That."

"Yes," she said. "That. There is a bottle of lube inside the paper sack; on the blanket."

He dug his hand inside the paper sack and did a double take: Jimmy did not care for what he saw in there: a black, rib-knit three-hole balaclava; a dagger with a four-inch hilt and a six-inch blade inside a leather sheath. Both had been mentioned in the instructions he'd received, of course, but hoped he wouldn't be asked to go this route. If they utilized them; say they did, he felt all this play-acting could prove far more dangerous than what he'd experienced at the hands of Nazi-idolizing Lisa Koch that night. He let it go. Hoped for the best. He would object later—if it came to that.

❧

He grabbed the lube, and inserted a good dollop in and around her butt.

"There is some lube inside from before," said the widow, "but we should make sure."

He did as asked. Wondered to himself if he ought to proceed, even while his middle finger entered her rump. He did so while adding a second finger to the procedure.

She sensed that something was wrong on his part; he was reluctant, and asked what was up.

"I wonder if we should."

"Do not deny me, Jimmy; I beg of you."

He had the fingers in there, preparing her for the business.

"You can't possibly take it," he finally said. "You're still tight; too tight."

"I need this," she said. "*Mon dieu*. It has been too long. Prepare the rectum. You know what to do. If you are *mon ami*, Monsieur Jimmy."

What choice did he have? The woman was insisting. Wanted to be fucked in the ass. She'd demanded that he lube her rear, play with it, prep it—and then slide his hard-on in there. This was not a first; there were women out there who got off being reamed. He'd been there, known one or two. What were you going to do? Did he mind? Not really. So long as one was careful. Yes; a person could end up with a damaged butt crack. . . . So, yes, caution was paramount.

There she was, though: wiggling her muscular ass and demanding that he drill her derriere. Okay, fancy lady, thought Jimmy, one anal fuck coming right up.

❧

He was nervous and he was careful. Spread the butt cheeks with his fingers, and made it possible to get the purple, mushroom-shaped head of his single-eyed wonder in there. He looked up, watching her face for any sign that it was suddenly no-go; waiting to hear her tell him to stop. Only nothing of the sort happened. If anything, she encouraged it. The widow was nodding her head.

"I am feeling the thick beast inside my French *cornhole*," she said in a quiet tone. "Ooh. More, Jimmy. Fill my French asshole with your glorious American bone. I want to feel it, the *Yankee Doodle*, inside."

Jimmy was more than cautious; he was scared stiff. For her—and for himself. Eye mask was on. He could be mistaken for—you name it: booty pirate, reprobate, exhibitionist, incorrigible browneye bandit, asshole violator, et al. But went on. Do it. Slide it in there.

As wary as he was, there was no denying how pleasurable it felt. My god. It was tight; the snugness and lube heightened the pleasure to such intensity that it was beyond belief.

"How does it feel for you right now, my fabulous American lover?" she said. "You do like it, yes?"

Jimmy could not help but smile. Yes, he was jumpy and in great fear that they might get caught, but there was no denying that it felt great to be inside this sexy woman's dumper.

"Wow, baby," he whispered in her ear. "*Mon cheri.*"

This made her laugh. His attempt to speak French increased her fondness of him.

"You had no idea I spoke French," he said. Reminded her that he'd taken it in high school one semester. "Being around you has helped, for sure. I'll be fluent in no time."

"Of course, Jimmy," she concurred. "This is why you should live with us."

He did not feel comfortable broaching the topic and stroked. He was in there. Not quite all the way, but there was no need, because whatever it was he was doing was certainly working. Her reactions with each and every thrust only confirmed it.

Jimmy, not missing a stroke, reached down for the industrial strength vibrator with his right hand, turned it on, and held it against her clit, all the while driving chubby home. She was taking it, and she was loving it—and screaming all over again. The orgasms came on: a series of powerful tremors. The vibrator doubled and tripled the intensity she was experiencing. Once again, he attempted to cover her mouth with his free hand, but nothing doing. She shook it off; wanted to be able to make all the sounds and noise she felt like making. This was freeing; this was what she had been waiting for all this time.

Jimmy withdrew from her asshole to give her rectum a break, and slid it inside her cunt. It was almost just as tight in there, but not quite.

It was all good. She never missed a beat; her explosions continued, as did the screaming and moans. Now she ordered that he return to the other hole.

"Again?"

"Do you have to ask?"

"You want more?"

"What a question."

"You won't be able to sit on it for a week."

She laughed. "I will worry about this, my friend, not you."

"Me worry?" said Jimmy. "Merely expressing concern."

The widow responded by demanding more sodomy. Insisted she had the uncanny and unusual ability to reach orgasm this way. He had read the piece of paper with the instructions and that's what it said. Not every woman could climax during rear entry; she was one of those who could, and her deceased husband had been eager to accommodate her, so long as her rectum was properly lubed. The topper, that she usually insisted on, after reaching her numerous orgasms, was to have it jammed in her mouth, including the balls, if possible—or at least one, if not both—in order to finish him off and give him a fabulous climax. She was very French this way. Free in her sexual escapades and loving it. Only her husband was no longer around to satiate her carnal hunger for it.

What it was about Jimmy, not so much as his looks and physique (that reminded her of her late husband well enough), but the shape and appearance of his organ. It reminded her ever-so-keenly of her long-gone mate. It was shaped, both in length and circumference as her late husband's had been. The knob? The smooth, purple-shaded, much larger than average knob, which she admired so much, was like her late husband's. Some men, so many men, had a cock head that was not very impressive; in fact, rather small, and the penis thin and unappealing in appearance. This was not Jimmy at all, and she was grateful. The thickness of it was beautiful, the shaft clear and devoid of scars of any sort, the helmet truly mushroom-like and a wonder to appreciate and fondle in every way, especially to receive in her mouth, cunt or asshole. Jimmy's face; his dark hair and blue eyes, his nose and strong jawline also reminded her so much of the man she had been married to and remained in love with and continued to miss and long for. No one would ever be able to truly replace her late spouse, but at least James G. Riff, aka Tubesteak, came so very close and was such a wonderful substitute. The man, even though having experienced so many sexual exploits, was big-hearted. Just like her late partner. There was kindness there, even though he had fucked for *d'argent*; even though he has had so many bed partners in his life, slept with so many different women . . . he was a good person, a genuinely nice man. And yet clearly knew how to be rough and in control when a situation such as this required it. She liked being manhandled, and he did what he was supposed to with such great conviction. There was force, brutal enough to be convincing, but not so much that it would scar or injure her in any way.

He seemed to know exactly what to do. The thrusts were effective in that he did not hammer away aimlessly, but kept a steady and prolonged pace. Moved at his own speed. She may initially have wanted him to move quicker, and her muffled cries may have demanded it, but he refused to go along, and continued as he wished—the speed he chose and maintained.

Finally she saw and reaped the rewards of it: when she began to climax; they were a steady stream of explosions, one after another. That made her feel as though the top of her head was about to erupt. It was splendor cranked up to the max. She was lost in it; lost all sense of time and space, her surroundings. She had no idea for the moment, where she was, who she was—or that she was even on planet Earth. She was drenched in sweat. It rolled off and dripped on down from her forehead, back of her neck and armpits.

The preacher's son was sopping wet himself. Yanked the eye mask off and ran his forearm across his brow to get at the beads of sweat that stung his eyes. This was some workout, and he doubted the lady was done with him. How much more would he be able to offer? Could he keep up? This woman was certainly older than him, but she was also in tip-top shape. Took care of herself, ate right. Yes, she had been grieving all along, but that did not hinder her from minding her health, staying athletic and in excellent condition.

His own blast soon followed, and he shot a considerable wad inside her *culo*. Held on. *Held on.* Needed to. Had his arms wound about her waist. Jimmy clenched his jaw; it was about all he could do to contain what could easily have resulted in a loud and powerful attention-drawing howl, instead was reduced to a more civilized and acceptable, if protracted, series of deep-rooted grunts and gasps. Subsequently topped off by a hearty chuckle or two.

Then he eased up. Kissed her gently up and down the back of her neck. His strong, manly hands massaged the area, as well as her upper back, shoulder blades. This was what she had been deprived of, what had not been hers for such a long time. . . .

One other thing was certain, she would not have trouble falling in love with this man, should he opt to stick around. No question; she knew she could easily fall in love . . . and it might even be happening right at this very moment. How could anyone explain it? They were orgasms, nothing more. They were fucking, having sex . . . when and how did this mysterious equation called love enter the picture? Not to be explained. Only that it was possible that it was taking place.

"My love," she moaned. "I love you so, Jimmy. . . . *Je t'aime; je t'adore.*" She said some other things in French that he enjoyed hearing. The sounds, words, her passionate way of uttering every single syllable made him smile and wish to go on pleasing her evermore.

Forgive me, Victoria, he thought. I want to do the right thing here. Anything worth doing is worth doing properly. And that's what is taking place right now at this very moment. I am giving it my all. I like the woman. No secret there. I said "like," not love. Her caring nature did get to me. Right where I live.

"Free my arms, darling Jimmy," she said softly. "There is something I must do."

He flicked the release mechanism on one of the cuffs as requested, and she turned, taking his sweat-drenched, handsome face in her hands. Held him still this way. Held him. With trembling lips, she said: "*Merci beaucoup.* Thank you so much, *mon cher.* My wonderful American *ami.*" She wiped sweat from his eyes, and kissed him full on the lips. Noticed that he had discarded the masquerade mask and she could not conceal her disappointment. "You promised," she reminded him. "The mask is part of the plan; part of the scheme, no?"

Jimmy nodded. Apologized.

Her smile was back.

"Look at us," she said. "Is this not the best ever?"

What was there to say? Jimmy was smiling himself. The physicality of it was certainly taking its toll. No denying that. But what a time they were having. She excused herself at that moment, then quickly ducked behind the tree.

Encore

It was not long before he heard the trickle. He walked back there to join her. Had to relieve himself. There they were: the passionate lovers, urinating in tandem. She squatting, he standing. You could hear the urine hitting the ground.

She hurried to be first to finish, then hopped up and gripped his shaft to do as she had before during his stay at the mansion: guided his groin and grinned with delight as she watched the urine arch up and over, the tail-end of the curving stream splatter the base of the tree.

"This is fun, no?"

When the last of the urine squirted out, she guided him back to the other side of the tree and was embracing him all over again. Had her arms entwined round his neck, alternately licking and kissing the sweat up and down the front of it; dropped lower to give his impressive torso some of the same attention, then lifted her face back up to meet his: kissed his eyes and bridge of his nose. Her lips drifted down to his chin, and her mouth was on his lips once again. And there she was, stroking him. Jimmy was at half-mast and felt for sure that they'd both spent themselves to the point of sheer exhaustion. He realized now that he was off the mark. There was no satiating the widow. Not at this stage. She needed more. Wanted more. Had to have it. *How much more?* How much would be enough? Good question—that he had no answer to. You just didn't go without sex for as long as this healthy woman had and be done with it after one tryst. Yes, theirs had been a marathon of a tryst—so far—but it would take something else.

He aimed to please, after all. He had set out to do so, had given his word, said that he would: and by golly, he would continue to fuck her brains out until they both passed out right here on the grass in this public park. And all else be damned. And if they got found out, busted, taken in . . . the loaded widow could always make a phone call to her prominent attorney to take care of that slight inconvenience. And as he completed the thought, she made the dreaded appeal: "Monsieur Jimmy, it is time for the headgear and the dagger, no?"

"Not the balaclava," said Jimmy.

"But we agreed," she said. "The dagger as well. It is part of the scenario, no?"

"Dag-aire" was the way she pronounced it. Made it sound cute and harmless—only it was anything but. Would she be able to snap out of the perpetual funk she'd been stuck in all this time without it? Another question he had no reliable solution to—other than to go along. But the underlying fear nagged at him; it was never far enough away. They both had to be insane to be doing what they were doing. Nuts. Foolhardy. Certifiable. For going through with it. And they were— *going through with it.*

She paused jerking him long enough to fetch the items and hold them up to him: ski mask and dagger. He donned the black wool balaclava with the small, decorative pom-pom on top. Held the dagger in his right hand, asking: What do I do with this?

She shrugged. "For now, take the dagger out of the sheath and bite down on the blade. Yes, so that it is across your face like so:

horizontally." This was a real effing blade, and Jimmy was careful: stuck it between his teeth, upper and lower jaw.

"*Oui*," said the widow, approvingly.

Jimmy Riff nodded. Go along. I am. Anything to help.

"Later," added the widow, "you will hold it against my throat. Pretend you are a real booty bandit, assaulting my backside. You must insist on making a rear delivery. *Sine qua non*; a necessity. You must sound like you mean it. Just as we did earlier."

"Sure," said Jimmy. *Only earlier there was no stainless steel blade to worry about and give me pause.*

"You are concerned," said the widow, back to jerking his dick, which was clearly in the process of rising. "I can tell. But I can also tell you will be careful. I am confident."

"I'm glad someone is," said Jimmy.

'We both are, *mon ami*."

She stopped talking. Had her hands doing the stroking, while his cock did the usual: got both fatter and taller. Growth was a natural state for this dude's "Moby Dick." It was usually hard, or in the process of getting there. The magic prick. There were times it felt like a burden. To be walking around with something this big and swollen hanging between your thighs all the time. Not unlike wielding a loaded .44 Magnum right there inside your shorts. Waiting to go off. And if you couldn't unload the stubborn mother, certain discomfort was the result.

He had lost count exactly how many times he had popped. And as far as her number went? Forget it. In the dozens. This was superwoman. Wonder Woman was a wimp compared to Solange Rodale.

She was kneeling before him again, her mouth open wide and taking him down her throat. She was able to accomplish above and beyond; certainly enough to impress. They say practice makes perfect. Here was absolute proof. Two-thirds of him was inside her throat and jaw. He was throbbing. The sight of what she was capable made his cock twitch and jump around inside her gullet, or maybe they were her tonsils that the head of his member rubbed against, perhaps deeper than that. He could feel the head of his one-eyed meat plunger tickling her tonsils for sure. Then she withdrew, to catch her breath, and had her mouth on top of him again—taking him back down, deep-throating.

How much juice did he have left? Was there enough scrotum nectar for another decent blast? He felt that there might be. Could he do it again? Possibly. If she stayed with it. It came down to the way she had of working the dome and giving it that winning corkscrew twist with either hand that increased and heightened the pleasure in and around it as well as—or rather primarily—the rim of the dome itself, the crown/corona (where a strong concentration of nerve endings resided).

She pulled it out. Took a look at it. The purple cock head pulsing with blood. She had had to pause to admire it. Spit on it, hard; repeatedly. In command and knowing it. Applied the corkscrew twist to the helmet with one palm, while stroking the shaft with the other this time. Jimmy's industrial-grade phallus was jumping around, jerking from side to side, back and forth. *Uber-sensitive* to the touch. She watched and smiled. Looked up at him from time to time and laughed.

"You love it, my dear Jimmy," she teased. "The way Solange makes you feel good, no? Monsieur Melville had his *Moby Dick*; but I do believe I prefer this one much better. And of course, I do this because you are the way you are: giving. A good man who makes this woman feel so terrific and whole. I am on my way to becoming whole again because of my friend Jimmy; with a little help from '*Moby Dick.*' Actually, he is a very big help, no?"

She ducked her open mouth over the bulb of his prick, inhaling him inside her mouth. She sucked this way, rapidly. In/out; in out, her own head bobbing in this unique fashion. In a minute, she was forced to yank it out and take a breather, all the while working on the shaft and cock-head with her hands, running lots of saliva over it.

"My heart is mending, due to my good friend Doctor Jimmy. My forever good friend, who reminds me so much of my dear, dear departed Clement."

She jammed his cock back in her mouth, getting quite a bit of it in there. Down her throat, it went.

He felt like saying: *Yes, Solange. Fine. I'd still like to drop the ski mask and the dagger.* Only he never uttered a word about it from fear of sounding like a broken record. Instead, Jimmy took the blade out of his mouth, leaned over and kissed her on the forehead. She took her lips off his cock for a second, lifted her face and their mouths met. Kissing. She returned to the task at hand. Stayed with it for a good while, then rose.

"Let us finish with a Big Bang, eh Doctor Jimmy Riff," she said, facing the tree as before. Her butt was out. Pressed against his groin. "What do you say, *mon cher*? We finish with a great big encore, yes?"

He was for it, following her lead. Made sure the balaclava was pulled down over his face, had the fingers of his right hand wrapped around the dagger hilt.

"What would you like, Solange?"

"A little bit of both: ass reaming, then put it in my pussy; then back to the bunghole," she said. "For the final explosion of pure ecstasy, fuck my bush—and let us attempt to climax at the same time, no? Should be fun." As an afterthought, an important one, she added: "You know what to do with the dagger. Make it look like a real assault."

"I still say I'd rather not," said Jimmy. "I'd rather skip that part of it."

"But you won't, will you, *mon cher*? I need your help in this."

Jimmy nodded. He was not for it, but would follow through. They needed to get going and get it over with. She suggested that he secure her to the tree; she wanted her wrists cuffed to the tree. As before, she wanted to be able to pretend to be resisting his less-than-welcome carnal transgression. This was pertinent.

"I got it," Jimmy said. Did as he was supposed to. Added lube to both: her cunt and butt. Slid it inside her behind. It was as good as ever. Amazing. They'd been fucking for quite some time now, and it still felt good. There was no getting enough of it. People were doomed. Sex could kill you if you were not careful; if you did not know when to quit and take a break. But this would be it—the final shag. He hammered it on in. Held the blade against her throat. That's when her next request threw him.

"Huh?" said Jimmy.

"I wish to be spanked! *Maintenant!* Now and how, *mon cher! S'il vous plait!* Take turns: first the left cheek, then the right! Use your open palm, spank me! Slap my backside! Then do the other with your other hand!"

Some BDSM couldn't hurt, and he was not against it—so long as it did not go beyond a certain point. She'd already shown interest in this area earlier, and he had easily complied because what she had wanted had been fairly mild and harmless. Only now she seemed to be after something else, a bit more intense. He was being asked to really slap her caboose. He felt his hesitation was prudent. Recalled all too well the encounter with Lisa Koch and the not-so-pleasant memories it had left him with. Only the widow was thrusting and jerking her ass around in a most impatient and angry way. He drove his member home. They were good, hard strokes, but it was not enough for her.

"Spank me, Monsieur Jimmy! I demand it! Be a *man*. Be *macho*. Be like Clement—or be a *wimp* and do nothing! I know you are not weak; you are no—what is the word? Wuss? You are not this, *mon cher!*"

"*Wuss?*" said Jimmy. Mildly perturbed. Because he was not eager to engage in violence in his *sexcapades*, he was being labeled a "*wuss*"?

"Hold the dagger blade between your teeth for now, Jimmy! Do the other! Do not be a *wuss.*"

"*Wuss?*" he repeated. "Me? James G. Riff? A wimp?"

He clamped down on the blade with his teeth. Both hands were free now and available to do whatever. Jimmy cocked his left arm, and came back and slapped the left side of her voluptuous behind with his open palm. Wham! He did the same with his other palm: whacked her hard across her right ass cheek. She winced, jerking her head back. Said something in French that he could not make out, only that she was liking it and wanted him to continue.

He did. First with the left palm, then with the other—and gave her more. She demanded that he *add* to it. *Something. Force.*

"Be like Clement! I wish you to! Need you to be like my darling Clement! That is the only thing that will help!"

He went on, believing he was delivering what she requested—and yet it was not enough. *"Make the fucking better; make it the best, the most pleasurable, Clement! Slap me; slap my backside! Damn it; goddamn it! I need it! I so need it!"*

She was calling him by her late husband's name now. So be it. Then she switched gears entirely and went into the play-acting part of it: demanding that the assault stop this minute. That he, as a stranger, had no right to ravage a defenseless widow like her in this vicious fashion.

"No, no! You must stop this instant, you horny bastard who gets his jollies by ambushing harmless widows like me! *No, no; a thousand times no!*"

"*No?*" said Jimmy. Confused, at the least.

"You know what I am saying," shouted the widow. "I am saying *do it! Yes!* When I cry 'No!' I am saying something else; I am saying: you know what I am saying!"

Jimmy put even more into it; the slaps were vigorous enough so that her ass cheeks were crimson at this point and his palm and fingerprints easily visible. He stayed with it, as well as with the thrusting. Gave her what she so vehemently demanded. Then there she was, screaming and moaning something else: *"No, no, no! Do not molest my bunghole and wet pussy! You must not! You cannot do this!"*

Slacking was not an option here, is what he gathered from all the mayhem she had cultivated heretofore and continued to encourage. Nor would he consider cutting her off and/or abandoning her at this far-gone stage.

The payoff kicked in. "Doctor" Jimmy watched her detonate a few times as a result of all that sweat and toil and effort. This woman fucked like a superhero. No shit. She was awesome. Even more than that: she was out of this world. She did take a moment to compose herself, catch her breath. Heard her say: "Whew. It was so good. I cannot explain." She laughed a bit. Nodded her head. Said: "Thank you." Did not waste time indicating that her bush needed some love.

"In the vagina," she said, "My vagina is lonesome for Monsieur Moby Dick, Doctor Jimmy. My vagina. Please make it happy."

He did what it took—to make people happy. Of course. Was that not his job? His vocation–as well as obligation. He was obliging. Happy to. This would be it, though. He liked the woman well enough; found her attractive and sexy enough. . . .

There she was: asking to have her muff tended to. He withdrew from one orifice, and filled the other. Drove the hammer in there. The lube made it work; she was able to take it. Just as energetic as before, she was. Impressed with her? What an understatement. How many women, or men—for that matter, had the ability to go on in this demanding fashion?

"Your American *beef Bazooka* makes my French pussy happy now, mon ami Jimmy! *S'il vous plait!* My pussy is in love with your Bazooka! I will fly this time; very much so! Due to the power of the American Bazooka! How do I know this? I will tell you; yes. Of course. Put your hand around my throat. Now! Do it! With the other you will hold the dagger under my chin."

"No," said Jimmy. "Too dangerous."

"Close to my mouth, then," she said.

Jimmy said no to that as well.

"What, then?" she asked. "What do you want? What do you suggest?"

He tossed the dagger aside. This was his answer.

She hadn't cared for it, but was too far along to do anything about it. She did have a new suggestion: a variation of the one just a moment ago: wanted both his hands around her neck, and she wanted him to choke her.

"Choke the caca out of me!" she insisted. "Choke me! Goddamn it; do this choking exercise now! Choke the shit out of Madame Solange! This very moment!"

Another request that he was uncertain about. Placed his hands on either side of her neck, but did not know what else to do, or if he thought and suspected what was expected of him next was once again reluctant to follow through.

"*I tell you, I will fly this time,*" she declared." Asked: "*Can you? Will you be able to fly with me? I wish for us to fly this time! Together! It is the very best way!*"

He was not sure what it meant. Yes, it felt great down there, the head of his groin plenty sensitive and the nutsack cream he felt being rapidly whipped up inside his scrotum. He knew it would be another terrific blast, but what was she after exactly?

"*Choke me,*" he heard her say. "*I want you to choke me! Now!*" She paused to catch her breath, then stated: "You do not know what this is? I am certainly letting you know what this is, *mon cher*! How can you not understand something this simple? How can this be?"

He applied pressure about her neck by squeezing his palms in a vise-like grip about her throat. Only it was not enough for her.

"*Yes,*" she yelled. "*You are getting there; but I need more! More pressure! Squeeze! Do it! I wish to soar! High! Above! Cut off my oxygen so that I cannot breathe; not completely, but close! You understand? Make it difficult to breath! So that I am gasping for air, mon cher!*" He applied more pressure, but was careful not to overdo. He knew by the time the thing was over that the woman would have red palm- and finger prints up and down both sides of her neck. This did not seem to faze her. She was urging him on. How much more could he do?—or be willing to render? There had to be a limit. A line had to be drawn somewhere— or else there would be consequences.

Her next request was a relief. She wanted her tits fondled and squeezed. "You have neglected my wonderful boobs, Jimmy. How is this possible?"

Well, he'd been tugging on them from time to time; he'd done his share of sucking on the hard nipples, but evidently she felt that her tits had been short-changed. All right, he thought. Let's take care of that right now. Ducked his head down, under her right arm, swung his own arm under and grabbed the breast. Drew it toward his mouth and sucked on the nipple, then more of the tit flesh.

"Bite them," she insisted. "*With your teeth.* I want to feel some pain when you do it!"

She was vocal enough. He did what he could to please the lady. Bit harder. Heard her wince. She squirmed with pleasure. Her body flinched in ecstasy.

"Like my dear, beloved Clement," she whimpered with pleasure. "Now the other; please, Jimmy! The other!"

He released the breast, shifted his head, then swung it over to the left. Pulled this breast toward him and repeated the process that she had been pleased with a moment ago. The biting went on. She winced her approval. Then it was back to the choking; she demanded more of it.

"Choke me, dammit! You weak American bastard! Choke me! I wish to be choked!"

He was there, hands clamped about her neck. And the name-calling? Being called a "weak American bastard"? Did not faze him one bit. He knew it was but a game. When someone like this woman was in the throes of passion, words escaped and behavior happened that had next to nothing to do with the actual person. It was part of the sex act; fornication, copulation; fucking; screaming and creaming—scaling that steep volcanic cliff with a singular goal in mind: to experience that lava ejaculation into oblivion: below in the groin region, as well as inside your psyche and brain, the grandest solar system of them all.

What else was there that topped it? Users/druggies were full of crap when they claimed that cocaine beat it, or that heroin equalled and/or even surpassed it. Bullshit. *Had to be.*

"I am soaring, Jimmy! Way up, up, up! Soaring." She could hardly get the words out, as his grip on her ever-so-feminine throat was quite tight, but not to the point it would choke her out and cause her to go unconscious. No way. It better not happen, thought Jimmy. That isn't me. Even though this is what she is after. Watch it. Careful. But he

choked the French nymphomaniac and both reaped the fruits of their labor.

Jimmy was breathing too heavily to say anything. Plowing took some effort; energy and stamina. As fit as he was, he felt it draining him; felt it slowing him down. And the violence? Even though clearly playful, and part of the game: smacking her athletic ass, squeezing her neck—took its toll on the one laboring away at it.

He withdrew his groin from her cunt and it happened: a *vart*. Vagina fart. Gas escaped her muff. She seemed a tad embarrassed by it. He assured her she needn't be, and had the anal impaler back inside her tight browneye: yes, the grand French asshole. Stroked it with great enthusiasm, then back inside that wondrous and hairy European joy box. Drove it. Sliced it in. Heard her choking. She wanted it this way. Insisted on it. This was what she meant when she said she wanted to fly, to soar. And he was giving it to her! Fuck yes! He choked the sex-starved bitch. He was indeed surprised to discover it heightened and underscored his own intensity as well.

This time, at this point in the romp, his pace quickened; he needed to do it this way—for he felt something brewing in his balls, felt a tsunami of spooge coming on; felt the explosion about to be triggered. Any second; any nanosecond. Kept at it. Stroke it. Pump the French lady's wondrous cunt. Pump it. Slam it.

She was screaming, as before. Loud; she was loud. Even though his hands were on her throat and she was having the shit choked out of her, she was moaning and saying stuff like: *"Bite my neck! You must!"* He did. She wanted to feel his teeth on her earlobes and neck, biting and biting hard enough for it to be painful. She needed to experience his teeth digging into her flesh, but not penetrating the skin.

"Hickeys?" said Jimmy. "You want hickeys?"

"Yes! OUI! No! No! Yes! Yes! Maybe! Possibly; it is possible! This is it!"

There were things in French she was screaming and crying out. Her body was jerking; she shook her head violently—and would not stop, that made it quite the challenge for him to continue with the nibbles and bites. There were explosions taking place inside of her, a series of powerful aftershocks. The ground, unmistakably, shook underneath their feet. Jimmy's own frothing orgasm was about to rocket out of the starting gate. He felt it blazing, rushing through the length of his cock, nearing the head, bursting forth something like his own mortal/humble version of the atom bomb.

"Fuck! Shit!" he cursed—and as he did, coinciding with the fireworks going on inside his skull, were gunshots from somewhere out there. He blasted! Shooting sperm inside the woman; and the other, actual shots, went on as well. *Gunfire! They were being shot at!* What the . . . *Someone was firing at them!* Just as he had feared: there was no time to yank the ski mask off with the dumb pom-pom on top and explain that they were merely play-acting; that the whole thing was part of a charade, a sort of psycho-therapy session recommended by the widow's head doc. Nothing of the sort.

They were being fired upon by a madman who was yelling something in a foreign accent: *"Halt! I said halt! Stop ravishing that helpless woman! Halt, rapist chien! Despicable cochon!"*

The man was stocky, wore dark clothing; a type of plastic Halloween mask that resembled President Jimmy Carter a great deal covered his face and head, a flaccid penis for a nose hung down and bobbed all around on a coil like one of those toy dogs people had in the rear window of their car, as the fool rushed up. There was definitely a gun. The masked man waved it around, still shouting in what sounded like a thick Euro accent. Perhaps on the gay side. Why not? This was the Bay Area, was it not? Only there was no time to bother with any of that.

The Good Samaritan, gay or otherwise, yelled: *"Halt, you reprobate! Rapist vermin from the foulest reaches of hell! Dirty bastard! Be still this instant! I order you to cease and desist, sir, or I must shoot you dead!"*

There was more firing. Shot after shot. Jimmy had no idea what the hell was going on, who this effeminate nut was. He went down, believing to be mortally wounded. If he did not go out completely, it was close. The total surprise and shock of the assault had taken its toll. The widow seemed to experience a temporary loss of her senses herself. His last glimpse of her, seeing through the holes in the balaclava as he folded, was this image of the lady leaning limply against the eucalyptus tree: wrists cuffed to it, the side of her face pressed against the bark. Still. Silent. Possibly out. Except there was no denying that a contented, calm smile had traced her lips. But this could have meant anything: she had given up her last breath as the final bullet entered a vital organ during orgasm.

❧

The masked shooter disappeared as quickly as he had appeared. He could not tell how much later, but someone, Emerald possibly, had rushed up with a bucket of water and had splashed them both in the face. The mother, the Widow Rodale? What had been her reaction upon waking? Tears of happiness, it seemed, poured from her eyes. Satiated at last; she could not stop crying at how unbelievably fabulous it had been and so freeing. She was out of the woods and no longer moping like a loveless, unwanted spinster. Was this what he was seeing? Was it? He yanked the ski mask off, and flung it at the ground. Yes, the woman was happy; not distressed at all. After what they had just lived through.

Jimmy did not understand it. What was going on? Looked down; inventoried his limbs, chest, abs, in search of bullet holes and blood. Where was the blood? And the pain? You got shot; there had to be pain, as well as bullet holes in your body. When he looked up, Emerald and her stepmom were hugging. The widow wept openly. Jimmy was first handed a towel to dry himself with, then given his clothes by the one-legged chauffeur, as well as a cold beer in a bottle. He took a long slug. Wiped his mouth with the back of his hand, then had another long slug. It was good, imported beer. He found himself staring off in the distance. And it dawned on him at last.

He had been set up. Used.

"Those were blanks," he said. "I wasn't shooting blanks into the widow, but that masked fucker sure as hell was."

No one answered him. Emerald walked her mother to the Bentley. Jimmy followed, pissed, for sure. No one had mentioned that there would be a shooting, that the reenactment would be pretty much the way it had happened before, only without real bullets. It hadn't taken much to add it up.

"Why didn't you tell me? Emerald? Mrs. Rodale? Why didn't you let me in on it?"

"It would not have worked as well," said Emerald.

"That's not good enough."

"Oh, please, Monsieur Jimmy, don't be angry with us," said Solange Rodale.

"You scared me half to death," said Jimmy. "You can't justify what just happened. It's inexcusable."

"Look at my stepmom," said Emerald. "Would you please look at her: smiling. Finally after years of suffering, years of depression and suicidal tendencies, she is smiling. Happy to be alive. And thanks to you, our wonderful, good-hearted Good Samaritan."

"Yeah," said Jimmy. Still shaking. "Look at my hands. Wonderful, huh?" He cursed under his breath. When compensation was offered, he refused to accept it. And he knew he had to get away from this scene. He'd had enough.

Some Good-byes Are Tougher
than Others

He had been packing what few things he owned in a single suitcase. Figured he'd be leaving the premises the next day. The widow had entered his room and found herself pleading with him to help her daughters in the same manner that he had helped her.

"Oh no," said Jimmy. "No more."

The widow had nodded, said that she understood. "May I have a good-bye kiss, my Dear Jimmy?"

"Of course," Jimmy had said. They had embraced afterwards.

"We part as true friends," the widow had said with a tone of sadness, and left him to finish his packing. It was not long before the twins entered. Emerald had confessed that Dagny, the porn actress, did not have VD that time; it had all been a ruse that she and and Mr. Bonaparte, the guy in the President Carter mask, had concocted in order to make Jimmy beholden to them and get him to stay at the house and help out Solange, bring her out of her shell. And it had worked. And now they were apologizing to him for it. Emerald with words, Saphyre in her own silent manner that she had. Asking his forgiveness. "The actors, Enzo Scorpion and his friends, got carried away, I am afraid. We specifically instructed Mr. Bonaparte to make certain that you were not harmed in any way. There must have been a misunderstanding and the jerks got carried away. Some of it must be envy. Men are envious of you, Jimmy. We said to Hercules, Mr. Bonaparte, to see to it that you were merely threatened, intimidated, if you will."

"That was an act of selflessness on both of your parts," said Jimmy. "There is nothing to forgive."

"You're not in the least bit angry?"

"Over what transpired at the tree? That was scary, but I'm over it; dealing with it; accept it. But this other thing? Actually, I'm touched that you and your sister would go so far out on a limb to help your stepmom out. You did what you did because you both love the woman so much, someone who thought the world of your dad. The make-believe rape scenes that they liked to play out? Not my business; I don't judge. It would have been fine, except it went wrong; took a decidedly wrong turn; as a result one good man is gone, and the other might as well be, because life behind bars, to be caged up like an animal, for some, is a fate worse than death."

Emerald's eyes may not have been welling, but there was a great sadness there; the other sister's look of longing could not be denied. Then both embraced him, holding onto him as if for dear life.

"Our darling man," said Emerald. "This angel named James Grayson Riff. . . . Can you stay awhile longer? Please, Jimmy? We can explain everything to this girl that you miss so much. She would understand."

"I've already put her through enough," said Jimmy. "I need to stop playing the heel. It isn't fair. She deserves better from me. There isn't going to be any more fooling around, no stepping out; no more sadness of this nature, anyway; not if I can help it. She's true. I owe her to do the same. I want to. I need to. . . ."

The widow had returned, joined in in pleading that he stay and live with them. "Your girlfriend can also live here with us. There is plenty of room. We can be one big happy family. You are both welcome. Truly, Monsieur Jimmy. You would not have to work; do as you wish. You can run one of the video companies, the distribution end. If you like."

"I am flattered, truly moved. But I can't." Here is where he paused. Asked who this Hercules guy was and what exactly his duties were. The widow was puzzled. Emerald said: "Our hearts are breaking and all you can think to say is 'Who is Hercules?' Very well: He was my father's personal valet. Had met him in Europe as well. Hercules Bonaparte, actually it is Her–cule, the 's' is silent; in any event, Mr. Bonaparte appeared in a few of our European gay productions. When his lover left him to return to his wife and kids he suffered a nervous breakdown. My father paid his medical bills and took him under his wing. Hercules is in charge of maintenance and takes care of the vehicles, seeing to it that they are kept up, washed and waxed, oil changed, etc., tires rotated, or replaced, as the case may be. He had begged my father to take him to San Francisco where at least he can live in a city where there are many penises in a relatively contained region; where he can be around his kind. The site of this many male buttocks in one place has restored his will to live."

"Now you know the 'histoire' of our 'Hercule' Bonaparte," said Solange Rodale.

"Yes, but what's up with the Jimmy Carter mask?"

"Ah," said the widow. "That one is a mystery. You see, Hercule wishes to keep that his own private little secret."

Some things were better left alone, and Jimmy did not feel a need to pursue it. The maid reminded Mrs. Rodale that lunch was ready.

"Thank you, Delphine," said Solange. "Jimmy and I will be

downstairs shortly. Emerald and Saphyre will be having their meal in the kitchen."

Emerald and Saphyre exchanged glances, then Emerald said to her stepmom: "We will?"

"Please, darling," said Solange. "I wish to speak to Jimmy in private over lunch."

A Widow's Request

They were in the parlor area of the dining room. Lunch consisted of a healthy salad and beef stew, which Jimmy had requested. "Anything to drink?" Solange had asked, while she sipped her wine.

"No, thank you," Jimmy had said. "I never was much of a wine drinker."

"Beer, then?"

"Water is fine," said Jimmy.

"I wish to take this opportunity once again to thank you, Jimmy, for restoring my will to live. I was lost; wondered if I would ever pull out of the black hole I was stuck in."

"It was Emerald, actually," Jimmy said, "who deserves the credit. She's very convincing. And, of course, you. Seeing you, the actual person, go out of your way to help others . . . convinced me to try and help out. . . . You and your daughters are pretty special. . . . I wish I didn't have to move on, but my uncle is waiting. . . . I'd like to find my own way. . . . It's about time."

"You may have noticed, Jimmy, Saphyre never speaks," the widow said. "She has been this way ever since her father was murdered. . . . And my other daughter, yes, they are not mine biologically, but they are still my daughters . . . it will always be this way. . . . Emerald, she appears to be fine on the outside . . . but inside, this is another story, a different story altogether, Jimmy. She is not living, not alive; she is like a zombie, truly. Inside. She is dead. There is no emotion, feels nothing."

Jimmy ate, listening, not saying anything. He would hear her out before responding.

The widow said: "I wonder, forgive me, Jimmy, if I am out of line . . . if it is asking too much. . . . What you did for me, I wonder if it would be possible to help my two daughters this way?" Her eyes welled. "Yes, we have access to many men . . . but they are not right; there is nothing special; always there is something missing. They do not know how to make love. It is like this, Jimmy: they jump on, do their thing, like robots; you have seen them in these silly adult videos. It is fucking like a machine. Never putting much into it, or anything at all: wham, bang. They shoot the sperm—and they are done. And the women, the women in these videos, they are all pretending to be enjoying themselves, but they are never enjoying anything. You know I speak the truth here."

Jimmy nodded. It was something he had never understood about the porn business. Why was it that the women and where *they* were coming from, was never paid any attention to? Why was there never any consideration there?

"The part I never got about porn," said Jimmy. "Without women you have nothing, and yet no time is ever taken to see to it that they are satisfied. Why? It's baffling."

"Yes," the widow said. "Not only baffling, but so selfish and careless. Unfeeling. I suppose I could try to do something about it. After all, we are the ones who hire the talent, at least pay them. We could urge our directors and the so-called studs to look into this part of it. Do not get off until after the woman has been satisfied. This is what we should do.

After all, I am in charge of my late husband's companies these days. I must admit: I have been neglectful about many things, not only the porn side of things."

Jimmy nodded.

"In that video you did with Raquel Renoir," said the widow, "I noticed right away that you were different from the other dicks-for-hire. You did not neglect her at all. You did not rush, you did not just bang away . . . you wanted to please her and satisfy her and took your time until she was fully satiated. Is this not true?"

"I tried, yes. That was the goal," said Jimmy.

"This is what I mean," said the widow.

"It's also true that Raquel had had a lot to say, since it was her production."

"Yes, but she mostly makes videos with lesbians. Very rarely will she do one with a man. I am not saying she does not like men at all, but she easily prefers her own gender. She likes bush. Is this not so, Jimmy?"

Jimmy had to agree here and wondered where it was all leading.

"I would much rather not appear in any more videos, Solange," he said. "That's not my life's goal. I did what I did to survive. But no, I have other plans. There is a girl who loves me very much . . . that I would like to apologize to . . . and maybe, just maybe, see if we can mend our differences, make a go of it; see if I can make it up to her and have her forgive me. . . . I would like to see if she and I can have something lasting. . . ."

"I understand," said the widow "This is what I and my late husband had. It is best this way. But I also wondered, because of what you clearly accomplished here with me, if you might consider doing the same for my two lovely adopted daughters: Saphyre and Emerald?"

"A couple of gems. They truly are."

Jimmy paused here. Sipped his water. He looked at her. This was going to be difficult, so difficult—to say no, to pass. Once again.

"I must decline, Solange," said Jimmy. "It is not easy for me, because I think the world of you and Emerald and Saphyre. Am so grateful for what you have done for me. But if I go through with this request of yours . . . how would I look myself in the mirror? How will I look Vicki in the eye? How would I explain it to her?"

"It is because I love my girls so much," said Solange Rodale, "that I ask this of you. . . ."

"I understand," said Jimmy Riff. "And it pains me to say that I can't. It hurts me inside to pass up this great opportunity to make love to your wonderful daughters."

She nodded her head. Wiped her mouth with a napkin. "I will let them know. It will break their hearts, but I will do my very best to explain."

"Did they ask you to talk to me about this, Solange?"

"No, of course not, Darling Jimmy," said Solange. "I am doing this on my own. I did mention that I would speak to you . . . as I am so worried about their well-being and general health. Saphyre has not said a word in so many years; and Emerald, as I have already mentioned, she appears fine, she functions, but of course she is far from happy. She cannot feel anything inside. I have had them both to my psychologist . . . and he has also suggested this to me . . . once he saw what your lovemaking has done for me. He has even expressed a wish to meet you." Solange Rodale smiled here. She shook her head. "I promised I would see what I could do. However, I did explain that you are not bisexual. You are all man."

Jimmy wondered when she'd had the opportunity to visit her shrink.

"Oh no," she said. "He was there."

"In the park?"

"Of course. He is very hands-on. Monitored all of it. Quite possibly took notes—in order to help others. He has many patients who are afflicted; dysfunctional in the boudoir."

Jimmy was at a loss. This was one unconventional head doc the lady was seeing.

"He has since telephoned me and expressed a wish to see you. He would very much like to be introduced. He has also offered to discount his usual rate for you, should you decide to visit."

"For me?"

"Yes," she said. "He has confessed he could not help pleasure himself while observing the two of us."

"While taking his notes?"

"*Oui*. Of course. He records his notes on a mini recorder and is quite the *multitasker*."

"I'm impressed," Jimmy said. "Unfortunately, I must pass on that score as well."

He rose, thanked the woman for the meal. Decided a nap was in order, in that he felt mentally exhausted. "So much has happened since I saw Victoria last. Not unlike Emerald: I'm calm on the outside, but inside is another story."

Reawakening

He slept in the buff. Victoria on his mind before dozing off. Many images were happy ones, but there was no denying that last image, of the two of them parting. . . . It ate away at him. Having made such a wonderful girl cry. . . . It was no good; it was not the way his life should have gone. He wished he could have wiped the slate clean, and moved on north, to the chicken ranch and begin anew. Start from scratch. Work with Uncle Orville and his wife, learn what there is to learn about raising chickens. . . . And should it turn out that this was not what he was meant to do, the direction his life should go in, well, then, he would find something else. But for now . . . that was where he was headed: Oregon. And the ranch.

How or why all these other images kept bouncing around in his mind's eye was puzzling, but he felt incapable of doing anything about it. There was that first time with Marcella, and slowly falling for her, developing feelings that he had no control over . . . and Willabelle, being discovered by Willabelle in the walk-in. . . . The lovemaking in Renata Blevins' kitchen . . . who did her best to help him heal. . . . Of course, the healing process had taken a long time, but at least the woman had showed kindness, plenty of kindness there, and then the final session with Marcella and Renata in her mother's bedroom. . . .

Meeting Victoria Chantal up at that wild party in Chatsworth. . . . Being assaulted by the porn goons, and Styles showing up and coming to his aid.

He wished he could make it all go away. All of it: Victoria, Styles, his past, childhood, fights with his father, images of his sister Betsy being committed, his mother in a coma after drinking the *Liquid Plumr*. . . .

He wished for nothing more than peace of mind. A good, restful nap, and then, the answers, it would all clear up, he hoped, as it often did. . . . It helped if you were relaxed to begin with . . . and things had a tendency to work themselves out as a result. This was what you aimed for. . . .

⚜

"Darling, Jimmy. . . ."

He vaguely heard a gentle female voice whisper his name. Oh, Vicki. Was it Vicki? Sounded like her, or was it? This was what he needed, ached for . . . to be spoken to in such a soothing, calming voice.

He was being kissed ever so tenderly on the lips and chin, his brow. . . . They were the sweetest and calming kisses that he was receptive to. It must be Victoria Chantal, he reasoned in this dream state that he was drifting in.

And once the kisses stopped gradually, and it was gradual, there was kissing, soft, soft kissing along his abs and below. It felt as though he were being fondled down there, caressed. . . . Felt his member develop growth. The pleasure as well as his organ stirring could not be denied. It was taking place; it was going on and he was not about to wake from this wonderful dream to see what exactly was taking place.

Someone down there, *perhaps two someones*, were licking his privates: both, his groin and his nutsack. A gentle tongue probed lower to seek out his butt crack. The perfume was exquisite and heightened the rising ecstasy that he experienced.

The touching was definitely female: gentle and soothing. Two females worked away on him down there, while a third—and this time he recognized this particular perfume—resumed kissing his neck and face, was that of Solange Rodale. He suspected. Was close to certain. Hoped Victoria Chantal was one of the bodies making love to him . . . but sincerely doubted it. And yet, he was not about to stop it. Inside, he may have resisted, emotionally he may have wished that it would not go on, but physically, he was not about to prevent being seduced in this giving and pleasurable fashion.

"How will I explain this to my girl?" Jimmy sighed. His eyes remained closed.

The widow shushed him. "Don't worry, *mon cher*, we will explain it all to her, or rather I will. She will understand. There is a difference between love and making love. Your love, what you feel in your heart, is for her, and only her—on the other hand, what we are doing here is having fun, celebrating life. Yes, there is feeling involved, but it is sex. Lust."

"You are being seduced, Jimmy," Emerald whispered from down below, between licks of his erect groin.

"Yes," said Saphyre, speaking for the first time in many years. "You are being seduced, James. And you are loving it, and you can't deny that you are enjoying it as much as we are."

"My girl Victoria will never forgive me," said Jimmy. "I will never live this down."

"She has forgiven you before, has she not?" said the widow.

"Those other times were different," said Jimmy. "We were not involved yet, not truly."

"Don't talk so much," said Emerald. And while she took him inside her mouth and worked it, with her sister concentrating on his balls and asshole, the stepmother remained at the other end, only she had maneuvered herself so that she was straddling his face, reverse cowgirl. Her buttocks were on his face, and Jimmy found himself burying his tongue in her butt and liked it.

He found himself taking turns with what he was doing there: his tongue would slip inside her butt crack, then probe her vagina. And he continued to work it this way, taking it slow and easy as usual.

He requested that Solange turn around so that he might have an easier time reaching more of her cunt, the clit in particular.

She complied eagerly, spreading her pussy lips so that Jimmy did not waste time licking her pussy and gradually moving up toward the clit. Woman was in utter state of bliss.

"Please don't be upset with them, Jimmy," the widow pleaded. "It is not their fault. I was the one who encouraged it so that they might rejoin the living, just as I have after that incredible session of lovemaking in the park."

Jimmy said nothing, and continued to concentrate on the clit. The woman's immediate reaction and urging that he stay with it was the big payoff.

The sisters switched off: Saphyre was the one grabbing his groin, while Emerald buried her tongue inside his asshole. They had him turn on his side, the right side, to make it easier to do what they desired: Saphyre sucked his cock, while the other sister continued to work away at the scrotum and his browneye. While at the other end, Jimmy had his face buried in the stepmom's hairy muff. The rawness was there, just as it had been during the pretend rape at the tree. Needy, hungry for sex, all three. There was no pretending otherwise: as often as he had gone through this, fucked so many women, gotten his rocks off so often, it was as though it was taking pace for the very first time; that's how horny and hard and desirous Jimmy Riff was.

Sex? Especially when it was this great? You could never get enough. You never ever got tired of it. Immediately after shooting your load you think you might not want to have any for a long long time . . . but it was never true. Because the need, desire, always, always returned. There was no use lying to yourself about it: We craved sex until the very end. So long as we were alive, we needed it; we thought about it, we had fantasies about it, we pursued it. . . . So long as we were above ground and breathing.

⸎

Then they switched off again: Emerald had taken the stepmom's place and was shoving her beaver in his face, while the mother was down there licking his balls. Jimmy was on his back and Saphyre had straddled him, and was fucking him this way, doing most of the work. It was not easy meeting her thrusts, being in this position, but that was all right; Jimmy was not complaining. Saphyre was young and was able to handle the physical exertion it required. Then something new took place down there: Solange had withdrawn him from her stepdaughter and taken him in her mouth. Jimmy lifted his head enough, had gotten Emerald off of his face, to be able to see exactly what was taking place down there. Solange sucked away, and sucked feverishly. The sucking was sloppy and enthusiastic, and he was loving it. There was saliva dripping on down to his balls and upper thighs. Saphyre had managed to get her own mouth in there herself and they were sharing his member, taking turns: one would suck for a few minutes, then the other would take over, sucking him in deep inside her throat. The sight of it added to the thrill, these gorgeous women sucking away, totally free and uninhibited. This was the way it ought to be: wild and crazy and unrestricted. The Frenchwoman, no doubt, had had a great deal to do with it. They followed her lead.

"Do not be inhibited," he heard her say to Saphyre. *"Never! Never! Go all out! Suck it, darling! Suck this beautiful cock! Lick his balls and then go deep in the asshole!"*

Saphyre did as instructed, and did it with relish. Then, once again, they switched off. His euphoria had been notched to such a heightened state that Jimmy was beginning to wonder if he'd be able to withhold from climaxing. He did not wish to blast just yet; no way. *Do not cum,* he kept reminding himself. All three women needed to be fucked and fucked properly. You have to last.

To save it, he withdrew for a while. Sat up, was on his knees. Positioned Emerald on her back before him, her legs spread open. He had Saphyre lie beside her and buried his face between her upper thighs and began to eat her out, while at the same time flicking her sister's clit with his left hand.

Down there, at the other end, the stepmom was lying on her back, her face pressed up against his privates, and she had her lips back on the head of his knob.

He took turns eating first the one's cunt, then the other, while being blown down there by Solange.

What a *ménage,* what a way to experience the sex act.

He looked up, searching for something. Saw it: a tube of clear lube. Handed it to Emerald. "Lube it," he told her. And did not need to say anything more. Her cunt, in fact, all three cunts were fully lubed with their own natural juices; it was their dumpers that needed to be primed for some righteous reaming.

Emerald was about to lube her backside, when Jimmy said not to, but to do her sister instead. She did that. Then handed the bottle to her sister. Saphyre proceeded to insert a gob of the clear gel into her sister's rectum.

Solange waited for her to finish, then brought her own healthy and athletic ass over to be processed, and Jimmy did her butt crack himself. Brown and tight and beautiful. All that tennis that she played, and time spent on the treadmill, hours and hours spent on the treadmill had kept her beautiful ass athletic and voluptuous and hot.

Hind Sight

He had them lined up before him, on all fours, their asses sticking out at him. It was a beautiful sight. Three wonderful and fuckable female assholes staring at him. He was on his knees himself, licking Solange's butt, who was in the middle, with Emerald to the left of her, and Saphyre to the right of the stepmother. While his tongue probed Solange's butt crack, he had his middle finger of each hand deep inside the others' butt cracks, stroking. Then his fingers left the rectums and probed the cunts, clits, then back inside the cunts, all the while driving his cock deep inside the stepmother's tight backside.

Dammit, he was close to exploding again, and he couldn't/wouldn't allow it. Pulled back for a while, the trio sat up and kissed until the crucial moment passed, and they were back at it again; only this time his groin was inside Emerald's inviting booty. And the woman was loving it: while pressing a dildo against her clit, she was climaxing and experiencing tears for the first time in years. *"Oh!"* she screamed. *"Oh my God! SHHHIIIT!"*

Jimmy stayed with it, a big grin on his face. Solange was grinning herself, so happy for her stepdaughter. At least, she was able to feel, be human. Jimmy stayed with it, watched as Emerald creamed repeatedly, screaming and moaning. She easily climaxed a dozen times, nearly passing out during the last and greatest of them all. Finally she did stop, freezing, weeping, her face against her pillow. Then laughed, a hearty laugh. Jimmy leaned over, kissed her on the cheek. She kissed back. He withdrew, unwilling to hold back any longer, and gathered the other two: Solange and Saphyre toward his exploding groin and shot hot cream at their open mouths! The stream of cum sprayed out as before, such a tremendous amount, that even Emerald had time to sit up and join in. The three women lapped it up, *nutsack juice* delivered by a man they were desperately in love with, sucking it, and devouring every drop and even fighting over it. It was a sight to witness, a feeding frenzy, as the stepmom and two sisters lapped up cum off of each other and his groin and balls. Jimmy was beside himself, nearly passing out; the orgasm was beyond belief. He'd blasted this much in the past and had experienced it being this intense, but in many ways, it felt as though it had been greater than any of them.

All four of them dropped back against the bed, clinging to one another.

Take Four

They had showered. Drank purified water. A break was in order. He was not about to leave the other two hanging; the other two being Solange and Saphyre. Emerald had rejoined the living at last and was fine now. She would merely sit in a comfortable chair in the corner of the bedroom and watch while masturbating herself to further orgasms. Jimmy's intention was to fully satisfy the stepmom and the other sister. And it all began rather slowly, calmly, gradually. This still remained his style. Marcella and her mother were to thank for it. In fact, he requested that they pop in that videocassette that he did with Raquel. It had been such a great fuck that he thought it might be fun to watch it while they continued their lovemaking.

Emerald had the cassette playing.

"It is one of our best sellers," said Solange. "For a MILF, Raquel is very sexy and in demand."

"Staying fit and tanned is always a big help," said Jimmy. "She's natural, too. That never hurts. No silicone."

"Yes," agreed Solange, as did her stepdaughters. "We do our best to hire girls who are natural, who do not have too many tattoos or earrings and all that other crap: tongue bars and whatnot."

"We find it all so repulsive," said Emerald.

"We hate it," said Saphyre.

"Yes," said Solange. "We hire talent with tats only because so many have them already; but we do try to hire those without. We tell our casting people all the time: please stay away from freaks; people who are tired-looking, on drugs, not able to look alive. No one is interested in seeing some wasted man or woman pretending to be having fun while barely able to keep awake. We hate the fake stuff, and so do our customers. We get a ton of mail. Our customers want people who look healthy and are enjoying themselves. This was why my husband was so successful. Years ago performers were natural and did not shave their pubic hair, did not go out and scar their bodies and make themselves appear ugly as they do nowadays. It is repulsive, if I say so myself. The actors who do this to themselves think it is attractive, but no, it is quite ugly."

"Well, I never found tats to be all that appealing to look at anyway," said Jimmy. "Same goes for fake tits. The scars are a distraction. Tongue bars? Yuck. They turn my stomach. Safety pins? Nose rings? It's all so unappealing. What I like about the three of you: you have none of that, you're clean and healthy; take care of yourselves. You're not drunk or wasted on drugs."

"Yes," said the stepmom. "Me and Clement did our best to keep drugs out of the house, away from our family. We do not even drink; only wine with dinner. This is acceptable."

"And you're relatively happy," said Jimmy. "What drew me to all of you. You're happy people. With all that you've lived through. You don't knock the male. You like men. You have treated me like a prince; so well. Too well."

"Not too well at all," said Solange. "*You are a prince!* You deserve to be treated this way because you are such a wonderful man."

"You are so loving, Jimmy," said Saphyre. "Why we fell for you. A real man who loves women; you genuinely love women. Thank you for what you are doing here, Jimmy, our *lovable prince.*"

He kissed her on the lips, then found himself searching out a nipple, and began to suck. He held the full breast in his hands and sucked on the areola until the nipple was rigid. He then worked on the other, sucking on the nipple and then as much tit flesh as he was able to take inside his mouth. The woman tilted her head back against the headboard, enjoying the moment.

Solange was in back of him on the bed, on her knees; she had leaned down and began kissing and nibbling on the small of his back. Worked her way down to the buttocks. Kissed each buttock for a while, then her tongue drifted between them, down to his butt crack, probing his asshole.

Jimmy positioned Saphyre so that she was on her back, while he buried his mouth down there again, licking pussy and butt, while Solange did the same for him; licking his crack and balls, and then made her way down toward his shaft, spun around and sucked on the large knob of his cock.

His groin twitched, and continued to do so while the stepmom stayed with it. She had him inside her mouth, sucking, then was back flicking the head again. Paused for a bit, paused long enough, to work her way out, over the balls and back inside his asshole.

Jimmy rose up and got off the bed, with the stepmom and stepdaughter staying close to him. He had one woman in front of him, Solange, while Saphyre remained in back of him, her tongue licking his buttocks. Solange stayed with the cock, would inhale him inside her mouth for a while, then stroke him with either one or both hands, then it was back inside his mouth. Jimmy was as hard as a brick. And as always, the prick twitching, jumping around, throbbing, hungry for both: cunt and cornhole.

They were back on the bed. The mother on her knees, ass stuck out. Jimmy had Saphyre lube her stepmom's butt crack and inserted his thick stiffie in there, and began stroking. He would stroke for a while, then withdraw and let Saphyre take him in her mouth, suck it good and long, then he would reinsert it back inside Solange's ass.

The sight of all this, the eroticism of it all, never failed to give it that extra dimension, and he stayed with it. Then he had Saphyre get down there on all fours, next to Solange, inserted his groin in her butt crack and worked it. Pulled it out, and had Solange suck on it for a good long while, then slide it back inside the stepdaughter's butt, and stroked.

He thought sticking it inside their cunts to see them experience orgasm was in order, and he started with the Frenchwoman, working it, while she rubbed her clit, then watched Saphyre get down there and flick Solange's clit and Solange went into spasms, creaming and exploding in a steady stream of climaxes; that amounted to at least a dozen times, and finally came close to passing out.

Jimmy paused long enough to catch his breath, then stuck it in Saphyre's jaw, watched her suck her stepmother's cunt juices off, lap it all up, then he had her on all fours again, drove his cock in her cunt and began the slow and steady thrusting, and it was not long before, she, too, started to moan and make loud, throaty sounds while climaxing multiple times.

"I love you, Jimmy!" she cried. "I love you so much!"

Over in the chair Emerald was getting herself off and emitting her own share of intense sounds and saying his name repeatedly. *Jimmy, over here! Lookit this! I love you, Tubesteak! I'm coming! Oh my God! I'm coming!"*

It made him feel good. Every bit of it. Yes, he was aware that this did not come close to being real love, no matter what was said, but it was good enough, because they meant it; it was clearly from the heart.

The one person he had feelings for, his heart wanted to be with, was Victoria Chantal; there was no denying it, but hearing these women say his name in this heartfelt fashion made him feel good.

He felt it rushing on, the cream, hot white ball gravy, spunk, scrotum nectar, whatever else you wanted to call it, surging, about to explode along the length of his stiff shaft, nearing the super-sensitive knob. He let them know it with sounds that emanated from somewhere deep in his throat. He winced, jaw clenched.

"Here it comes!"

The three of them surrounded him: stepmom in the middle, the other two on either side of her. He was up on his knees on the bed, jaw tightly clenched—watching them, the three women, mouths open wide, ready and willing and able to lap up cum, as much as he was able to shower them with.

He blasted! A tremendous, full-on hosing! He waved it from one end: Saphyre, on to the stepmother in the middle, and to the left of her: Emerald, and back again! It went on! Jimmy grunting, forever grunting, while the cream sprayed them, covering lips and noses and eyes and chins and forehead. Back and forth it went, the cock cream showered the ever-hungry and willing Rodales.

Then the sucking of the super-sensitive head began, as they took turns, that added and topped off all that had preceded it. My God, thought Jimmy Riff. It was unbelievable. What a finish! What a fabulous suck-off!

And the women? Made sounds themselves, battling over who would get the most; scrambling violently over every drop!

"Suck it," Jimmy encouraged the cum-starved sex fiends. *"Yes."* Mostly, he was out of words and simply making sounds and nodding his smiling face in agreement until he himself collapsed down there between them, his arms embracing them, and the four of them spent and satiated and needing rest.

Stork

From a cafe in the Embarcadero Nicky Horgan phoned his PI buddy Choo-Choo in LA and got him to help obtain the information they needed. While he talked, and waited for the call-back, Vicki began to suspect, but was not quite certain, that she might be pregnant. The symptoms were certainly there: ever-present nausea; her period overdue. Chances were she was, in all likelihood, "with child." It corresponded with what she had read in various publications with regards to morning sickness over the years and heard what other women had gone through in dealing with it.

Should she be happy or sad? She didn't know. What complications and fears would it bring on? And what about Jimmy? She had no idea how Jimmy would react to this. And then she thought: you're being nervous and jittery, and maybe for no reason at all. You'll have to go see a doctor first, and then . . . you'll have to deal with it. . . . She'd gone in the ladies' room just to be alone for a minute, to apply some cool water on her face and try to relax. After a moment, she looked up in the mirror and a confused young woman named Victoria Chantal Vevrier stared back.

If she were pregnant she would want to have this baby, she thought. Suddenly it meant the world to her. No matter what else happened, no matter if the true love she felt in her heart for this man were not reciprocal, no matter what her parents and others later would say, she would stand on her own two feet and decide her own fate and the fate of this child. "Impetuous," "careless," "nowhere near conducive to rational behavior"—both her mother and father would bombard her with clichéd terms like this and others. What do you know about this man? Her mother would say. What's he do for a living? Her father would question. Can't you see there's no future there? You'll be stuck with a ne'er-do-well! Don't judge a book by its cover, Vicki thought. How many "perfect" human beings are there out there in this world? How many men are anywhere near as decent as Jimmy? I'm going by what I feel in my heart, Mom. If people only trusted their instincts more often and didn't pay attention to what others told them they should do! You're just trying to justify this mistake, honey, her mother would probably say. It's not a mistake, Mom. How can you call love a mistake? You call that love, honey? Yes, Mom. It's love. I don't want Jimmy because he's a Wall Street genius and pulling down big bucks! I didn't marry your father because he was a success in his chosen field. Tell me another fairy tale, Mom! We find it so easy to label people, Mom! I know about Jimmy, Mom. I know he's had a tough childhood! Should he be blamed for that? Was that *his fault?* He's a little mixed-up right now, and who isn't a little mixed-up? He had his heart broken by a careless girl early on and it left scars. He never had real love in his life! He's never known what it is to be truly loved! What it's like to have someone truly care! *I can give him that! I can! I will!*

She turned her head away from the mirror, wiping tear-filled eyes. Splashed her face with more water and could feel the cramps tighten inside her belly. *And it isn't just because he's a great lay, either, dammit.* That isn't it. It's nice, of course. It matters. I'm not denying that it matters. I'll never be the one to knock sex. But there's more to Jimmy than anyone has ever given him credit for. I just know it. Don't ask how I know this to be true—I do, that's all. I just do. . . .

A woman walked into the restroom. Vicki gave her hair a few, quick brush strokes and walked out to meet a smiling Nicky Horgan.

"She live far from here?" Vicki asked.

"In the burbs," Nicky said. "Marin."

"God, the air seems so much cleaner," Vicki said. "Everything seems cleaner than LA. San Francisco is a romantic city."

"Definitely," Nicky Horgan said. "With an unmistakable European feel. Great town for a honeymoon."

It would be nice, Vicki thought, nodding.

"I hope," she said.

"Hope, nothing," Nicky Horgan said. "It will happen. Let's go find your Jimmy." And led her to the car.

Au Revoir, Tubesteak

"Is this the young man you wish to see?" the Widow Rodale said as Jimmy Riff escorted her down the winding staircase. Out of her black mourning attire, she was, and dressed in a bright print skirt and white blouse. Hair done up in a modern, fashionable 'do. She wore hose, beige heels. There was a touch of makeup even, lipstick. Nail polish. A changed woman, indeed. It was a sunny day, and she was dressed accordingly. Happy to be alive, in spite of the fact they would be losing Jimmy. There was, after all, a lot to be thankful for. Even if he left them, they would be friends forever. And stay in touch. If he needed help, anything at all, all he had to do was pick up the telephone. And she told him so. After all, Oregon was not very far.

The PI stood in the lobby, his hat in his hands. He was looking up at the vision who descended the stairs with Jimmy, her hand in his. Over in the home gym, to the right, the door wide open, there was a fellow with a mask that resembled President Carter a great deal, only this mask had a large penis for a nose and was dangling. The stocky gent was on a treadmill, walking, fast, and the imitation penis bounced up and down from that Pres. Jimmy Carter mask. Nicky Horgan did not know what to make of it. The gentleman was quite short and wore electric blue shorts that shone something like spandex.

There appeared to be quite a bulge in the crotch region. It was not that he needed to look; it was difficult to miss. Also, it was obvious the gentleman was giving him the eye. He let the thing go.

"Yes, ma'am," Nicky Horgan said.

"Who are you?" asked Jimmy Riff.

"I introduced myself to the lady a moment ago. I don't mind doing it again: Nicholas Horgan. Private Investigator. May we talk?"

"You working for Styles?" asked Jimmy Riff.

"No."

"If you gentlemen will excuse me for a moment," the Widow Rodale said. "I shall return shortly." And she disappeared inside one of the rooms in the back.

"I did at one time," Nicky Horgan offered.

"So you're the guy he paid to be my shadow."

"Something like that."

"The only way I'm returning to LA is in a coffin."

"Look," Nicky Horgan paused. "Styles is an asshole—we both know it. Yes, I'm supposed to bring you back—and I will do my best—but only because he's threatened to harm my family. The last time I talked to him on the phone I could hear my son screaming in pain. Styles was ready to break his arm unless I promised to track you down and bring you back."

Jimmy walked over to the sofa and sat down. Massaged his temples. Felt a headache coming on.

"This guy is just too much."

"You're telling me," Nicky Horgan said. "He's had me by the short hairs ever since I can remember."

Nicky Horgan sat next to him on the sofa.

"Look," he said, "I can't make you go back; Styles can't make you go back; no one can make you go back. . . ." He paused. "But I know this much: he's nuts, he's losing his mind. He'll kill if he has to. I'm begging you . . . come back to LA. We'll figure out a way to handle him. But you should go back with us before he does something drastic."

Nicky Horgan waited. He didn't feel well, either. He rubbed his face with a clammy palm and was about to light up. Jimmy told him it was not a good idea. Horgan shoved the cigarette back in the pack. He looked at Jimmy again.

"Please return with us? Please?"

"Us? Who's with you?"

"She needs you, Mr. Kidd," Nicky Horgan said.

"Don't call me that."

"I apologize. Mr. Riff."

"Why did you bring her here?" He walked to the window. Parted the curtain, and could see Victoria Chantal waiting outside.

"I don't understand," said Nicky Horgan.

"You shouldn't have brought her."

"Why the hell did you write that note if you didn't want her to follow you?"

"She found the note?"

"Yes, she found the note, and all the versions. I guess the motel maid hadn't yet had a chance to tidy up the room."

"She wasn't supposed to see it."

"But she did, and it destroyed her."

Jimmy Riff looked at him.

"That's a fine young woman out there," Nicky Horgan said. "She loves you more than anything in this world." He was quiet.

❧

Jimmy opened the front door and stepped outside. The second he closed it behind him, Vicki spun in his direction, ran up the marble steps, nearly losing her footing in the process, and threw her arms around him.

They hugged and kissed for a long time. She didn't tell him that she was carrying his child.

The Phone Call

The door creaked open. Emerald appeared briefly, looked Vicki up and down, attempted a smile, and went back inside.

Vicki looked into his eyes.

Jimmy nodded.

"Very pretty girl," Victoria said, while her eyes welled.

"I slept with all three: the two daughters and the stepmother. You happy? There. I warned you."

"I know," she said. "You can't help it. That's the way you are."

Emerald had stuck her head back out.

"That isn't true. It did not happen that way at all. He slept with our stepmom, only because we begged him to do it. And as far as the rest of it is concerned? He was tricked; an unwilling participant. He did it out of kindness." She handed her an envelope. "It's all there, the whole story." Jimmy picked up on the tears in Emerald's eyes. Another one. God. For all the good he tried so very hard to do, there were way too many people crying.

She kept walking this time. Got in her Corvette and drove off.

"Solange, the stepmother, had been grieving for over six years over the death of her husband. Nothing her doctors tried to get her to snap out of it worked. Family members were at the end of their rope. I didn't want to. Their tales of woe moved me. There was guilt then. There is guilt now."

He stopped, as if searching for the right words. Wondered if the words would ever be right. "I'll give it to you straight. Take it or leave it. I have much too much respect for you to lie to you or to try to sugarcoat any of it. When the widow's girls found me . . . I was in a bad place, psychologically, not to mention struggling financially. As usual. Was trying to make it up to Oregon and the chicken ranch. Got sidetracked, stranded. What else is new with me? Spent most of my money on that car I bought for the jerk. Ended up as part of a male revue strip show, did a porno. I helped the widow out; she helped me out."

"I could have given you money. Why didn't you take it?"

"I don't know." Then: "I do know: ownership. I don't want to be owned. Beholden. I can't live that way."

"I love you, Jimmy."

"After that?"

She nodded.

"How could you?"

"All I know is that I do." The tears rolled down the sides of her face. "I don't want to live without you. . . . I can't. . . ."

Jimmy drew her closer to him. He tried wiping the tears from her face. This proved futile. His own eyes teared and he buried his face in her shoulder.

"We need each other, Jimmy. We need each other."

The clouds roiled above them. The rain came down fast and hard. They clung to one another in the downpour.

"Please, Monsieur Jimmy," said Solange Rodale, poking her head out the door. "Shouldn't you and your lady friend come in?"

They both looked at her, at each other, smiled, and took the woman's advice.

"My word is gold"

"Benjy?"

"Speaking."

"James Riff here," Jimmy said into the phone.

"Where ya been?"

"Around."

"You're coming back, aren't you?"

"If you show me the ropes like you promised."

"My word is gold. You know that."

"Right," Jimmy Riff said. "I keep forgetting. How's the movie coming along?"

Only then did Jimmy notice Nicky Horgan shake his head sternly. He made a motion with his hand: Don't broach the subject.

"Long story," Benjamin Styles said. "Tell you about it when I see you."

"I've been thinking about what you said. You know your way around Hollywood. I could probably go very far with your contacts."

"Of course," Benjamin Styles said. "Finally got some sense into that head of yours."

"How are you feeling otherwise?"

"Ulcers giving me trouble, knees—other than that, can't complain.

Artie Gross is still anxious to meet you. Morey Grossbard's offer is just too good to pass up, if you know what I mean."

"I do know what you mean."

"Winifred Gail Sacks's been calling. Shit, you're more in demand than ever—'cause of your absence and all."

"Sounds good."

"By the way," Benjamin Styles paused. "I took care of the Lumberjack."

"Who?"

Benjamin Styles chuckled. "The Lumberjack. Asshole who knocked my teeth out. Busted him up good. You won't have to worry about him anymore."

"That's good," Jimmy Riff said, and thought: *But what about you? When do I get you off my back and stop worrying about you?*

"What I'm about to say I'm doing against my better judgment," said Styles. "Doing it so you don't think it's strictly about dollars and cents and business. That Blevins broad s'been calling. Renata? No, it's not an offer to appear in another one of her low-grade smut videos, only because I finally got through to her that that appearance you made in that crappy production of hers that time was a one-shot deal. Anyway, it's her daughter, who just might be the biggest porn whore in Porn Valley at the moment. Evidently she burned one guy too many and got her face rearranged. She's laid up in a hospital bed, I guess. Been asking to see you. Said I'd pass it on, and just did."

"What hospital?"

"Don't know," said Styles. "Want the mother's phone number?"

"Sure," said Jimmy.

Styles gave him the number, and said: "You can get the rest of the sordid details from Madam Blevins, or should that be Ms. Renoir? All she's doing is pimping out her own daughter. Couple of dumb bitches about to go down for the count. That's where that road is headed. Only they're too fucking stupid to see it."

"Listen," Jimmy said, "Nicky would like to talk to his wife for a second, if that's all right?"

"Put him on," Benjamin Styles said.

Jimmy handed the Hungarian the phone.

"Hello? Honey? Serafina?"

"Nicky, are you good?"

"Just fine, honey. Are you all right? Did he hurt you?"

"We are *bueno*, Nicky," she said. "We miss ju. Please come home, Nicky."

"I will, dear. We're flying back. We will be there before you know it."

"Nicky, ju be careful."

"You know me, honey," Nicky Horgan said. "Careful and tactful." Then he said: "Put the *loco* back on, honey."

"Nicky?"

"It's me, Benjamin," Nicky Horgan said.

"Kidd feeding me a line, or what? Is he coming back?"

"Sure he's coming back."

"He damned well better be."

"We're taking the next flight out."

"Remember what I told you yesterday, Pheiffer. You best show up with him."

"We're on our way."

"That's real good," Benjamin Styles said. "Real good."

The line went dead.

Bosko Lipschitzkowitz

Jimmy dialed Renata Blevins' San Fernando Valley number.

"Did I not tell her it would come to this, Jimmy? Go through life breaking hearts and it will come back to bite you in the ass. I knew him, Jimmy. He was not a bad kid."

"Who are we talking about?" said Jimmy.

"You remember the dick-for-hire who had trouble getting wood? In the bedroom scene? 'Lucky Woodcock?' A decent sort. Bosko Lipschitzkowitz was his real name. There's times I wonder if maybe that was part of the reason he had trouble coping in general. The handle, you know? Having to go through life with a name like *Bosko Lipschitzkowitz*." Then she said: "He was something like you, only the heartbreak was too much and he flipped out. His wasn't the only heart she shattered. There were others, many others, Jimmy, who threatened to tear her face off; to get back at her. She used them, in every way you can imagine. Would not listen to me. This Bosko kid broke Marcella's jaw and took his own life. Shot himself. Left a suicide note. It's all there. His pain was unbearable. The reason he couldn't get it up during the *bukkake* in the bedroom because he was in love with her, and when he saw all those guys doing her it just did something to him. Pushed him over the edge. He thought he'd be able to perform; I even tried to dissuade him. He insisted he'd be fine. And my daughter? Oh, she thought the whole thing was a joke, to tease him the way she did. You saw her; you were there. Was practically mocking him when he desperately tried to jerk his dick to attention. Only it didn't work, and he ended it."

"How is Marcella?" asked Jimmy.

"They wired her jaw. Can't eat regular food. Only soup through a straw. Can't talk, or perform. This is costing in more ways than one."

"Is there anything I can do? Benjamin said that she was asking for me."

"Yes, Jimmy. She has been."

"I thought she couldn't speak?"

"She can't. She writes notes when she needs something. What she writes is your name mostly. Where is J.G., Ma? She keeps asking. I told her I didn't know. Finally got the idea to contact that jackass Styles, and he was nice enough to relay the message."

"What can I do, Raquel?"

"Wait. She's writing: *Will Jimmy ever forgive me for what I put him through? Please let him know that I'm sorry. Please, Mom.*" Jimmy could hear Raquel blow her nose. She wept quietly. "She's a mess, Jimmy. Face swollen. What a sight. Like a mummy."

Jimmy said: "If you were to hold the phone by her ear, do you think she'd be able to hear me? Would it be all right?"

Raquel did as asked. Was gentle about it. Jimmy spoke into the phone.

"Marcella, we're all human. Humans make mistakes. I've made my share, and probably will make a few more before my time is up. That's just life. As far as me forgiving you. . . . I never held anything against you, Marcella. No one owns anyone in this world; no one should ever dictate how anyone should live or who to love. I consider that being controlling; I don't believe in it. It was tough going there for a while. I was heart-broken, true enough, but I never blamed you at all. If anything, I blamed myself for certain things. I was too young and didn't understand what was happening. We learn, as we get older, love is a crapshoot. It's always been that way. Most of the time we lose; now and then we win. If you need me to say it, I will: *All is forgiven, Marcella.* I've always wished nothing but the best for you." He could not think to add anything else to it. Asked Raquel if it had gone over at all? "Was Marcella able to get any of it? Is there a reaction?"

"There is a smile on her face," said Marcella's mother. "Her eyes; she has tears in her eyes. . . ." She excused herself, wanting to take a moment to dab at her daughter's tears with a tissue. "Oh, hon. Told you Jimmy was simply the sweetest." To James Riff, she said: "You're the best, James honey. Thank you."

"Not at all," said Jimmy. "I will never forget the support you showed me that time in your kitchen; and then, of course, all the love and affection later, with the two of you. That was absolutely memorable. I should be thanking *you*."

Before he and Victoria and Nicky Horgan left the mansion, Jimmy asked Solange Rodale for one last favor: to send flowers and a get-well card to Marcella Blevins.

Just a Gigolo

Louis Prima's "Just A Gigolo" ended on the record player, and Jesse, the nine year old, was playing some Mexican tune, and Benjamin Styles was willing to put up with it. He felt better now, having talked to Tubesteak and to Nicky.

Kidd was coming back. Sounded like he was doing it of his own free will. It only made sense. There certainly was a future here in town for him, and he finally saw the light. But he had to make sure he stayed away from Renata Blevins and her porn punks, all those losers who never stood a chance to make it where it counted.

He wondered if he had made a mistake by relaying the message. Hell, it made him look good, though. Sure did.

This called for a celebration.

He looked at Serafina Horgan, who was busy stuffing soiled diapers into the laundry bag. She was always doing something like that.

"You wouldn't have anything to drink?"

The woman stopped, looked at him. "*Como?*"

"*Cervesa*, maybe? Bourbon?"

"Si," she said, and hurried to the kitchen. He reminded her she had better wash her hands before bringing it to him. She did that. Reappeared with a bottle of Richard's Irish Rose. A cheap wine. One-eyed wetback damned near tripped on her own feet. Couldn't walk a straight line. Well, one needed two good eyes to do that.

"Winos drink that monkey piss," Benjamin Styles said to no one in particular.

"It is good wine," she said. "My Nicky drink all the time."

"He does, does he?" Benjamin said, uncapping the bottle. "That why he looks so healthy?"

"Como?"

"Ah, nothing," Benjamin Styles said, and took a swig. "Probably a lot healthier than I am."

"Si," she said, and returned to her diapers.

"Thank you," Benjamin Styles said, and picked up the phone, dialed his service. All the same people wanted to talk to him. He didn't have to jot their names down anymore. He knew who they were. He knew who wanted Jimmy's cock the most, and who had the most to offer.

Next, he dialed his home phone. Instead of hearing his own voice and the recorded message, someone else answered.

"Dad?"

"Sam? That you, Sam?"

"Yeah, Dad," his son said. "Got in this morning. Your landlady let me in. You got a nice pad, Dad. I like it."

"Where's your mother? Your brothers?"

"Came out by myself. To see what this film thing is all about."

Not another one, thought Styles.

"Thinking of going to USC," his son said. "Came to check it out. Didn't Mom write you anything about it?"

"She might have," Benjamin Styles said. "I don't know. It takes money to go to USC. That's where kids of the rich go. You'll starve. You need to come down to earth."

"I was offered a scholarship, Dad. It wouldn't hurt to look around," Sam said.

"How long will you be staying?"

"About a week," his son said. "Didn't bring much money with me. . . . I was wondering . . ."

"A week? I suppose it'll be all right," Benjamin Styles said. "I keep the place clean, as you can see. If you move anything, use anything—it gets put back."

"Same old Dad."

"Another thing: I don't want to catch you balling some broad in my bed, either. Understand?"

The line was quiet.

"I'm married, Dad."

"When?"

"Six months ago."

"How come no one tells me anything?"

"I thought Mom did. Sent you the wedding invitation myself."

"Must have got lost in the mail," Benjamin Styles said. He wondered if he sounded convincing enough, for he clearly remembered getting the letters and opening not a single one. All had been tossed into a paper shopping bag. Bills were opened only because he had no choice. Bills had to be tended to. All else was trivia. Bullshit. Time-consuming. Unproductive.

"I have to go now," Benjamin Styles said. "I'll see you later." And hung up.

⌘

He finished the wine and was feeling good and told the nine year old to stop playing the kind of Mexican crap he'd been playing and to find some Rosemary Clooney, or not play anything at all.

Quite a Man

Flight 405. Western Airlines. 4:30 p.m. James Grayson Riff, Victoria Chantal Vevrier and Nicholas Horgan were half-way to Los Angeles.

Not until Jimmy got up to use the restroom did Vicki take out the envelope with the folded sheet of paper inside that the widow's daughter had given her.

Dear Victoria,

You have quite a man there. Yes, it's true: he has made love not only to me and my sister, but our stepmom as well. Brought her out of her shell as a result of the way our father was murdered. She went into shock afterwards, we all did. What your man did, he did so to help out three unstable and lost women, well, two girls and one woman. It is true, in our stepmom Solange's case, he spared her from spinsterhood. Without a doubt. I will not go into how and why our father, her husband's life, was taken, only to say it was tragic. Jimmy, should he wish to go into the unsavory details, can do so on his own. He knows the entire heart-breaking tale. With his love and affection he has helped our Solange snap out of her doldrums and start living again. My sister Saphyre, who had remained mute since the murder, is communicating freely again as a result of Jimmy's loving support. As for myself, I was entirely numb inside for years and did not feel at all alive until Jimmy came along and did his magic by filling me with his special brand of love and affection and I was able to experience emotions like every other human: joy and laughter and even tears. We are ever so grateful to your man for this. He did what he did because he is a fine person, a rarity these days and a treasure. I also want you to know although he was in bed with us, screwing our brains out, bringing us to multiple orgasms the likes of which we shall never experience again, I am certain that his heart was with you. There is no denying that it made the three of us a bit sad when Jimmy continued to sigh and whisper your name while showering us with this tremendous fountain of cum, if you will. It was painful; both wondrous and frustrating: The wonder was all the sperm he was capable of ejaculating, the frustration of it was that he could never be ours.

It took us a while to understand. It was not easy to come to grips with this heart-breaking letdown. But eventually we did. We do. So does our wonderful and absolutely satiated and satisfied stepmom. Jimmy loves you so much. We envy you. All three of us envy you. You are wonderful people and so fortunate to have found one other.

Best of luck,

Emerald

Vicki lowered the note, and stared up, stared at nothing, unable to turn off the tears. Yes, she knew what had taken place had been for a positive and just cause, that it had been a good deed, still, there was no denying that it was painful. She understood; she accepted it, she would go on. She had her man, the love of her life, back and was determined not to let him slip away this time.

❧

Inside the restroom Jimmy had the palms of his hands firmly planted on the vanity as he stared at the face in the mirror that stared back. *How will you deal with Styles?* Horgan had told him that Styles was not connected and he would not have to worry about the Mob.

So it would be one-on-one.

Jimmy "The Kidd" Riff, versus Benjamin Styles, "The Prick."

Did Benjamin Styles have all his marbles still? Was he crazy enough to use a gun? If so. . . . If Benjamin Styles were to shoot him and kill him, or if they were to kill each other, if it came to that, where would that leave that tender-hearted girl out there? What would it do to her?

Deep down he knew it would destroy Vicki if he ever got seriously hurt or killed, and yet there was no way around this one. He would have to meet Benjamin Styles face to face sooner or later and settle the matter once and for all. He wasn't about to let some aging, out-of-shape crumb like that chase him out of town, not to mention he was hurting other people. He had threatened to hurt Horgan's family, to see to it that they got deported. Jimmy Riff felt he owed the man something. He had brought Victoria back to him. *He owed him.*

Jitters

The Porsche 911sc weaved in and out of heavy LAX traffic. Jimmy sat in front with Vicki. Nicky was in the back. It had been decided Victoria would take them to Malibu first, then he and Horgan would continue on in the Toyota to Horgan's place.

"Are you ready to meet Mom and Dad?"

"Today?"

"Sure," Vicki said. "They should be at the house by now."

"I wish you'd have told me earlier," said Jimmy.

"Why?"

"Gimme a chance to prepare—"

She held his hand between bouts of working the stick shift. An opportunity presented itself presently and she held the back of it to her mouth and kissed it lovingly. "You'll do all right," she said. "Besides, I'd forgotten all about it. The last time I spoke to Mom over the phone. . . ." She paused. "Over two weeks ago. Hope they're still there."

"Yeah," a worried Jimmy Riff said.

She wished she could have hugged him just then. Only there was no way to do both: deal with traffic and embrace her man. "Don't worry, honey. You'll do just fine." And she wondered how to break the news to him. *How does it feel to be a daddy?* She would wait for the right time to let him know, she concluded.

The PI brought up the coffin business he could not wait to get started on as soon as this mess with Styles was resolved. Vicki welcomed the change of topic. Earlier, while still on the plane, in an effort to provide her man with a bit of relief from all the stress brought on by his impending confrontation with Benjamin Styles that awaited them once they landed in Los Angeles, Vicki had briefly mentioned to him the somewhat unusual business venture their new friend Nicky Horgan was intent on pursuing and that she had kicked in a few bucks to help make his American Dream happen.

"I'd like to send you lovebirds a complimentary booklet soon as I get the business underway," Nicky Horgan said. "Truth is, I'd like to send you the materials, too—heck, all assembled. Why not?"

"Thanks a lot," Jimmy Riff said. "Kind of you."

Victoria shook her head. The Hungarian is a character, she thought.

"Nicky?" she said. "Do me a favor?"

"Anything," Horgan said.

"Don't do me any favors? Not for a while."

"Well, it'll be there waiting for you. Yours to claim whenever you want."

Guy's got some sense of humor, Jimmy Riff said to himself, cracking a grin.

"How about if *we* call you instead?" Vicki said to Nicky Horgan. Nicky Horgan did a gesture with his hands: sure. And was about to light a cigarette. He looked at Vicki and her beau for their consent.

"May I?"

Vicki rolled her eyes and looked out the window.

"I feel the same way," Jimmy Riff said.

Nicky Horgan crushed the cigarette and tossed it out the window.

"I'm gonna quit—one of these years," he said.

Dementia Rising

Hell, I'm way overdue for a shower, Benjamin Styles thought, as he stood in front of the mirror in the Horgans' bathroom; way overdue for a shower and some other things. But not here, he said to himself; I'm not washing in this dump, and looked around at the cracks in the walls of the bathroom and up at the ceiling and the progressively spreading stain caused by a water leak of some sort from the floor above. The place needed plastering, painting, cleaning, and fumigating. Hell, the whole building needed to be cleaned out and fumigated. What else was new? Look at the quality of the tenants in the place.

Styles took a leak. Got out of the sports coat and hung it on a hook on the door. Picked up the scissors that were lying there among the clutter of toiletries: toothpaste, toothbrushes, razors, bar soap, hair shampoo, combs, cough syrup, aspirin, Pepto-Bismol, Pinworm medicine (for the entire family), Alka-Seltzer, shaving cream, aftershave; lots of aftershave. Hell, he hated aftershave, the smell of it. Or just about any type of perfume or even deodorant. Aftershave was for sissies. Perfume always made him nauseous.

Guess I can always do that, he thought, trim the ol' whiskers. And he stood there, stared at the over-the-hill face that had taken its share of lumps in the ring way back when, a face that was no longer young and made to look ten years older, at the least, with all the whiskers. It did. Made him look about ten years older or more. Like somebody's grandfather. That didn't sit right with him. It didn't please him at all that he should look like he was ready to be put out to pasture. No way, nohow. Not Benjamin T. Styles. I still got plenty of get-up-and-go. I know it. There can be no doubt about that.

Being naturally left-handed, he started to use the scissors with that hand and the fingers and forearm just smarted too damn much from the encounter with Kerr that time. All in all, forearm's been healing rather nicely, he thought. He needed to adhere to caution when it came to using it, not do any heavy lifting. Other than that, it would be fine.

He switched hands, and trimmed some of the whiskers under the chin. Paused, and stepped back. Not bad, not bad. Earlier he'd shoved the kid aside and found a station that played the easy listening soft stuff he liked. Patty Page, or some woman singer, was on. "Hush Hush Sweet Charlotte. . . ." Hell, most music was crap, but at least this tended to soothe him out. He needed soothing. No denying there.

When next he moved in a bit closer to the mirror that was the medicine cabinet door to do some trimming above his upper lip, for a brief moment Benjamin Styles was seeing double. He shook his head, squinted his eyes, trying to refocus. Then he did nothing and held on to the vanity top for a moment and he was all right again. Just a slight dizzy spell. To be expected when you didn't put food in the belly. All you've been doing is drinking. When he straightened again the music was gone. The foreigner's nine year old was playing with the dial again. Benjamin Styles stuck his head out the bathroom. "Put it back on," he ordered.

Styles waited for the youngster to find the station, picked up a slipper off the floor and flung it at him and got him right between the shoulder blades.

"That'll teach you to mess with the radio," Benjamin Styles said.

The boy started to cry. Mrs. Horgan put her arms around her son and walked him to the kitchen to give him something to eat.

"Ju want *Jell-O*, baby? We have cherry, we have lemon, we have orange. What ju like, Jesse honey? How about some *Kool-Aid*? We got *Kool-Aid*."

"*Jell-O.*"

"*Jell-O. Good.* What kind?"

❦

Some folks never left home without this or the other: wristwatch, aspirin, hairbrush, mints, etc. In Ben T. Styles' case it came down to never leaving his apartment without a stack of the latest edition of his composite. His briefcase contained many prints of the 8½ x 11 full page version; inside his sports coat was where he had a moderate stack of a dozen or so of the reduced 5 x 8 calling card.

Man had to be prepared. You never left a casting director's office without dropping off your latest picture and resume; you never walked away with any type of production meeting with studio heads, major or minor, without doing likewise. It was tiresome and belittling, he knew it, but it was also part of the bullshit Hollywood game. One did what one had to as a professional actor to pick up work and continue moving forward.

He fished a composite out. Studied it. Compared it to what his eyes saw in the mirror. Difference was staggering. Pictures had been taken no more than a year and a half ago. He had aged at least six times that much. Let it go, he said to himself. It's the beard.

He still had about the best two-sheet composite money could buy. The front contained two reasonably large photos: Benjamin Styles with mustache, Benjamin Styles without. In large print across the bottom, caption stated: **FOR THE BEST — BENJAMIN T. STYLES**

He opened it. Two photos per page. Stills from films he had appeared in over the years. Two were from Westerns he'd appeared in with Robert Tanner. In one of the oaters he had played a vicious, lynch-hungry posse leader. In the other, his role had been that of a bartender.

Latter was a two-shot of he and Robert Tanner. Tanner's gloved hands resting on the butts of the guns in his waist, eyeballing Benjamin Styles. Styles in derby, striped shirt, suspenders, stogie in hand, leaning across bar. His expression clearly telegraphing: *You ain't shit, buddy.*

Upper right-hand corner: three-shot of Styles, a noted English actor, and another top-rated Hollywood thespian. The latter an Oscar winner. The English actor, a known lush, was still in demand, and Benjamin Styles couldn't understand it. Benjamin in white frock, eyeglasses in hand. Not so hostile looking. He played a bit part in that. A doctor.

Lower right-hand corner. Ben T. Styles sitting behind a typewriter, no mustache, looking up at camera with a smile on his face that made him look like Bugs Bunny. The Bugs Bunny reference was his own. Didn't mind it. You had to have a sense of humor to survive in this town. He took pride in that he was able.

The actor across the desk from him was another "superstar." Banana nose and all. How did they do it? Five feet five. Practically a dwarf. Eddie G. Robinson was short, but Eddie G. had incredible presence. On the other hand, this fuck with the banana for a schnoz was mediocre in most things he appeared in. Still, star billing each and every time out. How the hell do they do it? Better yet, whose dick was he sucking? He claimed to be straight, but Ben T. Styles wondered about that. Lots of these punks either sucked pipe or took it up the dirt road. At least early on, to give their careers traction, visibility. They "exposed" themselves to pick up exposure. They didn't have to go the BJ route once they made it, instead were the ones getting blown by the young up-and-comers.

Under each picture was a caption naming the film, director, and lead in said film. Very often, the budget was listed, if impressive enough. Why not? Let them know you had credits in major productions.

Back cover contained a trio of vertical photo booth images, one below the other, placed diagonally across the page: Styles with mustache, Styles in derby with a thick stogie between his choppers. A profile shot. There was a list of credits, parts he'd done on Broadway, television, and local theaters.

He raised the scissors to finish trimming and his face suddenly looked like a bad TV image, his sight impaired considerably. Not unlike what he'd experienced a moment ago. He shut his eyes and shook his head. Wait a minute, he said to himself. What's going on here? What's happening to me? There was not an inconsiderable, but brief ache that ran down the left side of his neck. Then went away just as quickly. Shit.

You haven't eaten anything substantial in days. That's what's the matter with you, and nothing else.

He regained his vision. Lowered the scissors all the same and got into his coat. He walked out to the living room and picked up the phone. He didn't like the idea of his son staying with him. Wine bottle was empty.

"Got any more?" he asked the woman.

"No more, *senor*," Mrs. Horgan said.

He asked her for a dictionary. Nicky Junior brought him a Webster's High School Edition. Benjamin Styles looked up the word SCHIZOPHRENIA and wondered if this was what was happening to him. Was he slipping? Losing it?

He ordered a pizza and another bottle of Irish Rose.

Mom and Dad

Investor/businessman Richard "Dick" Vevrier was a tall, bespectacled individual with neatly trimmed white sideburns that ran down the length of his earlobes. A sophisticated-looking gent at that, in a tan suit, who easily projected an image of wealth and accomplishment. The diamond-studded gold tie pin was worth plenty. There was also a substantial amount of gold on both hands, including a Rolex that retailed in the thousands.

Mrs. Vevrier stood an inch or two shorter than her successful husband. A well-preserved, attractive woman in her forties, who was dressed in miniskirt and pumps, an all-around outfit that would have been more suitable for someone half her age. It was hard to miss the long legs and golden tan. The frosted 'do cut short and stylish that showcased her appealing features and high cheekbones.

There were no wrinkles in the vicinity of their eyes, or anywhere else, none that were visible, at least. They were both smokers and the expression on both faces was not so much worry, but just plain weariness. They were booked to leave on a cruise bound for South America shortly, and now this had happened with Victoria. They wanted to know about the blood on the kitchen floor; they wanted to know where their daughter had been and what all the recent turmoil and commotion added up to. Who was this young man, James something or other, that she had been going on about in her all-too-brief phone chats with her mother.

They were in the living room of the Malibu beach house: Vicki, the parents, Jimmy, while Horgan waited in the driveway. Vicki introduced Jimmy to her parents and tried to tell them that everything was all right and that she would explain later. She walked Jimmy to the car.

"Jimmy," she said, and wanted to tell him that she was expecting. She kissed him instead. "Be careful," she said. And watched as the Toyota disappeared into the night and headed toward LA.

The Confrontation

They parked a safe distance away and snuck inside the building on the corner of Franklin and Argyle. They paused at the foot of the stairwell. Nicky Horgan pointed, indicating the door nearest the fire escape. Jimmy Riff nodded. He was alert, sharp. He was no stranger to the atmosphere, this feeling of tension, the calm before the storm, the lull before fists started flying. The poorly illuminated, seedy building almost gave him the feeling he was back on the East Coast somewhere: Boston, Maine, Brooklyn, Philly, or Midwest somewhere. Family moved around so much he couldn't keep track. All he knew he was usually the new kid in town, and about to get his ass kicked—unless he duked it; learned how to duke it out and keep from being a perpetual punching bag. He was seventeen in his mind's eye, back there, somewhere, about to kick ass, or get his own handed to him. Prelude to battle went something like that. So be it. He was ready. Here. Now. With this overbearing creep who used those around him at every opportunity. He needed to teach the user a lesson. Bad.

Both readily agreed they didn't want to put the kids in danger.

"Get him to come out," Jimmy said. "I'll be waiting for him."

Nicky Horgan nodded, and said quietly: "He's strapped."

"He's what?"

"Armed," said Horgan. "I'm not saying he's crazy enough to use it. . . . You never know. . . ."

"What choice do we have?"

"We could call the police."

"And tell them what? Has he killed anyone?"

Nicky shook his head. "Not that I know of."

"Damaged property? Shot his gun off?"

Nicky Horgan shook his head to both.

"He threatened to—"

Jimmy cut him off. "Threatened. What do you think they would do? He called you names over the phone. All that amounts to is an 'obscene phone call.' That's what they'd tell us. I want to see this prick get what he's got coming. I want to be the one to give it to him. We have to get him off our backs. This is the only way. Brute force is all he knows."

Nicky Horgan looked down. Unbuttoned his coat. Wanted to hand Jimmy the snub-nose .38, except Jimmy refused. He'd never cared for guns—and dreaded where it might lead should he take it. He was no criminal. He would face Styles on his own terms. No weapons. No guns.

"As a last resort," Nicky Horgan said. Shoved it at him. At last got Jimmy to take it, and cautiously climbed flight after flight of stairs until he reached the fourth floor. He paused at the door to his family's apartment. Knocked. Benjamin Styles appeared almost instantly.

"Where's Kidd?" he said.

"Parking the car," Nicky Horgan said. With an equal rush of emotion bursting from him and his offspring, he stepped in and hugged his kids. Soon his wife emerged from the kitchen to join the reunion— although she attempted, and easily failed, to conceal the bruise where she had been slapped. Nicky Horgan's face turned red with anger.

"In my book, guy," Nicky Horgan said, sticking his nose in Benjamin Styles' face, "that's low-life. Hitting a pregnant woman!"

"In my book, 'guy,'" Benjamin Styles said, "giving a woman nothing but a big belly is 'low-life.'"

"You hit my woman, Styles! I am going to get you for it, man! I will get you!"

Benjamin Styles warned him that he was standing too close. "Breath is strong enough to knock out a hog."

"Get out of my house, *'movie star!'*"

"Where's Tubesteak?"

"I told you: he's parking the car."

"What's taking him so long?"

"How should I know? Maybe he's afraid you'll work him over!"

"Hit him once. Only because he earned it. Had the whole thing planned out with McFluff, the director? I told Kidd to wait for me until I got back—but he couldn't. Pissed McFluff off; pissed me off."

Nicky Horgan shook his head. He couldn't help it. He had to give this blind dumb-ass some worthwhile advice, whether he wanted to hear it or not.

"Why don't you get smart?" Nicky Horgan said. "Do like I did. Teach. Focus on teaching. With your background you'd make a hell of a teacher. Why does everyone have to be a star? Does everyone have to be on the screen? Is it that important? Is it?"

Benjamin Styles turned away from him. He walked to the window, parted the curtain and looked at the street below through the pane.

"How old are you, Ben? Fifty-five? Fifty-six? You're not getting any younger. I left the stage; you can too. I quit the movies. You can too. Maybe I couldn't have gotten very far with my accent and all. The point is I had enough sense to see it. I saw the light, man, and decided I wasn't going to waste my life. Because I knew I couldn't make it. There are too many people out there who are far better, and twice as many who'll never cut it for one reason or another—just wasting their life away, groping for an illusion that will never materialize into anything. It's all so pointless."

"You should be on a cattle ranch," Benjamin Styles finally said.

Nicky Horgan looked at him quizzically.

"Where cow chips belong," Benjamin Styles said.

"Hey, guy, I'm not the one's got B.S. for initials."

"Someone ones said: Bullshit talks, money walks."

"Know what I think, guy? Half the time you're struggling in knee-deep manure and you don't even see it. Climb out, guy, before you drown in it." Inaudibly, he said: "Then again—won't be easy. You've been in it all your life."

"Mental ward advice I don't need."

Nicky Horgan said no more. What's the use, he thought. What the hell is the use?

"Where the fuck is Tubesteak?" Benjamin Styles said, and hurried out of the apartment and down the staircase.

Rage

"STYLES!" Jimmy Riff shouted, hurrying up the staircase and reaching the third floor landing just as his foe did same, having descended at the opposite end. Ground zero for both.

Benjamin Styles froze in his tracks. That all-too-familiar murderous look was in his eyes as soon as he realized that something was up, that he'd been mislead by both: the foreigner and this *wank stain* Jimmy Riff. Jimmy, too, had an expression on his face. *I've come to get you,* it said. *I've got a score to settle.*

"I'm here to kick your ass," Jimmy Riff hissed.

Benjamin Styles made a sound that was clearly mocking. "Oooh." Raised both eyebrows with all the sarcasm he was able to muster.

"He sounds like a man. Question is: Does he have the balls?"

"Come and find out, shit-head."

They moved toward each other, eyes burning with a powerful desire to unleash a ton of pent-up rage and frustration.

"You caused me a lot of grief, punk. . . . A lot of grief. . . ." said Styles.

"I'm about to cause you some more."

Benjamin T. Styles chuckled.

"Laugh, asshole," Jimmy Riff said. "You've been a thorn in my butt ever since I hit town."

"I tried to help you," Benjamin Styles said. "And all you did was cause me a bunch of shit."

"I hated everything, myself included; the way I lived."

"You're trash," Benjamin Styles said. "Pole-smoking punk. Face it. Sissy in disguise."

"You made me hate. But no more. . . . No more."

"You're nothing. Scum. Faggot. Filthy queer," Benjamin Styles leered.

Jimmy Riff shook his head, smiled. "I see it now. What do they call it? Latent homosexual? That's your problem, isn't it, Styles? Why you fear homosexuals. Why you're so quick and easy with degrading labels like 'fag' and 'homo' and 'queer' and 'sissy' and 'pipe smoker.' Afraid of turning fag? That it?"

"Shut up, punk."

"That's it, isn't it? Could explain why you work so hard to parade the macho image. Always on display. Like John Wayne. Look how big and bad I am. You poor, over-the-hill schmuck. I feel sorry for you."

"Just for that I'm gonna kill you." Benjamin Styles' face had become the color of a ripe tomato.

"I'm not the queer, Styles. I'm not the one who's afraid. I'm not the one who goes around beating up gays because I'm afraid of them, afraid I might turn into one. I know where my head is at. Do you know where *your* head is at? Do you, *old man?*"

"I'll kill you."

"I know you got a piece."

"Gun? I don't need a gun to take care of you. I'll beat you to a pulp."

"This I gotta see."

"You'll more than see it, *punk.*"

"Talk is cheap, big mouth," Jimmy Riff said.

Styles faked a right and stepped in with a left jab to Jimmy's chin that sent him spinning against the wall. Benjamin Styles' wolfish grin broadened, saliva dripped from his mouth.

"Look at him," Jimmy Riff said once he'd recovered. "Panting, just like the rest of them."

He cupped his crotch and puckered his lips and waited as Benjamin Styles' anger doubled. The man charged him like a bear, spraying his face with saliva. Jimmy Riff pivoted out of the way and sent a punch into the man's ribs. He was ready to follow through with a blow to Styles' face, but the man spun with both fists guarding the front of his head. He blocked the intended punch successfully and charged anew. He faked another uppercut, instead sent the tip of a cowboy boot up between Tubesteak's thighs, thinking he'd successfully connected with Riff's nut sack. Jimmy let Styles think whatever he wanted, staggered back and dropped on his side, making it look like the kick had been effective. There was plenty of pain, to be sure, but it was nowhere near as great had the boot thudded into his precious nuts.

Styles didn't waste any time. Dropped down beside him. More damage was in order. He grabbed at Jimmy's collar with his bad hand, wanting to hold him up just so, position him just right, while he cocked his good arm, made a tight fist, glaring with a kind of manic satisfaction, as this would be the *coup de grace*, a solid powerhouse of a punch to the gigolo's pretty face. He held the fist like that, savoring what it would finally do to this ignorant punk. That instant, Jimmy Riff's knee came up, plowed into Benjamin Styles' own groin. Styles' howl was deep and disturbing, as he backpedaled and dropped like a sack of cement, his features about as crimson as a briquette of coal in a barbecue pit.

Jimmy Riff stood over him, arms akimbo, waiting for his foe to get up. Only the Hollywood tough guy remained out of it and in severe agony.

Give him time, thought Jimmy. Maybe he's had enough.

Benjamin T. Styles' eventually recovered to the point he was able to reach inside his sports coat with the good hand and out came the .357 Magnum.

"Shoot," Jimmy Riff said. "You'd be doing me a favor."

"Sheeeyet," Benjamin Styles hissed under his breath. He emptied the chambers and tossed the revolver into a corner. Jimmy Riff withdrew the .38, and did likewise.

"Still waiting for you to get up," Jimmy said.

Benjamin Styles rose to his feet remarkably fast after what he'd just been the recipient of. He got out of the coat and tossed it aside. He jabbed and he faked. He had even begun to do some dancing, reminiscent of his Golden Gloves days. He was breathing pretty hard and he didn't care. Only the knees had begun to hurt and the dancing had to end. The rest of his agenda didn't, though: an uppercut to Tubesteak's jaw, a fist to the belly, a jab to Jimmy's ribs, a rabbit punch to the left side of his neck, another to the right.

Jimmy Riff stumbled into a corner. There was no denying the dizziness. He felt weak. His eyes were puffy, the face felt numb. Blood oozed from his nose and jaw. Everything went dark for a moment. He shook his head. It helped to clear things, but not much. He was able to make out the killer's fangs moving toward him again, fists moving in to pounce on him some more; knuckles stained with blood, his blood.

"You going to do as I tell ya?" Benjamin Styles said. "You going to do as I say?"

"You'll have to kill me," Jimmy Riff heard himself utter. *"You'll have to finish me. . . ."*

Styles' left came at him with the speed of light, it seemed. This was the arm that Kerr had driven the blade through, the arm that had never healed properly. And now Styles was about to suffer the devastating consequences. Jimmy Riff sank to his knees in time to avoid the punch, and almost felt the wall in back of him reverberate as the other man's fist put a considerable crack in the ancient plasterboard.

Styles whirled as if struck by a Mack truck. Jimmy Riff heard him howl like a wounded beast. Flesh dangled from his skinned knuckles. Jimmy Riff remained immobile. Watched as the man continued to spin and wave the busted fist in the air and moan. He lost balance and had dropped to his knees, holding up the presently useless hand, for what good it did him.

⌘

After a while, Jimmy Riff rose, dusted himself off, and stared at the pitiful sight before him. He felt both elation and its opposite. There was no denying the tremendous relief that surged through him at having broken free of Benjamin Styles, thug and bully like no other. And yet . . . seeing him like this, thoroughly defeated and hurting, hadn't made him feel exactly good, either. It was also true the man hadn't given him much choice.

He dug in his pocket for something.

"Keys to a new car," Jimmy Riff said. "Bought it for you once . . . when I didn't know better."

He let the keys drop to the floor and walked out of the tenement.

⌘

Benjamin Twitchell Styles stared at the car keys for what seemed like a long while, and soon enough drops dripped on top of them, drops that flowed from his eyes, teardrops mixed in with blood and mucus that slid down his aching face and covered the keys.

The Last Fart

After numerous failed attempts to contact Eddie McFluff and Morey Grossbard, a frustrated Benjamin Styles filed suit.

He was back drawing unemployment and was soon praying for an out-of-court settlement. Ordinarily, that was the way lawsuits of this nature got resolved, except this time a congenital son of a bitch by the name of Benjamin T. Styles was involved and a counter-suit was filed by both R. Edward McFluff and the studio.

Benjamin Styles was hurting for money.

⁓

It was on a cool evening in September, drunk out of his gourd, that Benjamin Styles turned to Sam for help. He owed him, figured Ben. Claimed he was only staying two weeks. That's a mighty long two weeks. Kid said he was testing the waters. Kept getting hired on as a PA on a variety of productions. Since he had overstayed his welcome a long time ago, Styles thought he'd run this one idea by him to see if it would fly: He gave his son specific instructions, telling him exactly what to do.

Sam, the tall, lanky young man, having feared his father his whole life, almost did as asked. But not quite.

One of the TV networks needed an actor for a lead in a weekly Western with Benjamin Styles' rugged looks and age. Benjamin Styles felt for sure he could land the part if Sam would only play up to the fag executive in charge of the show. Sam, instead, had packed his few things in silence; he'd had enough of both Hollywood and his father, and left the small flat without saying a word.

❧

Benjamin Styles persisted, with or without a gigolo to open doors for him. The need to become a success gnawed at him like a type of cancer, chipping away at his sanity and general well-being like a debilitating sickness. And a sickness it had most certainly become.

❧

The disease stopped gnawing away at him briefly on the day Benjamin Styles was called in to read and subsequently signed on to appear on the show as a regular for more money in one week than he made in a year. Thanks due in part to Reggie McFluff, as per their out-of-court settlement. Lawsuits were dropped by all parties.

❧

That very same day, in the Universal parking lot, while unlocking the door to his new car, Ben T. Styles strained, if mildly, to release a fart, not knowing it would be his swan song. The acute pain, the very same type he'd experienced in Nicky Horgan's john that time, was back. Ten-fold. And as he became aware of it, stumbled against his car door, slid down, down, to the pavement. Rolled over on his back.

"That's a wrap," he gasped with a lop-sided grin, and expired with his eyes wide open, eyes that stared at a perfectly clear, smog-free, azure Studio City sky for a change.

❦

Some said it had been the excitement of having signed a lucrative contract, steady employment, possibly a shot at fame; a dream come true by any standard. Others said it was the booze, stress, his own natural-born meanness that killed him finally. "Good riddance to bad rubbish."

The trades gave him five lines.

Character actor Benjamin T. Styles dead at 57. The former Golden Gloves champion had a long and varied career, both on stage and in film with some of the top names in Hollywood and Broadway. Services pending.

Escape from Oz

After two weeks of wandering about in Venice Beach, doing odd jobs, living like a bum basically and dropping weight, Jimmy Riff called Vicki up and asked to meet at a coffee shop on the boardwalk.

He looked tired, a shadow of his former self.

The moment she spotted him, Vicki rushed up and wrapped her arms around him. It was all she could do to keep from crying.

"Jimmy, you had me worried," she said. "What happened to you?"

"Sit down," Jimmy said. Indicated the nearest available table. Save for another couple at the other end of the patio, they were the only ones there.

"What is it, honey?"

"Please, Vicki," he said, and pulled out a chair for her. He waited until she sat, and followed suit himself.

"Couple of things you ought to know—and when I tell you, you'll know why we never stood a chance from the beginning. It was wrong from the start."

"You're at it again, huh?" Victoria said. "Inventing reasons why we shouldn't love each other the way we do."

"Wait until you hear what I've got to say."

"I'm listening," she said with a smile, and held his hand.

"The fact that you've got and I don't," he said, pausing, "has nothing to do with it."

"Translate."

"Three things: money, money, money."

Her smile broadened. She shook her head, then drew his hand to her lips and kissed it.

"So?" she said.

"Like I said, that has nothing to do with my decision. It's this other thing."

"I'm listening," she said, and kissed his hand again.

"I'm serious."

"I know you are, honey."

"I picked up an STD somewhere along the way."

A look of concern traced her face for a brief moment. "So?" she said.

"So?"

"Yeah," she said. "So?"

"You know how I got that new Toyota?"

"I don't need to know," she said. "Besides, that was then, whatever it was, this is now."

"You don't understand—"

"I do understand," she said, cutting him off. "I don't care what happened. The widow and her stepdaughters, and everything else. It was painful, but it's over. Behind us. People aren't perfect. We make mistakes. The past is the past. We have now; the future ahead. A life together. Don't you see? You suggested I make a wish before blowing out the candle that time; at my 'birthday party,' remember? Cheesecake you had for me? The most special ever, by the way. Know what my wish was? That we stay together. Forever. It was love at first sight for me. That was my wish, still is. True and ever-lasting love with my dearest man. You mean more to me than anything in the world. You're good, Jimmy. No matter how hard you work to run yourself down. Way too critical. You are. You're the most wonderful guy I've ever met."

"Me? You sure you got the right James G.?"

"You," she said. "*Tubesteak.* You mean more to me than my family. We need each other. No one will ever love you more than I do; no one will ever love me as much as you."

He looked at her without saying a word.

Vicki nodded. "It's true," she said. "I want to spend the rest of my life with you."

"Forever?"

"Forever," she said.

He stared at her for a long moment, unable to say anything. His eyes misted.

"I lied," he said. "I don't have anything. Not sure how that happened. Just lucky, I guess."

"It wouldn't have made any difference."

"I know."

"Guess what?" Vicki said, beaming.

"What?"

"I'm pregnant."

"Say that again. Slowly. Take your time."

"I . . . am . . . pregnant."

Jimmy Riff leaped up and embraced her. He held her pretty face in his hands and kissed her with all the love in his heart.

"This is great," Jimmy said.

"I'm so happy for us."

"Why didn't you tell me, honey?" He looked at her, and when it dawned on him that she hadn't wanted to use the pregnancy as a way of "blackmailing" him into staying with her, he hugged her again, and they walked the distance to the Porsche parked at the curb.

"Know something?" he said.

"What is it?"

"Lately I've gotten to hate this place."

"The beach?"

"Hollywood and everything in the vicinity."

"Me, too."

"What do you say we leave?"

"Sure," she said. "Where to?"

Jimmy shrugged. "Napa, Seattle, Salt Lake, or maybe that chicken ranch north of Portland I spent my last high school years on."

"Your Uncle Orville's place."

"Orville's Organic Cluck-Clucks."

"The university is not too shabby, either," she said. "From what I hear."

"Anywhere is okay with me, actually," Jimmy said. "I don't care. As long as it's far, far away from LA."

❧

They climbed in the Porsche, its front end aimed north. Victoria Chantal turned the key in the ignition and the motor roared to life and the sports car sped off, leaving the assholes of Tinseltown way the fuck back there.

THE END

LUSTMORD:
Anatomy of a Serial Butcher
Book One (of Two)

By KIRK ALEX

Blurb & Novel Excerpt

Who knew the minister next door
was also a sadistic predator?

Cecil Omar Biggs is not your average man of the cloth. By day, he appears to be a hardworking preacher, but once night descends upon the quiet Southern California neighborhood where Biggs resides, his darker self emerges. Living a double life as a sex fiend and brutal murderer, he enjoys luring innocent victims into his basement lair by any means possible.

Converting an old house into a church, Biggs becomes the perfect wolf in sheep's clothing, which also puts him in the ideal position to attract his unsuspecting prey. He lives to satisfy his sinister appetites without remorse or limits, indulging in his more violent tendencies as soon as the sun goes down by torturing and killing the women he abducts in his dungeon of doom.

But how long can Biggs keep up the nice-guy-next-door pretense while secretly living as a homicidal maniac? And what happens when the locals start suspecting that there's more to this seemingly harmless Bible-thumper than meets the eye?

A WORD OF CAUTION

**"And if you gaze for long into an abyss,
the abyss gazes also into you."**
–Friedrich Nietzsche

Translation: this one is not for the faint of heart, nor the weak of belly. Foretold is forewarned.

I started **LUSTMORD: Anatomy of a Serial Butcher** back in 1987, and it is January 17, 2013, as I write this. How many years is that? Twenty-six? Give or take. I say give or take because somewhere in there, during the mid 1990s, I had to lay off the thing for about five years. Why? Nightmares. Cold sweats. Unable to sleep. Why? Subject matter. Some of it was too damn horrific and the images wouldn't go away at the end of the day. Five years. Not to mention another three years when I could only face the book for about four or five months at a time. The shit was sick and depraved. Fucking brutal. I needed a break.

Why go anywhere near the subject matter, then? Why fool with it? Because I have to bounce around, move from genre to genre, or go batty—and because if I'm going to do a book about a sociopath, you better believe one thing: I am going to treat the material with absolute honesty. There is no other way. I did not want to whitewash (or sugarcoat) any of it, the way certain writers like to do, or the way some, rather, most Hollywood flicks treat the material: by having the unpleasant stuff happen off screen, or else it's done with gimmicks and cheesy effects. I wanted it raw, and I wanted it to be disturbing—because when it happens, the way it happens in real life, that's what it is: appalling, venal, sickening and twisted. So I repeat, read at your own risk.

The author/publisher is not responsible for any nervous breakdowns, facial tics, insomnia, depression, loss of appetite, loss of hair, sexual dysfunction, bouts of insanity, marriages and/or relationships disintegrating, time spent in therapy, stays in the bughouse, shakes, quakes, headaches, heart problems, vomiting, nausea, episodes of anxiety, suicidal tendencies or a sudden, inexplicable urge to do bodily harm to your fellow humans, and any other ailments, be they large or small, that you may experience as a result of having read **LUSTMORD: Anatomy of a Serial Butcher.** You have been thoroughly advised. Proceed at your own peril.

K. A.

CHAPTER 1

They were into it. Heard more than he wanted to.

"J.J., don't!"

"Shut your mouth, whore!"

"I'll be good! I promise, J.J.!"

"I told you to shut your hole!"

"Don't hit me, J.J. You better not hit me no more!"

"I'll beat you to death! Filthy heifer cunt!" Slaps and screams followed. "Why, you ain't even a good whore! Where's my whiskey money, bitch? Spent on shoes and ice cream for that worthless little shit? Why come? Since when are the little bastard's wants more important than mine?"

More slaps followed, screaming. The next sound was the male's, a deep grunt, as though on the receiving end himself. Furniture was thrown, dishes. The woman shrieked.

"We're out of ass-wipe, heifer, and you got nerve to waste money on ice cream and shoes for the little pissy!" Dogs barked; a real ruckus was in progress up there. The boy pretty much ignored it all. Went about in a calm way burning his spiders, tearing wings off flies.

The view from where he stood at the grimy rear window on this tenement landing between the third and fourth floors gave one about as much hope and peace of mind as the hell going on up on the fourth floor: a back parking lot with cracks in the pavement, pot holes and loose cement chunks and gravel that had, over time, become the unofficial dumping site for neighborhood wrecks. Autos of all makes and sizes, pickup trucks, vans, gutted. Some without doors and windshields or wheels, had been abandoned to rust on wood or cinder blocks, bricks, piled rocks.

Knee-high weeds grew from fissures in the pavement. There were scattered stacks and piles of threadbare tires and strips of black rubber throughout; rusted out mufflers, gas tanks, radiators and grills; engines that had long ago been stripped of anything useful.

Down, toward the right-hand part of the parking lot-cum-junkyard, where the dumpster was located and over-flowing to capacity with refuse, dead foliage, and an assortment of fractured and discarded bargain-basement, low-rent coffee tables and nightstands, sofas and chairs, toasters, crock pots, washers and dryers, refrigerators and other appliances, large and small, with additional mounds of plastic trash bags bloated and splitting at the seams, that surrounded it at the base, were a couple of stray dogs engaged in the act, something the boy had been exposed to enough times in the past, so that in and of itself held no real interest; only these two were caught up/entangled in such a way that he had never witnessed until now. Stuck, they were, ass-to-ass, literally; on all fours, heads at opposite ends. Evidently attempting to separate, to untangle, and not able to do so.

One would pull one way for a while, dragging the other with him, then the other mutt would pull, or try to, in his direction, forcing the other dog to back up, neither getting anywhere.

Mexican standoff? He couldn't say. All he knew was it was the Latino part of town. East LA. What was going on?

It was only moments earlier that they had been in front of the building. Fucking, to be sure, but doing it the way they were supposed to: the male, forepaws atop the other's hind end, while he pumped away from behind. The boy's mother, with whom the boy had walked up, having been thoroughly disgusted by the sight, had flung one of her pumps at them. The dogs hadn't bothered to separate—maybe even then had not been able to—instead had hopped the short distance to the left of the tenement to where the driveway and entrance to the lot in back was. And here they were, still at it, only coupled in this baffling manner.

He wondered what was going on, if only in a casual way. Because the mongrels, the junkyard, and the heaps hardly mattered beyond what went on in them at night, as well as during the day: local prostitutes, some who lived in the building, sneaking about with their johns, junkies in a crazy frenzy to slam a needle somewhere, bums seeking out vehicles with missing seats to take a dump in.

He'd taken more than one girl to one of the forgotten sedans himself, gotten them to pull their panties down and show him what they had.

None of that rated this mid-morning. No. What mattered and preoccupied his thoughts were the spiders and fat flies he enjoyed burning to a crisp on his side of the window, the flies who threw themselves mindlessly against the pane, and the spiders lying in wait in various corners of the window frame and the traps they had spun for the purpose of snagging a meal.

The boy stood at the window, book of matches in hand, doing the thing that sent the familiar sensation through him: setting things on fire, living or not; fire did it for him. Even though it was beyond his comprehension how or why the mere sight of fire and destroying things in this fashion had the effect that it did on him, it did not stop him from yearning for more of the same.

Drawing his attention above his head, in a web in the upper right corner of the frame, a newly trapped fly struggled to untangle itself to no avail. Spiders knew what they were doing. The web was sinewy, tough, and this spider's latest victim was not going anywhere.

As expected, the spider emerged soon enough from within its lair. Moved toward the prey. With bated breath, the kid waited until the predator was practically upon the doomed insect before striking the match, reaching up, and roasting them both.

There were other flies he pounced on, clutched in his fist, and dealt with. Large, glistening green flies, who made the loud buzzing, grating noise that added to the thrill, he caught and relieved them of their wings. They were incredibly easy to grab: dumb flies who kept throwing themselves against the grime-streaked glass as if they expected to be able to drill through somehow and escape out there to join up with thousands of their ilk at the dumpster below and anywhere else throughout the lot.

The boy snatched them up, yanked the wings off, and watched with something like inner satisfaction as they kicked out with their spindly legs on their backs, on the sill, kicking out frantically; that enhanced the experience for him. There was no denying it, no explaining it: the combo, fire and subsequent death, not only heightened the senses all around, but clearly left him in a state of arousal, just as there was no denying he felt responsible for what was taking place up there on the fourth floor.

Coco Garcia, the gap-toothed, obese Mexican woman who lived across the way from them in the other apartment and everyone knew to be a prostitute, who had, in fact, turned his mother on to some of her johns, poked her head out through her partially opened door.

"They're at it again, huh, kid? I wouldn't take that off no man. I hope she beats the shit out of his ass this time."

The boy said nothing. Looked up at her, then turned away to mind his spiders and flies. He was down to his remaining match and that bothered him. The big woman shook her head at the ongoing racket. She withdrew back into her place and closed her door.

"Lemme get this straight, bitch: You stayed out all night and a good part of the morning, and all you got to show for it is a handful of change? Why, you ain't even good at whorin'! To call you a whore would be an insult to all the hard-working whores out there! Hear what I'm saying, bitch? You ain't even good at whorin'! You don't rate!"

"It's the boy's birthday, Joe. I wanted to do something for the boy just this once."

"You ain't even got enough coins left here for a bottle of rotgut—"

"He needed shoes, Joe. It's his birthday."

"How many times I gotta hear about the bastard's birthday, goddamn you! I ain't got enough here for a taste, and you got nerve to spend on shoes and birthday cakes and ice cream!"

"Can't you do without this one time? We'll get some money later—"

"Why should I have to do without, bitch? Why should I have to suffer? Didn't I tell you to abort the bastard? Didn't I?"

"There was no money for it, asshole! You drank everything I brought in—like you're doing now!"

"You're blaming me? It's my fault?"

There was a loud slap. The woman screamed. There was tumbling. Someone being thrown against a wall. More screaming and yelling.

Mad dogs barked inside the apartment.

Eight-year-old Cecil Omar Biggs stood at the landing between the floors, struck the last match and burned a plump spider with it. Through with that, he was back on the green flies: easy to catch, while they kept at the filthy windowpane, buzzing away. He'd sever their wings and lower them on the window sill on their backs. Liked to watch them kick wildly this way.

He had an unusually large one now. Was desperate to burn it. Went through his pockets in search of matches. Dug up a book, but no matches left in it. Kept searching, found another. A single match left. Struck it. Lowered the flame toward the frantic fly: the fat fucker. He wanted to kill them all. Nothing gave him more pleasure than killing these fuckers. And then he got him but good. The last match. That was it. Gone. All of them. What would he do? Keep catching them and tear their wings off. He'd have to find some more matches somewhere soon. While happening to look up toward the top of the windowpane at a couple of flies banging their heads against the glass, his eyes wandered up toward the ceiling, up there in both corners, large cobwebs, too, but he couldn't reach those. He wished that he could. There were also plenty of dead moths along the window sill that he felt like frying . . . but he needed matches for that.

The landing was littered: beer cans and soda bottles, cigarette butts and empty cartons, bologna packaging and candy bar wrappers, used condoms and Tampons. He shoved his worn sneaker around in there, in search of a possible match, a lighter . . . and found nothing. He cursed. Needed fire. The yelling and fighting in their apartment kept on: more things being broken; his father's dogs barked. Then he heard John Joseph release a deep howl. The apartment door opened like a cannon shot, and his mother, heavily made-up as usual, both eyes swollen, mouth bleeding, with all that wild dark hair flying and not a stitch of clothing on her, scrambled down the flight of stairs toward him.

There was panic and terror in her peepers; even, incredibly enough, to some degree, a kind of glee. He noticed, too, a couple of her front teeth were missing this time.

She descended the stairs in her clumsy, harried way, with John Joseph, drunk and slobbering, nose and jaw bloody, in his soiled OD green army boxers and worn, mis-matched white socks, staggering in the doorway, the birthday cake haphazardly balanced on the palm of his left hand, while he held onto the doorjamb with the other to steady his aim. He cursed and hurled the cake at her, the birthday cake that she'd only bought moments earlier. J.J. sent the cake flying through the air as she neared the landing where the boy stood. The youngster turned his back in time. The cake grazed the top of her head, and a good deal of it deflected and spattered the back of the boy's neck.

"Half a whore!"

"Up yours, faggot!"

The boy's mother continued on down the next flight to make her way toward the lobby below.

"I'll kill you, bitch! Kill the both of you!"

John Joseph ducked back inside, to reappear seconds later with the box the boy's new footwear was in and pitched the shoes, one at a time, at the eight-year-old.

One shoe bounced off the top of the boy's head and went sailing through the windowpane, causing him to pivot enough for the second shoe to nail him between the eyes. The blow sent the kid spinning into the corner, his face buried in his hands. He wasn't crying, merely doing his best to deal with the throbbing pain.

John Joseph Biggs staggered back into the apartment, slammed the door shut, and could still be heard cursing and carrying on at the top of his lungs.

"That's right: kill you both, so help me! Cake and ice cream, when I ain't even got enough to wet my beak! Good-for-nothing, two-bit half-a-whore! Cake and ice cream! No ass-wipe in the crapper, but there she is throwing good money away on nothin'! Out of dog food, out of ass-wipe, nothin' left to drink—and the bitch throws money away with both hands! What I get for marryin' a madwoman! My own goddamn fault, right there. Could've married up—no, not me; I had to marry down! Insane heifer! Probably got Mad Cow. Wouldn't be surprised."

The boy was squatting in the corner of the landing and wiping his bloody nose with the back of his sleeve. There was no stifling the tears by now.

He heard the door to their apartment open again. Looked up to see Juicer Joe leaning against the door jamb and pointing a shaky finger at him.

"What was you doin'? Playin' with matches, boy? How many times I gotta tell you not to play with fire? Wasn't enough you burned our home down—forced us to have to move to a place like this what we can't even afford."

"I wasn't playing with matches."

"Like hell you wasn't. What you sittin' there for like an asshole? Get that twat in here before she goes out and kills herself!" his father yelled at him, barely able to hold onto the jamb, vomit and blood dribbling down his chin. He had one of his barking large mutts with him on a leather belt, the belt buckle end of which he had a difficult time holding on to.

"You heard what I said, Pissy? Go get your mother! What are you waiting for?"

"What can *I* do? She never listens to me. . . ."

The father swiped at his chin with his hand, staggered back inside, to reappear a short while later with a beer bottle. Noticed that a good swallow of brew remained. He drained it, and the bottle was hurled at the cowering boy, caught him across the lower back and knocked him off his feet.

The kid was doubled up on the floor, wincing in pain.

"*You heard what I said, Pissy?* Quit your fakin' and bring that tramp in here before she throws herself under a bus. Wouldn't break my heart any if she did. Trouble is ain't got no insurance on the bitch. Can't never scrape enough together to take out a policy on the confused heifer! Understand what I'm sayin', boy?"

Cecil looked up. Could not move from the pain and remained lying on the littered floor of the landing.

The door directly across the way from their unit opened, and the same tired, wasted street whore who lived there stuck her head out.

"The fuck you want, skank?"

The woman's eyes were about half open, not that it mattered, because the appallingly bad bleach job that was her hair hung over them. She had on a black bra that was several sizes smaller than it should have been and revealed a far greater amount of the flab that made up the enormous bosom than was flattering. The large, moth-eaten black underpants she wore managed to detract even further from the overall bloated and disagreeable appearance. This was a big woman who easily weighed in excess of two hundred pounds.

"Can you spare a drink, J.J?"

"Get your *nasty, hog bitch ass* back in that *smelly sty* you crawled out of. This is family business."

"*Besame culo, pendejo.*" She flipped him the middle finger.

"Who you calling '*pendejo*,' you tub of shit?"

John Joseph yelled at the dog to go after her. The woman withdrew quickly enough back into her place, slamming the door shut in time.

J.J.'s attention was back on the boy. Yanked on the makeshift leash, pulling the dog back, who would not stop barking and tugging on the belt. This was one manic animal. Out for blood. Anyone's blood.

"Get up, you little turd! I'll turn this beast on you, so help me!"

The canine tugged too hard, causing the drunk to trip on his feet and stagger against the door jamb, driving his face into it, exacerbating the bleeding nose. He cursed. Wiped the blood with the back of his hand. The man gave the dog a few whacks on the head with the buckle end of the belt, then pointed at the youngster.

"Get him, Mojo! Get the little snivel snot down there! Get him!"

The dog charged, pulling the drunk to the stairs. Caused him to miss a step, and down he went, falling on his backside and tumbling down the rest of the way to the landing, cursing both: child and dog.

The boy managed to scramble out of the way in time, crying for help, pleading.

"Daddy, don't! Please, Daddy! Please, Daddy, no! I'll get her! Daddy! Daddy!" Clearly wetting his pants by now.

John Joseph rose to his knees, hissing, in a rage. "Who you callin' 'Daddy,' Pissy? If I told you once I musta told you a hunnerd times: I ain't your Daddy, boy! Just 'cause I married that whore mama of yourn that don't make me your Daddy! I ain't nobody's Daddy!"

He probed for something to pick up out of the pile of litter to throw at the kid. Settled for a nondescript bottle. Flung it. Found an empty whiskey fifth. Threw that down the flight of stairs at the fleeing boy. Missed. The bottle hit the wall. John Joseph could be heard shouting over the breaking glass.

"Don't you *never, never, ever* call me 'Daddy,' boy! I didn't ask to be your Daddy! Only married the nasty heifer on account I musta been outta my mind at the time!"

He felt like chasing after the kid. Was in no condition. Only the dog didn't get that. Kept tugging, and forced the man down to his knees once more.

John Joseph rose, kicked the animal, then began whacking away at it with the belt buckle, drawing blood. Yanked hard on the makeshift leash, and made it back up the stairs to the apartment door. Went in. Slammed it shut.

ZOOK

By KIRK ALEX

Blurb & Novel Excerpt

**Some very strange things are taking place
at the New Pueblo Funeral Home . . .**

War vet, Ray Zook, a PTSD afflicted former grunt, is about to regret that he ever set foot in Tucson, Arizona.

All he wants is to gain the courage to face his inner-demons and somehow explain to the widow of his best friend what *really* happened to him during their stint in the military. But when Zook is mugged and takes a temporary job working the night-shift at a crematory run by a couple of unsavory employees, those plans get derailed.

After witnessing a series of disturbing incidents—like the shady "after hours" business taking place—that hurl him into an immoral world of grave robbing, coffin swapping, and even disappearing bodies, Zook finds himself caught in the middle of a twisted power-struggle to control ownership of the funeral home.

If Zook hopes to escape this utter mess with his sanity intact, he must rise above his fears and confront the dark deeds before he ends up back in the looney bin . . . for good this time.

Chapter 1

I had just gotten off the bus and the two of them followed me: the dim-witted young chick with the dishwater hair and the beastly two-hundred-pound butch dyke with her: all tats and rings and studs and chains. Lots of black leather. Blue/black crew cut. Demanding money.

"For what?"

"BJ."

The other one was quiet. Just wasn't there mentally. Didn't seem like it mattered to her, either. It was the bitch built like a dozer who was after my cash. I dared her to take it, which hadn't been a wise move at all. She cold-cocked me. By the time she was done I was on the ground, nearly out. She'd flipped me over on my belly and sat on my back. I could hardly breathe, let alone do much of anything else at this point. She'd taken my wallet, extracted the bills, tossed it back at me. Spit in my direction, and they walked off. With close to eighty dollars of my jack. My roll. A good chunk of it. If it hadn't been for the paper money I'd kept stashed inside my sock I'd have been up the creek. I was, but at least with what remained I'd be able to rent a room, buy something to eat, a newspaper, and look for work.

I had been sound asleep, as comfortable as one can possibly be on a Greyhound bus. Been pulling on a bottle of hooch all the way from

Phoenix. The idea was to stay on in Tucson long enough to beef up the roll and continue on to Ft. Worth. The ex had family there and I hoped that's where she'd ended up. I didn't have a need to connect with her. It came down to my kid. In her early teens by now. Hadn't seen her in years. I'd been to LaFayette, Indiana; Bowling Green, Kentucky; Lawrence, Kansas, and dozens of other towns, large and small. I stayed on the move; perpetual motion seemed to keep the demons at bay—at least I had myself convinced of it. I had war-related nightmares I couldn't shake, and some other things I was trying to live down. Staying on the move seemed to be the answer. Only how in hell do you get away from yourself? I'd been given the boot by more apartment managers and motel desk clerks for kicking the floor and walls in my sleep than I cared to remember.

It was usually some indiscriminate setting, me unarmed, being chased by the enemy in some far-off land. Commies? Mid-East zealots? Your run-of-the-mill America haters? Who knew? Or maybe I was in denial. Unwilling to face my demons. It took a lot to deal with that shit.

That was where they got on, though: Phoenix. The young one: couldn't tell how old, didn't look half bad in tight jeans, pink blouse, although the heavy one with the butch cut made me want to retch. This was one unappealing broad. And wouldn't you know it, she was the one who dropped her sweaty and mean ass in the seat next to mine. She wanted a hit off my hooch. I told her to piss off. Took the occasional nip from the bottle, pulled the blanket up to about my neck. I had no idea how long I'd be staying in Tucson. Didn't know a soul in town, not really. It was just a place to drive through, or maybe spend a week in, look around. Been in the "Old Pueblo" before. Worked as a busser at some sports bar some years back, did a bit of panhandling.

What nudged me awake was the two of them switching seats. Now the young one was sitting next to me. Before the fat one gave up her seat, she whispered in my ear: "My cousin gives great head."

"How much?"

"Forty bucks."

I told her to get lost.

They switched seats, and before I knew it, "cousin" had her hand under my blanket. Inched it slowly toward my crotch and was rubbing it, just running her fingers gently over it, and I'll be damned if my groin didn't begin to stir. All that vino, and there I was: getting wood. She proceeded to unzip my fly. I let her; pretended I was asleep, and let her do what she wanted. I figured if I acted like I was dozing, they wouldn't be able to claim I owed them money later, her and the beast she was with.

She had it out, stroking, slowly, taking her time. Then she ducked her head under the blanket. I let her. Of course, I let her. It had been a while. No love, no sex. Traveling the country on buses, when the money was there, hitching when it wasn't.

She had her tongue on it, licking; then she had the shaft inside, all of it. I didn't have a tremendous whole lot, but it was all right; there were some poor bastards who envied what I did have. You lived with the hand the Dealer laid on you—and this time the Dealer had shown me some kindness, I thought. That head of hers bobbed up and down, not fast, gently, gradually, taking her time. And the fact it was night provided adequate cover. Passengers were zoned out, with the exception of some punk in his teens, across the aisle, watching out of the corner of his eye. Let him. Probably wished he was me, the big shot, getting his nuts off on a Greyhound bus to nowhere.

The licking went on. She played with the head, flicking it thoroughly. This chick had been around, knew her business when it came to licking balls and sucking cock. It had been such a long time, too. Probably did this to get by: sucked off strangers for whatever they could pick up. Who knew? Did it matter? Only I'd had too much wine. Couldn't make it. It was no good. Wine and sex didn't mix, not for me.

She lifted her head. I pulled out my wallet. Extracted a tenner for her effort. She did what she could. Not her fault. Before the young hooker had had a chance to even take a good look at it, the beast, her freakish "relation," stuck her hand in and snapped up the sawbuck. She sniffed it. Looked it over. She was not pleased. Tough, I thought. That was a ten dollar try.

"My name is not Bill Gates and I don't own *Microsoft*. Besides, I never got off."

"You're lying." She yanked her "cousin" out of the seat, and lowered that wide posterior next to me.

"We agreed on forty."

"Like hell we did."

"That was a forty dollar BJ. You never had anything that good in your life."

"How would you know? Maybe I had better." For a fact. Only my ex-wives wanted nothing to do with me, especially the last one. I had no idea where she was. Ft. Worth was nothing more than a guess, a vague one, like all the other towns I'd been to. She'd taken the kid and disappeared off the face of the earth. Could explain the roaming. If I admitted it to myself. I didn't need the exes back, only ached to see the kid. A girl. Must have been six years ago I saw her last. I didn't blame the wife for leaving me. Couldn't take the screaming in the middle of the night, the kicking at the floor with my feet, the times I was stationed out of the country, or stuck in some bug bin here in the states. I drank to fight the demons. Only made everything worse. They had me on *Prozak*, then *Paxil*, at the VA. While I was in the whack ward the wife dropped the bomb: wanted out. I couldn't stop her, didn't try. She never mentioned custody, only because she figured she was entitled. She'd given birth to the child and that was that. Frankly, I was in no shape to take care of a kid, couldn't even take care of myself. I let it go; let them both go. The ex had a man, in fact, had been shagging a neighbor while I was stationed overseas. The way it usually went. I'd had it done to me once before. Kid could be his, biologically. Probably. Don't matter. I treated her like she was my own. You get emotionally attached. Kids are all right. Always wanted a family. Always did. Things kept going wrong somehow. Something would always happen to turn things upside down. This was divorce number three. You know what they say: three strikes and you're out. Three marriages, three divorces. I was defective, a loser. Something was seriously the matter with me. It was the war; it was other things.

"I doubt it." She looked at me. "Not with that nose and those teeth." My nose was bent, both ways, in bar brawls that I usually started and lost, so were my teeth—born with them that way—the ones still there: black, yellow. Of the uppers in front, I had but one left. In the middle.

I pulled the blanket up, and pretended to go to sleep. Only she wouldn't let me.

"Thirty bucks. You can't deny that was worth thirty bucks."

"You got what it was worth. And that's the end of it. I never got rocks. You bitches came on to me. Before I knew what was going on, your nympho girlfriend was molesting my privates."

"You owe us money."

"Fuck off, or I go to the driver."

"He's our friend. That wouldn't get you anywhere."

"What does *he* pay for it?"

"That's a different case. He gets a discount—and has nothing to do with you."

"I feel drained for some strange reason and crave rest." And this time

I shut my eyes and kept them shut. I could feel them switch seats again. As she got up, I turned my head, and caught her cousin going down on some geezer way in the back. I guessed the freak was on her feet in order to collect payment, and before I knew it, the young bitch was back sitting beside me. It wasn't long before she had her hand under my blanket again. This time I slapped it away, and she left me alone.

We got off the bus. I had my old backpack; walking down in search of a cheap motel along Drachman. Then I turned down an alley. Big mistake. They'd had friends waiting for them. Indians. Looked like. I was jumped, knocked down. She stood on one side, while one of those drunk Indian friends of hers stood on the other, and they took turns delivering a couple of very effective, if unsteady, kicks to my kidneys. The beast had emptied my wallet, rummaged through the backpack, spat in disgust and left me lying there in the puke and blood.

Welcome to Tucson, Arizona. To be fair, this was no slam against the Old Pueblo, and besides, the bitches had hopped on in Phoenix.

I was up, wiped vomit from my chin. Dug my hand inside my left sock. At least I still had that. Jammed the spare socks and underwear, photo album, toiletries, back in the pack. Checked into a motel, washed my face, showered, then plopped down on the floor and slept the rest of the night and most of the next day when I had to go out and find a bar, or *Circle K*, to buy a can of *Spam* and a 6- Pack of *Red Dog*, a newspaper. At this rate, my money wouldn't last long and I'd be stuck here indefinitely. Taking a look at the job ads was in order.

About the Author

Kirk Alex's novel *Lustmord: Anatomy of a Serial Butcher* was a finalist in the Kindle Book Review's Best Book Awards of 2014. He is also the author of *Zook, Fifty Shades of Tinsel,* the story collection: *Ziggy Popper at Large,* the *Love, Lust & Murder* series: *Throwback & Backlash,* the Eddie "Doc" Holiday Private Eye Series, and a few other novels & shorts.

IF YOU ENJOYED THIS BOOK . . .

Dear Reader, if you enjoyed this book, won't you please consider posting a review wherever you deem suitable. Thank you kindly.